The Backward Boy

The Backward Boy

Kenneth Cameron

FELONY & MAYHEM PRESS • NEW YORK

All the characters and events portrayed in this work are fictitious.

THE BACKWARD BOY

A Felony & Mayhem mystery

PUBLISHING HISTORY
First UK edition (Orion): 2013
Felony & Mayhem edition (first US edition): 2020

Copyright © 2013 by Kenneth Cameron

ISBN (trade cloth): 978-1-63194-228-0
ISBN (trade paper): 978-1-63194-229-7

Manufactured in the United States of America

Library of Congress Cataloging-in-Publication Data

Names: Cameron, Kenneth M., 1931- author.
Title: The backward boy / Kenneth Cameron.
Description: Felony & Mayhem edition. | New York : Felony & Mayhem Press,
  2020. | Summary: "Denton tries to help a woman clear her husband of
  suspicion in a murder case and in the process discovers the family's
  tragic past-and its possible connection to a present mystery"-- Provided
  by publisher.
Identifiers: LCCN 2019045213 | ISBN 9781631942280 (trade cloth) | ISBN
  9781631942297 (trade paper) | ISBN 9781631942303 (ebook)
Subjects: GSAFD: Mystery fiction.
Classification: LCC PS3553.A4335 B33 2020 | DDC 813/.54--dc23
LC record available at https://lccn.loc.gov/2019045213

To Paul Schullery
the eloquent angler

ACKNOWLEDGEMENTS

One person is always invaluable to these books: my editor, Bill Massey.

A number of books on the Metropolitan Police of the period were used: *Hargrave Adam's Police Encyclopedia* (8 vols, c.1911); Frederick Porter Wensley's *Detective Days* (1931); J. F. Moylan's *Scotland Yard and the Metropolitan Police* (1929); Sir Howard Vincent's *Police Code* (15th edn, 1912); and H. Childs's '*Police Duty' Catechism and Reports* (11th edn, c.1910). As well, as in all the Denton books, I used *Yesterday's Shopping: The Army and Navy Stores Catalogue*, 1907 (reprint, 1969); Baedeker's *London and Its Environs* (1894 and later years); and the *Booth Poverty Map, 1898–99*, at the Charles Booth Online Archive (booth.lse.ac.uk. cgi). My notion of the Oxford women's colleges of the period was suggested by *St Hugh's: One Hundred Years of Women's Education in Oxford* (ed. Penny Griffin, 1986) and Margaret E. Rayner's *The Centenary History of St Hilda's College, Oxford* (1993), but they should not be held responsible for the result.

The icon above says you're holding a copy of a book in the Felony & Mayhem "Historical" category, which ranges from the ancient world up through the 1940s. If you enjoy this book, you may well like other "Historical" titles from Felony & Mayhem Press.

———————•·◆·•———————

For more about these books, and other Felony & Mayhem titles, or to place an order, please visit our website at:

www.FelonyAndMayhem.com

Other "Historical" titles from

FELONY&MAYHEM

The Backward Boy

The late-afternoon air was heavy with a heat that made the people beyond his first-storey window move like waders in some soft jelly. Even a dog, stopping to sniff at a plane tree, seemed almost too oppressed to put his nose to the trunk, then hardly able to raise a leg. To Denton, just back from ten months in Naples, the London heat felt normal, although the wet, soft slap of it was not so pleasant. The worst heat in fifty years, he had heard somebody say, although how the man, who looked to be forty, knew, he couldn't tell.

His house was silent. Everything was silent; even the city undertone, as if too hot to groan, seemed to have given up its usual bang and thump and grind. A horse's hooves, seeming muffled, intruded; a large black dog, asleep until then on his carpet, raised his head an inch and tried to wag his tail but had too little of it to make a noise against the floor. And too little energy; the head fell back with a bump.

'Yes, it's her,' he said. The dog opened an eye. 'Not that you give a damn.' The dog wasn't his but his servant's, the only person whose step on the pavement would rouse the dog to delighted wriggling.

A hansom drew up outside. The horse's head went down and stayed low. A female foot, then a skirt appeared, a hand: Janet Striker. She said something back into the cab, then turned her head up and spoke to the driver and motioned at the horse. The driver looked morose, then stubborn; she said something fiercer—Denton could see her back straighten, knew what expression would be on the face even though it was turned away—and the driver made a child's grimace of phoney resignation and began to climb down. Janet turned from the cab's door.

The driver waded through the heat to the horse's rear, then bent to lift, with enormous effort, an empty canvas pail that had swung between the wheels. He stood holding it, looking up and down the street and then right at Denton as if instruction, or possibly water, would flow his way. Denton raised the window. 'Try the Lamb!' He pointed at the pub two doors along. The cabbie actually put his hand over his eyes to search the distance.

'Oh, you're home, good.' She stepped over the dog and came to him, touched his lips with hers, kept a hand on his chest. 'You look quite cool, you wretch. It's like an oven out there.' She passed him and looked down at the street. 'The fool.' He supposed she meant the driver. 'He'd let that horse totter to its death before he'd move his fat arse off his perch and give it a drink.' She turned back to him, pulling out hatpins. 'I told him that if he didn't water it I'd give him not a cent, and he could go to the police to collect it.' She exhaled loudly, threw her hat into a chair and came back to lean slightly against him, almost as tall as he, slender. 'It's too hot to be physical, though I rather feel like it.' She kissed him again. 'I've brought somebody with me.'

He tried to hide his irritation: if she was going to bring somebody, she should have warned him. 'I wondered.'

She moved away, letting her jacket slide down her arms and fall on the floor behind her. She wore a plain white blouse, which she pulled at in front as if it were a bellows. 'I'd like to drop all my clothes in an untidy trail behind me and go about like a South-Sea Islander. I'm wearing wool, would you believe? Everybody in London is wearing wool because the calendar says it's autumn. Except you. What is that—linen? You look like a planter who's going to go out and give hell to dark-skinned people.' She threw herself down in his armchair and put her head back and closed her eyes. 'Was it ever this hot in Naples?'

'Often.'

She opened one eye. 'That dog stinks. I suppose it's the heat. The woman in the cab is named Snokes. Her husband's been taken in for questioning, but he hasn't been charged yet. The woman came to see Teddy today about it.' Teddy was Theodora Mercer, Janet's solicitor, who had taken Janet on as a kind of novice: Janet had decided she wanted to be a lawyer, and working as a clerk for a solicitor was one way to start. Women couldn't become barristers, so Theodora Mercer—suffragist, socialist, activist—was the best that Janet thought she could do.

'The police going to charge him?'

Janet nodded, her eyes still closed.

'With what?'

'It looks as if he's murdered a woman.'

Denton glanced at the window, then at the collapsed woman in his chair. He smiled. She opened an eye and asked him what he was grinning at.

'You.'

'Well, stop it.'

'Three days on the job, and you're bringing another stray dog home.'

'It isn't a job; I'm paying Teddy, not the other way round! And it's not a stray dog, it's a client, and I'm not bringing her home; I'm bringing her here.' True, this house was Denton's; Janet's was behind, their back gardens separated by a wall that had a door to which they both—an innovation, part of the resolution of a nearly disastrous split—had keys. Still, she hadn't brought her stray dog to her own house, so he said, 'You're bringing her to me, you mean.'

She grunted.

'If you don't let her out of that cab pretty soon, she'll go away.'

'No she won't. She's frantic—in a stolid, corseted sort of way.' She got up and raised her arms. 'I'll get her. You'll see her, yes? Teddy wants her to see you.'

Now he let his irritation show. 'For God's sake, why?'

'It's complicated.' And she went out.

Outside, the horse had its head in the water bucket. The cabbie was standing next to it, looking as if, having got that far, he could no longer move. Denton saw Janet, foreshortened, appear from the front door, walk the few steps to the iron gate, go out and say something into the cab. It swayed on its springs. A massive female behind presented itself, covered in dark-blue silk; it backed down to the pavement. The woman turned, revealing a red, round face under a small, dark hat. The dress, Denton thought, was several years out of the fashion, not expensive when it was new.

When the woman came through his sitting-room door, she was panting from the stairs. Short, broad in the hips, she had a puffy face whose focus was a baby's mouth; her nose seemed insignificant, her eyes little currants in all that dough. She might have been fifty but he thought her younger; it was fat, not time, that had given her pouches and dewlaps. One of those wanly pretty, round-faced girls who had done nothing to stay young, too much to get old.

'This is Mrs Snokes,' Janet was coming in behind her.

'Mrs Arthur Snokes,' the woman said. She looked at Denton as if she hated him. He thought she was simply distraught, maybe far closer to an edge than she let on. He tried to think himself into her place—having her husband arrested, going to a solicitor, getting fobbed off on somebody else. The woman rubbed at the flesh beside a nostril; the finger was trembling.

He eyed Janet, showed her he should have been warned earlier, got Mrs Snokes into his armchair, established that nobody wanted sherry, pulled up a hard chair for Janet and stood in front of his own fireplace, his right side towards the window, behind him a wall of books. 'I'm afraid I don't know my part in this,' he said.

Janet handed him a single sheet of paper, some typewriting on it. 'Teddy says you must sign this. And take this.' She held out a shilling.

Denton renewed the you-should-have-warned-me look. Tempering his words, not always so mild, he said, 'Now you've really lost me,' and laughed what was meant to be a hearty male laugh, ho-ho-ho. The sound fell into the room like plops of manure on the street.

Janet, usually outspokenly anti-male, didn't rise to it. Her voice neutral, she said, 'Teddy thinks Mrs Snokes needs somebody besides a solicitor.'

'To do what?'

The woman spoke up. 'To get my Arthur out of this horrible tragedy!' She had a harsher voice than he'd heard at first. Maybe it was worry.

'I'm afraid,' Janet interrupted. 'Teddy thinks it should be looked into before everybody goes off half-cocked.'

'The Metropolitan Police don't go off half-cocked. Usually.'

'Teddy thinks it should be looked into.'

'Then Teddy needs an investigator. London's full of them.'

'Mrs Snokes isn't made of money. Anyway, she doesn't want one.'

'Nasty people,' Mrs Snokes said. 'Prying.'

Denton looked at Janet, got from her a slightly wide-eyed look that meant they would talk about it later, with the implied threat of what might happen if they went on talking about it now. He looked over at the pudgy Mrs Snokes, thought she looked harmless and uninteresting (but the novelist in him said that there were no uninteresting people—and, a second thought, the old lawman in him said that there were no harmless people) and therefore (why therefore?) could be got over quickly. He shrugged. He looked at the paper Janet had given him. For the sum of one shilling, he, Denton, agreed to consider the matter of Amelia-Anna Snokes, wife of Arthur Snokes, thus making him a creature of Theodora Mercer, solicitor, and so sheltered under the same umbrella of confidentiality as the solicitor herself. 'Ah,' he said.

'Sign.' Janet looked severe.

'Mrs Snokes, you have to understand, I'm not—'

Janet was holding out her fountain pen. Denton put the paper on the mantel, signed it, and then took the shilling and put it on the paper. In a flat voice, he said to Mrs Snokes, 'What just happened means that I'm bound to keep your confidence and not repeat anything I hear from or about you, and that includes any dealings I might have with the police.' He glanced at Janet. 'Which I don't mean to have. Now, what's this about?'

Mrs Snokes began to weep. Janet passed her a handkerchief and rolled her eyes at Denton to suggest that Mrs Snokes was as big a pain in the neck to her as she was getting to be to Denton. 'Mrs Snokes came to the office about four. Teddy was busy with a barrister and asked me to chat with her. I explained that I had no legal stature—'

'You were kindness itself!' Mrs Snokes wailed.

Denton wanted to say *That's because she isn't a lawyer yet* but didn't.

'Mrs Snokes wanted legal advice for herself—*not* for her husband. You see the distinction? Her husband *has* a lawyer, she thinks. Mrs Snokes is concerned about her own legal situation.'

Denton frowned. 'Is she...involved?'

'No, no! Oh dear me, no!' Mrs Snokes was dabbing her little eyes with the handkerchief, or as much of it as could be stretched over one plump forefinger. 'No, I am certainly not—' She shuddered; her voice dropped into her bass notes. 'Involved.'

'She was concerned about what sort of testimony she could give. I reported all this to Teddy, who spent a few minutes with Mrs Snokes and advised her about her position and then told her she thought she needed, as I said, somebody to tell her at least what the investigative possibilities were. Mrs Snokes refuses to pay for an investigator, and Teddy suggested you, Denton. It wasn't my idea, I swear!'

Teddy Mercer and Janet were friends, of a sort. Teddy had got Janet a bundle of money in a lawsuit that had lasted for years; she knew that the five-inch scar on Janet's face had been made with a knife, and that Denton had shot the man who had held the knife. She knew Denton's reputation. And she knew that both Denton and Janet were easy marks for the stray dogs of the world. *And she thinks she can trade on it.* He felt more irritation, followed at once by resignation: it was what Janet wanted that mattered.

'Well.' He turned to Mrs Snokes, then drew another chair over so that he would be on the same level as she. 'Mrs Snokes, can you tell me why you think you need a solicitor?'

She looked down at the now-balled handkerchief. Her unpleasant voice was almost inaudible. 'They say he killed a…a girl. A woman.'

'Yes.'

'He didn't.'

He looked at Janet. She barely shrugged. Denton said, 'He didn't kill a woman, so—'

'He didn't kill anybody because he was with me, and the police won't believe it!'

Janet started to speak, and Mrs Snokes was still going on, and he lost them both until Janet stopped and Mrs Snokes was saying, '…at first, I was as sure as sure they believed me, and then they came back and said he would have to come down to the police station with them and they didn't believe me any more! I said I'm a witness, he was with me, I'll swear it on the good book, and they said just that he had to come with them. Is that fair, I ask you?'

Now Janet said, 'That's the gist of it, Denton. She's the husband's proof of innocence, and it looks as if they have reason to think she's—'

'I'm not lying! D'you think I'm the kind goes about telling lies? As God's my witness, he was with me!'

Janet almost whispered, 'Her husband found the body.'

Ah. He said, 'How?'

Mrs Snokes started to weep again.

Janet murmured, 'What we could gather from Mrs Snokes is that Mr Snokes found the woman about ten last night. He had been with his wife until only a short time before. The police asked her about the period from seven o'clock to nine or nine-thirty, so…'

'*How* did he find her, is what I asked. *Where?*'

Mrs Snokes seemed to be washing her hands with the hand-kerchief. 'He said there was ever so much blood. It was terrible, he said. She was lying on the floor, not…she wasn't…all clothed. He thought it was her throat, but he was so upset he ran out and ran for three streets before he thought to call for the police. He did! He was that upset. He said it was like looking into Hell.' She looked up at Denton. 'We're Church of England, but we believe in Heaven and Hell.'

Denton contained his impatience. 'Where, Mrs Snokes? *Where* did he find the woman?'

She looked aside at Janet, the way a child will look for help to a parent, and she muttered, 'In her room. Rooms. Down Sadler's Wells way.'

'What was he doing in her rooms?'

'I suppose he heard something. Maybe a scream or a cry. Or things falling. He said there was a great mess in there. Like… broken things.' It must have sounded as appallingly weak to her as it did to Denton. She sagged into her hips; her shoulders rounded; her head fell forward and she sobbed. Denton wanted to put her out of her misery, send her away. He was going to say that there was nothing to be done tonight, say something that would let her down a bit easily and get him completely out of it, but Janet gave him the look and nodded towards the far end of the long room and stood.

Denton got up. He murmured something to the woman, who now looked like a minor figure on a funeral monument, and followed Janet down the room.

The room ran the depth of the house. The far end, by a window looking into their back gardens, was deeply shadowed. Janet said, 'We're trying to get the facts from the husband's solicitor and from the police. There hasn't been time to do either. Apparently the husband didn't get home until long after midnight last night because the police kept questioning him. She was frantic by the time he came home. She says he was in a bad way—actually weeping, she said—and she made him a hot toddy and gave him some chloral and he went right to sleep. This morning, he seems not to have told her any more than she just told you before the police came back and took him in. She went to the police station about noon and got the run-around from them and was told only about half-two that he'd been moved to New Scotland Yard. When she got there, they told her he wasn't there. Apparently she tried to tell them again that she'd been with him, and they said she should go back to the police station.'

'Why was he in the woman's rooms?'

'It's not clear.'

'It's clear to me. He killed her.'

'Oh, Denton…Look here, I'm trying to think like a person of the law. *Not* about guilty or innocent. What is the evidence? What's the defence?' She poked a finger into his chest. 'That's *your* speciality.'

'I don't get it. Why do you or Teddy care? Oh—because it's a woman.' He looked down at her, her shadowed face unreadable. 'Because it's a woman who's been lied to by her husband. Is that it? Because it's a woman whose husband had another woman. Yes?'

'Denton, *she needs help.*'

'But not legal help. There's nothing about the law in her side of it. She's not accused of anything; if she's lying to protect him, the coppers are used to that; they won't prosecute her. Let be, Janet.'

She caught the edge of his waistcoat in her fingers and pulled him a little towards her. 'I want you to find out what happened. For *me*. You're not working on a book just now. You haven't started anything yet. You're at sixes and sevens, I know you are; when I walked in, you had nothing better to do than stand by the window and watch us all melting in the heat. Now goddammit, Denton, *do it!*'

He knew what she meant. He had friends in the police, a knowledgeable solicitor of his own who always had his tentacles out. He said, 'Do it for you because I love you, you mean.'

After a moment she said, 'Yes, that's what I mean. I know it's wrong of me.' Because, she meant, she didn't love him. They'd been round and round about it; she had left him because of it a few months before, come back within hours. He had begun to realise, nonetheless, that 'not loving' meant for her a good deal more than being neutral to him. A great deal more.

Denton looked down the long room at the huddled figure. 'I guess I can ask some questions.' He kissed Janet. 'You expect a lot for a shilling.'

CHAPTER

2

He came through the gardens in darkness, the day's heat now cooled by a summerish rain. Thunder rolled like distant guns and the clouds above London, pale yellow-olive already from the city's never-extinguished light, showed a dull flash to the west. He passed through the gate into his own garden and looked back at her house. A light still burned in her bedroom. He would have preferred to be there, but she had argued that she had to be up and off early; she wouldn't have time for him. She was starting her last year at University College—somehow she was going to do that and work for Teddy Mercer at the same time. He waited a few seconds longer, hoping to see her, then closed the gate and locked it.

Atkins, his 'soldier-servant', as a newspaper had called him, was waiting in his tiny sitting-room, which Denton had to cross to get to the stairs to his own part of the house. Atkins was wearing a green silk dressing-gown, apparently new—certainly so to Denton, anyway—and a brown cap somewhat like a soldier's pillbox but rather collapsed and, startlingly, made of crushed velvet. Atkins said, 'Do you know what time it is?'

'Watch broken?'

'Oh, ha-ha. Me and Rupert have been in bed for hours, now you come traipsing through my room like the Melton through a wheat-field. How'd you like it if I went through your room on the way to bed!'

'You often do.'

'Because I'm paid to do it. Rupert thought you were a burglar.'

'Mrs Striker and I went out to dinner.' He didn't say what else they'd done; he hardly needed to.

Atkins, normally cheerful, seemed particularly narky. Now that Denton thought about it, Atkins had been grumpy ever since Denton had got back from Naples. 'What's the matter?'

'What would be the matter?'

'You don't seem yourself.'

'That'd be a gain, I should think.' Atkins pulled his gleaming silk robe closer and looked down at the black dog, Rupert, who had at first sat, then lain down, and was now on his side snoring. 'You want tea?'

'You talking to Rupert or me?'

'I couldn't sleep. Haven't slept good for a while.' Atkins was going towards the old kitchen, where he had a gas ring. He began to make noise among the dishware.

'Something wrong?'

'What would be wrong?'

'You've been in the sulks since I got home. Is it me?'

Atkins was staring at a small kettle, willing it to boil. He sighed. 'No, it isn't you, Major. Sorry if I've been a bit of a sore-head. Didn't know it showed.'

'What's up?'

Atkins shook his head. He hugged himself in the robe. 'Sit yourself down, General. You want biscuits? I could manage anchovy toast, if you'd like.'

Denton said no, wondered why he wasn't on his way to bed, and sat in an armchair whose springs told him that he ought to buy Atkins some decent furniture. He was still wearing his light mackintosh, so squirmed out of it and then sat in the cushion it had made wet. 'You're not going to talk about it?' he said.

Atkins came out of the alcove with a tray. 'Not yet. Ask you to put up with me for a bit, Colonel.' Atkins had been a real soldier-servant for thirty years; Denton had been a lieutenant for a few months in the American Civil War. The ranks given him by Atkins, which varied from 'left-n't' to general, were a comment on both of them.

Atkins put a plate of biscuits down, immediately gave one to Rupert. 'How's the missus doing with the law?'

'Don't call her "the missus", and after three days she still likes it. In fact, she brought me one of her—or Miss Mercer's—clients.'

'Oh cripes, now what?'

'Woman's husband killed a woman.'

'I knew it! I knew it! Oh, crikey, now we'll be all winter solving a murder. Just when I thought things couldn't get worse.'

'I thought you'd be interested.'

'I got mysteries of my own to solve. Come on, Colonel, you got a book to write, you told me so yourself: a new one was due last spring and you can't even start it yet. You forget the missus's "clients" and just put your nose to the inkwell. We need the money!'

'I'm stuck. Anyway, we always need money. I can always go into the funds if I have to.'

Atkins waggled a finger at him. 'Don't you touch the funds!' Denton had got several thousand pounds for being shot a year before, and he'd invested it. Denton had lived a scatty life, could tolerate not knowing when the next cheque was coming; Atkins, on the other hand, saw the wolf always at the door.

Atkins fell into a chair. 'You write that book.'

'That robe a gift?' Denton said.

'What robe?' Atkins looked about as if the robe might be in one of the room's corners. 'Oh, this? You've seen this a thousand times.'

'It's new. You always used to wear something that looked like it had mange.'

'You're thinking of some other party. Had this a dog's age.' Rupert lifted an ear at 'dog'.

'I like the hat, too. Fetching.'

'Do I make comments about your wardrobe?'

'All the time.'

'Because if I didn't, you'd look like a bleeding tramp. One of us has to have an eye for fashion. Not to mention respectability.' Atkins served the tea. He sipped some. 'All right, so the missus brought home a lost soul. Would she, by any chance, be the wife of what the gutter press are calling the Barnsbury Butcher?'

'You know all about it!'

'I know the police have arrested somebody for murdering a woman in Barnsbury. Hard to miss.'

'The wife said Sadler's Wells. Not that far.'

'Denmark Road. Also "committed indecencies upon her". Also "caught in the act".'

'The wife says he found the body and went to the police.'

'Oh, yes, a likely tale. The wife say anything about how he got into the house?'

Denton shook his head. He sipped his own tea. 'Evening papers said they've charged him?'

'Laying charges as we go to press. Quick-march to magistrates' court.'

'The wife says she was with him all the evening. Until he went out about ten.'

'And marched right off to Denmark Road and just happened to stumble over a body inside a locked house. Oh, yes. I'm sure the police have taken all that into account. He'll hang by Christmas.'

Denton finished his tea. 'The wife thinks otherwise. She would, wouldn't she?' He collected his hat and coat. 'Thanks for the tea.'

'You're not going! It can't be a minute after two in the morning.'

Denton eyed him. 'Want some time off? Would that help?'

'Cripes, no. I'd go non compos with nothing to do.'

'Need money?'

Atkins shook his head. Denton eyed the silk robe. *It's a woman, then.* He knew how that went.

To Atkins's satisfaction, Denton went next morning to his publisher's with a manuscript tucked under his arm. Fresh from Mrs Johnson, his typewriter, it was not the months-late novel that had dismayed Atkins but *The Ghosts of Naples*, a travel book he'd researched and written in Italy.

'Ah!' his editor cried when he saw it. The cry was fairly famous in the publishing world, much envied by editors who hadn't thought of it themselves: it seemed to say everything and actually said nothing. 'Ah, at last.'

'You owe me some money.'

'When it's been accepted, of course, of course. A mere formality in your case, but we do have to be seen to follow the rules. The Ghosts of Naples! How splendid. And how is the, mm, the, hm, the...The title escapes me.'

'The novel.'

'Exactly.'

'*The Secret Jew.*'

The editor winced, hardly more than a twitch that could have been a facial tic up near the left eye. He murmured something about a less than fortunate title; Denton murmured back that it was about a man who thought he was a Jew.

Diapason Lang was thin, in fact almost emaciated, perhaps sixty, perhaps fifty, perhaps Denton sometimes thought twelve, or maybe eighty. Unmarried, unattached, unsexed so far as anybody knew, he had the sensitivities of one of the late queen's ladies-in-waiting. Yet he was a good and a successful editor. 'About to *finish* it, are you?'

'I haven't started.'

'Oh, you must have.'

'I'm stuck.'

'Oh, that's just something that happens. You probably need a holiday—go away somewhere by the sea—but you've just got back from Naples, haven't you? Well.' Lang inhaled mightily, ending with a sniff that compressed his nostrils as if he'd pinched them with his fingers. 'Why don't we put the *The Secret Mmm-hmm* aside for a bit and you can write us a *different* novel. One of your specialities. Horror.' It was an old argument. Lang had tagged Denton as a horror writer after his first book. Denton could have written moral tracts for small girls, and Lang would still have seen him as a master of horror.

'I don't have another sausage waiting in the machine.'

'Sausage? Oh, I see. Ha. You mustn't denigrate your considerable talents. Henry James spoke very highly of you in the *Lit Supp*. Gosse, too. Somewhere. Perhaps a novella—something short, rather curt, very tight—something frightening, delicious—release it at the same time as *The Ghosts of Naples*—eh? Eh?' He leaned a little over his desk, an apparently genuine antique (Denton was learning about such things from a dealer he'd met when a woman had gone missing) that looked as if it had been stored in the damp for several decades and then used by somebody who threw knives. Denton had asked about it once; Lang had said that it was 'part of the firm's history'. Now he said in a confiding voice, 'You *owe* us a book, Denton.'

'Yes, I do. And you owe me the second part of my advance on the one you're leaning on. To write another book, I have to eat. A failing in authors, I know.'

'Oh, please don't be ironical! It isn't at all kind. We do our best for our authors here. You know that. But really, the author must reciprocate.'

Denton stood. 'Back to the sausage machine, you mean.' Lang's tic returned. 'Well, I'll cast around, see what I can do. Something short to go with the Naples book isn't such a bad idea.' He went out.

He walked. He wanted to re-establish himself in his London, so he walked. Denton was American. He had lived in London long enough to know the great city, but he would never

own it the way natives did. Walking was his way of laying temporary claim to it. It also helped him to think.

After ten months away, he had a lot of reclaiming to do.
He walked west along Fleet Street and the Strand, cut up the
Quadrant to Regent Street because he'd thought of the Café Royal,
but it was too early for those louche banquettes, his equivalent of a
club. He was thinking of what Lang had said. (Denton really had
been bad about the overdue novel; Lang had every right to ask for
that advance back, was being good by not doing so; Denton felt
indebted.) A short novel about a ghost? He didn't actually write
about ghosts and spooks and monsters; he wrote about people
who were driven by demons of their own making. Did the sausage
machine have another one of those in it? A small sausage?

He dropped down to Piccadilly and strolled. The night's rain
had brought cooler air behind it; there was a sense of briskness, of
relief in the faces, the faster pace, the noise. Narrowly missed by a
horse-drawn 'bus, he escaped to the other pavement and then made
his way across Green Park, thinking now about Mrs Snokes and
the foolishness of doing what Janet wanted. He'd learn nothing
that would help Mrs Snokes, he knew: it was her husband's lawyer
who would find things out. He'd hire a real investigator, learn the
rest from the public prosecutor if it went to trial. But that begged
the question. Why, he was wondering, did Mrs Snokes think she
needed a solicitor's, and therefore Denton's, help?

He marched across a corner of St James's Park and kept
going, the idea and the question flipping back and forth in his
mind like people going in and out of doors in a French farce—
something short and horrible for Lang, then Mrs Snokes, then
something for Lang—until at last he stood at a rear entrance
of New Scotland Yard, which was where he had of course been
heading all the time.

'You're a sight for sore eyes. Those clothes Italian?' Donald
Munro was a detective inspector, a massive man with a slight
limp not earned in the course of duty. Canadian by birth, former
RCMP, he knew Denton well enough to mock him. Inside the
mockery, however, was obvious pleasure at seeing Denton again.

'If you tell me I look like a pimp, I'll assault you, right here in Met HQ.'

'You armed? You usually are.'

'And licensed. If we'd had to get licences for pistols in the American West, we'd have seceded.'

'Like set up your own country? I thought that's what you fought a war about.'

'Well, this time the rebels would have won. How've you been?' They were striding down an echoing corridor towards the CID detectives' rooms. Munro, having been told by a porter that Denton was there, had come out to meet him. Munro said now that he'd been fine, never better; his roses were the best he'd ever had, wonderful blooms, but the heat was causing some leaf fall; how was Mrs Striker? By the time he'd waved Denton into a hard chair by his untidy desk and got tea, they'd been over the courtesies and Munro asked Denton outright what he was there for.

'You know me too well.'

'Too well indeed. I didn't think you'd've been back long enough to get into trouble. What is it this time?'

Denton handed over his copy of the paper he'd signed for Janet. Munro said, 'Judas Priest. What're you working for some solicitor for? Novels selling that bad?'

'Janet likes her—she won her a lot of money.'

Munro waved an enormous hand. 'And you're doing it for a shilling? Cripes, you must be hard up.' He tossed the paper down. 'This is crap, am I right? What, it makes you confidential? All right. So?'

'A woman was murdered—'

'I saw the name, yeah, Snokes. Killed a woman in Denmark Road. So?'

'He was brought here yesterday.'

'Like hell.'

'That's what the wife said.'

'She's wrong. Divisional CID'll be handling it. She got a bum steer from somebody at the local station. Happens. What probably happened, they stuck him away while the tecs went to the Crown. Why the hell would we move a prisoner about?' He leaned back; the chair groaned; he folded his hands and hooked his thumbs under his chin. 'What's your interest in the wife?'

'She says he's innocent.'

'What would you expect her to say?'

'She says she was with him all the evening. Almost until he found the body.'

Munro laughed. 'You know better than that. It isn't my case; I don't know what the medicos say about time of death and et cetera, but the divisional tecs will have dotted their i's. If they don't believe the wife, it's because they've got something better. Go ask them.' Denton groaned. Munro laughed again. 'You have it coming, Denton, putting that big nose of yours into it. Go see the tecs at division. It'll be N, Islington—probably the Angel sub-division. Or better yet, mind your own business. I say that as a friend.'

'I know you do.' Denton made a sighing sound, half exasperation, half resignation. 'It's something I promised Janet I'd do.'

'Oh—it's the lady, is that it? Yeah, well, that makes it harder.'

They talked several minutes longer. They liked each other. Munro, however, was always a copper first, Denton's friend second; neither of them ever forgot it.

When Denton was going, Munro said abruptly, 'Why does the wife need a solicitor? Or you, more to the point?'

They were walking down a corridor again, this time on his way out. He went all the way to the end and was balanced at the top of a flight of stairs before he said, 'That's what I'm wondering myself. I think it's really why I'm doing it.'

The detective in charge of the Denmark Road murder was not at the N Division station behind the Angel. The officer at the desk wouldn't say for sure that Sub-Divisional Detective Inspector Masefield was in Denmark Road, but he didn't say he wasn't, either.

Denton wanted his work—no, it wasn't his work, his prying—for Mrs Snokes to be finished; still, he had to show Janet that he'd tried. He ambled to the house where the woman had been killed, thinking again by turns about Mrs Snokes's murderous husband and a novella for Lang, and he thought he had one. Oddly, it had come to him while he had been talking to Munro. Odd because it had nothing to do with Munro or Snokes, rather with Lang's love of ghoulies and spooks: a man haunted by himself from another period of his life. His past? His future? The future was tempting, exciting, but he didn't see any story. The past, on the other hand…

Denmark Road was a short street of terraced houses, none very prepossessing. When Denton turned into it from Barnsbury Road, he was able to pick out the correct house by the man in the black bowler standing outside, and the uniform next to him. Denton strode towards them, watching them; the uniform said something to the detective and both men watched him approach.

'No access for gentlemen of the press, sir.'

Denton smiled. 'Do I look like the press?'

The detective came down the single step to the pavement. 'I know you from someplace.'

Denton didn't recognise the man but knew the type. He was not as big as Munro, not as tall as Denton, but he had size— fifteen stone, some of it fat. He wore a coarse tweed suit he'd about outgrown, looked to be in his late fifties, grey hair with a black beard.

'My name's Denton.'

'The sheriff!' The detective pointed a finger, thumb up like a revolver hammer.

Denton was tired of saying that he hadn't been a sheriff, he'd been a town marshal, but he let it go. Thirty years before in the American West—three minutes' work with a shotgun, and he'd been famous. Still was. Annoyed, Denton skipped the man's title and said, 'You Masefield?'

'I'm the sub-divisional detective inspector.'

Denton said, not quite truthfully, 'Munro at the Yard suggested I drop by.'

'Munro at the Yard isn't on this case. You're some kind of writer now, ain't you? Not such a far toss from the daily papers. Nothing doing.'

Denton held out the piece of paper that said he was working for—representing? doing the legwork for the file-wallah of?—Theodora Mercer. The detective frowned at it. The uniformed cop frowned at Denton. The detective thrust it back. 'Don't waste my time with such stuff.'

'It says I'm—'

'It says cock-and-bull. There's nought in that gives you more claim to ask questions or look inside than that dustman coming down yon street. I've work to do, Sheriff; so have you, I'm sure. Push along, if you please.'

Denton tried once more. 'I represent the man's wife.'

'And that's a mystery in itself I won't go into. Tell her if she wants knowledge, she should ask her husband. Off you go now.'

And off he went.

Atkins was wiping the windowsill in Denton's sitting-room as he walked in. Muttering something about dust and summer, Atkins carried his duster off to the window at the far end of the room, where he raised the sash and shook the cloth out with vengeful vigour.

'Doesn't that just put the dust back into the air?' Denton said.

'That's for the neighbours to find out.' Atkins hooked the cloth into the back of his trousers. 'I picked up a couple of the early papers for you. Thought the *Times* would be too nice to have the blood and guts in it. Also, there's mail.'

There was always mail. The post came several times a day. Denton sorted through the half-dozen envelopes, lowered himself to his armchair and sat on the front part of the cushion, one leg forward, arm on thigh, looking at letters. 'What do the papers say?' he said.

'He did it; he's to be charged; inquest Thursday at the Line and Leger. Which is a public house. Took me a bit to see what they was getting at with that name: New River used to have fish in it. Flowed nearby. Anyway, it's over and he's for it.'

Denton threw papers at the grate, bent with a grunt to pick up those that had missed. He held one sheet high in his left hand, then waved it to make sure Atkins saw it. 'We're to have a caller.' He straightened, a little red. 'You remember Mr Hench-Rose.'

'*Sir* Hector Hench-Rose, Baronet. The late, and much missed he is. Of course I do.'

'His son. The new baronet.' The father, Denton's close friend, had been killed the year before by a bomb. Denton still believed that the fault had been his. 'He wants to "come by" on "a matter of some delicacy".' Denton held the note out.

Atkins took it, felt the paper, raised his eyebrows. 'Didn't get that at the Army and Navy Co-op. Best laid cream stock. Like the best laid plans. You want to give him tea?'

'He says half-six.'

'Sherry, then. Whisky?'

'He's only nineteen or so. Make it tea and put the sherry handy—the dry stuff, the same as I drink usually.'

'He's a bleeding baronet!'

'We don't want to seem to have rushed out to get something better. Hmm?'

Denton settled down with the newspapers. The *Daily Telegraph* had the most details:

LATEST NEWS OF DENMARK ROAD OUTRAGE

Snokes Led Away for Detention
'Innocent!'—Accused Man's Wife
The Metropolitan Police, led by Sub-Divisional Detective Inspector F. Masefield of the Islington Division, reported themselves 'fully satisfied' that Mrs Bella Wilcox, widow, was murdered in her rooms

behind her confectioner's shop on Denmark Road by Arthur Snokes of De Beauvoir Town. Although Detective Inspector Masefield declined to give details, he said in the hearing of our reporter that 'We have the right man. We have the proof. We will go to the Crown for prosecution for murder.'

The accused man's solicitor, Mr A.M. Drigny, told the press that Snokes 'is no more guilty than any of you' and he welcomed an appearance in court to prove so. Sources close to the police investigation said that Snokes himself, under advice from his lawyer, has refused to make a statement throughout his many hours' examination, except to ask twice for water.

Reached by our reporter at her pleasant home in De Beauvoir Town, the accused's wife Amelia-Anna said that her husband was innocent and she can prove it. The man Snokes spent the entire evening of Tuesday, the day of the murder, with her, she said, and left only about a quarter to ten to go to his position as assistant night office manager for the Cosmopolitan Steam Railway Company, Ltd. Though distraught, Mrs Snokes was quick to explain that her husband was a trusted employee with an important position. 'They tally the fares at night,' she said, 'and the whole night-time repair scheme of the underground is run from that office.' A subsequent visit to the Cosmopolitan offices confirmed her words. Mr F. Warrenton-Blatch, deputy assistant director of the scheme, said that Snokes had 'never given any trouble' and was 'a quiet man who gave no warning of a violent nature'.

Mrs Wilcox, the victim, was stabbed through the heart with a silver carving knife apparently taken from a nearby sideboard, where the knife rest still reposed when the police arrived. Her clothing was disarranged and there was evidence that a violation had been wreaked upon her. A widow, Mrs Wilcox,

38, had operated a shop for the sale of confections that she made in her own kitchen since the death of her husband nine years ago. A canvass of the street produced such opinions of her as 'very sweet', 'an angel to the children', 'a great loss', and 'she led a blameless life and done nothing to deserve it'.

Our reporter found also that the man Snokes was unfamiliar to the residents of Denmark Road. However, a source close to the Metropolitan Police told our reporter that there were indications in the Wilcox premises that Snokes was less than a complete stranger to them. No details were forthcoming.

We suggest that this horrible act has the hallmarks of a 'crime of passion' but, since the perpetrator has been caught and is to be charged, it was a singular event and will not begin yet another chain of atrocities of the sort that have terrorised Greater London as the polluted tide of modernity has risen ever higher.

Denton let the newspapers drop to the floor beside him. Amelia-Anna Snokes was cooked. Her husband had had a little something on the side—the 'sweet' widow Wilcox—and he had killed her. Crime of passion? Mrs Snokes was not somebody he'd have associated with passion, even at second hand. Well, poor woman, now she had to cope with the knowledge that her husband had been unfaithful, as well as the worse realisation that he and his income would soon be gone. And unless she had money somewhere, she'd be on her own at forty or fifty or whatever she was.

And *that* was genuine horror. What Lang wanted was laughable by comparison.

Sir Ivor Hench-Rose, even at nineteen, was enough like his father that Denton felt himself briefly unable to speak. His throat closed; the threat of tears prickled along the inside of his nose. 'Your father was a very good friend,' he managed to say. 'A very good man.'

'Thank you, sir.' The boy—boy he was to Denton because of his pink cheeks and his smooth skin—still wore a black armband. Seeing Denton see it, he said with a faint blush, 'My mother decreed a year's mourning.'

'Of course, of course.' Denton gestured towards a chair. Tea things were already set out. Atkins appeared, now the perfect servant, murmuring small offers to the boy: tea, Sir Ivor? Milk? Jam tart or biscuits? Denton took the opportunity to study the young man, wonder what his 'matter of some delicacy' would be. Not another murder, surely? In debt? Gambling? Some sort of blackmail? People came to Denton with things like that because of his thirty-year-old reputation: 'The man who saved a town!' They thought he could save them. He never seemed to, but he did get involved in those things in a way that irritated Atkins and Detective Inspector Munro. 'Your big nose.' Well, it was a big nose, in fact a huge nose, looming over a grey Manchu moustache whose ends came almost to his jawbone. And eyes to make most men look away.

'Sir?' The new baronet looked frightened, and Denton realised he had been staring at him.

'I was thinking how much like your father you look.' In fact, he'd been thinking that the boy had his father's heft but not his authority, and certainly not his chin. He had the body of a 'hearty', but there was something in the face that seemed uncertain. Maybe it was only youth. 'You're at university, I believe.'

'Oh, yes!' The boy reacted too strongly to that. He babbled about Oxford. None of the babble was about learning or knowledge; it seemed like a disorganised muddle of touristic treats, as if he thought because Denton was an American he'd want to know which restaurants were best. The best walks. Getting a carriage to the Trout. Best places for a bunch of good fellows to have a midnight swim together.

He's nervous. He's a baronet, for God's sake. How unlike his father. Although to be fair, Hector had been confident because he had been narrow-minded—a perfect John Bull.

'I think you met my father in your own West,' the boy said, giving over babble at last.

'In the States, yes. I took him buffalo hunting. There were still some buffalo then.' Denton gave an ironic half-smile.

'Aren't there now?' The young man reached for a jam tart.

'No.'

'Why not?'

'Indians ate them. No buffalo, no Indians. We got rid of the buffalo and starved the Indians.'

'Oh. That sort of thing is for the best, isn't it?'

Ah, there spoke his father!

Finally, the two-tiered folding table of cakes and biscuits pretty well emptied, the tea drunk, Denton said, 'You wanted to discuss something with me.'

'Ha!' The laugh was surprising. 'Yes, well—Yes, I did. Was coming to that. Ha! You were over the fence before I had my seat secure! Ha!'

Denton waited. He was tired of the boy and his babble. Saying nothing and looking him straight in the eyes seemed the best way to move him along.

Young Sir Ivor stared into his teacup, drank the nothing that was in it, set it aside. He frowned at his fingers. He looked up at Denton and smiled. He looked ready to weep. 'I've a bit of a quagmire,' he said.

Denton nodded.

'This is the sort of thing that chaps are supposed to take to their fathers or favourite uncles, but...' He chewed his lower lip with one tooth. 'Father said if things ever got in a tangle, I could count on you. Those were his words. "You can count on Denton."'

Denton nodded. He hoped that Hector Hench-Rose's son could count on him, although he was having trouble liking him. But that should make no difference.

The boy put his palms together and bent forward, hands squeezed between his beautifully trousered knees. 'I've decided to go into the army. The varsity is wasted on me. I want—*substance*. Not a lot of undergraduates preening and posing and trying to please a herd of dried-up old men.'

His father's son, then. 'What does your mother say?'

'Oh, Mother's a champion. My father was army; so was his father. It's what we do. I think I'd far better—and far rather—spend a year as a soldier, working towards promotion, than spoil my eyes over a *book*.' He looked at Denton, perhaps remembering that Denton wrote books. 'You were in the army, Mr Denton!'

Denton nodded. 'You'll want a commission.' Denton had been three years an other-ranks.

'Yes, of course. That's relevant to the, mmm, delicate matter I wanted to discuss. On which I need advice. *Aid*.'

'I don't know much about the British army.'

The boy waved a large hand, one of his father's gestures. 'Not that sort of advice. I want…' He sat back and looked Denton in the eye. 'I've made a mistake. It's a girl—a young woman.'

Denton thought the obvious—somebody from town, not his class, a pregnancy. It fell on him with the depressing weight of a cliché come to life.

'Oh, not what you think!' Young Sir Ivor seemed to have guessed his thoughts. 'Quite a nice girl, *quite* nice. She's at a college, too.' He looked away, picked at something on the arm of his chair. 'A bit older than I, but hardly enough to matter.' He cleared his throat. 'An Old Student, in fact. Some sort of tutor.'

'A professor?'

'We don't call them that here, but, in a way, yes. A sort of professor. Reading and doing the odd lecture. Quite brilliant, supposed to be. Don't know what she saw in a chap like me.'

A title, maybe. Denton said, 'How far did this go?'

'Not what you think, not what you think at all! There was nothing. No—nothing of that sort. It isn't about her going to have a baby, if that's what you think. It's only that…' He sounded suddenly older than Denton, a bit patronising. 'I don't know what you know about the British army, but we have good regiments and then others, most of them, that a chap of my—in my position would rather not join. It's quite important to be in the historically low-numbered regiments, the Guards and so on. I can't get into a low-numbered regiment if…' He opened his hands as if in surrender.

'If you're encumbered with a woman who isn't of your class?'

'Well, not to put too fine a point on it, yes. And I can't *marry*. That's quite out of the question. Subalterns need their CO's permission to marry, and in the best regiments, it just *isn't done*. I'd be throwing my career away.'

'Like Cornwallis-West.'

Sir Ivor gave him a look that Denton recognised: Hector's look of glassy-eyed incomprehension, usually given when Denton made reference to something that Hench-Rose hadn't learned at school.

'George Cornwallis-West. Married Randolph Churchill's widow. Winston's mother.' Denton might as well have been talking about American baseball. 'He had to give up his army career.'

'Yes. I see.' He didn't see. 'Exactly my point.'

'Tell the young lady the truth.'

A rather sick look passed over the young face. 'I can't.'

'If you've come to me for advice, that's my advice.'

'It sounds absurd, but…I'm afraid. I don't know what I'm afraid of! She's only a slip of a girl. She doesn't even raise her voice. But…'

'Are you in love with her?'

'No, no.'

"Did you tell her you were in love with her?'

After a long silence, the boy said, 'I'm afraid I might have done.'

'Is she in love with you?'

'She's never said that. No. She's very strong. Very strong-minded. But she's said things that suggest—assume—well, you know, a future and being together and…that sort of thing.'

'Did you propose marriage?'

'No, no. Not in so many words. I never said marriage. I'm sure I didn't. My father told me in no uncertain terms how seriously I must avoid that unless I really meant it. As the heir, I mean.' He licked his lips as if they had gone desert-dry. 'She wouldn't be acceptable to my mother. As the baronet's wife.'

'Then tell her the truth.'

The boy hesitated. He tried to smile. 'I was hoping I could prevail upon you to do that.'

Denton was dumbstruck. Then he saw how the boy must see it—this older man, unconnected to him by family, a foreigner, classless: the perfect one to tell his girl, at arm's length, this heartless truth. 'I don't think you know what you're asking.'

'It would be nothing to you, sir. She's nothing to you. She would see you as a representative of my father. It's what fathers do.'

'In opera. This isn't opera. What your father would do is tell you to your face that you're a coward and maybe a blackguard.'

Surprisingly, that didn't send the baronet storming out of the house. All he said was 'No, he wouldn't. He'd know how important it is that I get rid of her. To my future!'

Denton locked his fingers into each other and, his elbows on the arms of his chair, rested his lower lip on the thumbs and studied the young man. The egoism opposite him was impenetrable. There was no point in explaining or arguing. But the boy had a point: he had been raised to be a credit to his title and his class, and Hector would have understood him. Might, indeed, have called him coward and blackguard, but he would have done what the boy wanted—badly, probably, offering the woman money and saying awful things about duty and higher callings. Denton said, 'She's got something on you.'

'How do you mean?'

'You're afraid of what she can do to you somehow. Otherwise, you needn't do anything. You could just walk away. Join a good regiment. How bad is it?'

'There's nothing!'

'Letters?'

'No, no—I don't like to write—'

'So there is something. *Is* she pregnant?'

'I told you, there was nothing like that!'

'And you lied.'

The boy made a quick gesture, hand to head, that was interrupted halfway with a spasm, as if he'd lost control of the arm. He held his forehead very tight. He was sweating; Denton could smell it. The boy said, 'There was some kissing. You know—'

'No, I don't know. Kissing and...?'

'Only some...fondling. You know.'

'And?'

'That's all!' It was almost a scream.

'Then what are you worried about?'

'She'll *tell*!'

It was so much a child's cry that Denton had an instant's impulse to laugh. But the boy was serious. 'What's she going to do? Write a letter to the *Times*? Take out an advert—"I was fondled by Sir Ivor Hench-Rose, Baronet?'" Young women don't do things like that, Ivor. For God's sake. They're too afraid of their own reputations, too puritanical, too...Oh. I get it. She's a New Woman.'

Sir Ivor Hench-Rose was hiding behind his hand.

'She's a New Woman, and the New Woman calls a spade a spade. You think she wouldn't draw the line at writing your commanding officer a letter, once you get one, telling him exactly what went on.'

Hench-Rose nodded, still holding his head with one hand. He muttered, 'I'd be ruined.'

'Commanding officers don't take that sort of stuff as wild oats? Boys will be boys?'

Ivor took the hand away. The skin around his eyes was red. 'She's ferociously intelligent. And sarcastic. She can argue me into knots. It might be all right with a CO if she was some townie bint, but she knows people. She knows how things are done. And she's *fearless*.'

'Why do you think she'd stay quiet if I asked her to, any more than if you did?'

The boy's eyes brightened. 'She's talked about you. She's read your books. You're her kind of person—kind of, you know, *arty*.'

If there was one thing Denton never wanted to be, it was arty. He despised arty. He thought about that for some seconds, actually thought *There might be a story in this, might please Lang, older man goes to plead with young woman—and what, falls for her? 'Speak for yourself, John',* no, that won't do for half a second and then found he'd made a decision, and he said, 'Give me her name and address.' When he had those before him on a slip of paper, the handwriting touchingly like the boy's father's, Denton said, 'She'll be there now?'

'Term doesn't start for a week. More. Yes, she does some sort of extended special thing—I don't understand it. She'll be there.'

Denton put the paper in an upper pocket. 'I'll write to her.'

CHAPTER

'He actually said he was afraid. What has he to be afraid of?'

'You're afraid of me.'

'That's because I'm in love with you. He said he didn't love her.'

'Yes, it's different if you care. Then you're afraid of upsetting a balance.' She looked up at him. 'He sounds rather a pill.'

'He's nineteen. Nonetheless, his father was my friend.'

'And you think he died because of you, and so you'll do what his baby boy wants out of guilt. You're quite amazing, Denton—you're worth the two of them put together, and yet you'll do something like that scene in *Traviata* for them.'

'It's only going to Oxford. I thought we could go together, spend the night.'

'Not on such an errand, I wouldn't.'

'You'd never see her; I'd do that part.'

'While I wait in some hotel? I'd rather be shot from a gun. You can do your dirty work alone.'

'It isn't—' He got up and took a turn to the window. They

were in her little parlour, a place of unfashionable white walls and bright clashes of colour, Janet most of all, in uncorseted draperies of purple and pale blue and yellow, on a dark red couch. He looked out on Millman Street, dusk falling, the street lamps just come on, summer ended in a smell of dust and horses. 'You're right; you're always right; it's a shameful job. But I said I'd do it.'

She pushed herself back on the couch, reclining almost full length, and patted the space she'd made. He sat, feeling her warmth, kissed her on impulse. 'Should I tell him it's off—I've thought better of it?'

'Get it over with. It won't be your finest hour, but I won't turn you out. What did you learn about Mr Snokes?'

He leaned back, fitting his right hip against her abdomen. 'A lot less than I learned from the papers.' He told her about seeing Munro and his visit to Denmark Road. 'Being Teddy's minion was about as much use as a dead cat.'

'Mmm. Oh, well, Teddy simply wanted to get rid of her. She sent me off to meet with the husband's solicitor first thing— that shows how little it matters to her—and I told her what I'd learned and she said, "Good, that's that, then."'

'And what did you learn?'

'That the solicitor's an utter geek and should be fired. Tries to be charming, but it's beyond him. Breath like a spaniel. Shabby clothes. Says things like "Where there's hope, there's acquittal." He's got a barrister he knows—God help Snokes—and says that the defence is all in the timing. Can't have done the deed because he was with his wife and so on.'

'The coppers seem to have obliterated that already.'

'I know. Poor Snokes.'

'Why do we care?'

She stirred, then stretched behind her to take a cigarette from a box. She handed matches to Denton. While he struck a match she said, 'We care because Mrs Snokes, awful as she may be, is a woman who's going to have the world kicked out from under her.' She inhaled and blew out a fine stream of smoke. 'They have a child. That's the only thing new that I had to tell Teddy.'

'She didn't mention it last night.'

Janet shook her head. 'Elegant Mr Drigny referred to him as "the idiot kid". There's something wrong with him. He lives out—some sort of institution.' She shook her head again. 'Christ, what's the woman going to do? Snokes will hang, you know he will. How is she going to support herself, much less a mental case?'

'"Idiot kid" was a diagnosis, or a manner of speaking?'

'Drigny also referred to "the half-wit". With the sort of shake of the head and laugh that indicated I was supposed to find him hugely entertaining. I suppose the boy is retarded, pretty badly so, as he can't live at home.' She blew out more smoke. 'What d'you suppose it would cost a year to keep her and the child going?'

'Janet, you can't go giving your money away!'

'Don't tell me what I can't do. I've plenty of money. I was only thinking aloud. A couple of hundred pounds a year would hardly break the bank.'

'You don't even know Mrs Snokes. She may be an axe-murderer for all we can tell.'

Janet leaned her head back and let smoke escape straight upwards. 'So it's all right for young Sir Ivor to ask you to tell his girl to go to hell, but it isn't all right for me to ask you about giving money to a stranger.' She lifted her head and looked at him. 'I think of you as my moral compass, Denton. What's happened to you?'

'I'm human.'

'Oh, that.' Her head dropped back and she stretched for another cigarette. She sighed. 'Sophie's in heat, by the way. Tell Atkins to keep that monstrous dog of his out of my garden.' Sophie was a likeable mongrel she had brought back from Naples.

'You don't want little Sophies?'

'Least of all if they look half like Rupert. Mind you tell him. He's got quite careless about the gate.'

Denton shifted and leaned back against her with his right hand on one of her ankles. 'Something's wrong with Atkins. He's not himself.'

'Another one of his schemes gone bust?' Atkins had a passion for losing his money in bad investments.

'I think it might be a woman.'

She smoked. Outside, the light slowly failed. She said, 'Not everything bad that happens to men is the fault of some woman.'

Sir Francis Brudenell was a solicitor, not a barrister, but he had a reputation and an income that most barristers might envy. His offices were in a tall house in Chancery Lane, handy to the inns and the Temple. A bit older than Denton, he wore the most beautiful suits to be seen this side of Buckingham Palace—and a good deal smaller round the middle—and was driven about London in a succession of motorcars that seemed bigger and shinier each year. Noted as the brain behind three barristers famous for their criminal cases, he had been called within Denton's hearing 'the law-courts' puppet-master'. Denton found him congenial, if expensive.

'I'm wondering if you could find something out for me,' he said now.

Sir Francis, who looked a little as you might expect a Houyhnhnm to look (long, equine face, intelligent and stoically amused), gave a sly smile and said, 'You're the one with the investigative turn of mind, I should think.'

'You have resources.'

Sir Francis looked modest.

Denton went on. 'You've heard about the woman who was murdered in Barnsbury?'

'I heard something said but I didn't give it my attention. I don't have a horse in that race, as they say. One of your hobbies?'

Denton gave him a quick sketch of what he knew.

'It's the husband for certain, is it?'

'The police think so.'

'Who's defending him?'

'He's got a solicitor named Drigny.'

Sir Francis's eyebrows rose. 'Not one of the names to make a solicitor's heart beat faster.' He burrowed in a desk drawer, pulled out a blue-cased book that might have been a parliamentary report. 'Drigny—Drigny—Aloysius Michael. That the one? Clerkenwell. My, my. I am not heartbroken to admit I don't know him.' He dropped the book back into the drawer. 'Are you curious about Mr Drigny?'

'I'm a little curious about the murderer's wife.'

Sir Francis smiled. 'The *accused's* wife.'

'Right. She came to see me. It doesn't matter why. But she refused to have an investigator. Said something about how they were "nasty people". I'm wondering why.'

Sir Francis opened his mouth, then closed it and tilted his head back as if to study the ceiling. From that position, he said, 'This has to do with the murder case?'

'Curiosity.'

'Killed a cat.' The solicitor's head dropped to its normal position. 'Curiosity also costs money.'

'Well—look at it this way: I make a living by figuring people out and making novels out of them. That's how I can pay your bills.'

'What is it you want to know?'

'I thought—your contacts, your sources—maybe you could find out why she's so down on hiring an investigator to defend her husband. I thought she might have had some kind of bad experience with an investigator in the past. Maybe hired one? Or maybe the husband did?'

'Ah. Oh, yes, I see. Well. I might have someone who could try to find that particular needle in a haystack.' He passed across a leather-bound book and a gold pencil. 'Write her name and address in the book. We might start with where she lives—she isn't WC1, I suppose? Didn't think so. London has hundreds of investigators, as you must know, a great many of them unlicensed and most worthless. I could have Doty grub about, I suppose. But it will cost. Doty's materialistic.' Doty was his own investigator. Doty was paid only slightly less than the king's equerry.

'I don't mind paying a *little*.'

Sir Francis named a figure; should he advise Doty not to exceed that? Denton, who had hoped for half as much, swallowed and said that would be fine.

'Do you Americans know what we mean by a "wild goose chase"?'

'We have them, too."

'It's what this will prove to be, I fear.' That warning issued, Sir Francis became sociable, asked about the year in Naples, then 'that fine woman, Mrs Striker', about whose dark past he knew as much as Denton. Then he turned to motorcars. 'I have my eye on a new Italian model! You remember the Benz? I mean to get rid of it. Now I think of it, it would make a splendid motor for you. Are you still daring to appear in that three-seater French machine?'

Denton had bought a Barré a year before. 'I forget I own it. I haven't taken it out of its garage since I got home.'

'And no wonder. What you need is a proper motorcar and a chauffeur to drive you in it!'

'I can't afford to pay for two drivers, Sir Francis. I'm already paying for yours.'

Sir Francis was delighted. He loved being expensive. His fondness for Denton had a lot to do with that. He saw Denton out, patting his shoulder and saying he must, he really must think about the Benz. And do send him something about this murder case, which sounded more interesting than he'd at first thought. Meaning, he saw dinner-table gossip, at least a couple of good stories, in what would prove to be the ineptitude of lawyer Drigny and whatever luckless wig he put into court.

Denton was met at his front door by Atkins, who was pulling the door open just as he was trying to put his key into it.

'Snokes is out,' Atkins said. 'Early papers. "Insufficient evidence".'

'Could I come in?'

'Well, nobody's stopping you. I thought my news would be welcome!'

Denton was handing him his hat and gloves. 'What d'you mean, he's out? The last I heard, he was headed for police court!'

'Bit of a mystery. They never got past the magistrate, it seems. His lawyer said that justice had been done. Well, what would he say? Any road, Snokes is back in the lovely home in De Beauvoir Town, and him and the missus are having a love feast, with the main subject what he was doing in the lady confectioner's house, I'm sure.' The speech had taken them all the way up the stairs and into the sitting-room. 'Struck speechless, are you, General?'

'Confused, anyway. "Insufficient evidence"? That pompous detective at her house sounded as if he'd got it on a stone tablet from the Almighty.'

'Yes, well, shocking as the idea is, I suppose even policemen stretch the truth now and then.'

Denton frowned at his wall of books. 'He had something and it fell through.'

'Rushing his fences.'

'Mmm. I'll have to talk it over with Mrs Striker. Which reminds me, her dog's in heat.'

'Oh, don't I know it! That bitch has poor Rupert tying himself in knots! Using her wiles or whatever they are on him. Rupert doesn't know any more about procreation than I know about the Irish Question. He's fair frantic with it.'

'Don't let them get together.'

'You think I want Rupert doing the unspeakable with some Eye-talian cur? It's embarrassing enough when he pokes his Johnson out while I'm walking him. Little kids point and ask their mummies what that thing is on doggy. He trots it out at the worst times, the very worst. Of course, he doesn't know any better. It's Nature.'

'So is Sophie's being in heat. Let's not let Nature take its course. Mrs Striker would have our hides.'

He should have been thinking about the novella for Lang, but instead he grabbed his hat back from Atkins and headed for Teddy Mercer's office in Goodge Street. When he burst in, Janet looked up from a littered desk and said, 'What are you doing here?'

'I've come to see my employer. And you. Snokes is out.'

She stared at him. 'Oh, well, that's better for her. And the child.'

'The coppers sounded dead sure he did it. Now he's out. Oh, hello, Teddy.'

'Come to give me my shilling back?' She was short and squarish, seemingly combative because she carried her shoulders back and her large chin forward. 'You certainly didn't do anything to earn it.'

'I tried. There was nothing to learn.'

'Amateurs.' She threw several bundles of paper tied in blue tape on Janet's desk. 'File those except the top one, which is Hatton, and look up the references in that one because I smell a rat. Are you still here, Denton?'

'I thought you might know something about Snokes.'

'Neither know nor care. I don't do murders. We told the wife to see the husband's man. You could do the same. That's an impolite hint to move the goods off the premises.'

Denton looked at Janet, who smiled and then frowned and bent her head over Hatton v. Somebody.

'You're heartless, Teddy.'

'I'm a lawyer, ain't I?'

He might as well have stayed home, he told himself as he headed that way. Nonetheless, it gave him a chance to think more about his story or novella or whatever it was: man haunted by self from past. His youth—selfishness, sexual urges, ignorance? Or farther back. A child? Haunted by a child? Too Henry James?

Drigny, Snokes's solicitor, had his office in Clerkenwell in an old house that included a gem-polisher and a firm of commission agents, whatever they were. A sign said that clients had to make an appointment, and when he got inside he saw why: people, mostly men, came and went through a stuffy little ex-parlour from an inner door as if from some sort of takeaway. They were in and out in about the time it would have taken to put a chop and two veg into a dinner bucket, take the money, give change, and call out 'Next!'

Drigny was perhaps forty. He was pale, round-shouldered, expressionless, as if he had seen everything and didn't want to see more. Denton suspected that he was tired of the law but would keep on with it until he dropped, as if he had taken on something that had once seemed interesting but had disappointed. He was wearing a dark lounge suit on which his scalp was slowly falling in white flakes. He broke wind occasionally without seeming to notice, only lifting a buttock, probably unconsciously.

'Mr—Denton, is it? I charge for my time. More as you didn't have an appointment.'

'It's about Snokes.'

'You're in luck that I've nobody for fifteen minutes. That's two and six. My clients pay as they go.'

Denton put some coins on the cheap oak desk. 'I just want to know what happened that Snokes was let go.' He handed over Teddy Mercer's useless piece of paper. Drigny read it through glasses that he held up without unfolding the bows. 'I don't know her, but that's all right. You're some sort of investigator?'

'Mmm.'

'I can always use a good investigator if you don't charge the world. Snokes. This Mercer woman was engaged by Mrs Snokes?'

Denton grinned. 'If *you* ask the questions, I'll have to charge two and six.'

Drigny waved a hand, not at all impatiently but resignedly, as if humour, irony, bad temper, even irritation had been ground out of him.

Denton said, 'Mrs Snokes thought she needed a lawyer when the police wouldn't believe her about where Snokes was that evening.'

Drigny had his head on one hand. He was giving half his attention to Denton, half to blue-bound papers on his desk. He said, 'Wasted her money. She should have come to me. Water under the bridge now.' He pushed a paper away and looked at Denton. 'The police thought they had Snokes. As it happened, they didn't. When the prosecutor's solicitor saw that, he gave up.' Head on hand, he stared at Denton as if he was done.

'Tell me what happened in the magistrates' court.'

Drigny looked at him. No change of expression. 'What happened had happened the day before. I went to the scene of the crime. Demanded to. Police didn't want me to, but they know better. You've been there? Well, picture a room had been a dining-room, now was a bit of everything. Worn carpet, soaked with blood. Coppers had taken the body and the knife away. I asked to see the knife, was told it was "being tested". Told them I'd give them twenty-four hours and then I'd howl to the magistrate. So I looked about the scene of the crime, found three marks on the bare floor where the carpet ended. Fingerprints. You understand about fingerprints? Well, then. I thought, *oho*. See?

'Next day, I went to magistrates' court with my client. So the magistrate comes in, and—'

Denton interrupted. 'I thought solicitors couldn't argue cases.'

'*Magistrates*' court. Solicitors welcome in magistrates' court. Half my income would go out the window if I wasn't. Where was I? Oh, in court. Well, the prosecutor's man—also a solicitor—asks for remand and says, "We have incontrovertible evidence" and so on, no question of guilt, la-la-la. I had Mrs Snokes there but I didn't want to use her unless I had to—matters of time are always dicey—so I get up and say, "Am I to understand that the Crown intends to submit evidence drawn from fingerprints at this time?" Because, as you know, they haven't risked a case solely on fingerprints as yet, so it sounded as if what I was asking was if this was going to be the test case of the fingerprint theory.

'The Crown's man says—he's a pompous sort, chap named Gregg, not bad at what he does but not Blackstone, either—

he says, "The Crown does not intend to submit fingerprint evidence at this time." And he sits down, as I knew he would, thinking that's that. But I say, "Why not?" Now, if the police had instructed Gregg properly, he'd have been ready and he'd have said that the theory wasn't established and let it go at that, but Gregg, who hadn't been properly instructed, hemmed and hawed and la-la-la'd, and I say, "But there *were* fingerprints found, were there not?" Well. Gregg can't lie and say no. So he says yes. And I say, "Whose are they?"'

Drigny smiled. If Denton hadn't been looking right at him, he'd have missed it. It hardly moved Drigny's lips and it certainly didn't show his teeth. Still it raised Denton's estimation of the man, who might have been a husk stuffed with legal sawdust but who was no fool: he had laid a trap, and he had sprung it. Janet had underestimated the solicitor. Denton, who liked a good story, said, 'And what happened?'

'There was a wrangle, of course. Gregg tried to say they chose not to submit certain evidence at this time, et cetera, and I said that in that case I requested immediate release of the accused. Gregg argued that this was a first appearance and remand was the issue and they didn't need fingerprint evidence at this time and place, even though they knew it was incontrovertible. That was what I needed. I said, "Then tell us, as we will grant that fingerprint evidence is incontrovertible, whose fingerprints have the police found? *Are they those of the accused?*" Well, of course they weren't. I knew they couldn't of been or they'd have used them in court. And Gregg had to say it out loud— the three fingerprints on the varnished floor weren't Snokes's.' Drigny's spectral smile came again. 'I pointed out that therefore my learned friend had just proved that somebody else had been in the room, not Snokes. The magistrate scolded Gregg, and they withdrew the charge.'

'Is he still a suspect?'

'Of course he is. He's the only suspect. They'll take him in again; I've warned him. The minute they come up with some other evidence.'

'Is he guilty?'

'You must know better than to ask me that.'

Drigny was looking at his watch. Denton tossed another shilling on the desk. 'I'll run behind if you stay on,' the solicitor said.

'Can I talk to him?'

'Can for all I care. Watch out for the press if you go to his house. They're like fleas on a dead cat up there.'

Denton stood. 'If he didn't kill her, who did?'

'Not my concern. You don't intend to investigate this and then try to bill me, I hope. You'd die of old age before you saw a penny. No contract, no payment.'

'I was hired to serve the wife. That's what I'm doing.'

Drigny, his face as expressive as a corpse's, looked him in the eyes for several seconds. 'If you find anything, you know, *funny*, let me know. I pay for good information.'

'You think there's something funny with the wife?'

'There's something funny somewhere.' Drigny picked up the shilling and pocketed it. 'As you go through the anteroom, sing out the name "Shuttling", will you? Or just say "Next."' He lowered his dead face to his papers.

At the door, one hand on the brass knob, Denton said, 'Did Snokes ever speak at all?'

'No.'

'Not even to you? Why not?'

'No idea.'

Denton let irritation show in his voice. 'Can you get me into the crime scene?'

'No.' Drigny's head never moved.

'Next!'

Getting to see the Snokeses was more difficult then he had expected. The problem was not the press, but Mrs Snokes. Denton sent a note; she refused by return post. He sent another note; she replied that her husband was recuperating and could not be troubled. Denton sent a third note, pointing out that he had gone out of his way to help her, had been sought out by her (not quite true), and had made a special trip to New Scotland Yard on her business. Might he please have a few minutes with her and her husband?

The answer didn't come for twenty-four hours. This time, she supposed he could see them, but he was not to come until Saturday, by when she hoped and prayed the vultures of the press would have cleared off the doorstep and left them in peace.

'Why do you give a damn, General?'

Denton was silent for a good long time. 'Have you ever had an urge to go through other people's houses while they're out?' He glanced at Atkins, who was looking disapproving. 'Partly it's the risk. Partly it's...' He shrugged. 'Maybe it has something to do with writing novels.'

So he went to Oxford.

CHAPTER 5

The train ground into Oxford with a clatter and clang and a belch of steam that hid the dreaming spires, of which Denton had heard, although he didn't know the source. He carried no luggage but planned to go back that night.

It was still summer in Oxford, the air sultry, looking thick at a distance, some of the more distant spires almost invisible. He walked. He had a map he'd picked up in London, already knew that it was a trudge from the station to her college. He tickled his brain, as he had on the train, with that fleeting notion of a story about the encounter to come: a man goes to a woman to do some unpleasant duty for a friend. Then? Then, perhaps, to his astonishment, she is lovely, smart, charming. They spend hours together; she doesn't seem to mind that he is older. On the contrary; it's she who proposes that they meet again. He leaves her to go home, remembers something, goes back, hears her say to another young woman something like 'Of course I shall have to get rid of him once he's done what I want. He's hooked for now, at any rate.' With the same rich, sensuous laugh that had enchanted him.

A bit obvious. Needed thought.

Oxford surprised him by not being medieval, in fact by looking a lot like parts of London, manufacturing not unknown. Closer to the colleges, he got the sense of the great institution— pubs, bookshops, the assertiveness of the mighty architecture. The lack of students, however, seemed to him to tilt it out of kilter: a stage setting with no play.

Her college was north of the men's, by location neither in nor of the university so far as he could see. Janet had told him that the women had been 'allowed' there for three decades but couldn't take degrees; he wondered why they were there, in that case. The atmosphere? Assertion of a right they couldn't yet demand?

'Mr Denton to see Miss Gearing.'

The porter was male, a little to his surprise. Neither young nor large, so not there for defence. The man consulted a book, nodded, rang a bell, sent off the maid it produced. Denton was invited to sit on a long bench like a church pew. He wondered if this was filled in term with young men like Ivor Hench-Rose. He was reminded of Rupert, sniffing at the garden wall.

She came into the lodge by a different door. He supposed it was she: she seemed right, not at all girlish, apparently serene; she looked at him with about the expression he expected. *My lady Disdain*. Who said that? Had to be Shakespeare, because that and Dickens were all Denton could quote from. She was—disappointingly, for magazine-fiction purposes—not pretty, in fact from some angles homely, long-faced, olive-skinned, a wide nose with nostrils that seemed crushed against her cheeks; her eyes were large and somewhat bulging, as if she were being choked. Her lips seemed permanently pressed together in a slight smile, the kind that isn't sincere; maybe it was nature, not choice. She had a good, possibly voluptuous, figure, more than suggested by the light dress that blew against her in the breeze.

And she was American. From the South: an accent he hadn't heard in years, only a trace in the 'I' that became 'Ah', the slight temptation of 'you' to elide into 'yew': 'Ah won't let you take me to lunch, thank yew.' She held out a large but short-fingered hand.

'I'm Rosamund Gearing.' She seemed self-possessed, convinced of her own place in the world. Her voice was rich, cool, faintly ironic.

'I'm Denton, as you guessed.'

'Oh, I knew your face. Should you like to sit somewhere?' The Southern accent, perhaps trained away and resumed out of nervousness or simply meeting another American, seemed to fade. The 'should you like' seemed to him deliberately British. 'Most places are private now with the students gone, of course. You wanted to speak privately, you said.' She didn't smile any farther than her habitually pressed lips already offered, but she seemed amused. He saw why Ivor Hench-Rose was frightened of her: she had great presence. Also why he had been attracted. There was some French expression for being at the same time both alluring and homely.

He said, 'You're American, aren't you?'

She laughed again. 'Don't expect a Daisy Miller.'

He skipped over the submerged hostility in that and said, 'Maybe you could show me this part of Oxford.'

That didn't please her much. Maybe she wanted to get rid of him more quickly. Still, she said to the porter, 'I'll be back very shortly, Jenkins,' and led Denton out into the air. They walked for a hundred feet towards a grassy meadow and a row of willows that would produce, Denton supposed, a stream, and she said impatiently, 'Say what it is you've come for, please, Mr Denton.' The Southern accent was entirely gone.

'You seem to think you know already.'

'"A matter of some delicacy", your note said. There are so few of those in my life that I can pretty well guess what's meant. However, you're going to be the one to give it a name.' Her right hand rested on her left arm, seemed to caress it; she looked down, apparently to study her own arm.

He was acutely embarrassed. For all his talk of opera (which he didn't like), he hadn't really faced the moment. 'How did you recognise me?' he said as a way of putting it off.

'Something in a mag, an engraving of you, maybe. I admire your books.'

'Are you studying English?'

She laughed. 'I took a first in English lit because that's one of the few exams they'll let us sit, but my interest's really in some grey place where philosophy washes over into psychology. Do you know who William James is?'

He wanted to say *Do you take me for a dunce?* but muttered, 'Of course,' and let it go at that. She said she had affinities with James but her interest was 'less humanistic'.

'I'd think philosophy and psychology would be entirely humanistic.'

She laughed yet again. She held up a hand and studied it in the sunlight.

As he'd expected, a smooth stream of water appeared through the willows. A couple of punts—he knew they were punts; they had punts at Hammersmith, where he rowed for exercise—were tied up, nobody in them. She made no attempt to play the guide; the river might as well have been the Nile, for anything she told him about it. Nor did she in fact say anything. Facing the inevitable, Denton said, 'I'd like to talk to you about young Hench-Rose.'

'I see.'

She led him under the willows. There was an iron bench there, all scrolls and leaves and chipped paint. He thought it looked both ugly and uncomfortable. She stood by it, her fingers touching the back, more or less inviting him to sit if he wanted to, her face and light dress dappled by shadow. She looked calm, even at ease, as if this were her house and he would be the one leaving it soon, not she. Inside the light summer skirt, however, he saw one knee moving, small jerks.

'He's a boy, Miss Gearing. Boys change very quickly.'

'What's your interest, Mr Denton?'

'His father was a good friend. If he hadn't been killed last year, I think he'd have been here, not me.'

'At least you're embarrassed to be here; I doubt he would have been. He was here once, seeing Ivor. Not one of the broadest minds in the room.'

'You met him?'

'I didn't need to.' She laughed. 'Nor was I asked to. Come, come, Mr Denton, get it over with.' Her left hand rested just above her right breast, the fingers moving back and forth.

He disliked her brutality, so was brutal in reply. 'How far did it go, you and Ivor?'

'You must have heard that from him already.'

'You know what he wants me to do, I think.'

'I always know what Ivor wants. He's transparent. I know what he wants, Mr Denton, but I want you to go through the pain of saying it.'

He disliked that, too. It made him more brutal. 'He wants to be rid of you.'

'Of course he does. Are you going to offer me money?'

'No.'

'What, then?'

'Nothing.'

'Oh, that *is* hard to resist.' She laughed again; it was, he saw, a too-often-used tactic. 'A matter of honour!' She tipped her head back. Her bulging eyes seemed half-closed, appraising, maybe mysterious or trying to be. She said, 'Ivor is rid of me already. There was never anything much. As you say, he's a boy. I'm four years older than he; I have a position here. There's been nothing to do with him since term ended. I've been on the Continent.'

'He's concerned.'

'What is it now? The army? Has he settled on that? I shan't stop him. What did he think, that I wanted to marry him? Dear God! Have you met his mother? Can you imagine being related to that? I've no desire to be a baronet's brood mare, Mr Denton. "Lady Rosamund"? That was never on.'

'What was, then?'

She shrugged one shoulder. 'Play. Something different. One can't do much in my position. I can put up with women only for so long. The students are too young, the senior fellows too old.' She turned her head and seemed to look at the river, then turned partway back and looked at him more or less sideways. Her profile was better than her full face, he thought, and he was aware of what Ivor must have seen: that full body, pretty breasts under the summer clothes, which she kept touching as if wanting to find herself inside them. She said, 'You can tell Ivor I shan't go out of my way to say anything—but if I'm asked, I'll tell the truth.' She smirked. 'Did he tell you I held up the handkerchief for him?'

The expression was a new one to Denton. It didn't take any brilliance to figure it out, however. 'He said there'd been some "kissing and fondling".'

'In the meadows at night. All very furtive. That was a good part of the fun of it.'

'If asked, will you say that he forced you?'

She laughed. 'Forced! He *begged*. And begged and begged. Did he tell you that? I rather despised him for begging, but he so wanted me to touch him that I was curious to see what would happen. It was in fact a case of what Professor Mikkelson calls "spontaneous neurasthenic early release". Cribbing from Krafft-Ebing, I think.'

'Ivor, or Professor Mikkelson?'

'It's a clear case of hyperaesthesia—excessive desire for the female.'

'Cribbing?'

She looked at him with what he thought he was supposed to interpret as disdain. 'I don't like ragging, Mr Denton. I don't respond to it.'

'It looks to me as if you do.' He was smiling.

'You are not free of hyperaesthesia yourself. I see it quite clearly in your novels. All your male characters—these "demons" you invent for them.'

'I thought we were talking about you and Ivor Hench-Rose.'

She turned to face him again. He was thinking about what she had said, the couple on the dark grass, those cool-looking hands on the erection. Thinking, too, about his idea for a story and how ridiculously short of her he'd come.

She said, her left hand back on her right breast, 'What does he think, that I'm going to write a letter to his mother saying that

I did for him what boys did for him at school and that I let him put his hand down my knickers? Tell him for me he's a fool.'

'There's no chance of a baby?'

'Not unless they've changed the mechanism of insemination. I'm a rational being, Mr Denton; I'd hardly be swept away by what you novelists call "passion", by which you mean the sex urge, if you'd only put things honestly. I'd be as likely to let Ivor Hench-Rose inseminate me as to put my head through the bars of the lions' cage in Regent's Park zoo.' She tilted back again, gave him that half-appraising, half-contemptuous look. 'Though I mean to have a child when I find the right father. The race needs more minds like mine.'

She was trying to be shocking, he thought—testing him. He made his voice bland and said, 'So I can tell Hench-Rose that you won't say anything.'

'I told you—if I'm asked, I'll tell the truth.'

'I hope that'll satisfy him. He's really worried.'

'He should have thought of that while he was begging.' Denton snorted. 'No wonder he's afraid of you.'

As if he had finally said what she wanted to hear, she surprised him by taking his arm and leading him farther down the river. She said, 'Is that part over? We're done with Ivor, are we?' She began to tell him about the swans that appeared around a bend.

They walked for another ten minutes and then she said she would go back. She had talked about his novels, which she actually seemed to have read. She admired his 'psychological percipience' but thought his use of personal ghosts and demons was cheating. She suspected that he had read too much Swedenborg but thought he would do better to read Nietzsche. Denton, who had read both, thought about the couple on the dark grass. He thought about her touch on his arm, her hip's brushing his, suspected he was being seduced, or at least teased. At one point, to contribute something, he asked her what part of the South she was from.

'I don't have any interest in where I'm from. I care about where I'm going.'

Outside the porters' lodge, she extended those cool fingers. 'I'm coming to live in London after Michaelmas term. I want to call on you.'

This was too like his story idea. He muttered something polite.

'I want to be introduced to people. I mean to be somebody, to be known. The easiest and quickest way to do that is to write something. You can give me pointers.' She squeezed his big hand. 'You will help me, won't you?'

Was there an implied threat, maybe the suggestion that she could withdraw her promise to say nothing about Ivor? He said, 'Maybe you should send me something you've written first.'

'Better if you introduce me to your publisher and a few reviewers. Not the old guard, Gosse and that lot—the younger ones. And not the ones who are part of the pederasts' clique. I know all about how that works; I see it here among the Sapphists. Goodbye, Mr Denton.' A mysterious smile. 'You'll see me again.'

He found that he hoped not.

Travelling back on the train, he wondered what it was he disliked about her, realised it was temptation. And some essential falseness. He changed the ending of his story: the man doesn't hear her say anything about him but goes home, realises he's been a fool. Next day when a note comes from her, he throws it away unread.

'A New Woman? Not your sort, Denton.'

He and Janet were lying up in bed in her house, each with a book, each wearing eyeglasses, remarkably chaste and marriage-like.

'I don't know what else to call her. Anyway, yes, not my sort, but…mmp-mmm, a wagon-load of life force or whatever it is. Like something out of Shaw.'

'Sex, you mean.'

'It has that effect, sure, but…There's something…uneasy about her, too. She keeps touching herself. One of her knees kept jumping, too, but the rest of her was still as a statue.'

'You were watching her knees?'

'I had the feeling that she…She's interested in psychology. I wonder if that isn't a kind of narcissism. *That's* what bothered me! She made everything about *her*. As if…there was the world, and there was her.'

'Maybe if people're interested in psychology, they do it because they're trying to find out what's wrong with them.'

'Well, that's narcissism, isn't it?'

She went back to reading. He interrupted her to say, 'I think Ivor Hench-Rose got off easy.' He waited; she had glanced up from her book but went back to it. After some seconds, he said, 'Have you ever heard of "holding up the handkerchief"?'

'Sounds like what we used to call "hand work".' She made a gesture—fingers curled, hand moving up and down.

'She said he begged her. Then Ivor apparently—what do the horsey people say? —"rushed his fences".'

'What, rushed her? Oh, you mean finished before he started—one of those.'

'She made it sound like he was a toy she played with. A game. But more intellectual than physical.'

Janet made the gesture in the air again and returned to her book. After a dozen seconds of staring at it but apparently not reading it, she said, 'You may be right about the narcissism.' She looked again at the book and then said, 'Maybe the life force isn't good for the brain.'

6

Back in his own house the next morning, Janet sleeping late because it was Saturday, he made coffee of the Italian kind on his gas ring and took the cup to his desk. In two hours, he had a draft of the story about the older man and the girl. Purely magazine stuff, but money.

The weather had broken at last, the heat driven ahead of cool rain that fell in great splashes on the pavements. He had got wet making the crossing from her house; now, heading down-stairs again, he wore old bags and a tattered smoking jacket, no necktie or scarf.

'You look like a tramp,' Atkins said, coming up from his lair. 'Don't you dare put your nose outside the door in those clothes.'

'I've decided to become a Bohemian.'

'You can decide to do without a manservant, in that case. Look at that coat! I've seen dossers under a bridge in better.'

'It's comfortable.'

'If that was the standard, where'd respectability be, I ask you. You going out to them Snokeses today?' When Denton said he was, Atkins muttered something about putting out 'one of the cheap suits'.

Denton sprawled in his armchair. 'What d'we have for breakfast?'

'I *suppose* I could produce an egg. Two, if you're peckish. Loaf's stale, but I could toast it. I suppose you'd want jam. We had some very nice greengage, but I finished it. Golden syrup?'

'On toast? What do you take me for? What happened to the marmalade?'

'Oh, marmalade. I've some Society Old Fashioned somewhere.'

'Well, produce it up here. Bacon? Gammon? Ham? What the hell!'

'I haven't been to the shops. I'm not myself.'

'Atkins, what's wrong?'

Atkins was standing with his arms folded. He dropped his chin into one hand. 'I don't know. I really don't know.'

'I think you do. You're in the dumps. Is it me?'

'You? No, no. It's...' He took his hand away, seemed to shake himself out, as if he were a wrinkled suit. 'We'll have a talk one of these days.'

'How about now?'

'No—no.' He sighed. 'Rupert tried to dig under the fence.'

'I saw. She'll kill both of us if he gets to Sophie.'

'Butler five doors down suggested I have him clipped. Be like getting my own cut off. Can't do it. It's his nature.' Apparently reminded, he said, 'How'd you do with the female in Oxford?'

'She's going to be good about it.' That wasn't quite true, he thought: goodness was probably not in Rosamund Gearing's vocabulary.

'So,' Atkins said, 'once you've seen these Snokeses, you can get to work on the writing, isn't that the way of it?'

'I've already put in two hours on something while you and Rupert were snoring downstairs.'

'That novel?'

'A story. A definite ten-quidder.'

'You said you'd think up a plot for that novel on the train.'
'I don't "think up" plots! I said I'd think on the train.
Which I did. And it came out as this story. Stop nagging.' His
other idea for some horror for Lang, the thing about a ghostly
child who is or may be the protagonist's own once-innocent self,
hadn't gone anywhere. *The Secret Jew* was still its own secret. 'I'll
keep on thinking.'

'Thinking, General, to quote yourself, "don't get the hay in".
I'll fetch breakfast.'

When Denton had eaten and changed and was going out,
he said to Atkins, who was waiting to hand him a mac and an
umbrella, 'Is it a woman?'

Atkins's small face contracted, giving Denton a vision of
what he would look like in old age. In a hoarse voice, Atkins said,
'Well, what if it is?'

Denton met his eyes. An expression of great misery
appeared around them. Denton patted him on the shoulder.
'You've got my sympathy. Let's talk about it. I've had some experience in that department.'

Atkins, muttering that he'd think about it, handed over the
umbrella and helped him on with the mac. As Denton was going
out the door, Atkins said, 'It's never fatal, is it?'

'"Men have died and worms have eaten them, but not for
love."'

'Cold comfort's better than none, I suppose.'

Denton had the pleasant surprise of finding a motor-driven
taxicab in Russell Square. Chugging up to De Beauvoir Town, he
was reminded of Sir Francis Brudenell's Benz.

The Snokes house was a semi-detached stucco in a terrace of
lookalikes that Denton's scanty architectural sense told him were
not very old, but old enough to have come down in the world.
They were better, however, than the mean houses and little facto-
ries along the Regent's Canal, and they got some second-hand
lustre from nearby De Beauvoir Square and Kingsland Road. The
Snokes house was different only because of the three men in bad
suits who lounged outside it—newspapermen from the tabloids.

'You're the sheriff, aren't you? Name Denton, isn't that right? Know you anywhere. What're you doing here, Mr Denton? Mr Denton? You working on this murder, Mr Denton? What's up—come on, now, you be good to us, we'll be good to you. Mr Denton!'

He simply looked at the three of them, raising a warning finger at one who came too close. When at last the door was opened by an unhappy-looking housemaid, they were all around him, panting like dogs who had been run too hard. Denton tipped his wide-brimmed hat to them and stepped inside.

'Denton,' he said to the maid. She was middle-aged, red-faced, with smallpox or acne scars, grey hair that looked as if it spent too much time in a steamy atmosphere. She led him a few steps to the doorway of a small parlour and stood back, her arms out to take his hat and coat.

Inside, Mrs Snokes was sitting in a hard-looking armchair to his left in a furniture- and aspidistra-crowded room, much of the space taken up by a huge square piano; what caught his eye, however, was a couch directly across from the door, lying flat on it a man covered with a yellow blanket. Seen sideways, his face looked narrow, his moustache very red, his skin putty-coloured, his nose large. Denton stepped in and made a kind of bow to Mrs Snokes and hoped she was well.

'Well!' She sniffed. 'With Mr Snokes suffering palpitations and journalists at every door and window, I can't say I'm well. What can the neighbours think, all this uproar?'

Denton crossed the few steps to the couch and bent down, extending his hand. 'I'm Denton. You're Arthur Snokes, I think.'

A smaller hand appeared above the blanket—not before, Denton noted, the man's eyes had flicked to the woman as if for approval—and they shook hands. Snokes's was cold, the fingers long but strengthless. Up close, his moustache was not red but ginger-coloured, as was his hair.

'I'm sorry to hear you're unwell, Mr Snokes.'

'I've been better.' The eyes flicked again to his wife. 'It's been a trying time.'

'It's ruined his health! He used to walk every day from here to the canal and back, and look at him now! He can't even climb the stairs! I'm that rattled, I don't know my own name, Mr Denton. Will you have something? Tea? No, it's morning, you're right. I'm all at sixes and sevens. It's good of you to come. Very good.' She seemed to have forgotten she'd put him off twice.

'I'm afraid I wasn't any help to you, Mrs Snokes.'

'It was good just to know a man of your reputation was behind us. I said to Arthur, it gave me strength to know we had allies like Mister Denton and that nice lady who brought me to you. Such a help in a difficult time. Didn't I, Arthur?'

'Great help,' came from the blanket.

'I wanted to make sure that you were satisfied, Mrs Snokes, about the things you came to see me about. The police, and you being with your husband that evening.'

'And what wouldn't have satisfied me? Yes, all satisfied. I was being foolish, I see now. Jumping at bushes that look like bears, as they say. But I was sorely tried—sorely tried. Wasn't I, Arthur?'

The man's head nodded. To Denton's surprise, Arthur Snokes's eyes seemed fixed on him. They were, he saw now—Snokes had shifted upwards—large and dark brown, set a little too close to each side of that nose. But the look he was giving Denton was not that of a sick man. Rather, perhaps, that of a very worried one.

Denton said, 'I hope your time in the lockup wasn't too rough, Mr Snokes.'

Before he could answer, his wife shrilled, 'It was horrible! To lock a man up on what they call suspicion, and they knew he was innocent! I told them he was. And then there was evidence of what they call fingerprints, which weren't his. It's a scandal! There should be an investigation! I've been on to our alderman about it and I won't let it go, no, I won't!'

Denton, who had taken a chair without being offered one, leaned towards Snokes and tried to turn a shoulder to his wife in hopes that that might keep her from jumping in. 'Did they ask you about a particular time of day, Mr Snokes?'

'The very time I was with him!' she cried. 'I told them. *And they didn't believe me*. It's a scandal.'

Denton kept looking at Snokes. Snokes licked his pale lips and muttered, 'Seven o'clock. They harped on seven o'clock.'

'But your wife had told them you were with her then and for a long time after. Didn't they admit that?'

Snokes shook his head. His wife gave a kind of cry—outrage—but Snokes said through it, 'They didn't care. Kept telling me I'd done it. Said over and over if I'd sign a confession they'd go easy.'

'But you never spoke.'

Snokes shook his head again. 'Not till my lawyer got there, that was some godawful time of the morning. Then every time they asked a question, he said he was advising his client to remain silent. Which I did.'

'Did they get rough with you?'

'What's rough? One of the detectives came behind me and clapped me hard on both shoulders when I wasn't expecting it. My lawyer wasn't there then. And they shouted in my ears.'

'He's partly lost his hearing,' Mrs Snokes said. 'He can't hear me the way he used to. It's criminal, is what it is.'

Denton was thinking that the detectives had more on Snokes than Mrs Snokes understood. For most of the day after the murder, they must have believed they had fingerprint evidence, too; then, when they had found the prints were not his, they had gone to the magistrate anyway. Why? Denton's guess was that they had evidence or statements, maybe from the neighbours, that Snokes had known the dead woman—hard evidence. Perhaps fingerprints, even clothes of his, in her bedroom. He said, 'How did you find the body, Mr Snokes?'

Snokes glanced at his wife. When he looked back at Denton, his face was miserable, but the eyes had the same intensity. 'I stopped sometimes at the shop to buy sweets to take to my office. For me and some of the others. It was a kind of a joke in the office. I liked her place—Mrs Wilcox's. She made her own. They were very good and they were genuine, if you know what I mean. And

I liked to help her out. Her life was a hard one.' He glanced aside at his wife. Denton wished he could see her face but didn't want to take his eyes off Snokes, whose own face underwent a quick change, an expression of fear and, perhaps, dislike passing across it.

'Maybe her shop seemed a little out of your way to the police.'

'A bit over a mile to walk. Or there's the Favourite omnibus down Essex Road.'

'But the Cosmopolitan Railway offices are at Liverpool Street, aren't they?'

She thrust in with 'My husband is a great walker. Didn't I say he walked for his health? He's remarkable for a man of his age. Or was, before this calamity fell on us.'

So he could walk to the confectioner's shop in twenty minutes— and get himself something sweet? No wonder the police made him their best suspect. Denton leaned back and looked at one and then the other. The husband was looking away from the wife now, but she was looking at him as if willing him to turn to her. To send him some message? Denton wanted to ask how well Snokes had known Mrs Wilcox, but he didn't dare. It was too close to the bone: Mrs Snokes must have been as aware as the police of what it meant that her husband had found the body.

He got up, a sign that the guest would be leaving soon. Mrs Snokes, unable to keep relief out of her voice and not caring, he thought, said, 'It's been so good of you to visit us in our hour of need.'

Denton was looking around the room, however. The piano and the pictures above it interested him, the usual curiosity, the novelist's eye always hungry. The piano itself was an important piece of furniture, rosewood, beautifully polished, huge, now twenty years out of date but apparently kept with great care. A paisley shawl was hung across it. Music was open on the music desk. Denton said, 'Does one of you play?' but he was bending forward to look because the lines of the musical staff had been decorated with writhings of what looked like vines and minuscule insects. In colours.

Snokes started to mutter something but she said, 'No. Nobody in this house plays.' And added in a lower voice, 'Any more.'

He couldn't stay looking at the strange music and he moved to his right. The photographs above the piano told their own story. A little boy in a Fauntleroy suit and collar stood with one hand on a photographer's prop pillar, in his other hand a conductor's baton. Above the photograph was a certificate in elaborate calligraphy, 'For Excellence in the Art of Music, WALTER ALLENBY SNOKES: Piano.' Next to it was a framed newspaper clipping: *Six-year-old Conducts Surbiton Euophonion*. Denton had time to read, 'On Thursday last in Victoria Rooms, the six-year-old child prodigy Walter Snokes—'

'That was my little boy,' Mrs Snokes murmured. 'He was a prodigy. A prodigy. He played *Beethoven!*' She pointed at the music on the piano. 'That is his own composition. His first sonata. Opus one.' Her voice broke. 'Unfinished—like Schubert's—'

'Now, Mother—'

Denton took the opportunity to step closer to the music and have another look at the vines and the insects. He felt the stirring of story-teller's excitement, not sure why—something about the former prodigy signalled to him, a flash of mirror light from across a valley. He looked at the Snokeses. One or the other, he knew, would tell him about the boy if he said nothing. He waited. Finally, Snokes pushed himself up on an elbow and said in a groaning voice, 'He lost…He grew out of it.'

The woman snuffled back tears. 'He didn't *grow out of it!*' She was scornful. 'He had an accident, a dreadful accident, and it changed him. Destroyed his genius. Now, he…he doesn't touch a piano, I suppose.'

'He's still with you, then.'

The man threw the same fearful, almost hateful look at her. She said, 'He lives out.' When Denton again said nothing, she squeezed her mouth into a crumpled line like the opening of an old leather purse and said, 'He isn't our little boy any more. He's sometimes difficult.'

There seemed nothing to say to that except 'I'm so sorry.' But inwardly, Denton felt that excitement mount, cued by her 'sometimes difficult'. A child who had been a prodigy and suffered a change so severe that he was now 'difficult'? And decorated his music with strange designs? There was a character with promise...

They each made some polite sounds, and she eased him out of the room and called the maid. She appeared from somewhere at the back with his mac, then handed him his still-wet umbrella. Mrs Snokes watched him go as far as the front door and then, with an insincere smile, faded back into the parlour.

The maid held the front door for him. As he went out, she whispered, her eyes glancing behind her, 'Right pocket. Don't say nothing.'

Then he was in the street, feeling in his right-hand pocket and finding a folded paper there.

He made his way across the gardens in the rain, noting that Rupert's attempt to tunnel under the wall had been filled in and he had started another. In Janet's house, he went to the first floor and called. Silence. Maybe she wasn't home yet from the law office. Or she was at University College. He called again.

Distantly, her voice came down to him.

He walked up the steep stairs, shucking himself out of his mac. The bath was at the far end of a corridor. He dropped the coat on the floor. 'May I come in?'

'Of course.'

She was in the bath. She had had it installed when she had rebuilt the house with her new money, walls of pale green tile and a rectangular box of gleaming mahogany with the ceramic tub set in it, long enough for her to lounge in. At shoulder height, a row of nasturtium tiles swept around the room, orange with green tendrils, the flowers frosted now with condensation. She lay in the water, her hair in a towel.

'What did you learn?' she said. She was smiling.

He got down on both knees, kissed her breasts, her bright pink nipples. He might have been kissing the feet of some saint on a plinth.

'Shall I get out?'

'Yes!'

'I'll be wet.'

'All the better.'

He was stripped by the time she had arranged herself on several towels, he hugely aroused. The air felt tropical, lush, exotic. She said, 'We should have a parrot in here,' and then neither said anything until she said, 'How good you are to me.' Her legs were still wrapped around him.

'Me!'

'How good we are to each other. Get in the bath with me.'

They faced each other from the ends, he with his back being drilled into by the taps but delighted to accept the discomfort. He told her about the visit to the Snokeses. 'And I'm to meet somebody at the Rose at ten-thirty. The Rose is a pub in the next street, actually the Rose and Lyon.'

'Mrs Snokes has fallen for you?'

'Not likely. Nor the maid, who looks too worn down to care any longer. No, I suppose it's Snokes.'

'Who doesn't want his wife to know? What's he up to?'

'I suppose I'll find out at ten-thirty. I hate having to go all the way back to De Beauvoir Town at that hour.'

'Maybe he wants to confess.'

'To me? It would be an odd way to go about it.'

After several minutes, she said the water was getting cold. They got out and dried themselves with Turkish towels as big as bedsheets as the water gurgled from the bath.

They went to the Café Royal. They were early; there was none of the noise of voices or the sense of nervous activity that he knew would come later, people drinking too much and making themselves seen. Upstairs was respectable, fairly famous; down here in what was still called the Domino Room despite the lack of domino players was a more relaxed set of rules. 'Bohemian' was a common charge made by respectable people. Quite a few writers came there, in fact, although likelier to be journalists or magazine hacks than Denton's sort, also editors and publishing people, these usually up at the far, Glasshouse Street, end. Musicians had their own enclave near the Regent Street side; painters of the non-RA sort wandered through to wherever they could find a seat. Oscar Wilde had had a reserved table until he had gone to prison nine years before.

'Is there any pasta?' Janet said to the waiter. Like Denton, she was suffering the returned expatriate's withdrawal. They both missed Italy.

'Pasta?' The waiter seemed never to have heard the word.

'Pasta. Spaghetti, macaroni—'

'Madame, that is *Italian*. This restaurant is Continental.'

'Pizza?'

'*Pizza?*'

Denton expected him to clutch his heart. But Janet persisted. '*Ma, lei e italiano,*' There was no escaping his accent: like most of the waiters there, he was indeed Italian.

'Madame, if you want Italian food, you got to go to Soho. Previtalli's. Such places.' He left them with menus and went away. Janet grumbled that a place whose most famous dish was chicken cooked with hardboiled eggs was in no position to cock a snook at pasta.

'The joke is that I think the place was founded by an Italian. But of course it's an English institution now.'

When the waiter returned, he took their orders—the chicken pie for the gentleman, the *vol au vent* for madam, a bottle of the house claret; he wrote nothing down—and then bent slightly towards Janet. 'If you want *good* Italian food, Clerkenwell.' He glanced around as if the cordon bleu police might be listening, then leaned still closer and almost whispered, 'Clerkenwell Green. Farringdon Station. Walk up Turnmall Street.' His right hand made a quick curving motion, fingers stiff. 'Around the green, cross the road, left'—another hand gesture—'into little, little street so small you think is not there. Halfway down is a *salumeria*.' He gave another furtive look. 'At the back is three tables. Sit. They bring you food.' He formed his lips as if to whistle but breathed air in, not out, got a thin, high sound. He put his hand on his chest. '*I* eat there. Eh-eh-eh.' He shook his right hand, fingers open, up and down. The food was that good.

'Can I buy pasta there? To cook myself?'

'*Home-made*. Also from Italy, dried.'

'Pizza?'

His eyebrows went up. 'Ask. But I tell you, *signora*, you want to make pizza, make a good bread. Not English bread—real bread. Use that.' Later, as he served their food, he told her about an Italian bakery in Clerkenwell where he thought she could buy pizza dough if she went early. She asked him where he was from in Italy.

'Brescia.'

'We lived the last year in Naples.' His eyebrows went up and then down, as if to say that the English would go anywhere.

'You're going to cook?' Denton said to her.

'If I have to. I know how now, you know.' She was cutting into the remains of the flaky pastry. 'Mr DiNapoli taught me.' DiNapoli had been their mentor in Naples.

'It doesn't seem like you.'

'If I had to do it because somebody came home at seven and threw his necktie in the corner and demanded his dinner, I wouldn't. But I can *choose* to do it, if I like.'

He thought of Rosamund Gearing. She wouldn't be knuckling under to some husband either, he thought.

She had a dessert; he did not. She seemed able to eat anything and not gain weight, perhaps because she had been ill the year before and was only now winning back what she had lost. He touched her hand. 'You have your colour back. I thought that this afternoon.'

'In the bath? That's *not* what you were thinking about. Colour? I was always sallow. My mother used to make me pat my cheeks to bring colour into them before we met people. She thought that men like rosy-cheeked women because they think they're more fertile. She was full of such notions.'

They paid—she insisted on her paying her share—and went out into Regent Street. She took his arm and said she wanted to walk. 'I miss Naples,' she said.

'Me, too. We could go back this winter.'

'DiNapoli would find a flat for us.'

They walked in silence for so long he had forgotten what they had been talking about; suddenly she said, 'No, it's too soon. Next winter, perhaps. We'll try the restaurant in Clerkenwell. You'd go there with me?'

Denton knew London pretty well from years of walking. 'It isn't Mayfair.'

'It isn't Bethnal Green, either.' Before she'd got her money, she'd lived on a pound a week and supported her mother, by then a raving drunk. 'Would you eat my pizza if I made it?'

'I'd make you my *pizzaiuolo*. By Appointment.' She laughed.

So they went on up to Millman Street and her house. He thought they were now completely comfortable together, the idea dangerous because they'd come so close to splitting so recently. Yet he felt as if they'd come out on some plateau with a long view ahead.

'Should I stop by after I see Snokes?'

'I'll hit you with the fire tongs if you do. I plan to be asleep.'

He left her at her door and walked the three streets to the tumbledown outbuilding where he kept his automobile. Behind it was a long rank of horse barns. The smell was strong. Now and then, a hoof thudded, a nose whinnied. He wished that like them he was in his stall, munching oats, not starting out for the unknowns of De Beauvoir Town.

He had located the Rose and Lyon that afternoon. Leaving the car seemed all right: the street was empty, the neighbourhood sombre enough. The pub itself, despite its *ye olde name*, seemed to him only a few years old. It had made the usual nods to High Victorian pubhood, but its polished wood looked to him cheap and its frosted glass merely obligatory. He took a seat in a corner where he could watch the door and began to nurse a pint of best-something-or-other that was arguably better than what the horses were leaving in the barns.

He was twenty minutes early. After forty minutes, he had to ask for another pint and rid himself of the first one. The urinal did nothing to make him want to recommend the place—a zinc wall with a trickle of water running down into it so as to splash on everybody's boots. Back on the worn plush of his place, he eyed the door, his soft hat pushed back on his forehead and his mac open. He'd been thinking of removing it the whole forty minutes, didn't because he thought Snokes would want to take him outside as soon he got there.

He was wrong. Snokes beat the closing bell by five minutes, planted himself firmly opposite Denton and ordered his own pint before the landlord could say 'Time!'

'I thought you weren't going to make it.' Denton didn't try to sound forgiving.

'Devil's own time getting out of the house. She watches me like a hawk. Eyes in the back of her head.' He seemed a different man. Certainly not one to kowtow to his wife now. Of course, she wasn't there. 'She's got me on toast because of Bella. No avoiding it—she couldn't help dropping to it once everything came out, eh? Had me crawling, I don't mind saying. Well, you saw. Cheers.'

So far as Denton could see, they were now supposed to be men together, the threatening woman a common enemy. He didn't say anything. Let Snokes go on.

'Bit different from this p.m., what? Wasn't sure you'd get the note. Parsons's a good old soul, though. Bit sweet on me, if you can believe. Gave her sixpence, which I had to steal out of Anna's purse because she'd taken my money away, would you believe it? Some men would give her a wallop, I know, but that isn't my way. More flies with sugar. Drink up, he's going to lock the door.'

'Are we going somewhere?'

'Thought we could walk. This is the first time I've been out since they picked me up. Can't tell you how you get a hunger to see a street and a bit of life. Starved for it.'

They went out. The rain had ended, but a thin fog had followed, the air cold and clammy. Denton pulled the mac closed and buttoned it. He pulled his hat down. He was tired of Snokes already. 'Did you kill her?'

'What? You can ask that? Of course I didn't! I thought you were on our side.'

Our side. What did that mean? 'Any idea who did, then?'

'How would I? Not a hint. You think I'm a detective? I found her is all. Absolutely did me in. Bella was a nice little thing, very kind and all. To find her like that—it undid me. I mean it. Cripes! If I'd put my hand in the blood and then put my hand somewhere! I just thought of it. My God. What a narrow squeak.'

'She, on the other hand, was dead.'

'Yes, poor little thing. She'd been good to me.'

'You didn't see anybody? Hear anything?'

'She'd been dead a while; the police made that clear enough with their questions. Whoever did it had scarpered.'

'Then why did they fix on you?'

'Because I found her, didn't I?' Snokes had his hands jammed into his overcoat pockets, a huge, hairy winter coat with the collar turned up. 'Besides which, they found things of mine there. Things I'd left. Handkerchief with my initials, cufflink I'd dropped somehow; the wife said they came looking for the twin at the house. Found it, I'm sure. So I was the adulterer who got tired of his bit of stuff and killed her. As if I'd do *that*. Christ, I've got rid of a dozen women who'd clung tighter than Bella; are the police so thick they believe you've got to kill them to get loose?'

They had walked around the streets surrounding the Rose and Lyon and passed it again. As if reminded, Denton said, 'Why did you want to see me?'

'You're good at investigations, aren't you? I've read about you.'

'I don't do investigations.'

'You know what I mean. I don't mean for money. You've got the knack and you've got the ear of the police.'

'You mean you think I can get you off.'

'Well, if you find who did it, you *would* get me off, wouldn't you? Anyway, I don't for a minute mean you'll go straight along and find who did it. I mean you can cast doubt. Convince the people who really decide those things that it wasn't me but somebody else. You don't have to produce the somebody else to shake me loose, eh?'

'I don't have any evidence.'

'But you don't believe I did it, do you? No, you don't. I can tell. I could tell this p.m. Well, you can put in a good word with your connections, can't you?'

'Why should I? I know some people, Snokes; that doesn't mean I run to them with an opinion about every crime that's committed.'

'But where you know an injustice's been done—'

'And been corrected. You were released.'

'Yes, and living on tenterhooks waiting for them to grab me again. They've got one suspect—me. My God, can't you put some sort of bee in their bonnet?'

'Like what?'

'Like I was having a bit on the side and that was all! Cripes!'

'It wouldn't do any good.'

They were halfway around another circuit. Denton was determined it would be the last, but there were things he wanted to know. 'Tell me about your son.'

'What? He's nothing to do with it.'

'How old is he?'

'Sixteen now.' Snokes sounded angry. 'What about it?'

'Your wife said there was an accident.'

Snokes marched along another dozen paces without saying anything. Then he growled, 'He had an injury when he was eight. It was like we'd traded him for a different kid. I was glad at first—it was the end of the ancey-prancey velvet suits and the bloody piano and all that. Like he just forgot it all. Then you could see he was different. And got more so.'

'How?'

They had turned into the street where the pub, now dark, waited. As if he, too, didn't intend to make the night longer, Snokes stopped. 'He got moody. I thought it was just moods. But it was like he couldn't get things into his head. Or all he could get was the…the bones of it, not the meat. Like if you said, "She's a sight for sore eyes", he'd ask how eyes got sore. Then he'd ask what you saw with sore eyes. Then he'd ask if your eyes were sore.' Snokes looked down the dark street. 'And he never laughed. Nor smiled. And he got…They wouldn't keep him in school. He fell behind and behind. A teacher showed us his paper from an examination. The question was to write what you knew about Guy Fawkes. He'd made the letter G and then decorated it, made it bigger and put leaves and flowers and then little figures crawling in and out of the leaves. And that was all that was on the paper.' He shook his head. 'He wasn't our little boy any more.'

'Is he in an institution?'

Snokes came back from somewhere. 'He lives with some others like himself. A house. We pay.'

'Do you see him ever?'

Snokes shook his head. 'The wife does. I can't face it. When he was little, I could, but once he—' He shook his head again, this time as if he were shaking something off.

'Is he dangerous?'

Snokes walked away into the fog.

CHAPTER

7

On Sunday mornings after Janet had been to church, they lay about his house or hers and read, usually the *Times*, the custom already re-established after months away. Atkins would be out, Sundays more or less his own; the Jewish couple who took care of Janet's house treated it like any other day.

'You're interested in the boy,' she said the morning after his meeting with Snokes.

'The boy agitated Snokes. Something's wrong there.'

'A child who was a prodigy and now has to live in some sort of institution is wrong enough.'

'He didn't make it sound like an institution.'

'Bad enough, whatever it is.' She had spent four years in a prison for the criminally insane, thanks to her then husband. She had a horror of such places. 'But it hasn't anything to do with somebody murdering the woman in Denmark Road.'

'Bella Wilcox. He called her Bella. She was "good" to him. His little bit on the side, as he put it. He also let drop that he'd got rid of a dozen others. Not by murdering them—that was the point. Getting rid of women being easy when you knew how.'

'One of those.'

'What'd that girl at Oxford call it—"hyperaesthesia"? Although I guess I'm suspicious of the "hyper" part. A lot of men will jump at sex if it's offered. Like Rupert.' After a moment's thought he said, 'Snokes may be a bit extreme. He's a perfectly ordinary man to look at, but unless he was trying to come it over me, he seems to have done a lot of tomcatting. How does he afford it? Surely even Bella Wilcox cost him something?'

'Some women have to give it away, if they're lonely enough,' she said drily. 'Or simply if they miss sex. Wasn't she a widow?'

'You suggest a world of available women.'

'That's the one that Snokes manages to inhabit.'

'There's men that can't find a free poke if their lives depend on it. How d'you suppose Snokes does it?' Before she could answer, he went on, 'And why doesn't his wife care? Or does she? Better he pokes somebody else than bother her?'

'You said he thinks she knows and it's why he's afraid of her.'

'Yes, and...I've asked you this before—what's he afraid of? When did I ask that? Oh, of course, Ivor Hench-Rose and that girl.'

'Woman, Denton; she's a woman. Him treating her like a girl doesn't make her one.'

'Anyway, what are they afraid of? I'm afraid of losing you, but I'm not out tomcatting all over Metropolitan London. In Snokes's case, what has he to lose?'

'Her.'

'Dear God.'

'You know better than that. "Love" isn't just about sex. It may be nothing more than habit with somebody like Snokes. But it's their history. I'd say he's afraid of losing twenty years of his life. Not that he won't have somebody new "on the side" within a month or two.'

Denton was sitting in an armchair, the *Times* crumpled on his lap. She was on a couch, vivid in a dress of a red so dark that out of the sunlight it looked black, with slashes of pink in the billowing sleeves and the bodice. They were in the room he said he never used, next to his sitting-room.

Looking up, he said, 'You have anybody left from your old life who could do some digging in a library for me?'

'Mmm. I'll think of somebody. Let me read now.'

Next day, he tried to telephone Munro at New Scotland Yard, but he was told that Munro was out for the day, confirming Denton's dislike of the telephone. He knew it was irrational, but it seemed to him that if he telephoned, people were out; if he went to see them, they were in.

He walked to the Angel police station and asked to see the detective in charge of the Wilcox case, then had to explain that he meant the Denmark Road case, which seemed to be the local police name for it. He should see Divisional Detective Inspector Masefield, he was told. That was fine as far it went, but Detective Inspector Masefield was out. Perhaps with Munro, he thought sourly. So much for his theory about the telephone and personal visits.

'If you come back just before lunch-time, sir.'

Denton walked to Denmark Road, hoping that the detective would be there, but the confectioner's shop was locked and a sign on a wooden stand had been put up, *Police Premises Keep Out Under Penalty of the Law.* No uniformed copper—the press had lost interest.

In for a penny, in for a pound, he thought, and he headed southwards into Clerkenwell to Wynyatt Street, where Snokes's lawyer kept his office. *I was in the neighbourhood, I thought I'd drop in.* He didn't think Drigny would bite on that one. Better just to say, 'I've brought another two and six.'

In fact, Drigny had three clients ahead of him, and Denton sat in the grim anteroom, nothing to read or look at, wondering what the medical facts were about the change to the one-time prodigy, Walter Snokes. When the three had been into the office and done whatever they had to do and come out, three more—no, four—had piled up behind him, the same grim faces, the same look of smallness—small incomes, small fears. But problems that couldn't have seemed small to them, he thought. And in each one, a novel he ought to be writing if only he could prise it out of their faces and their unpressed clothes and their scuffed boots.

'Two and six.' He dropped the coins on the desk.

'I don't have time for you. Make an appointment—write it in the book by the door; my clerk's out.'

Denton sat down. 'I'll make it quick. What do you know about Snokes's son?' He surprised himself; he'd thought he was going to ask about Snokes.

'Did I tell you I don't have time or didn't I?'

'You have time to argue with me; why not answer the question?'

Drigny looked disgusted. He pocketed the coins. 'The son's a mental case.'

'Where is he?'

'You can't see him, so don't think you can. What's it matter? It's nothing to do with the death of that woman.'

'What's the matter with the boy?'

'I told you, he's a mental case.'

'That doesn't tell me anything.'

'Well, it's all I know. What're you putting your nose in for?'

'I'm nosy. Have the police shared their evidence with you?'

'They're short on generosity.'

'Autopsy report? Fingerprints? They got a warrant to search Snokes's house, I'll bet.'

Drigny was nodding. 'You're not slow off the mark, are you?' He opened a drawer in the wooden desk, took out an accordion file and put it near Denton. 'Take this out front and read it and then pop it back in here. And leave.' He nodded at the file. 'It's all in there. Say "Next" as you go out, will you?'

'I haven't used up my two and six yet.'

'Yes, you have. Higher rates for surprises.'

Denton chuckled and went out, saying 'Next' and ducking back as a young man with a centre parting and slicked-down hair launched himself from a chair and headed for the office. Denton sat in the chair he'd left empty, six other people now in the small room, half of them standing. He unwrapped the soft cotton tape from the file, felt dust between his fingers. The file had been used before, maybe for more than one case: *Snokes* was written on the front, but above and crossed out were *Witham* and *Goldsby*. Inside were several sheets of paper, all filled with the same copperplate hand. Drigny's clerk, sent to the police station to copy them?

The autopsy report was medical and dense and told him only that Wilcox, Bella, female, aged about thirty-five, five feet four inches, one hundred and thirty-one pounds, white, had some moles on her back and a vaccination scar on her left upper arm, had been in good health generally except for bunions and five missing teeth; that she had been stabbed once between the third and fourth ribs with a wide blade that had penetrated five inches; that she had bled copiously; that her stomach had contained partly digested toast, a sardine, and dark fluid believed to be anchovy sauce. She had a contusion on the occiput resulting in minimal bleeding that had matted the hair, the extent of the bleeding suggesting that the contusion had been dealt her at least several minutes before death. Semen in the vagina and slight abrasion, suggesting possible force. No other injuries. No sign of struggle on hands or arms. Time of death was estimated to have been between seven and nine p.m. Cause of death: stabbing to the heart with resulting bleeding.

The fingerprint report was pretty much what Drigny had told him before. There had been five prints in all, three on the floor and two on the knife, those on the floor clear, of a size consistent with a man's or a large woman's hand; those on the knife were unreadable because of the surface (Indian stag) of the handle. No match to the fingerprints of Arthur Snokes.

The next sheet was headed 'Summary of Warrant' and recorded the warrant issued by a judge to Frank Masefield, divisional detective inspector, to search the premises of Arthur Snokes. The last sheet was a list of items removed from the Snokes home, including one imitation-silver cufflink. The other things seemed to Denton to have been taken for the sake of taking something—a man's hat and overcoat, a copy of Dr

Treadwell's *Married Love According to New Science* and a pair of boots, black, men's.

When he opened the office door, two faces turned to him, Drigny's sallow and expressionless, the slick-haired young man's angry. Denton tossed the file on a chair. 'Thanks.'

Drigny waved a hand as if he were swatting a fly.

Outdoors under a low, grey sky, Denton reminded himself that he was in Clerkenwell. He remembered being told something else about Clerkenwell. Ah, the Café Royal, the waiter. He looked at his pocket watch. If he set off now, he could be back at the Angel before lunch-time, but he'd miss the Italian grocery with the three tables in the back; if he hoofed it over to Clerkenwell Green, he could find the Italian grocery with the restaurant behind, but he'd miss Masefield. For the second time.

He headed back northwards. At the police station, he was directed to wait, but as he was sitting there the detective he'd seen in Denmark Road the week before came down the stairs with two other men and started for the door. Denton got up so as to be in his way.

'Detective Inspector Masefield.'

The detective was going to brazen it out for an instant and then he thought better of it. The other two scowled but held back. It was very British, Denton thought: they wanted to tell him to get the hell out of the way, my lad, but a thousand years of class prejudice made them leery of offending a suit that well made.

'Well, well, if it isn't the sheriff. I'm just headed out on a case.'

A case of bangers, Denton thought, but he said, 'I can come back. I *will* keep coming back.' Smiling as he said it.

Masefield looked at the other two. Maybe he was thinking that, before, Denton had mentioned somebody at the Yard. The swells always had pull. 'You go on without me. I'll tend to the business here. I'll be right along.'

They looked at Denton. One touched the brim of his hat.

Masefield led him up the stairs and into a big, draughty room that needed painting. Where the edges of the narrow floorboards met, they were worn almost white; the middles of the boards were still yellow-brown with vestiges of varnish, the whole floor marked with scuffs like short strokes of dark paint. The room was a long step down from the CID room at New Scotland Yard, although it had what seemed to be the same bank of telephones, their horns jutting towards him like hungry mouths. To Denton's surprise, several of the desks had a typewriter on a separate metal stand next to them. Masefield led him to a smaller office hardly less battered than the detectives' room and superior only because it was separate.

Masefield kept his hat on. He waved Denton to a hard chair. 'Be quick, if you please. Sir.'

'It's about Snokes.'

'I can guess what it's about. What's your interest?'

'I've just come from Drigny, his solicitor. We were going over the autopsy and fingerprint reports.'

'Oh, you were, were you?' Masefield look disgusted. 'We didn't have to give him those yet. Those were given to further the cause of justice.'

'The cufflink you found in his house. That's your evidence?'

'We don't have to tell you what it is. You figure that out for yourselves.'

'Does it match the one you found at Mrs Wilcox's—which you didn't mention in the papers you gave Drigny?'

'That's for us to know and you to find out.'

'Autopsy puts time of death between seven and nine. You know he was with his wife then.'

'I don't know anything of the kind. I know what she *says*.'

Denton hadn't yet asked what he really wanted to know. Leading up to it with other questions wasn't working, however. He said, 'What did you learn from the neighbours?'

'Not a reason in the world I should tell you that. Go back to the law shop and tell him to apply to the magistrate. He knows how.' He leaned forward on his folded arms. 'You want to know something? Snokes isn't paying him enough to make him spend the time now. He'll wait until Crown Court and then he'll tell the barrister to make the application, and then it's the barrister's time.'

'You're pretty sure it will go to Crown Court.'

'I know it'll go to Crown Court! He did it. And he isn't going to skip.'

'You know, not telling Drigny suggests to me that you found something from the neighbours that helps Snokes, not implicates him. You're not supposed to keep evidence back.'

'Don't you tell me what I'm supposed to do! I'm the head of CID here!' Masefield was on his feet. He slammed his knuckles on the desk. 'I'm bloody tired of amateur questions!' He pointed a stubby finger. 'I've been patient with you. Now I'm bloody sick of you. Move your rich arse out of here.'

Denton stood. 'If I was rich, Masefield, I'd have sent *my* solicitor. How about I buy lunch and we keep on talking?'

'You keep away from me. Keep away from my division! You lot think you're cute because the mouthpiece the Crown sent couldn't tell which hand he was supposed to grab his Johnson with. Well, *they* made a balls of it; *we* didn't. We've got the goods. Go tell your legal genius that. Now move yourself out of here.'

Denton straightened the folds of his overcoat. He adjusted his hat. 'The offer of lunch still stands. When you want to talk to me.'

Behind him, Masefield was making a sound that could have come from a dog.

Now Denton regretted having missed lunch, even more having given up the Italian grocery. He was less than a mile from his own house, but there would be nothing to eat there. He cut around the Central Post Office at Calthorpe Street, made his way to Gray's Inn Road and so down to Holborn, where a coffee stall sold him a mug of tea and something mysterious but edible on a surprisingly fresh roll. Fortified, he made his way to Chancery Lane and Sir Francis Brudenell.

'I'm just off to lunch and can't linger, Denton. Clients should be disciplined enough to make appointments and not disturb the great ones unwarned. However, as you're here, I'll give you two minutes.'

'Anything new?'

'On the Rialto? Ha. I do hear things of Brother Drigny, who does seem actually to exist and has an office in the wilds of—yes, Clerkenwell, you already know. Well, well, it's not a hundred miles from Gray's Inn and so within the penumbra of the law. He seems in fact to be a not uncommendable fellow. Someone I know had actually heard something good of him.'

Denton told him about Drigny's *coup* in magistrates' court.

'Aha, yes, splendid. Crude, but splendid. Was the name once Dérigny, do you suppose? Huguenot. There was a Dérigny family that was not without means. As for your other interest, Doty is still nose to the ground for investigators connected to your Mrs Snokes. He is not sanguine, however.'

Sir Francis had been moving Denton out of his office, down a flight of stairs, out to the street, having acquired a topcoat and very black bowler along the way. His Benz was rumbling in the hackney lane. 'I shall charge you for the minutes we just spent together, as punishment for not making an appointment. But I shan't charge much. Ha!'

There was no offer to drop Denton somewhere.

He thought of going to see Munro but knew that Munro would tell him to see the people at N Division. It wasn't Munro's case; it was Masefield's case, and Masefield wasn't going to tell him anything. Denton trudged back northwards, frustrated by having no wedge with which to open CID confidentiality. But to what end? He was, he knew, using Bella Wilcox's murder to keep himself from flailing about in search of something to write. And to keep him in touch with the Snokeses because of their son, who interested him beyond any proper measure of curiosity. Better an empty mind intrigued by a peculiar child than a mind filled, like an asylum, with the screams and groans and chain-rattlings of characters with no existence.

At four-thirty, he got a message from Janet telling him to come to Teddy Mercer's office in Goodge Street if he wanted to talk to a woman about doing some research for him. He had been trying to nap and failing. Delighted by the change, he almost ran out of the house, Atkins stopping him at the door with an overcoat. Indeed, the day had turned colder and greyer. Summer was over.

Janet had spent a dozen years working for the Society for the Improvement of Wayward Women; as a result, she knew a lot of women who needed work. The one he now found at Goodge Street, Nellie Strang, was in her thirties, stout, a little cheerless. Janet had muttered that 'Nellie's brighter than she looks.'

'I write a good hand and I went to school to the legal age.' That meant eleven, he thought. 'I've had work in the ladies' garment trade and I've done canvassing and I've done office work for Mrs Striker. I brought my references.' She had papers in her hand.

'If Mrs Striker recommends you, that's enough. What's important is that you be a good reader.'

'Oh, I read.'

'Have you ever done research?' She looked blank. 'Looked things up in books or newspapers? Have you ever used a library?'

'I use the penny library for Miss Carey. I've read all of Miss Carey.'

'That's good. Good.' He wasn't sure who Miss Carey was, but books were books. 'Do you think you'd like doing some work in a library for me?'

She glanced over at Janet, who was working at a long table. She said, 'I need work.' The kind, he thought she meant, didn't matter. Liking it didn't matter.

He told her what he wanted—everything she could find about a child prodigy named Snokes. He had to explain what a prodigy was. She should start at the British Museum's Reading Room. 'It would have been about ten years ago. If you don't know how to go about it, ask a librarian.' He gave her one of his cards and a scribbled note. 'Give them this and tell them you're doing research for me, and if there's any question, refer them to me. You'll get the hang of it quickly.' They made an arrangement about pay—four shillings a day, two days in advance because he thought she looked as if she needed it, an increase to five a day if she did well—and he asked her if she'd mind going to Surbiton.

'Not if you pay the fare, sir.'

'Of course.' He told her about the concert by the Surbiton Euphonic Society. 'It was probably a local newspaper. Track it down. But do the Museum first; they just might have a copy. And while you're in Surbiton, locate the Euphonic Society and get a name, if you can, somebody I can talk to. All right? I think you should let me know how you're doing by...Friday?'

'Here, sir?'

Denton was aware of Teddy's disapproval. He was also aware that Nellie didn't want to meet him alone. 'At Mrs Striker's, I think. You make an arrangement with her. Maybe you could meet her here and walk home with her; it's nearby. All right?' He looked over at Janet, who had turned her grave working face on him. She nodded but didn't smile.

'That's all right, then? You'll start tomorrow? Good. Good.'

He wondered if he was throwing his money away.

8

Sir Francis Brudenell had said that the investigator was 'not sanguine' about tracking down the private detective whom Mrs Snokes might have used, but halfway through the next morning a commissionaire handed in a message from him. *Doty has struck gold. Half-eleven if you can make it.* Denton had been pacing his bedroom-study, throwing himself into his desk chair and getting up again, staring at a blank piece of paper and a pen as if he'd never seen them before. And might as well not have, for all the good they were to the frozen mass of *The Secret Jew.* When Atkins climbed the stairs and handed in the message from Brudenell, Denton felt relief like a rush of blood, to be followed by guilt at having accomplished nothing.

'Any answer?' Atkins said. 'Commissionaire's waiting.'

Denton scribbled 'I'll be there' on the message slip and handed it back. He picked a sixpence from coins on his desk. 'Give him that.'

'He'll be beside himself with delight.' Atkins turned to go down the stairs.

'You still in the dumps?'

'Deeper.'

But he came back up and laid out Denton's clothes—dark grey double-breasted suit, five-buttoned so that it closed very high on the chest; a black-and-purple necktie; black elastic-sided boots. 'I'll have the black kashmir overcoat by the door and the grey Homburg. The grey gloves, I think. Umbrella.'

'I hate umbrellas.'

'Can't be helped. It's raining.'

'Hell.'

He wouldn't let Atkins fetch a cab because of an ingrained egalitarianism that he simply couldn't shake, although he saw that it was ridiculous to let somebody else lay out clothes for him and then say it was unfair for the same person to get him a cab in the rain. If it hadn't been raining, it would have been all right. Or something of that sort—he found it hard to grasp the minor rules of his own code.

Sir Francis was sitting behind his desk. A medium-sized man—medium everything, in fact: colour, amount of hair, weight—was sitting in a side chair. He had a medium-brown moustache of no great size, eyes not quite either brown or green. He wore no wedding ring, no lapel pin, no watch fob.

'This is Mr Doty,' Sir Francis said. 'The finest private investigator in London.'

'Now, now,' Doty said softly. He'd got up and was putting out a hand. 'I've heard of Mr Denton.' The H in 'heard' was quiet but not silent.

'And I of you. Sir Francis says you have something for me.'

'Well, we'll see, sir. It may be nothing much.' Doty sat again; Denton got a chair. Sir Francis said he'd like to move right along as he'd another appointment. Doty put on a pair of eyeglasses and took out a pocket notebook and leafed through it and found a page. 'Mrs Arthur Snokes,' he said.

'Yes.'

'I was asked to look for a connection with an investigator. I found three.'

'Three.'

'One in Kentish Town, one in Finsbury, and one in Hackney Wick. The Kentish Town one came first to me, as my researches discovered that the family once lived nearby.' He looked over the glasses. 'Thought it prudent to look through the directories.'

Denton thought, *Why didn't I do that?*

'The Kentish Town investigator happened to be somebody I know. He knew one of the others. Hackney Wick. Mrs Snokes a bit of a joke between them. They both seem to have had trouble with her.' He looked over the glasses again. 'A bit sordid. She wanted her husband followed. Then when they found something she said they were making trouble.' He went back to his note-book. 'The third investigator was found by one of my employees, doing basic shoe-leather work in Finsbury. This one doesn't want to tell us anything—but might, I think, for a consideration.' He closed the book.

'Mrs Snokes suspected her husband of being unfaithful?'

'That seems a reasonable presumption.'

'And they found something.'

'I didn't ask for details, sir, as these matters are confidential, but I believe what was to be inferred was that the husband was followed to an address and spent more time there than was consonant with a social call.'

'Were these all recent?'

Doty opened the book again. 'The Kentish Town was ten years ago. Hackney Wick about four—after they moved to the present address. Finsbury as yet unknown.'

'I think I need to know about the Finsbury one.'

'We can try that, sir. Of course, it's a violation of confidentiality. However, my employee believes there was an implication of openness to a consideration.'

'Try it.'

'Very good, sir.' Doty put away his eyeglasses and notebook and gave signs of being about to stand. 'I can't promise anything, sir.' He stood. 'On the other hand, it doesn't seem hopeless.' Having covered all outcomes, Doty smiled.

Denton walked to High Holborn and then to Red Lion Street, and he had crossed to the south end of Lamb's Conduit Street and was within a few hundred feet of his own house when a stern voice at his shoulder said, 'Now, sir, I must ask you to come along to the station, if you please!'

Denton whirled. A uniformed constable was frowning at him. Denton was thinking the constable was off duty—no armband—so what was he doing making an arrest? And then he looked into the face, which was young and stern, and he was about to protest when the face broke into a great grin and laughter rang out.

'Maltby!'

The young man was so pleased with his joke he could hardly stand still. He stamped his boots on the pavement. Then they shook hands and Denton clapped him on the shoulder. 'You young pup!' He had met Maltby months before in Naples, when he'd been an unhappy and obviously incompetent beginner at the British consulate. 'And now you're a proper copper, are you?'

Maltby had been a dour young man in Naples; now he seemed a happy police constable. 'Passed the examination with flying colours, was taken in the day I turned twenty-one. Thanks to you!'

'Nonsense. You saved my life.' Maltby had put himself in the way of a bullet that might have hit Denton. 'That wound all healed? Good. Munro said you'd get a medal—did you?'

'I gave it to my father. Wouldn't dare let the other chaps know about it. They call me things like "the gent" and "the toff" as it is. But it's just good-natured ragging. I'm the one they come to when they're having trouble writing a report.' Denton tried to picture Maltby, product of a middling public school, with the rest of the police recruits. His mother had meant him for the Foreign Office; destiny had meant him for the Met.

They strolled towards Denton's house. Maltby explained that he had just called there. 'You passed me right by, Mr Denton! My sergeant would blister me for not noticing a face I was supposed to know.'

'But you do look different to me.'

'Gained ten pounds. All muscle. Been training.' They passed the Lamb; Denton's was the next house. Maltby said, 'You expecting a lady? One was waiting. We coppers are trained to keep an eye out for that, you know—loitering's not to be allowed.'

'A woman loitering?'

'She was standing across the road by that entry, but looking at your house. I thought perhaps she was early for an appointment. Quite respectable-looking, actually. Not, you know—a woman of...'

'Not much of that here. The street has that reputation, but it's from decades ago. Maybe a woman I've hired to do some research.'

'She made off very smartly when she saw me look at her. A bit suspicious, I thought.' Maltby patted a pocket. 'Thought I might get a pic, but she was too fast.' He grinned again. 'Oh, yes, I bought myself a folding camera with my first pay. "The possession of a camera or Kodak by a constable may be in many cases of the greatest advantage." That's right out of the *Code*. Vincent's *Police Code*, that is. We just call it the *Code*.'

Denton hid his smile at this eagerness. 'Come on in.'

'I can't, sir. I was just going to pop in and say I'm in the police, thanks to you, but I can't stay. I get only one day off in fourteen, so I have to whiz.' He gave a proud smile. 'A copper's time's never his own.'

Now Denton couldn't help smiling. 'You like the police.'

'Yes, sir, I—' He looked embarrassed. 'I love it. My mother's heartbroken, of course. But I was meant to be a copper!'

Denton said he must come back, and Maltby promised to come to supper one day. They parted, but Denton looked back from his gate to find that Maltby was looking over his own shoulder at him. Maltby called out, 'I'm going to make detective, Mr Denton! I will!'

Atkins was waiting inside the door. As he took Denton's hat and coat, he said, 'Young constable was just here. Left a card. Said he'd known you in Naples.'

'I ran into him up the street. He's all right.'

'I didn't say he isn't. Thought he was going to tell me the story of his life, though. New copper. Bit excitable, I thought.'

'You were young once, weren't you, Atkins?'

'Couldn't prove it by me.'

Denton started up the stairs. 'Did a lady call?'

'Wouldn't I of told you if she had?'

'Maltby thought he saw somebody over the way.'

'New copper. Sees suspicious types in his sleep.'

'Mmm.' But Denton by then was thinking about what Doty had told him about Mrs Snokes and her investigators.

To his surprise, Janet sent a note that evening telling him that Nellie Strang was at her house and wanted to talk to him. He crossed the gardens without hat or coat, a cold wind blowing, flecks of rain flying. He brushed the moisture off his shoulders as he climbed to the first floor to find Janet and the researcher in the sitting-room.

'There you are, Denton.'

Janet made no move to leave, and Nellie Strang didn't seem to expect her to. Because she didn't want to be alone with Denton? No: it was quickly clear that she expected Denton to be angry and she wanted Janet's protection.

'I didn't do it the way you said, sir. I did it all backwards.' Her colour was slightly up, but she looked right at him and she didn't seem apologetic. Defiant, perhaps. 'I went to the Reading Room, and they all but turned me out into the street. A very snooty young fellow barely half my age said didn't I know any better? "Application is to be made in writing in advance." I said it was only for the day, and he said he wouldn't bother the Principal Librarian for a day ticket for somebody like me. So I went to Surbiton.'

'Aw, Miss Strang, I'm sorry.'

'It's Mrs.'

'I should have gone with you.'

'Sticks and stones, Mr Denton; although you'd think a *gentleman* would know common courtesy. Anyhow, I went to Surbiton. I didn't do like you said there, either, but went straight to the police station and asked about a newspaper and the musical society. They didn't know about music but they did know the newspaper, which is weekly and up the road. So I went there and a very nice and polite woman helped me find what was wanted, which I copied out.'

She handed him two sheets of paper. She wrote a good, plain hand, easy to read. It was apparently the same article that the Snokeses had framed on their parlour wall: the 'child prodigy' Walter Snokes had conducted a concert of Sir Arthur Sullivan, Hubert Parry, and Richard Wagner at Twining's Rooms, to the 'extreme delight of a crowd of the town's most enlightened citizens'. The reporter had got quotes from Mrs Snokes and from the prodigy's 'delighted ten-year-old sister Eunice, who said breathlessly, "I am so very proud to have so gifted a brother."' After the concert the musicians, all citizens of Surbiton, had 'mingled with the approving crowd' for tea and cakes furnished by the Ladies' Garden Society.

'You did well. Very well.'

'There's more.' She looked at him as if for approval. He nodded.

'The Euphonic Society doesn't have its own premises. It's only a club of ladies, I think. They weren't in the directory, but the woman at the newspaper said she knew somebody she thought her mother had been in it. Well, the long and short of it is I traipsed up and down Surbiton talking to ladies and finding that the Euphonic Society went out of business three years ago, but the chair lady who was is still alive and could be finally tracked down. She'll talk to you, I suppose; she wasn't very eager to talk to the likes of me. What I did get was that she'd been there when Walter Snokes conducted, and he was a dear little lad, and his mother was a tartar. Not her word, but it's what she meant.'

'In what way a tartar?'

'She wouldn't say it right out to me, but I think what she might say to you is she was pushy. Pushy for her boy and pushy for herself, was what I got. Reading between the lines, so to speak. I thought maybe you ought to talk to somebody who was in that orchestra he conducted, too, because what I got from the old chair woman was maybe the boy was a sell and the musicians had conducted themselves.'

'She said that?'

'Oh, no. What she said was something like "he waved his wand just like a real conductor, and I'm sure the musicians weren't distracted by it". I made notes, which I'll write up tonight and you can have.'

'A sell? You mean you think she meant he wasn't a prodigy?'

'She didn't say that. She just seemed to say they could have got on without him. And that the mother was the reason he did it. So I thought you might want another authority and I asked her who had recommended the boy and she told me, like I was supposed to be impressed, "Oh, the Trinity College of Music in London!" like it was the home of the Archbishop of Canterbury.'

'Ah. He had a certificate from that place on the wall.'

'Oh. You knew already.' She looked as if she might pout.

'No, no! I knew it but I hadn't thought of it. Of course. Well, you did a lot. A tremendous lot! You did brilliantly.'

'I didn't do it the way you wanted.'

'You did it better. I think we should move you up to five shillings a day. Tomorrow, you and I'll go to the Reading Room and get you a ticket, and I'll give the snooty young man a piece of my mind. What I want you to do then is go to the Newspaper Room—I'll show you where it is—and look for other stuff about Walter Snokes. Something happened to him two or three years after the concert. His father said he had an accident; maybe it made a newspaper. Not Surbiton, because probably there was just the one appearance in Surbiton. But they lived in Finsbury and then in De Beauvoir Town; we'll ask if there were local newspapers up there. London's full of newspapers—more than fifty, the last time I had to dig for something. Hard work—probably no index, but maybe something. The librarians will know. And we'll see to it that they help you. All right? You'll stay with it?'

'Oh, yes.'

'It's boring work.'

'You run a sewing-machine six days a week, then tell me about what's boring, Mr Denton.' As if she had to have confirmation from Janet, she said, 'I really did all right?'

'You can believe what he tells you, Nellie. Yes, you did very well. Very well.'

Mrs Cohan, who lived downstairs, produced tea. As they drank it, Denton learned more about Nellie Strang: she had three children; her husband was 'a sea-faring man'.

'Royal Navy?'

'A coaster out of London. He's somewhere up by Leith just now. Home in a week or two unless they get something for the West.'

'Steam or sail?'

'Sail. It's that hard on him in the winter, the rigging. I want him to stay home, but he says that a job's a job, and he's right.'

After she left, Janet said, 'How could you send her to the Reading Room by herself? Those little men must have taken one look at her dress and rubbed their hands and licked their chops. Denton, you should know better!'

'I didn't think.'

'Well, after this, think! She was humiliated. The famous British class system.' She snorted. 'The nation's premiere "public" library—just try using it if you're a woman and are wearing a hand-me-down dress and drop your H's. Really, how could you!'

'I didn't think.'

'No, you didn't. And why? Because you're too damned preoccupied thinking about the Snokeses! I'm glad you're giving her work, Denton, but why—why do you bother? What in the name of God do you care about a middle-aged couple and their once-was and has-been child prodigy?'

He told her the truth: something about the boy tickled him or irritated him. A grain of sand, he hoped, in an oyster.

Next morning, he read the Riot Act to two young men in the Librarian's offices of the Reading Room. One was the snip who'd patronised Nellie Strang; the other happened to be in the way. He complained to the Librarian himself, got an apology made to Nellie, and was able to hand her her reader's ticket within minutes. 'It's all contacts and who you know. It's all nobs and pull.' He had been a guest of the Library trustees at a dinner; he had met the Librarian there. It was all very like the Masons, with the Nellie Strangs of the world not members.

She said, 'I've seen it all my life, haven't I?'

Before she went to the Newspaper Room he told her what else he wanted. 'Somerset House. We're looking for the little boy's sister. Eunice. You found the name in Surbiton, and that's a big step forward. I hadn't thought of it. If we can locate her, maybe she can tell us something. She's older, so maybe she's married. She certainly wasn't at home with Ma and Pa. So I want you to look out for a marriage of a Eunice Snokes within the last—oh, five years. You may not find it; I think a lot of marriages are still kept only in church registers. But try. People at Somerset House are nicer than the Reading Room. Then, if you don't find her, you'll have to get at her through birth records, as the mother, I mean; if she married a few years ago, she's likely had a child by now. I think you can go into them by the mother's name.' He had a gloomy thought. 'But maybe not the maiden name. That'll be bad.'

'One step at a time.' It was as if she was now telling him how to do it. 'Where there's a will, there's a way. I want to get to work, Mr Denton.'

'Well—yes, fine.' Denton stood. 'Keep me up to date. If you don't find anything more on the sister, come to see me again. We'll, mmm, work it out.'

He had started back towards the main entrance and turned to call after her, 'And maybe the Census of 1901,' but she was gone. And the census wouldn't have been any good unless she had a married name and an address, anyway.

Atkins was out when he got home, but he had left two notes on top of the first mail of the day. One said, 'I saw that young policeman friend of yours from Naples across the road again, what's he up to?' He'd printed 'IMPORTANT' at the top of the other and circled the block of handwriting. 'Somebody named Doty telephoned. The Finsbury man will see you. Name of Frank Pinkert. 125 Worship Street. Near the Artillery Ground. Mornings best.' Denton, who had planned to spend the rest of the morning at his desk, staring at a blank sheet of paper, threw himself back into his coat and ran down his stairs and out the door as if he were afraid that somebody might stop him.

Worship Street would not be the worst street in the parish, he thought as he left Moorgate Street station and started up Finsbury Pavement. Things would be worse to the north, probably. Finsbury had had a big population in the eighteenth century; now it was much shrunken. He had walked through these streets but remembered none of them well, but he was aware of Liverpool Street station and its sprawling rail yard only a little distance away.

When he turned into it, he found Worship Street as he had expected, neither mean nor great, bustling with little shops and shoppers, as wide as the City Road it joined. Number 125 was a few hundred feet along, four storeys of blackened brick with stone lintels and a cornice that suggested better days and an earlier architecture. Pinkert, Investigations and Private Consultations, was at the top of a stairway that started with wide treads and a handsome newel post and dwindled to scarred wood and hand rails before it reached Pinkert's level.

A young man, really a boy, sat reading a pink newspaper behind the door. Sandy-haired, spotty, he looked up as if he'd been caught at something; the newspaper disappeared.

'I'm here to see Mr Pinkert.'

'Appointment?'

'He'll see me. Tell him Mr Denton. Courtesy of Mr Doty.'

The boy got up, brushing crumbs from his lap. The place smelled of fish; could he have been eating fish and chips in mid-morning? Or maybe that was somebody downstairs.

The boy squeezed himself through a doorway, opening the door only far enough for him to go in sideways, as if he were hiding what lay beyond. After a full minute, during which Denton heard a mumble of voices, no words discernible, the sounds sinking into the rumble of the street outside, the door opened again and the boy came out to stand beside the doorway. A face appeared, fleshy, tough, suspicious. It was as if the boy were saying *See? See for yourself. Is he a specimen, or isn't he?* The face disappeared and the boy held the edge of the door in his left hand and said to Denton, 'You can go in.'

Denton got up. The hand let go of the door. It started to swing closed; Denton hurried and stretched and caught it. Beyond it was a stronger smell of fish, a room that might once have been a bedroom, about twelve feet square with windows looking out over the roofs and backs of other houses. Five stiff chairs stood around the walls, perhaps for dealing with whole families—maybe those were the 'consultations'—and against the right-hand wall as he came in was a desk with a high comb along its back, so that whoever sat behind it must have had to stretch his neck to see anything else in the room. A general feeling of discomfort radiated from it.

'I'm Denton. Doty said you'd see me.'

The man grunted. It was his face that had looked out the door. He was big, maybe a former policeman. He was just starting to get a bulge of fat under his chin, which had probably been scraped that morning with a razor but was already dark with stubble. His eyes, except that he kept them slitted against the world's betrayals, were large and, once he opened them, well-shaped, the irises dark blue. His dark hair hung in oily-looking curls around his temples and ears; the very top, Denton thought, was darker, perhaps not his own, and hung over the rest like a tarpaulin on a haystack.

'You're Pinkert?'

The man grunted again. Denton wondered if he was hung-over, husbanding his energy. Denton said, 'Do you know why I'm here?' He was still standing so he could see over the top of the desk. Pinkert reached a hairy-backed hand to a chair and pulled it out and nodded at it.

Denton sat. 'You're a man of few words.'

'Nothing to say yet.'

'This is about a Mrs Snokes. You did some investigating for her.'

'Did I say that?'

'You told Doty that.'

'Never met a man named Doty in my life.'

Denton was getting tired of it. 'You told one of his people, then.'

He seemed a man who practised self-control, certainly of his face. 'Might have done,' he said.

'I'd like more information. About the investigating you did for Mrs Snokes.' He used the name again deliberately to see if Pinkert would connect it with the Denmark Road murder.

Evidently he didn't. 'Illegal to give out information. I'm licensed.'

'The law won't come after you.'

'You a lawyer?'

'What did Doty tell you about me?'

Pinkert looked again at him without expression, then

turned to the desk and pulled from a pigeonhole a brown folder tied with a paler brown ribbon. He didn't open it but looked at it, tapping it with a fingernail as if he thought somebody would open it from inside. 'I'd have expenses if I let you in on this.'

'I guess I could cover some expenses.' Although he hated it, hated the dickering and hated the illegality. A bribe was a bribe.

'Half a quid.'

'That's a hell of a lot!'

Pinkert shrugged. He sat back in his armchair, not a proper desk chair at all but something that might have come from a dining-room suite. He kept his eyes on the folder. 'Shut the door on your way out.'

'Look—all I want to know is what you told Mrs Snokes about her husband. And what she did when you told her.'

'Oh, that's all? You think you can come here and get the world with a dollop of icing on it for half a quid? What are you, a bloody Hottentot, you don't know how things are done in Britain?'

Denton almost got to his feet and left. He almost reached out to gather Pinkert's shirt-front and punch him. But if he left, he'd have got nothing and would have to do it all again; if he punched Pinkert, Pinkert would punch him back, and he'd know how. He forced himself back down into quietness, picturing himself doing it, pushing himself back into the chair, saying *Now, now...* He said in as level a voice as he could manage, 'What does half a quid buy?'

'Some of my notes. If they can be done in three minutes.'

Denton thought it over and produced some coins—more than half a working-man's wage for a week.

Pinkert opened the folder. He took out small pages that looked as if they had been torn from a pocket notebook and spread them in front of him so that they were upside-down to Denton. They were covered with pencilled handwriting, impossible for Denton to read from where he was, probably hard enough if he was standing over them: bad handwriting. Pinkert got to his feet. 'I have to step out. Three minutes.' He manoeuvred his bulk around Denton, big but not clumsy, and was gone, the door pulled tight behind him.

Denton saw how it was to be done: he would look at the notes while Pinkert was gone. *Mr Denton, did Mr Pinkert show you his notes? He left them on his desk. Did he tell you to look at them? No. How did you see them? He left the room and I read them.*

Denton hated it. Still, he stood and leaned over the desk, a hand on each side of the pages, and tried to read. The handwriting was worse than bad, but worst of all was finding that crucial details had been blacked out. '8 p.m. followed S to an address on [blacked out]. Stayed [blacked out] hours. Followed to [blacked out] station and underground to [blacked out] and to place of work. Gave up for night because S works nights.' The next page was the same, another evening of following Snokes, although this time he seemed only to have gone to some blacked-out street to a tobacco shop, then to a blacked-out station and so to work. A third night produced only a visit to a blacked-out street with a long name, of which Denton could make out a C at the beginning and an E at the end, then, after turning it and holding it to the window light, either an L or an H after the C. *Charterhouse? Is there a Charterhouse Street? Maybe Claverhouse?* Otherwise, the pages were useless, their dates blacked out so that he had no idea of even the year when they had been made.

The door opened. Denton tossed the pages on the desk. 'Give me back my half-pound.'

'You've been reading my private papers. That's actionable.'

'So is extorting money under false pretences.'

'I don't think you'll report it.' Pinkert dropped the papers back into the file. 'I reported what I found to the wife and that was that.'

'When? What year, at least?'

'Look you, I'm not the most honest tec in the world, but I'm not the worst, either. You've had all you're going to get.'

'That's all?'

'What'd I just say?'

'What did you tell the wife? *Exactly* what did you tell the wife?'

'None of your business.' He gave Denton his blank face.

'Did you tell her what he was doing in the house you followed him to?'

'Didn't know what he was doing, did I?'

'What did Mrs Snokes do?'

'She paid.'

'Was there a woman at the house he went to?'

Pinkert tied the ribbon around the file and put the file back in the pigeonhole. 'You got your money's worth.'

'Not without the other woman's name and address and the date, I didn't.'

'If I tell you somebody's name, you'll maybe find her—or him—and ask more questions. Or try to pry money out of them. Or God knows what-all. And then it comes back on me and I lose my licence. Close the door when you go out.'

Denton saw that he meant it. He wanted to say something that would insult Pinkert, but he couldn't think of anything right then, and what good would it do? Pinkert must have been sloughing off insults all his life. From the door, Denton did manage one last try. 'How did Mrs Snokes behave when you told her?'

Pinkert thought about that—or thought about whether it would come in under the same half-pound. 'I never saw her again. Like I'm not going to see you, right?'

Denton accepted the defeat. He went out, not earning even a glance from the boy, who was bent over his pink rag again. He wandered down to Finsbury Square, then on down again to Finsbury Circus. He could have gone back to Moorgate Street underground but had nowhere to go, and so he wandered, finding himself in Smithfield Market and then Bart's. Realising how close he was, he walked up to Clerkenwell Green and found the Italian *salumeria* that was supposed to have the restaurant in the back. It was the right place but not the right day. 'Only Thursday, Friday, Saturday,' a black-haired man told him, 'only' coming out as 'on-a-ly', 'Saturday' as 'Sat'day'. Denton said something in Italian; the man became voluble and went too fast for Denton to follow. He managed to get that the 'restaurant' was mostly for family and friends, but, as Denton had been in Naples and liked Italian food—he did like Italian food, yes, for certain, yes?—he would be welcome to come one of those evenings. Denton bought Italian coffee and a chunk of real *parmigiana-romagna* and a pound of spaghetti (*'importata, da vero'*) and was escorted to the shop door and shaken hands with before he could get out.

He wandered some more—to Old Bailey Street and Fleet Lane, then Lincoln's Inn, King's Cross Road—and, after an hour of which he remembered nothing, Glasshouse Street, with the entrance to the Café Royal beckoning him. He looked at his watch: it was after one.

He took his usual seat on a banquette near the Regent Street entrance. The Domino Room was far from full. That was just as well, he thought. He didn't want to jabber. He ordered *choucroute garni*, a strange choice for him but right for the day, which was still wet and blustery. He drank a glass of the house claret greedily. He was cutting into his last sausage and topping it with mustard when a voice said above him—it could have come from one of the caryatids on the green-and-gold columns—'What're you doing here at this hour?' The speaker pulled a chair over from another table and sat.

'Do sit down.' Denton was chewing his sausage. He watched Frank Harris toss off the rest of his brandy and reach for Denton's wine carafe. 'Do have some wine.' Harris was an editor and writer, better known for his sexual adventures—or at least his tales of them—than his work.

Harris poured himself wine, sipped, made a face, and looked for a place to empty his glass. Denton took the glass from him and emptied the wine back into the carafe while Harris hollered at a waiter for more brandy. Denton said, 'Drinking your lunch?'

'I'm doing a temporary job on a magazine for mothers that's driving me to it. "Baby's Tummy Is Mummy's Altar of Love".

Truly. That was the original title. I've got to change it. Can't think of anything better than "The Perils of Pabulum". Any suggestions?'

'You know anything about music, Harris?'

'I know everything about music.'

'Ever hear of a child prodigy named Walter Snokes?'

'There can't be a child prodigy named Snokes. They're mostly Italian or German and dead and have names like Mozart. Ask me another.'

'This one played the piano and composed. Conducted something in Surbiton wearing a velvet Fauntleroy suit.'

'They all do that.'

'Somebody told me he may not actually have conducted. Waved the stick around.'

'That's usual. How young? Six or seven? Would you do what a six-year-old told you? The child gives the downbeat and then they're off and playing, and he waves his arms about and middle-aged women are so entranced they find they're sitting in puddles of pee. He didn't conduct anybody any good, I'll wager. A bunch of Surbiton ladies! Good God. I wish I'd been there; the sexual sweepings after such events are always good. You can pick up more damp muff at a middle-class musicale than you can in Drury Lane. I've known the time I could hardly get one out the door before she was pulling down her knickers.'

'Ever had a woman talk about "holding up the handkerchief"?'

'An offer you should never refuse. Leads to better things. Anybody I know?'

'She was talking about another fellow.'

'Tell me another. Women don't use the expression unless they've something in mind. They love the situation—the man powerless with his pego in their hands. They can't resist thinking that they could cut it off. Like Judith. What are you frowning about?'

'Judith cut off a head, I think. You know anything about idiocy?'

'You ask that of a resident of Britain?'

'I mean in children. Backwardism, whatever you call it. Not growing up right in the head.'

'Is this connected with holding up the handkerchief?'

'The prodigy.'

'Ah, an *idiot savant*.'

'He had some kind of accident and lost his prodigiousness.'

'Went insane?'

'Somebody's called him a half-wit.'

'And the music stopped? Huh. That's one I haven't encountered. I hate to say it, Denton, but you've stumped F. Harris. Might make an interesting piece for my mummies' mag, though. "The Day the Music Stopped—How Little Willie Lost His Tone". Better than every baby's belly an altar, eh? I could go three pounds for a couple of thousand words, nothing longer than three syllables, and no sex.'

'Mothers already know all about sex.'

'You'd think, but the mag goes on as if it had been just them and the Holy Ghost. I could go four pounds if there was some suggestion of thrilling nastiness in it—Nurse dropped the kid on his noggin, or Cook made his breakfast with coal oil. "Mother Beware—A Vicious Servant Drove the Music from My Baby's Soul".'

'I'm having enough trouble with a new novel. What I want is some information about what happened to this kid!'

'Ask a doctor. Although you'll find they know even less than you do. If all the physicians in Harley Street were laid end to end, they'd make good paving stones.'

Denton finished his coffee. As he was going away, Harris shouted after him, 'Five pounds if there's a scandal in it!'

It was raining again. There were no cabs; when it rained, everybody with the money hogged one. He dodged from awning to awning, doorway to doorway, to Harley Street, the office of an intrusive physician named Gallichan who'd got him through being shot but had tried to open a peephole into his psyche. Denton wanted to ask him about Walter Snokes, but the soonest Gallichan could see him was three weeks. Denton slammed out into the rain again. By the time he reached home, both his hat and overcoat had soaked through. When Atkins opened the door, Denton said, 'And what bad news have you got for me?'

Atkins looked startled, then hurt. 'There's a woman waiting for you upstairs.'

'Throw her out. Wait—is it a woman named Strang?'

Atkins looked at a card he took from a waistcoat pocket. 'Miss Rosamund Gearing.'

Denton groaned.

'A very forceful young lady. American, is she? I tried to send her on her way, I really did. She all but threatened me with the police. She's upstairs in the sitting-room eating crumpets with butter and the best marmalade, as she says she missed whatever she calls what she eats in the middle of the day. Probably lunch. Hearty appetite she has.'

'You go up and tell her I'll be with her in a jiffy. I've got to get out of these wet clothes, but you don't have to tell her that. You go up the front stairs and I'll go up the back from your place.'

'She'll see you.'

'Can't be helped. Off you go. Distract her.'

'Oh, yes. My hat.' Atkins put the hat and coat on an appalling hall stand and went up the stairs. Denton rushed to the back, through Atkins's sitting-room, across Rupert, and up to the first floor, where he paused on the top step until he heard Atkins's voice. He walked quickly across the dark end of his own sitting-room and went up the next flight of stairs without looking towards the far end of the room, as if by not looking at the woman he would become invisible.

He came down several minutes later, drier but not very well put together. After apologising to Rosamund Gearing, he poured himself some whisky and stood in front of his fireplace, in which, bless him, Atkins had a brisk coal fire going.

'Well, Miss Gearing, this is a surprise.'

'Oh, I had hoped it wouldn't be. I mean, I hoped you'd want to see me.' Her protruding eyes opened even wider and for some reason her eyebrows went up.

'Um, mm, well, yes of course. I didn't expect you, is what I meant. You said you'd be in London after, um, is it Michaelmas?'

'Term. I was in town for the day and I decided I wanted to see you.'

'Yes?'

'I want to know you better.'

'I'm not sure I'd recommend that.' He tried to make a joke of it. She didn't smile. He thought of his story and how wrong he had been about her.

'I looked again at several of your books. They're *quite* good.'

Denton finished his whisky and put the glass down. He was wondering if Rosamund Gearing was the woman whom Maltby had seen. It was an odd thought—if she was in town for the day, what would she have been doing here yesterday?

'Have you children, Mr Denton?'

'Two. In the States. Both grown.' He smiled. 'Did you wish to be introduced?'

'I am interested in everything about you. I was asking really after your fecundity.' Denton felt himself blush. He could think of nothing to say. No matter; she went on all by herself. 'I told you at Oxford that I want to have a child. It's my moral responsibility to have a child. I think I should like you to be the father.' Some of her Southern origins crept back in as she said this— 'fa-thuh'—and he wondered if that was a sign of something. Nerves? Aggression?

'Ahmm...' He felt himself trying to smile and knew that he looked wide-eyed with fright. 'I'm afraid I don't want any more children, Miss Gearing.'

'Oh, it wouldn't be yours; it would be mine. Do you not like the idea of impregnating me, Mr Denton?' The pop eyes got big again.

Was this the New Woman? *Good God.* 'I don't think we should be having this conversation, Miss Gearing.'

'It embarrasses you? You disappoint me. When we were talking about poor Ivor and I was describing what we'd done, I found that I was thinking how much I'd rather it had been you. And that's led me to think—'

'That's enough, Miss Gearing.' He actually said next that he was old enough to be her father. She laughed.

'Well, I've moved us beyond *La Traviata*, haven't I! Are you really old enough to be my father? You don't seem it. You look very fit. In fact, it was your body I noticed first. You are healthy, tall, long-lived, all qualities I should like to join my own to. And you are an artist and yet intelligent, which is rare. You are interested, Mr Denton—aren't you!'

He was thinking *Damn her*, because of course he was; he had been 'interested' in Oxford. He hadn't been able to keep from thinking of the couple on the grass, the darkness, her hands. But how had she detected it? She hadn't, he thought; she had simply expected it. Her egoism. He said, 'Miss Gearing, you're mistaken about me. I'm flattered. But you've put the cart before the horse. At least in my case.'

'What does that mean?'

'What you call impregnation is the end, not the beginning. And not the means, either.'

'Oh. Courtship and so on. I don't have time for that.'

'Nor I. Nor the inclination.'

She frowned. 'You don't like me?'

'Miss Gearing, I live with a woman I'm very fond of.'

'That hardly matters, does it? What's important is that when I reach that point in the cycle when I'm most fecund, we need to meet each day in some private place, and then your part will be over. I shall ask nothing more, I promise.' The frown was replaced by a rather sweet smile that parted the lips, seemed to give them more flesh. 'I can't believe you're immune to the idea of intercourse with me.'

Although he was blushing again, he said, 'I'm not immune; I'm flattered, but it's one of the crazier ideas I've ever heard.' At the word 'crazier', her frown returned. 'I don't like to be rude, but I'm going to ask you to leave. We won't talk about this any more.'

'And what if I say that your attitude would change my promise about Ivor?'

'I'd say you were being dishonest.'

'Honesty—truth, fidelity, ethos if you like—is for me to define, not you. If I were to change the promise, it would be your fault, after all.'

'I won't go into court with a Philadelphia lawyer, Miss Gearing. You've got a crazy idea into your head, I don't know why, but you can just get it out again. A woman your age, and *me*? You have to see there's something queer about the idea.' But thinking, some of the whores I went with not so long ago were her age, or younger.

'It is Nature.'

'Nature doesn't like the old; she favours the young, especially in procreation. Read Darwin.'

'I've read Darwin.'

'Then you know it isn't Nature. It's nuts.' He was deliberately rude, rather a relief.

Her face took on a very strange expression; she might have been a different woman. The jaw seemed to have grown downwards, although her mouth was closed; her eyes seemed larger than ever. The effect was certainly of anger, also of a kind of grossness. He thought *Jekyll and Hyde.*

She stood. 'We will have this conversation another time. Please ring for my things.'

Denton didn't like to ring for Atkins—egalitarianism again—so went to the top of the back stairs and said, 'Would you bring up Miss Gearing's things, please?' The doors to the dumbwaiter stood open, so he guessed that Atkins had heard at least part of it. Atkins confirmed things by saying, 'I'm getting them, ain't I?'

She was halfway down the stairs to the front door, Atkins leading, when Denton said, 'Were you here yesterday, Miss Gearing?'

It was hard to interpret her from the back, but he thought he saw some movement of her head and neck. From the bottom of the stairs she said, 'Of course not.' Seconds later, she was gone.

Upstairs, Denton poured himself another whisky. He held the decanter up towards Atkins, who shook his head. Denton said, 'You heard it. Well?'

'Some men have all the luck.'

'Now, now.'

'Just joking, General. Not got quite all her bolts tightened, has she?'

'Well, she's outspoken. Likes to call attention to herself.'

'She's loonier than that.'

'The idea is loony, yes.'

'Not the idea—*her*. She's nuttier than Aspearn's Almond Cake!'

'Just because she wants me to father a baby? I'll admit she works at being kind of shocking, but that doesn't make her crazy.'

'It isn't the baby. It's *you*. If you think that once she wraps her legs around you, pardon me, she'll let you go, you're as loony as she is.'

'I'm not much of a catch.'

'It's just because you're *you*. It's something she's after, Colonel, and I don't mean a toss in the hay. It's your—lustre.'

Denton stared at him. Atkins waggled his eyebrows and said, 'Why do you think she picked young Sir Ivor? Because of his brilliance? His *joy de veever*? No, because he's a baronet and she made him beg. You don't believe it? I do. I've seen it before with women, and I'll bet you have, too. But I've never seen it brought right out and hung up like knickers on a wash line. In her, it goes too deep and too strong, so she's loony!'

'You think the baby's just a, mmm, ruse?'

'I think she tells herself she wants a baby, and if she has one she'll show it off for a while before she packs it off to her mum to raise, but what she's after is the, the…power. Sir Ivor's power and your power and God knows how many other poor chaps' power before she packs it in.'

The Backward Boy

Somebody else had said something very like that—cutting Johnsons off. Frank Harris. *Good God.*

'You going to tell the missus?'

'About Miss Gearing? Of course. And don't call her "the missus".'

'Can I leave off giving you advice and mend the buttonholes in the tweed suit?'

'Unless you want to tell me *your* troubles.'

Atkins groaned. 'Not yet, General, not yet. I can't—I can't...' He went to the stairs and took one step down. 'But mark my words—that woman's a loony, and we haven't seen the last of her.'

CHAPTER
9

Janet listened to the saga of Rosamund Gearing without laughing as he thought she might, smoking throughout and scratching Sophie's silky ears. On the whole, she seemed to agree with Atkins. She said, 'If you want to, you can. After the things I've done, I'm in no position to be jealous.' She was still grieving over the death of a former lover, Ruth Castle; he could see that loss in a curious, abstracted look she got at odd times.

'I'd rather you were jealous.'

'Oh, I don't think so. Jealousy isn't very pleasant.' She brushed dog hairs off her skirt. Sophie was a pretty mutt, mostly black and white, in love with Janet. 'Sophie's about through her heat and still a virgin. A few more days. Atkins is to be commended.'

'He still won't tell me what's wrong in his life.'

'You worry too much about other people's troubles. How's the novel?'

'Ha, ha.'

The next evening, Mrs Strang had information for him

from Somerset House and was again in Janet's sitting-room, Janet on the couch with most of Sophie beside her, the head on her lap. Mrs Strang had got nothing more that was useful from the Newspaper Room—a mention of the Surbiton concert, some unrelated squibs about the music school but nothing about Walter Snokes's accident—but she'd found Eunice Snokes's marriage record and then, although it was irrelevant, a record of her recent baby.

'She's Mrs William Bonney. I fancy that name; wish I had it. Seems a happy name. She lives in one of the streets above Victoria Park. Her husband's something in the gas works, must be making a decent salary because those are nice houses up there.' She had written out the details. 'You want me to keep looking in the Newspaper Room?'

'No. What I'd like is to know who was the boy's teacher at the music school. Can you find that out?'

'I can ask. I daresay they can't be worse than the Reading Room.' He asked her for more—most of it, he knew, make-work—a list, for example of private places that might house somebody like Walter Snokes. It wasn't the way to go about it; he simply wanted to give her work and keep her handy in case something new came up.

'That was good of you,' Janet said when Mrs Strang was gone.

'I can't keep it up indefinitely. I really do need to put some money in the bank.'

'I've plenty.'

They'd been over it and over it. She did, in fact, have plenty. But he wouldn't take it. She stopped petting Sophie and put her hand on Denton's. 'You say you love me, but you won't take my money.'

'That's right.'

'Is that consistent?'

'Probably not.'

'And you think Miss Gearing is unbalanced.' She stood, causing Sophie to have to move. 'Why don't you spend the night?'

The Backward Boy

Eunice Snokes Bonney in fact lived in a house above Victoria Park that was not very grand. It was one street too many away from the park, but maybe, he thought, it would seem a good house to Mrs Strang. And that thought seemed churlish to him, unfair.

He had not sent a note, admitting to himself that if the young Mrs Bonney told her mother he wanted to see her, he might not be allowed to visit. An Irish maid answered the door and took in his card and the paper he'd signed for Teddy Mercer. A young woman he supposed was Eunice Bonney squinted near-sightedly at him from the far end of a central corridor and then disappeared.

'This-way-if-you-please-sir.' The maid looked about thirty and a veteran, no fluster or fuss about what to do or how to do it. Denton wondered if Eunice Bonney could manage her or if in fact she ran the household. She led him to a front parlour that was very much in Mrs Snokes's taste, heavy manufactured furniture and a lot of feathery greenery. A quick glance around told him that there were no mementoes of Walter Snokes's prodigiousness, however, nor was there a piano—a bit unusual in a modern house.

Eunice was a thinner version of her mother, although her face had her father's long chin and, when she squinted her eyes, some of his look of perpetual fatigue, with dark pouches under them. Her hair was his, too, gingery and thin. She had pulled a shawl around her upper body as if for protection.

Denton thanked her for seeing him and said he had talked with both Mr Drigny and her father. She looked uncomfortable but asked him to sit. He still had his overcoat on and his hat in his hand. He selected a platform rocker in machine-carved wood and a blood-coloured plush seat, lowered himself into it and put his hat on the floor. The overcoat stayed on: the room was cold and had no fire in the grate. Her shawl was explained.

'I asked Mr Drigny, but he couldn't tell me—about your brother Walter, Mrs Bonney.' He was worried about her recognising his interest as selfish curiosity, but he thought it best to get right to it before she asked him why he was coming to her.

It was not a good opening. Her face looked as tightly buttoned as a publican's waistcoat. 'I don't see him.'

'Your mother and father are sensitive about the subject, and I thought I could ask you.'

'Why wouldn't I be sensitive? I'm his sister.'

'Can you tell me what happened to your brother?'

She got her back up. He had started off wrong. 'What's this to do with my father? I thought all that was over.'

'Drigny's putting together a brief for a barrister. Just in case.'

'But it's over!' Her voice was shrill.

'The police don't seem to want to give it up. Were you there when your brother had his "accident"?'

She shook her head.

'What do you remember about it?'

He thought she wasn't going to say anything, except maybe to ask him to leave. Then, as if asking her about herself rather than Walter had released something, she said, 'I was at school; I stayed beyond age eleven and studied three more years. I came home and Ma said something terrible had happened and my brother was in the hospital. Then after he came home, it was never talked about.'

He felt the excitement again, the writer's curiosity—that lust. 'What had happened?'

She began to close up again. 'I think he fell. I don't know. They never said. He hit his head.'

'And he changed?'

She made a small, snorting sound. 'It was like they'd sent the wrong boy home. He was just entirely different.' She stopped; so did Denton's breathing. Then she started again and seemed to gather momentum. 'At first he was just sulky all the time and then he got, well, you wouldn't want to be around him. He made my life a little hell, I can say, and I wasn't half glad to find my Will and get out of it. There, that's what you came to hear, I suppose. Well, I don't try to hide it.' Again, she stopped, but only for an instant before she rushed on. 'My brother destroyed our family, that's the sum and substance of it! People say he changed and wasn't the same after, well, none of us was the same after, either. You think you can live with a monster and not change, you've another think coming. Call me cowardly, but it was the happiest day of my life when I got out of it!'

The word 'monster' delighted him. 'What was he like?' His own voice sounded hungry to him.

'What wasn't he like? He was an infant in a body as big as me! He screamed at the least little things; he demanded and demanded and if he didn't get his way he screamed. He soiled himself, on purpose I used to think. Maybe not. But he was nine years old when it started, nine and growing, and when he was eleven he was a big boy and strong. Imagine if you can an infant as big as me and stronger! My mother was black and blue from him—I've seen bruises up and down her arms like she'd been fighting off somebody in the boxing ring. If you said anything at all to him he didn't like, he'd put his hands over his ears and screw his eyes up tight. Then he took to hitting his head on the walls. Hitting his head on the walls! My mother had to hold him so he wouldn't do it. I wouldn't go near him for fear of him, but Ma would put her arms around him and hold him, him beating at her and hitting her and using his head to hurt her. And when I asked her why she did it, she said he was her little boy.' She sat very straight and sniffed. 'I wasn't her little girl, I can tell you. I grew up pretty fast. Especially when he got—when he matured. I won't give a name to what he tried on me.'

Denton took that in, said gently, 'And there was no more music?'

'Like he'd never played a note.' She sniffed again. 'At first, he tried. He'd play a page of something if it was put in front of him, and he'd get to the bottom of the page and start over. You couldn't leave him alone with it or he'd drive you mad with playing the same thing all the day long! If he made a mistake, he'd have one of his tantrums. Banging his head. Screaming.'

'His ability was just—gone?'

'He'd been a pest with his music before. He was always practising, morning, noon and night. My mother egged him on, but he didn't need nagging like some kids; he *liked* it. Loved it. You couldn't go anywhere in that match-box of a house and not hear it. I thought I'd give anything for him to stop sometimes.' She brushed hair back from her face, smiled thinly. 'You get what you ask for, don't you?'

'Do you remember when he conducted in Surbiton?'

'I had to go. I remember there were cakes.'

'Did he really conduct?'

She shrugged. 'It was probably Ma's idea. But he really was musical. I don't have an ear for it, myself.'

'And now he lives out.'

'They put him in a home with others like himself. Where he belongs. But it was too late to save our family. Everything that's happened I blame on him. This business with Pa...I suppose you can say Walter didn't know any better, his mind was gone, but he should have been put away as soon as they saw what he was. Not ruined three lives because Ma couldn't let go!'

'Do you know where he is now?'

'I do not, nor want to. Ask Ma or Pa.'

'You don't visit him?'

She snorted.

'Do your parents?'

'Ma's there two days of every week for sure, rain, shine, or fire and brimstone coming down. She says, "Oh, he's getting better, he's getting better." Better! She means he didn't give her bruises for once.'

'Does Walter know people?' Now he saw himself as scavenging in her brain, trying to find tasty bits he could use later.

'What, remember them? I suppose he does. Yes, he must. He isn't...an idiot. He reads books. Ma says he can talk very smart when he wants to. But he's—or he was; I haven't seen him since they took him away—it's like he never *sees* you. Like he didn't really see you there as another person. If you said like, "Time to go to bed, Walter," he'd say, "No," like what he said was what mattered. Or if you said to him something anybody would understand, like...oh..."once in a blue moon", he couldn't let go of it. When is that? Will I see it? Why is it blue? Why do we have to wait until then? Show me the blue moon. Like he didn't have any sense!'

'And if you frustrated him, he banged his head on the wall.'

'That's exactly the way it was. Made himself bleed. It made me sick to watch him.'

Denton was thinking of a scene about that. From the boy's point of view? Or some horrified person who loves him? 'Does he still do it?'

'I don't know, I'm sure. Ask Ma. Why aren't you putting all these questions to her?'

'I thought it would be too painful for her.' *Liar.*

'Well, she doesn't need more pain, that's plain as paint. Her life's been no bed of roses. This business of Pa being called a murderer must just about have finished her.' She squinted and looked at him as if she suspected him of something. 'Is that over, or isn't it?'

'It's only the police—'

'He couldn't have done it, *couldn't* have done it. He hasn't the gimp.' She tilted her head and turned a little sideways to him. 'But he knew the woman, didn't he? The one was murdered.'

'You'd have to ask him that.'

'Pa has a roving eye. You think I shouldn't say it about my own father? Everybody always knew. Poor Ma! She had enough with him, and then Walter!'

A baby's cry sounded from the back of the house.

'That's baby. I can't go on jawing. I suppose I've said too much already.' She gave him the sideways look again. 'Ma'll give me the dickens if she knows what I said.'

'I told you, I don't want to upset your mother.'

The door opened and the maid looked in. 'Baby's hungry.'

'Coming, coming.' Eunice Bonney got up, pulling her shawl tighter in the cold room. 'Why're you're so nosy about Walter?'

He had the lie ready. 'It's background.'

'I suppose you could get Pa some sympathy in court by trotting Walter out. You might think of that, if push comes to shove.' She put out a thin, very cold hand. 'Goodbye, Mr...'

'Denton.'

He wondered if she had been waiting for some stranger to say all that to. Or was she so filled with resentment and self-pity that she said it to everybody? Another case of egoism. He didn't much care. What he cared about was a boy who had been a prodigy and had turned into a monster, and how he might be the key that unlocked *The Secret Jew*.

In his own chair, chewing over what Eunice Bonney had told him, he had fallen asleep. Waking, he knew he had heard a sound, but he was disoriented by the light, actually the lack of it; the room was almost dark. Then the sound came again—a throat being cleared.

Atkins was standing next to him with a tea tray. Denton could smell anchovies. 'What?'

'I thought it was time we talked.'

Denton pushed himself up in the chair, shaking his head to arrange his hair, then swiping at it with a hand. '"We"?'

Atkins cleared his throat again. 'I've been putting this off. It's cowardly of me. The time has come. I have an announcement to make.'

Denton groaned.

'I'm trying to get married.'

Denton opened his mouth and then closed it. He opened it again and said, 'Trying? Do I say "Congratulations" for trying?' He was thinking that he was looking at a personal disaster: Atkins was going to leave. *Ego.*

'I thought you ought to know.' Atkins cleared his throat. 'You already know the, mm, prospective bride.'

'How so?' Denton was thinking of the housemaids up and down Lamb's Conduit Street, but he was also thinking of what marriage meant: *He was going to lose Atkins.*

'It's Mrs Johnson.' Atkins looked like a small boy waiting for a hiding.

Denton sat up still straighter. Atkins started fussing around him with a folding table and the tray and the tea, his hands trembling. 'My *typewriter?*' Mrs Johnson had typed his manuscripts for years. She had always behaved towards him as if he were an axe-murderer; he had thought she was terrified of men. And now *Atkins?* '*My* Mrs Johnson?'

'I took the stuff you sent from Naples up to her to be typed. I didn't mean for nothing to happen, but...we hit it off. You know—first one thing, then another.' Desperately, he said, 'She's a jolly soul.'

'Mrs *Johnson?* Well, that's, that's...wonderful, Atkins.'

Atkins had poured three cups of tea. He stared at them, then handed one to Denton and took one himself. In a terrible attempt at a humorous voice, he said, 'I guess I thought Rupert was coming for tea.' He stood there. Their eyes locked.

'For God's sake, sit down, Sergeant.'

'Yes, sir.' Atkins fell into a chair as if the backs of his knees had been hit with an axe handle.

'This is what you couldn't talk about.'

Atkins nodded. He tried to drink the tea, but the cup rattled against the saucer and he had to put it down. 'It's very painful.'

'Weddings are supposed to be joyous.'

'Supposed to be.' Atkins's voice was a whisper. 'There's complications.' He looked at Denton and then at the tea tray. 'Have some Eccles cake.'

'Forget the Eccles cake. What's wrong?'

Atkins sighed. 'We're going into business together. That's how it started. The Johnson-Atkins Modern Typewriting and Recording School and Company, Limited. My knowledge of the recording business and her expertise in typewriting.' Atkins had been a partner in a short-lived recording company. 'To teach typewriters to type directly from the recorded human voice and without the intervention of the shorthand tablet. It's a revolutionary idea. Stuns the mind.'

'That's not what you want to talk to me about.'

Atkins shook his head slowly and mouthed but did not speak the word *No*. 'She don't like the idea of marrying a servant, and she's very firm about not living like one. She says if she did, she'd be like a servant herself. That means I won't be able to live here.' He looked at Denton, his face miserable. 'She's a proud woman. I wouldn't force it on her for the world.'

'You're leaving me?'

'It wouldn't be for a while yet, because Lily's...' He rubbed his head. 'Lily's *Lily*. And, if you listen to a proposition I'd make you, it wouldn't be as you'd say *leaving* you.' He began to talk fast. 'I had in mind requesting to stay on the books and being here between let's say eight in the antemeridian and like seven at night. That way I could do all my usual, do the clothes, get the door, answer the phone, straighten up the rooms, replenish the coals in the grates, do the washing-up for whatever dishware you use...' He ran down. '...and all the other little things you pay me so generously for.'

'While running a typewriting and recording company.'

'Lily can do the day-to-day. What I'm needed for is the advertising and sales, plus a bit of tailoring of the recording devices. I can do that evenings.'

'You mean to sleep out, in other words.'

'Connubial bliss, if I may say so, Colonel.'

Denton glared at his shoes and massaged his upper lip. Janet had said once that Atkins was his best friend. He'd denied it, said that he paid Atkins double what other manservants got so he wouldn't be his friend. Now that he was going to lose him, he saw that Janet was right. And lose him to Lily Johnson! A woman Denton had thought of as one of those who would inherit the earth under some other management. The type who wouldn't say boo to a goose. Butter wouldn't melt in her mouth. He said in a groaning voice, 'Is this all decided?'

'Well...' Atkins sighed again. 'Yes and no.'

'Goddammit, Atkins, "decided" means yes *or* no!'

'There's something else.' Atkins looked at the grate, the coals burned down now to a whitish mound with a pink interior like some sort of cake. He leaned back, lacing his fingers together in his lap. 'I can't keep Rupert.' His voice broke on the name; he pressed his lips together.

'She doesn't like him?'

Atkins shook his head. 'No dogs.'

Denton wiped down his moustache with thumb and finger. 'That's a poser.' He handed over Atkins's tea. 'Drink your tea; you'll feel better. I suppose what you're saying is, you want to work for me from eight to six or seven, and you want me to keep your dog.'

'Except he wouldn't be my dog, would he? He'd be your dog.' Atkins's voice broke again. 'He sleeps on my bed.'

'Well, he won't sleep on my bed. I don't know, Atkins. It sounds as if you're going to try to live two lives at once.' Denton rubbed his finger rapidly back and forth across his nose. 'Have some of the Eccles cake. My God, Atkins, not to have you around in the evening—'

'You could get somebody else in.' Atkins cleared his throat, said, 'I thought you might find somebody to come in at night—answer the door and the telephone, fix breakfast as needed. Fred Oldaston, for example.' Oldaston had been a prize-fighter, then the muscle at the late Ruth Castle's whorehouse. 'You like Fred. He's looking for something.'

'What, and he'd play Cox and Box with you in the downstairs?'

'Well, I won't need the bedroom, will I? A place to sit is all, in the few minutes I get in any day to sit, which is rare.'

Denton pulled himself up in his chair again. 'I don't need somebody in the house at night at all.'

'And what if somebody dumps a bullet into you again, what of that? What of the time I found you halfway to the attic and gasping like the pet goldfish has leapt out the bowl? What then?'

'Sergeant, if somebody shoots me again, I give you permission to come in nights and fuss over me.' Denton smiled. He filled their cups. He thought, *We sound like an old married couple.* He put the pot back on the tray, handed across the cake plate, now mostly crumbs. 'The truth is, one of the things I value you for is our talks. Those often happen late at night. I can't talk to Fred Oldaston that way. Fred's a *prize-fighter.* You and I've talked through several crimes, and you've given me insight. That'll all end.'

'You're not making it any easier, Colonel! Anyway, I talk perfectly well during the day. I'd point out, as well, that when a great heavy doorstop thudded down on my skull, courtesy of a vengeful murderer, it was at night. If I'd been living out, it wouldn't have happened.'

'He'd have got me instead, you mean.'

'He did anyway.'

Denton gave a grunt. The truth was, he'd lived all his life until he came to London without a servant—born dirt-poor, dirt-poor until he was forty—and he was as capable of taking care of himself as anybody on the planet. He let the grunt turn into a chuckle and the chuckle into outright laughter. 'I'll miss your company, is what I'll miss, Sergeant. But as the night-time is usually when there's least call on you, I guess I'll have to live without you then. If what all this has been about is whether I'll agree or not, then I agree, although not with a lot of clapping of hands and shouting Hosannah. And Rupert's a problem. But tell Mrs Johnson she's getting a good man.'

Atkins said in a voice that was hard to hear, 'Compliments not called for. Trying to have a business-like discussion. But I'm grateful, General. That you see it as, um, possible.' He put his cup and saucer carefully back on the tray. 'Well—all that said, I'll push off below stairs.'

'Sit a minute.'

'I can't talk much more, General. I'm bushed.'

The Backward Boy

'I want to tell you about Eunice Bonney—the sister of the prodigy. You'll help me to think."

'You always tell me my ideas are rubbish.'

'That's how you help me.'

He told his story about the visit to Victoria Park and what the prodigy's sister had said about him after his accident. 'Uncontrollable. Violent. Clearly something sexual, too, when he matured. I find him interesting as a character, but...It's a question of how dangerous he might be.'

Atkins's face was screwed up into a suspicious sneer. 'You don't mean to tell me that you're thinking this barmy lad might have something to do with the murder up on Denmark Road!'

'It hadn't really occurred to me until she told me he was violent.'

'Oh, crikey, you're off on a wild hare again!'

The business offices of the Cosmopolitan Steam Railway Company, Limited were in a business block behind Liverpool Street station. At night, the lights in the windows above the ground floor were at first startling, then reassuring, as if some oasis had been reached in the city darkness. Denton had come in a horse cab, not on foot for once. He prowled the deserted railway station, then went outside and walked a few hundred feet up Bishopsgate Street Without. He had a Remington derringer in his overcoat pocket, but there seemed little danger here. Goods wagons were drawn up in the alleys that led to loading docks along the railroad tracks beyond; above him, the lights burned in the offices. He walked back down to Liverpool Street and across the front of the station, then turned again into North Broad Street. Here at last he found the entrance to the offices above, a fairly modest doorway with a small portico and double doors. A wispy, aged porter waited inside.

'Snokes, sir? Yes, we have a Mr Snokes. Is this on business, sir?'

'I'm sure you know that Mr Snokes has had some notoriety lately. It's in connection with that.'

'Are you a policeman, sir?'

'From his solicitor.' Denton produced the paper he'd signed for Teddy Mercer, which seemed to have more impact on civilians than it had had on Detective Inspector Masefield.

'I see. Well, that's all right, then. Shall I just send a boy up with a message to come down, sir?'

'Or I can go up.'

'Better if he comes down.' The porter lowered his voice. 'Private matter, isn't it?'

He sent off a slightly younger old man—the 'boy', presumably—who disappeared up a flight of stone stairs. Denton and the porter agreed that the night air was cold, shocking; that Indian summer was over and it would be a long winter; that there could be frost soon. They had been sharing a long silence when Arthur Snokes at last could be heard on the stairs and finally came into view, feet and trousers first. The 'boy' seemed to have been absorbed by the upstairs.

'This is irregular,' Snokes said. He was leading Denton away from the porter's cubby-hole. 'Not supposed to have visitors.'

'I won't be long.'

'Nowhere to sit.' Snokes looked around as if the marble floor might be made to produce chairs. Nothing appeared but scuff marks and several crushed cigarettes.

'I want to see your son,' Denton said.

'God, no.'

'I'll need a letter giving me permission. Also directions how to get there.'

'It's not on. Anna'd kill me.'

'She won't know. I'll be careful—I understand the situation.'

'No—that's flat. Why in the name of God would you want to see him?'

'You wanted me to help you.'

'Nothing about Walter can help me.'

They wrangled for five minutes, Snokes looking at his watch and at the porter and giving off signs that he was about to leave. Denton simply insisted and insisted and didn't explain, finally saying in a voice that was meant to be a threat, 'Do you want my help with the police or don't you?'

'Well, yes, naturally, but—'

'Take it or leave it.'

'I *can't*.'

'I talked to your daughter this afternoon. About Walter. It's imperative I see him. Or I'll give it up—all of it. And I suppose if my friends in CID asked me why I gave it up, I'd have to tell them that, frankly, there's something here that has a smack. That would be the honest truth.'

'If my wife hears of it, she'll kill me. She doesn't let even *me* see him.'

'I need that letter.'

Finally, Snokes went off. Denton thought he wasn't coming back, and he was right: ten minutes later, the 'boy' came down the stairs, carefully, his eyes on the treads as if he were afraid of falling, and gave Denton a sealed envelope. Denton slit it with his pocket-knife and saw that it was addressed to The Manager, The Oaks, at an address in Camberwell that made him think, *She has a long trip, two days a week*. On the letterhead of the Cosmopolitan Steam Railway Company, Ltd., it gave him permission to see the writer's son, Walter Snokes, and was signed in a very large, showy hand Arthur P. Snokes, Esq.

Denton gave the 'boy' sixpence and handed another to the porter as he went out. *I've got to stop giving out money and start making some.*

His breath showed in the cold air. Overhead, an apparently solid mass of cloud reflected pink-yellow light down on him. The street lamps were haloed with balls of pale colour, faint rainbows. For London, it was quiet: he could hear only the goods wagons, a train, somebody cursing. Pigeons huddled on the window-ledges stared at him.

The Oaks stood at the top of a low rise, set back from Bushey Hill Road behind a wall that might once have given protection but was now mostly fallen down. A gatehouse still sat beside what must have been a carriage drive; the gates were gone but the gateposts still more or less remained brick topped with stone, one leaning a little towards the house fifty yards beyond it as if bowing. The house was four storeys tall, many-chimneyed, with two side-by-side gable ends at the top, the angled edges broken into stair-like steps—stairs to nowhere, Denton thought. The house's bricks were mostly hidden by creeper in the process of turning from green to red; its high windows, some half-obscured by the creeper, looked like dark gashes in the mass of rusty green. Denton didn't know much about architectural styles; if asked about this one, he'd have said it looked like something out of Dickens. Or one of the Brontës. Or Poe.

He steered the little Barré between the decrepit gateposts and up the weedy remains of the gravel drive. As he approached the corner of the house, he saw an even weedier branch going off towards the back, the ruins of other buildings back there. Perhaps a carriage house, once upon a time.

He stopped the car under the browning leaves of an enormous oak, presumably the last of those that had given the place its name. He kept his eyes on the front door as he removed his gloves, then his motoring cap, then his duster. Nobody appeared. He put on a Homburg hat and dropped an overcoat over his left arm because he thought it might help if he looked respectable. And the derringer was in the overcoat pocket.

The door was set back inside an alcove, up four steps from the ground. One of the steps had broken loose as a single chunk of brick and cement and lay slightly askew on the one below.

He looked all the way up the façade of the place, seeing nobody; he tilted his head back and studied the oak above him, looking for the branch that would fall on his motorcar. None likely. There was no wind, only a damp cold and a thickening of the air that made any idea of seeing the city across the Thames ridiculous.

There was a bell-pull. He gave it a good yank, half expecting the chain to come loose in his hand or the hanger to come out of the wall. Nothing happened. He yanked again. He stamped his feet and turned away to look around what had been a front garden—weeds, two clumps of bushes gone wild, a stone bench almost hidden in the growth.

'What is it?'

He hadn't heard the door open. Startled, he swung around. A big, sallow, almost bald man was standing in the doorway looking at Denton's car.

'I've come to see one of the guests.'

'We don't permit visits. Without notice.' The man had one of those local accents Denton couldn't identify; they were all 'cockney' to him. He sounded as if he was tired of telling people that they didn't permit visits.

Denton got out Snokes's letter and showed it to him. The man studied it. He had a bony, intelligent face, deep-set eyes that, with the bald dome, made his face seem skull-like. Still, Denton thought, he was solid but lean, certainly not frail. If what Eunice Bonney had said about her brother was true, frail wouldn't do for somebody who had the care of him.

Reading the letter seemed to take more time than Denton thought it deserved. He said, 'Are you the manager?'

'I'm Tonk.' He seemed to start to read the letter all over again, then said, 'The manager ain't here.' He raised his eyes and met Denton's. 'I'm in charge.'

'May I see young Snokes?'

The man handed the letter back. 'What do you want with him?'

'I'm handling something for his father.'

'Because of the woman was murdered? We don't want Walter hearing of that. He gets very easy upset.' He had the ability to keep his eyes on Denton's and not blink or look away. The lids were always kept slightly lowered, as if he might have taken a drug or he was partly asleep. 'Anyway, I can't be doing these things for nothing.'

Denton wondered if he could have shown up without the letter and got to the same point. 'How much?'

'Half a crown a visit. Not that there's many visitors.'

'Except Mrs Snokes.'

The hooded eyes didn't react. 'Yes, she's here aplenty. But we have an arrangement. If I let you in, the rules are that you do exactly as I say, and if you upset the patient you leave at once or I throw you out, which I can do. Does Mrs Snokes know you're here?'

'Her husband does.'

'I saw that. Well, if she doesn't and you don't want her to, it'll be *two* half-crowns.'

Denton paid.

The space into which he was led looked battered but probably intact in more or less an original state, dark-panelled walls and heavy oak doors and oak staircases. Above the ground floor, however, interior walls seemed to have been added, cornices and mouldings ending abruptly. The original doors had been replaced, Denton thought; up here, they were heavy, with smooth faces in which was set a single small hatch. The windows at the ends of the corridors had interior vertical bars, the corridors themselves empty of furniture, bare-floored, twilight-dark. He saw a few gas fixtures that were not lit.

There was a smell of urine and cooking and excrement and disinfectant.

'Where are the patients?'

'In their rooms.'

'These?' He made a small gesture towards the doors they were passing.

'One a room. Thirteen in all. Wear me out, they do.'

Denton stopped and listened. Without the clatter of his own footsteps, he thought he could hear human voices, muffled and distant. Were the walls padded or filled with something that deadened sound?

On the second floor, they stopped by a door. Tonk opened the hatch silently. He looked in, then stepped back so Denton could look. He could see part of what had once been a bedroom, now apparently cobbled into a smaller room. Old wallpaper on two of the walls—faded nosegays on a dusty-looking yellow— but covered with ink designs in vivid colours, curlicues and spirals and coils and twists. He was reminded of something else, thought of the music on the Snokeses' piano, the vines and tendrils curling around the staff. He could see one barred window, a closed-up fireplace. The far corner to the right had been curtained with what looked to him like old, even rotten, paisley—more colours, more curves and twists. Set against the nearby wall were a washstand with a bowl and pitcher and, on the lower shelf, a large metal chamber pot with a lid.

'You have central heating?'

'No.'

Tonk closed the hatch as silently as he had opened it and, pushing Denton back from the door with one hand, ran his other hand down a thin chain from a braces button to a side trouser pocket and took out a ring crowded with keys. Finding the one he wanted immediately, he put it in the door's lock and swung it open. At once, there was sound from inside the room. And smell.

'You don't touch him, you mind me? No touching.'

Denton heard a thump and the clatter of something falling. A figure appeared near the doorway, understandable at once as an adolescent boy, slightly fat, dark hair disarranged, a huge smile on his face. He wore a green tweed suit, the fabric old and spiritless and filthy; one side of his shirt collar was caught inside, a necktie wrapped over it but not tied, vanishing in a wrongly buttoned waistcoat. He was already looking beyond Tonk and saying, 'Mummy! Mummy!' And then seeing Denton back there in the gloom and his smile fading.

Tonk moved in; the boy backed away.

'Where's Mummy?'

'This isn't a Mummy day, you know that.'

'I want Mummy! I want Mummy!'

Tonk turned and said over his shoulder to Denton, 'Get in here, get in; we don't want to set the others going.'

'I want Mummy!' The boy stared at Denton and then put his hands over his eyes as if denying his ability to see. He bent forward, then squatted, repeating in a lower voice, 'I want Mummy, I want Mummy—'

'You know what happens if you misbehave, Walter.'

'But I want Mummy!'

'If you wake anybody else, you know what will happen, Walter.'

Denton could hear the boy's breathing, hoarse, almost panting. Some kind of struggle was going on—Tonk still, his tone of voice unchanged, the boy rigid and breathing noisily. Abruptly, the boy took his hands away from his eyes and said, 'I don't like him.' Looking towards Denton but not at him, then looking up to appeal with his eyes to Tonk.

He was good-looking, Denton realised, but unhealthy and filthy. His skin was pasty from being too long indoors, his body slack and puffy from lack of exercise, yet he had a handsome face and beautiful, feminine eyes. His chin and jawline carried several days of dark stubble; some of it straggled to his upper lip. Denton looked for the little boy in the Fauntleroy suit and the shoulder-length hair, couldn't see him. The room's smell was entirely adolescent, unwashed clothes and sweat and the chamber pot and perhaps sex.

'Walter, this is Mister Denton. Den-ton. Say Den-ton.'

'I don't like him.'

'Say Den-ton, Walter.'

Denton saw the boy's eyes swing his way again but again not make contact. 'Den-ton.'

Something passed from Tonk's left hand to the boy, who popped it into his mouth. Denton hoped it was only a sweet, winced slightly at the thought that it had been bouncing around in Tonk's pocket for God knows how long with no wrapper.

Tonk turned and walked to the door. As he passed Denton he murmured, 'Half a crown buys five minutes. No touching, remember.' He stood with his back to the door as if to say he wasn't leaving. Denton wondered what would happen if somebody else rang the bell downstairs.

Denton asked himself if he should sit on the floor at the boy's level. He didn't want to, certainly. The floor was filthy, dust balls and threads and bits of paper and crusted stains. He was holding his hat and coat. He said, 'Can I put my hat someplace, Walter?'

'You mean "may I". Not "can I". We don't say "can I" unless it's a question of possibility.' He had a strange voice, rather deep, monotonous, certain vowels too long extended; he sounded to Denton like a man he had known in America who was deaf but could speak.

'Thank you. May I put my hat down someplace?'

The boy looked around the room. 'Certainly not in the grotto. Not on my bed.' Denton noticed the bed now, pushed against the same wall that held the door; what he could see of a sheet was wrinkled, limp, grey. Above it was a bookshelf with a dozen books. 'Not on my desk or my chair. You may put it…on the floor.'

'My coat, too.'

'I didn't give permission!'

'May I?'

'I don't know. Tonk, may he? Tonk knows all the rules. He may? All right.' Without ever looking at Denton.

Denton folded his overcoat and put it on the cleanest spot he could see and put his hat on top of it. Walter had stood up and walked off to Denton's left to a small desk, where he sat and took up a pencil and a ruler. At once, his head was bent over a sheet of paper. Around him were watercolours and brushes. Denton wished he dared to take notes. He took two steps towards the boy and bent to see.

'Don't watch me!'

Denton found he was flustered by the boy's hostility, an absurdity; sane adults could rarely do this to him. 'What are you drawing?' He almost stammered. He saw a sheet of music paper, but there was no music, only tendrils and leaves and what, at a glance, he took to be tiny bugs.

'Don't watch me! Tonk, make him stop watching me!'

Denton stepped back. 'I won't watch.' He was poor with children, even at best, but this boy was almost a grown man. He tried to think of what to say. 'Are you writing music?' He sounded stupid to himself—an adult speaking in sickly-sweet tones that were so false he wanted to apologise. What he wanted to do was to embrace the boy and say he understood, he had lost his childhood, too, but he couldn't. To the contrary: his very being there offended the boy. 'I promise I won't watch.'

Walter looked at a space near him as if surprised and perhaps pleased. 'Mind you don't.' His head went down again.

'I write stories.'

Again, the head came up. 'Do you do magic? I ask and ask for Mummy to send somebody to do magic, but they don't send him.'

'Writing stories is kind of like magic. I make things happen. Like you're doing.'

The boy covered the paper. 'Tonk, I don't like this!'

'Aren't your pictures magic? They look magical.'

'Tonk!' He looked up at the ceiling. His hands were fists, going back and forth above the desk at the level of his chest. 'This is a private place! Don't you know the rules? A private place has a door and if it has a window, put up a curtain so nobody can see in. Private places are for doing private things. The WC is one. Your bedroom is another. You can do it in those places if nobody sees. You have to clean up afterwards and use a towel and wash your dinkus. That is what private is! This is a private place!'

Denton looked at Tonk. The man's eyes seemed dead. Denton said to the boy, 'If I cover my eyes, will it be all right?' He felt helpless and thought he sounded desperate.

'I don't like you!' Denton covered his eyes anyway. The boy's voice changed, so Denton thought he had turned back to the drawing. Denton said, 'I understand about private places. I have to go into my private place to write. To make up my stories.' The boy said nothing. Denton heard the sound of the pencil on the paper. Afraid he had lost Walter Snokes, he said, 'I make things happen that aren't…real. Is that magic?'

'What is "real"?'

Denton cut through thickets of philosophy to say, 'What everybody knows.'

'That's stupid.' The voice changed again; he had turned back towards Denton. 'You can look now. I don't care. I took the magic out, so you can look.'

Denton opened his eyes. The boy was holding up the sheet of music paper. Nothing on it seemed to have changed. 'What did you do?'

'I made a magic mark, stupid. Are your stories about elves? I know a lot about elves. You don't.'

'I know a man who believes in fairies.' He meant Arthur Conan Doyle.

'Has he ever seen them? I see them. But I have to be private. In the grotto. They come into the grotto. Do you know what fairies eat? They eat the honey from nasturtiums. Then they excrete it through their skins. They don't have anything down there like humans. They don't have to have WCs and they don't have to have privacy. They don't pee or have b.m.'s. They never get a bone on. They never have to get a sally or have somebody do them or do themselves. I'm tired of this and I want you to go away now.'

Denton looked at Tonk, who bobbed his head towards the corridor. Defeated, Denton bent to get his hat and coat. 'Could I have your drawing?'

'No!' It came out as a scream.

'I'd take good care of it. I know it's magic—'

'It isn't magic! I took the magic out, I told you! Tonk, make him go away!'

'I'm sorry, Walter, I didn't mean—'

'Make him go away! I don't like him! I don't like him!' The boy ran across the room, his hands over his ears now, crawled under the paisley drape and apparently curled up on the floor, the soles of his shoes showing with the curtain caught over them. Tonk bobbed his head again and opened the door with his back still to it, then slowly stepped forward and let it swing, his hand still on the knob as if he were trying to keep some small animal from escaping.

In the corridor, with the door locked again, Denton said, 'I'm sorry.' He meant it. He felt as if he had been in a battle, his knees weak. Awful as Walter Snokes was, he had touched Denton. And exercised power over him. 'I'm sorry he didn't like me.'

'You did pretty well.' Tonk opened the hatch and looked in. 'He'll stay in there with his thumb in his mouth for a couple of hours. As good a way to pass the time as any.' He closed the hatch. 'Pull his Johnson, like as not. He does that a lot. They all do. Put saltpetre in the food, you might as well use caster sugar.'

They walked back along the dark corridors. Denton thought he heard somebody shouting, but the sound seemed to come from deep under water. He said, 'Do they get exercise?'

'Twice a day, they carry their chambers down to the cess pit and back.'

'Is Walter ever trouble?'

'They're all trouble. Why do you think their families won't have them? If they give me too much trouble, back they go.'

'Are they all like him?'

Tonk looked aside at him. 'They're all kinds. We have four idiots—pinheads. They're the easiest. I'd fill the place with them if I could.'

'Still, it's not much of a life.'

'Go have a look at an insane asylum.'

They had reached the front door. Denton felt cheated: the experience should have given him more, he thought; as it was, he felt saddened, dirtied, guilty for his own curiosity. He said, 'Could you get me one of the papers he draws on?'

'Get you a dozen.' Tonk met his eyes without expression. 'He's made piles of them. He forgets them; we throw them out. I might have some in the dustbin.'

'Can you have a look?'

'Cost you.' Tonk turned and walked away. Denton assumed he was to follow, sure that Tonk would let him know if he wasn't. They went off towards the back of the dirty house, down a flight of narrow stairs, the house deeper on that side because of the slope. The cooking smell was stronger down here, cabbage or Brussels sprouts and maybe a root vegetable, old grease. Tonk turned right, leading him past what had perhaps been a pantry, then into a cold room with a stone floor. Dustbins almost filled the space. Tonk passed by the closest ones and lifted the lid of one near the centre, stared in, lifted something, dropped the lid and looked into the next one. After some rooting around, he pulled out a wad of paper.

'Been folded.'

'That's all right. So long as I can make out the drawings.' Denton took them to a small window that looked out on the back, weeds with dirt paths through them, a hundred yards away a terrace of grey houses. The papers were dirty but the drawings were clear. He was surprised that his heart beat faster. 'They'll do.'

'Sixpence apiece. Call it five shillings the lot.'

Tonk led Denton back the way they had come. 'Who does the cooking?' Denton asked.

'Woman comes in.'

'Otherwise it's just you?'

'There's Malkin.' Denton would have to figure out for himself who Malkin was.

At the door, he said, 'When Mrs Snokes visits, does she stay in his room, or is there a visitors' room, or...?'

'She takes him out. I don't know where. Gets him shaved sometimes.' Tonk was closing the door. When it was so nearly closed that only one of his eyes showed, he said, 'I'll fix it so Walter doesn't tell her you were here.'

Denton pitched the hat and coat into the passenger seat of the little car and struggled back into the duster and the cap. He hadn't bothered with goggles—foolishly, as it turned out, because the dust from the streets was as bad as from any unpaved country road. He let the car coast down the drive and braked at the gateposts so he could look back. The Oaks seemed to rise like some slender animal, peering over the hill; its twin gable ends pointed into the sky like ears. Walter Snokes had caught its look of menace quite well, he thought: his few seconds of looking at the papers from the dustbin had told him that several of them began with a tiny drawing of The Oaks. Because it was his new beginning? Because it was all he remembered? Because it was the end?

CHAPTER

11

'He isn't stupid. He's got books, and not all kids' books, either.'

'Having books doesn't mean people read them.'

'All I saw was the spines—one on anatomy, one with some title like *Secrets of the Egyptians and the Masonic Rite*, or some such. An old kids' book about locks. One down at the end of the shelf about fairies and ghosts.'

Janet was leaning back in his armchair, weary from her day. 'Fairies are for little children, aren't they?'

'He used words like "excrete", Janet. He gave me this daft explanation of why fairies don't need a WC, but in its own way, it made sense. I mean, it showed that he can reason things out. In his own fashion.'

'Well, that's the clanger, isn't it? I suppose one definition of madness would be that you see the world "in your own fashion" and without regard to what everybody else sees.'

'He isn't mad! He's…touching. At least I don't think he's what we usually mean by "mad". He's like a child, almost like an infant, but he isn't…Oh, hell, I don't know enough. I've been through some of my books; they don't talk about somebody like him. He isn't pathological or criminal, so Krafft-Ebing doesn't have him. He has a sexuality, by the way, but it's nothing that would catch a psychologist's attention—he knows about erections and getting himself off.'

'Doesn't every sixteen-year-old?'

Denton poured himself more whisky. 'You?' He held up a bottle of Italian vermouth, which she'd started drinking in Naples. She raised her glass; he poured in a little and she said, 'Enough, enough!' He walked back to his place in front of the grate. 'Every sixteen-year-old knows all about tossing himself off, yes, but he doesn't talk about it to a stranger as if he was talking about the rules of cricket. Walter turned a whine about me violating his privacy into a harangue on what "private" means, something he seemed to have memorised, and then went on and on as if he was reciting a manual about privacy as a place where you could get yourself off and nobody could see you. As if he'd been *taught* it.'

'This man Tonk, probably.'

'Maybe.' Denton sounded grumpy to himself. 'It's as if his idea of how you behave with other people is just all out of kilter. He said right off the reel, "I don't like him." Meaning me.'

'Only a mad person could say such a thing about you, Denton.'

'I don't mean it that way. English boys just don't say that about their elders to their faces. It's as if—'

'He doesn't know the rules?'

'He knows the rules about privacy well enough. No, it isn't that, it's…Something about other people. About not giving them their due. About…Oh, hell, I don't know!' He thought of Ivor Hench-Rose and Rosamund Gearing, their self-centredness. 'It's egoism carried to some limit. But it's different somehow.' He shook his head. 'It's a puzzlement.'

She sipped the horrible drink. 'Nobody exists but him?'

Denton thought about it. 'There's some of that. But that's

the infant in him, isn't it? And him thinking I was "Mummy", and he was so pleased, so happy, and then crushed when it wasn't Mummy. That's infantile, too. I don't know.'

'Well, the real question is—don't deny it—can he do you any good with your book?'

He drank most of what was left of his whisky and didn't want to answer her because it seemed to invite bad luck, so he said that if they were going to get supper somewhere they should go. She groaned.

'I could make some pasta,' he said.

'Oh, *would* you? I don't want to move.'

'Atkins is out with Mrs Johnson. He says they're working on "instructional materials". I hope they're doing something more interesting than that. Anyway, the kitchen's free. Come down with me while I demonstrate my cooking prowess, courtesy of Mr DiNapoli.' DiNapoli had taught Denton some rudimentary Italian cooking, too.

'I can't move.'

Denton knew how to cook one dish, spaghetti with olive oil and garlic and anchovies, for which he'd stocked the pantry. The olive oil and the anchovies were easy—the Army & Navy stores—but the spaghetti and the garlic had had to be got from the Italian grocery in Clerkenwell. They had yet to try the tiny restaurant in the back.

After ten minutes he came up and said, 'I've found some bacon. You want that in it?'

She was asleep.

Inertia, always a problem with him when he wasn't working, settled over him on Sunday like a too-warm blanket. Janet had church and then university work. He read the *Times*, walked miles, wandered through his house, stared out of windows. Atkins was off. Rupert was a distraction when he had to go into the garden to pee, the same when he had to be chivvied back indoors before he could get too interested in whatever odours Sophie had left in Janet's garden. The day dragged into evening, then night, the only change a glimpse of two policemen on the opposite pavement, one reading something from his notebook to the other, and then too late Denton's realisation that the one with the notebook was Maltby. He went down, but by the time he reached his gate, they had gone. So much for Sunday.

On Monday, he went to see Walter Snokes's piano teacher. Mrs Strang had found his name at the Trinity College of Music and the hours when he was likely to be there. 'You'll have to catch him between pupils, or whatever they're called, I suppose. But he can't be showing people how to play the piano from sunup to sundown, can he?'

Trinity College was in several houses on Mandeville Place, only a couple of streets from Portman Square. Not, he thought, the usual haunt of the Snokes family. Little Walter must have impressed somebody to have been allowed to study there.

'Yes, impressed very much.' Anton Reishak looked to be in his sixties. He had the remnant of a German accent—slightly uvular R's, an in-and-out sibilant S—and an un-British look: long, rather bushy silver hair, a flat and pudgy nose, small but very bright eyes of a pale yellow-brown. 'We do not take children in the usual manner here. This is a serious place.' The eyes flashed; Denton was meant to take 'serious' with a little mockery. For himself, he thought it was very serious, indeed; around them, practice rooms tinkled and pounded with what seemed to be expertly played pianos.

'His mother says he was a prodigy.'

Reishak chuckled. 'Every mother says her child is a prodigy.'

'He wasn't?'

'What is a prodigy? Mozart was a prodigy. Why? Partly because he was Mozart and partly because he had Leopold for a father. Mozart was playing in public at seven.' He smiled. 'Walter did not have a Leopold. However …'

'He had promise?'

'I would say more than promise. His mother brought him

here. I was sceptical. The little boy played. He was rough, he had many bad habits, but—he had music! How to explain? Many children can be brought to play with technique when they are ten or so. One listens, one says "Very skilled, very nice." *But no music.* It is all technique. If we could teach monkeys to read music, they would be technically skilled only. Walter was not a monkey.'

'What bad habits? He can't have taught himself.'

'No, some local lady. They are all the same. Tuppence a lesson, no theory, enough technique to keep Mama and Papa supplying tuppences. His fingering was poor; he had silly flourishes she had taught him to make a show at her recitals. And so on. But we got rid of those quickly. Very quickly. Walter was a very, very good student. A remarkable student for such a little boy. He *practised*.'

'He's supposed to have conducted an orchestra.'

Reishak made a face and shrugged. 'The mother, the mother.'

'Could he have conducted an orchestra?'

'I am not a conductor. I suppose a monkey could conduct an orchestra if the players knew enough to ignore him. Walter would have done what Mama told him. He would do whatever Mama said. If he had…gone on doing what she told him, he would have concertised, I am afraid. She wanted to push him. She talked of it. He was eight, not ready.'

'She said he was playing Beethoven.'

Reishak looked pained. 'There is Beethoven and there is Beethoven. There is what we call "easy" Beethoven, Beethoven *leichte*. The Opus 49, the "Für Elise", the "Easy Variations". They are Beethoven, *but they are not the Beethoven of the concert hall*! He might have been ready by fifteen. Better, twenty. She pushed. I would have told her that if she forced him into some kind of freak show, I would not keep him as a student.' He pulled out a fat pocket watch. 'I have a student in two minutes.'

'I'll be quick. What happened to Walter Snokes?'

'But you know. He was injured somehow; I never understood how. She brought him after several weeks he had been away, and when he tried to play...It was heart-breaking. He could not remember. And when he made a mistake, it was terrible! I thought he might have a fit. He screamed. He hit his head against the piano. I had to tell her to take him away. I said, "Bring him back when he is well."' He shrugged, spread his hands. 'He never came back.' He put a hand on Denton's arm and steered them both towards the door. 'You have seen him?'

Denton nodded.

'How is he?'

Denton couldn't put it into words. 'He's grown. He's not... normal.'

Reishak nodded, went on nodding. 'And no music?'

'No.'

Reishak went on nodding. He said, 'It left him. I thought when he tried to play and could not, "He has lost his soul." Poor little boy.'

'He's still a poor little boy. In a grown-up body.'

He went on his way, passing a young man with music under his arm and an impatient glare in his eyes.

Sitting at his desk with Walter Snokes's 'drawings' spread out in front of him, he was trying to think himself into the mind that had created them. This was a state rather like the moments before sleep, half-conscious, what Janet called her 'fugue state' when she improvised at one of her pianos. If asked what he was doing, he would have said he was looking at the drawings, but in fact his mind was wandering over the conundrum of Walter Snokes. Why was he as he was? What identity did he have? Was it reachable, or was it simply alien, not insane but *different*?

He took a magnifying glass and studied one of the drawings for the dozenth time. He was familiar now with the leaves and vines and the tiny human-like figures he had thought were bugs. They crawled or climbed along the vines, even along the lines of the music staff. Their clothes were those of some perhaps never-existed past, perhaps pasts—Denton was not strong on period clothing but saw what he thought was 'medieval' on some figures and other periods on some—a very long coat on one of the men, little hats like trilbies with long feathers, here and there a cape. The women wore long skirts and laced bodices and looked hippy and bosomy, one of them grotesque, breasts like funnels.

For the first time, he understood that the figures were *going* somewhere. Every staff was a journey, then, beginning always at The Oaks or one other building, a house, going through a world of Walter's imagining to—what? He found three other buildings, probably houses, that recurred on some of the pages. Each was quite individual, quite identifiable. One was a semi-detached, one probably part of a terrace, the third an oddly triangular structure with conical towers that seemed to Denton to have come from a book of fairy tales. The terraced house had a peculiar porch in front of the door, rather ecclesiastical, with what seemed to be a weather-vane on top, although its little peaked roof reached only halfway up the second storey. But if the figures got to these buildings, nothing seemed to happen there; the journey went on. Twice, the building itself seemed to move from one staff to another, making no sense to Denton.

He scribbled on a piece of paper: *See Mr Snokes—make appointment. Ask about the houses. Can he get me the music on the piano in their house? Is it different?*

And every time Walter started in on a new sheet of paper, he did the same things all over again. With variations, to be sure; this was work by hand, after all. But was he in fact writing a kind of music, or was he living and re-living and re-living an obsessive fantasy?

Denton dozed.

He dreamed.

It was the old dream but it was transmuted into something new. The window of the little house in Iowa; his wife; the lye jug. In the old dream, lived through again and again, less often since he'd started with Janet, he looked through the window and saw her walking towards the meadow where she would drink the lye, and he knew she would do it and would die after days of screaming; and he stood by the window and watched and waited for those screams. But this time, Walter Snokes was with her and they were both smiling and were walking hand in hand, as if she had Walter instead of the lye jug. Out to the meadow where she would die, but both of them smiling and happy and paying no attention when he rapped on the window and shouted. And he knew that Walter Snokes was also himself despite the velvet suit. Himself as a child. Happy and smiling and walking away with—was the woman his mother? he wondered as he woke. He had never known his mother. The dream began to withdraw but left a sense of joy.

The man who's haunted by the ghost of his childhood. It had been a bad idea for a ghost story but it would work wonders in *The Secret Jew*. He sat sprawled at his desk. It came whole, the way such happy discoveries sometimes did, the fruit of something grown in sleep. In the dark.

He has an accident and becomes like Walter and he's obsessed. Reishak's voice: *He has lost his soul.*

And as if a microscope slide had been moved under the focus of his attention, he thought—no, not thought, intuited, understood—Walter could be my central character in *The Secret Jew*.

It came like that. A flash, it was often said, like one of the lights on the new advertising signs that the English called 'flash-lights', out of nowhere, but this had not been a flash, rather a calm acceptance, a comprehension.

Accepting him as he is.

The very thing that Walter's parents couldn't do.

A Walter who grew old in pursuit of a religious obsession as strange and as fixed as Walter's pursuit of these houses through the thickets of his leaves and vines.

Not a religious fanatic, but an alien being with a different psychology.

Could you write such a thing and hope that readers would understand it?

He began to write.

'I've got it, Lang! I've got it! No need to worry. I've cracked it and it's going like a house afire!'

'This is a *real* break-through, Denton? Not mere hysteria? Pardon my saying that; it was a dreadful thing to say. What I meant is, I hope you aren't letting the euphoria of the moment—'

'I've written forty pages in two days. It *works*.'

'Oh, my dear, how wonderful! Gwen will be delighted, too.' Gwen was the publisher.

'It's all because of a boy I met. He lives in a—not a different world, not entirely; it's as if he's taken a step to one side of the rest of us, sees things from a different angle, doesn't...You have your frightened look on, Lang.'

'Are you saying he's mad? Is your new character going to be mad?'

'No, he's sane. But he's—*different*.' Denton leaned forward over Lang's desk, his face eager, his voice filled with his new idea. 'Imagine somebody who came here from the planet Mars. He looks like us and he talks like us, but he's different. He thinks differently. He reacts differently, because he doesn't understand us. He's fascinated by us, but he's afraid of us and he's irritated by us. It's his own psychology to follow an idea to its end; he's relentless; he's obsessed. But to us, he'd seem—'

'Mad. Mad as a hatter.'

'You haven't understood.'

'Is he a monster?'

Denton liked Lang. They were entirely different from each other, but Lang had been good to him and they understood one another. Sometimes, however, Lang seemed wilfully obtuse. Denton's voice got low and quiet and slow. 'Lang, what have I been saying?'

'Does he have *feelings*?'

'I've told you, he's obsessed. With religions. Pursues them, no matter the cost.'

'But he has feelings?'

Denton thought of Walter Snokes. 'Only for himself. I don't think he understands our feelings or the ways we express them.'

'Aha, then he *is* a monster. Oh, good! You're at your very best with demons and monsters and so on. I may tell Gwen, then, that your idea is in the very best sense *horrible*.' He laughed, then abruptly became sombre. 'I hope there's no undignified, that is to say, *vulgar* action. You originally had him murdering his wife and children, which I thought beyond the bounds of good taste. You cited Medea, but what an example!'

'I don't think they're his wife and children any more. I don't think he's capable of having a wife. Although children, yes—the sex drive is very strong.'

'Oh, no, no, no! You mustn't! We can't publish a book that offends.'

'Do you mean the sex or the murders? I'm not sure I'll do anything with the sex, anyway. But the murders, yes. But they're in the way somehow. I haven't figured it out yet. But I need them so he's always on the run, so there's a terrific sense of movement—driven from behind by the murders, drawn from the front by religion. I wonder now if he doesn't start his own religion—a sort of Joseph Smith. Starting this tremendous movement, a cause of enormous violence, uproar, and then he moves on because it doesn't satisfy him—it isn't the religion he's seeking. Mmm?'

Lang stared at him, cheek on hand. He shook his head. 'Sometimes I think authors are all mad. Where do these things *come* from?'

Denton got up. 'It'll be fine. You'll see. I'll have it done in three months.' He got his hat and overcoat from the floor. "It came from a boy I met, I told you. He's part of a murder case.'

Lang groaned.

He had arranged to meet Snokes at the Rose and Lyon on Tuesday night. It had taken two notes back and forth, Denton's sent to Snokes at the Steam Railway offices because he didn't want Mrs Snokes interfering. He needn't have bothered; Snokes himself was unwilling to meet. Denton had had to remind him that the police might still take him back to magistrates' court and that Denton might be a help to him if he got the information that he needed.

When they were sitting together in the pub, Denton said, 'I went to see Walter.'

Snokes looked unhappy but said that was good; he'd given Denton the note, after all. 'How was he?'

'How long since you've seen him?'

'Oh, it must be...' Snokes ran a hand through his already messy hair. 'Since he went to that place. Four years, it must be.' He looked at Denton with real anguish. Not that Snokes was incapable of faking anguish; he was somewhat an actor, Denton thought, perhaps the reason he got loose from his women with so little pain. And got them in the first place. Snokes said, 'He's changed, I'm sure.'

'He needed to shave—had a couple of days' growth. He's not as tall as I am, but he's above the average.'

'I know what it's like in that place,' Snokes said. 'I know I sent him into Hell. But he couldn't stay at home. I had to put my foot down.'

'Why?'

Snokes shook his head. Not a drinker, apparently, he was using his glass of beer as something to keep his hands busy, running a finger around the rim, making circles on the tabletop with it, rocking it back and forth and watching the line of froth just touch the rim.

'What happened?'

'Not your business, sorry.'

'It's my business if the cops pick you up again.'

Snokes ran his finger around his glass several times and at last said, 'He offered an outrage to my daughter.'

'How?'

'*How?* What did I just say?'

'He touched her? He used violence against her? Look, Snokes—I've talked to your daughter. Yes, I was able to find her; she actually seemed glad for somebody to talk to. She gave me a pretty good picture of what her life was like when Walter got older, but all she said was that he'd "come on" to her or something of the sort. What happened?'

'Damned if I'll tell you. Lay off it. It isn't connected.'

Denton, still wearing his overcoat and hat, folded his arms and studied Snokes. It was cold in the pub. Snokes seemed to know he was being looked at but didn't look up at first, then at last raised his eyes, and Denton said, 'Tell me.'

'He didn't succeed, but he tried, all right? She said he pulled her skirts up and showed her his thing. He didn't know what to do, but—oh, cripes, you always know, don't you? Cripes, he was twelve years old, he probably had a horn like a grown man! She was frightened out of her wits. Screaming. I was downstairs, I go running up—it was right then I decided he had to go. You can't have that in the same house with a young girl. You can't!'

'Do you think that he was capable of a rape?'

Snokes looked off into the fug. He sighed. 'Walter wants what he wants when he wants it. He can't bear to hear "no". But you know, with Eunice, he was frightened when she screamed. I mean, frightened for *her*. As if it wasn't him that had her screaming. Maybe he thought somehow that he was offering her something nice. It sounds crazy to say it, but he wasn't a bad boy. He had his tantrums, and he could fight like a demon if you crossed him, but he had a soft spot for females. As if he was protective. But he wasn't, was he?'

'I don't know. I wasn't there.'

Snokes got to his feet. He started to go, but Denton caught his sleeve. 'I want to look at those music sheets on your piano. The ones with the drawings on them.'

'Why?'

'Never mind why.'

'Anna'd kill me. They're part of the shrine. Oh, yes, she's made a shrine to Walter-the-prodigy, didn't you notice?'

The Backward Boy

'I've brought you some other sheets to put in their place. Get them for me, please.'

Snokes shuddered as if he were already out in the cold. Shaking his head, he shambled to the pub door and went out.

CHAPTER

12

Denton was up at five and at his desk at five-thirty. He wrote as if he were being driven with a whip; the words gushed out, covered the paper, demanded more. He knew the risk of writing too much too fast but went on.

Two hours later, Atkins knocked on his door with tea. When he handed over the little tray, he said, 'There's been another woman murdered. Thought you'd like to know.'

'Where?'

'Finsbury. The Artillery Ground.'

Denton had crossed it only days before, coming from—what was his name?—that money-grubbing private detective's. *Pinkert.* He shrugged, took the tray and then stood there with it, trying to get his mind out of the novel and into what Atkins was telling him. 'This sort of thing happens in London.'

'Woman, "outrage" perpetrated on her, not all that far from Denmark Road.'

'Knifed?'

'Bludgeoned.'

'Well, there you are. If it was some lunatic who was going to kill and rape women, the likelihood is he'd do it the same way. No connection. Anyway, Arthur Snokes isn't stupid enough to murder two women in a fortnight. But save me the paper.'

He put the tray down, poured himself tea from the brown pot, sipped. Still standing, he read over the last of what he had written. It was all right. Maybe it was even good. But he saw that there was something he should do: show how his twisted protagonist had got the way he was. A little of his childhood. An accident. And then...? Could he make that believable? Did he know enough about Walter Snokes to do it?

He sat and wrote for another hour. The childhood scene remained at the back of his consciousness; he would leave it there for a while, confident that it would 'work', as his grandmother had used to say about food that spoiled or fermented. *This cider has worked.* It would have a smell of alcohol, a tang, effervescence; it would have become something new while it sat in the jug in the dark. He'd do that with the childhood scenes.

He shucked himself out of his wool robe and pulled on a tattered smoking jacket that he had in fact never worn to smoke; he put it on as a kind of badge of comfort after work. He went downstairs, negotiated with Atkins about breakfast, sat and went through the first mail and then read the newspaper. Atkins had left it folded open to the article about the new murder. The cheap papers would have more in the afternoon, he thought; if the body had been found overnight, there would hardly have been time to get it in the early editions.

WOMAN'S BODY DISCOVERED IN FINSBURY

Another Outrage
Has the Barnsbury Butcher Struck Again?
A police constable on his regular round discovered a woman's body behind a cricket pavilion in

the Artillery Ground, Finsbury, late last night. An outrage had been perpetrated on the victim, and she had been bludgeoned to death.

'We have good information as to the murderer's identity,' said Detective Sergeant G. Guillam of the King's Cross Road station. 'We expect an arrest very shortly.' He would not elaborate. The victim was identified only as 'a resident of Cherrytree Street', which is only a short distance away.

More details are expected before the day is out.

Cherrytree Street. It was like a riddle—'What London street starts with C and ends in E and has many letters?' He had seen a street-name of crossed-out letters in Pinkert's notes—a C legible at the beginning, an E at the end. He remembered that he had wanted to ask Mrs Strang to look in the directories for streets with those letters. And maybe an L or an H after the C.

Well, Cherrytree begins with C, H and ends with E. But he remembered it as seeming longer—maybe Pinkert's handwriting?

And the detective who had the case was George Guillam! Denton groaned.

'What's that about?' Atkins was coming up behind him with the breakfast tray.

'The detective who's quoted in the newspaper about this murder. George Guillam.' He had a history with Guillam, and Atkins knew it.

'Oh, crikey. Well, happy days you don't have to deal with him, hey?'

'I'm afraid maybe I do.'

Atkins was setting out the folding table. He stopped with it half-opened and gave Denton a suspicious look.

'I think maybe there's a connection,' Denton said.

'You said there isn't.'

He explained about Cherrytree Street as Atkins put out a plate with a thick slice of back bacon and two scrambled eggs, another with a high stack of buttered toast and a mound of

Seville marmalade. 'You fancy cinnamon and sugar? I brought it along.' Atkins put the castor next to Denton on the bookshelf.

'Coffee?'

'Of course there's coffee! You don't think I'm a bleeding juggler can carry everything at once, do you?'

'Don't you get sick of waiting on me?'

'Often.'

'I'll start making my own breakfast.'

'Not in my kitchen, you won't!'

'Maybe you should just get out of it—give it up.'

'And starve, oh thank you very much. It isn't *you*, General. It's…the condition of servitude.' He went off to the stairs, clattered down; when he came up, Rupert was panting behind him. 'Rupert's suffering.'

'He doesn't look it.'

'Denial of conjugal rights. He keeps getting his Johnson out and looking at it.'

'It can't go on much longer. You bring two cups?'

Atkins put a cup in front of Denton and showed another for himself. 'I thought we might be about to have one of our late-night talks. In the morning, notice.'

Denton poured coffee into both cups. 'If it turns out that that private detective actually followed Snokes to this new dead woman's house, Snokes is bitched.'

'I don't see why. Well, it does look bad, I suppose. But it could be coincidence.'

'That doesn't play too well in the dock.'

'You mean to say you think he had two women on the string at the same time? And he's murdered both of them?'

'I think that's what the coppers will want to think. It's especially what George Guillam would think.'

'Don't tell them.'

'I think I have to.'

'What are you going to say—"I bribed a private tec for information and got this titbit about Cherrytree Street"? That'll go down well, I'm sure.'

'I can't withhold information.'

'Maybe the tec will tell them.'

'He might. If he even remembers. He'd crossed the street name out in his notes. If he does a lot of cases of that kind, "Cherrytree" probably makes about as much impression on him as a stone in a pig wallow.'

'Best you stay out of it.'

Denton had eaten his way through the bacon and eggs. He sprinkled cinnamon and sugar on the toast, watching the glistening of the butter turn into a pale brown crust as the odour of the cinnamon swam up to his nose. 'If it was anybody but Guillam. If it was Munro, it would be all right.'

On the other hand—and he didn't say this to Atkins— Denton knew something about Guillam that might put a damper on Guillam's usual zeal: Denton had once walked in on Guillam's having sex with another man. He hated the idea that that knowledge, on which he hadn't acted and never would, might serve as unspoken blackmail. *Still*...He said, 'I'll give Guillam a shout.'

'You can never let well enough alone. How's that novel coming?'

'Like a steamroller.'

'That's all right, then. Stay with it.'

'How're the marital plans?'

'Oh—well.' Atkins looked at Rupert, who was finishing a piece of toast. 'Sale pending, as they say in trade.'

He went off when he had finished his coffee. Denton sat and read the rest of the newspaper and, when at last there was nothing to keep him from doing it, got up and went to the telephone. He hated the telephone, but more and more people whom he knew had one; more and more, it was becoming part of London life. He looked up the King's Cross Road police station's number in the directory pamphlet, now grown to eight pages. He got through to Central and then to the station sergeant's desk without needing Atkins's help, and then he waited, listening to distant voices, bits of conversations—incomprehensible, not unlike Pinkert's notes—and the crackle of the lines. After two good minutes, a harsh voice said, 'Guillam.'

'Denton.'

The silence that followed went on so long that Denton thought the line had gone bad. He was going to say his name again when Guillam said, 'What do you want?'

'I may have information about the killing in Finsbury.'

Again, the silence was long. When Guillam spoke, his voice sounded different, perhaps relieved: had he thought that Denton was going to say something about his secret life? 'I have to go up there now. You can meet me there. The cricket pavilion on the Artillery Grounds—green, wood—can't miss it.'

'I'll take the motorcar. You want to meet me at the garage? You remember where the garage is?' One of his encounters with Guillam had had them trying to trail an anarchist in his little motor. 'You're closer to the garage than you are to Finsbury.'

'All right.' He sounded as if it wasn't all right.

Denton threw on the clothes that Atkins had laid out, grateful that they were old and informal and meant for a day at home. Downstairs again, he grabbed a cap and a duster and shouted at Atkins that he was going out.

'I thought you were working!'

'I am.'

Atkins met him at the front door with a different hat and a kashmir overcoat. 'You're a sight.'

'But I'm comfortable.'

'You'll freeze your properties in that duster.'

'Better than getting that coat filthy. Oh, all right, I'll take it. I'll get lunch out. What day is it?'

'My afternoon off.'

'All right. Before you go, hop over and ask Cohan if he'll box with me this afternoon. Here. About three. Say hello to Mrs Johnson for me.'

He didn't stay to hear how Atkins took that. Should he be that familiar with his servant? Probably not. He'd never understand the English.

Guillam was already at the shed where he kept the little car. Guillam was big, even for a policeman, seeming fat but actually heavy with muscle. His face was pocked from some long-ago problem, lined not with worry but cynicism. He had black eyebrows and a black hairbrush moustache. In his forties, he seemed to Denton ageless and indomitable and difficult because he had disliked Denton at first sight. Denton's discovering what Guillam had later called his 'sickness' hadn't made things better.

Guillam was standing by the unpainted boards of the sagging shed doors, hands shoved into his overcoat pockets, a black bowler pushed a little back on his head. He had been looking at the ground but looked up as Denton approached. Denton expected some sarcasm about the time he had taken getting there. Instead, Guillam said, 'Well, you haven't told, have you.' It was a statement, not a question.

Denton was surprised that he had decided to be so forthright. He had wondered, would they ever mention it, or was it now the unspeakable? He said, still a dozen feet away, 'I told you I wouldn't.'

'I didn't believe you.'

'How's it going?'

Guillam looked away from him. He had a hard look, useful to a policeman. 'It's always there.'

'Risky.'

Guillam moved his shoulders as if he were cold. 'I almost bought it last summer. Somebody I was eyeing turned out to be another cop. But he arrested another poor sod, and I showed my warrant card and helped him.' Guillam's self-disgust filled his voice. 'The righteous man of law.'

'I told you before, you're too hard on yourself.'

'Right I am. Let's go.'

Denton didn't want to shout his information over the noise of the car as they drove to Finsbury, so he waited until he had pulled up at a place where he could park by St Paul's churchyard, just north of the Artillery Ground, and he turned off the motor and explained about the private detective's following Snokes.

'Bloody fool shouldn't tell you things like that. He'll lose his licence!'

'He didn't tell me. I looked at his notes.'

'Did money change hands?'

'Look, Guillam—'

'Did you give him money?'

Denton turned sideways in the little seat and looked right into Guillam's eyes. 'Munro taught me long ago that one of the hardest things for a young cop to learn is when to let things go. All right?'

'Don't throw Donnie Munro in my face. His shit smells just like mine. And yours.'

'You can't arrest everybody in the world, Guillam.'

Guillam gave him the look back, holding it long enough to show he wasn't impressed. He turned and put his hand on the door-handle. 'We'll see.'

Walking to the cricket pavilion, he asked about the detective who had followed Snokes. When had it been? How long ago? What did he see? What did Mrs Snokes do? Was he sure the notes had said Cherrytree? Denton gave the same answer to each question: he didn't know.

'You don't know! Cripes, if you paid the tec more than tuppence, you were strung for fair. And from tuppence you should have had change.'

A constable was standing behind the pavilion where a patch of ground had been roped off with sisal cord strung through iron eye-bolts and their shafts pushed into the dirt. Guillam went to the rope and stood staring down at the thin, trampled grass inside the barrier and close to the pavilion.

'That's where he found her.' He exhaled noisily. 'I was here from midnight until five this morning. The gents of the press weren't half a pain in the arse. Not to mention my betters in the force.' He wiped a hand over his mouth, blew out more air, and pointed into the roped-off area. 'Her clothes were up over her face; her knickers were down. Duff in her, or that's what the surgeon thinks; they're going to test it. He'd about pounded her head in with some kind of club. I've made a fuss with the surgeon about that—I want to know what he used. Either something heavy or he was a strong bastard. Or in a frenzy.' Guillam continued to look at the space by the pavilion. 'You want to work on this?'

Denton was astonished. 'You're *asking* me?'

'Masefield from N Div telephoned me after you visited him. He wanted to know how big a pain in the arse you were. So I knew you were sniffing around. Now you bring this Cherrytree connection to me on a plate.' He shifted his weight and moved his legs as if they might be cold. 'If I tell Masefield there seems to be a connection with Snokes, he'll grab this case.'

'You want it yourself.'

Guillam shrugged.

'What did you tell Masefield about me?'

'I said you were a handful but you were good at putting two and two together. You want to work with me on this, and the Cherrytree things pays out, you can, but it's understood that it's my case and I can freeze you out whenever I want. If Masefield takes it away, that's that. I'll give you a pass on bribing the private tec.'

'Kind of a change, isn't it?'

Guillam's shoulders moved up and then down with a huge breath. He said, 'I don't trust anybody in this world, Denton, but I come close with two people—my wife and Donnie Munro. And now you. And you know why. But you're on probation.' He began to point around the roped-off space at where the first constable and his sergeant thought they had found some footprints, at where one of the woman's shoes had lain. 'They took casts of what they thought were the right boot marks, but by then there'd been half a dozen people milling around here in the dark, so God knows. The constable's only two months out of probation, so he didn't do everything he should have. You teach them the catechism, but they can't keep it all in their heads.'

Denton knew Bride's *'Police Duty' Catechism and Reports*, one of the little books that all probationers and most seasoned constables carried. He had one on his own shelf, in fact. 'What about the shoe? Definitely hers?'

'It matched the one on her foot, didn't it?'

'Was she dragged?'

'No sign of it we could make out in the grass, but God knows after the trampling that went on. Maybe she tried to run and it came off. Or maybe he hit her so hard it knocked the shoe off, then she staggered over to the pavilion.' He nodded towards the painted wooden wall. 'There's some blood smears there—her hands as she slid down. Maybe from her face, too. Her nose bled like a stuck pig. He'd hit her both front and back, more than once.'

'And then raped her?'

'We don't know that yet. Probably won't, will we? Does that kind of maniac care whether the woman's alive or dying or dead?'

'She was lying on her back?'

'She was.'

'You saw her that way?'

Guillam nodded.

'How were her legs?'

'Not what you might think. One curled up a bit and laid over the other, that one pretty straight. Not as if he'd just pulled out of her and left her and she stayed like that. Maybe she did some thrashing about, that's the way she ended.'

'Bruising?'

Guillam shrugged.

'Any impressions from his knees or his feet? The ground's soft from the rain we've had.'

Guillam pushed out his lips, frowning, then stepped over the rope and walked the few steps to the pavilion. Denton, expecting to be sent back, followed. Guillam was looking at the ground. 'Cops have big feet.' He pointed at a line of small wooden slats that had been pushed into the ground to show where the body had lain. 'Chief Inspector insists those sticks aren't enough.' He pulled a roll of white tape, the sort that seamstresses used for hemming, from a pocket and began to pull off a length. 'This's more or less where she lay. Her feet down here ...' He tied the white tape to one of the slats, which Denton saw now were the sort that Atkins used to mark his rows in the vegetable garden. 'The tape should have been put down last night. That's why I came back.' He squatted as he wrapped tape around another slat. 'If there were impressions from his knees, they'd have been covered by her legs. His feet about here—where a million coppers' boots have been.' He squatted again. 'Nothing.' He stood. The place where the dead woman had lain was rather neatly marked off now in white; there was no suggestion of a human form, perhaps more of a coffin.

Denton went close to the wall of the pavilion. He found himself not stepping over the white tape into the place where the dead woman had lain. The green paint was chalky with age, bubbled, chipped; dark patches of dried blood lay on it like fungus. He supposed he could make out what Guillam had meant about marks from her hands, although these were only smudges. Bare wood showed in places where blood samples had been scraped away.

'Handbag?' Denton said.

'Purse in a coat pocket, nothing more. Nothing in it but a bit of money and some calling cards. That's how we identified her, by the way. Name of Mary Adger. Married name, anyway.'

'Peculiar that she had only a coin purse.'

'Maybe. Women don't pick up a big bag every time they run out to a shop.'

'Is that what she was doing?'

'How the hell would I know? Cherrytree Street is over there.' He nodded eastwards. 'But the shops are over there, too. Was she going to walk across the Artillery Ground at night to get to some other shop over the other way? Or maybe visit a friend? PCs are doing a canvass now to find out who saw her. Maybe she talked to somebody.' His face was dark, almost sneering. 'I doubt we'll be that lucky.'

'Husband?'

'Widow. Has a son who's a motorman on an electric tram, nights. He was at work; we've already done that. She was found before he ever left his car. Otherwise, he'd have been the first one I pulled in.'

'How did he take it?'

'Chief Inspector went and told him. Said he looked like a cow who's been hit with the sledge but doesn't go down. Not apparently like a man who'd hired somebody to beat his mother to death, if that's what you're thinking.' Guillam, clearly fighting exhaustion, shook himself and said, 'I want to see this tec of yours.'

'Now?'

'Now's the time. The sooner I know that's where your tec followed Snokes, the sooner I can pull him in and ask where he was last night.'

Denton felt sheepish. 'I can tell you where Snokes was until after nine.' He grinned. 'He was with me. In a pub.'

Guillam's face filled with blood. 'I'll want a statement. Judas Priest, what else have you been holding back?'

Denton didn't rise to the taunt. 'Hadn't we better move along? I have something at three.'

For answer, Guillam walked away.

Denton steered them into Worship Street and along to number 125. The same youth was in the anteroom, apparently reading the same pink trash. He looked up, and, if he recognised Denton, gave no sign.

Guillam said to Denton, 'What's the name again?'

'Pinkert.'

Guillam put a hand over the boy's reading and loomed above him. 'Tell Mr Pinkert that Detective Sergeant Guillam of the CID wants to see him.' The boy looked at him with his mouth open. 'Not tomorrow, son—today. Move.'

'He's with somebody.'

'You march yourself in there and tell him in a nice low tone what I said, and be quick about it.'

The boy put his face a little into the inner office, then moved part of his body in, and finally went far enough that only a foot was left showing. Voices murmured. The boy backed out and said, 'He says five minutes.'

The Backward Boy

Guillam took out a silver hunter and popped the lid and made a show of reading the time. He closed it with a snap and eyed the boy. 'Why don't you fetch us each a cuppa?'

'Not supposed to leave the office.'

'We'll watch your penny paper for you.' He put a coin on the desk. 'There's a coffee stall in City Road. Hop it.'

'I know where it is,' the boy said in the voice of an aggrieved and overworked adolescent. He was quick, however: he was back before the five minutes were up, although the five in fact stretched to eight before a harried-looking woman in peacock blue sailed out of the inner office and down the stairs. Denton felt slightly foolish, carrying the white mug of milky coffee into Pinkert's office, but the warmth and the sweetness of it were welcome.

Guillam presented his warrant card to Pinkert and then drew two of the chairs over so he and Denton could sit where they didn't have to crane over the desk. Pinkert barely glanced at the card; contempt for the power of the police was implied.

'You did an investigation for a Mrs Snokes,' Guillam said. Pinkert looked at him and said nothing. Guillam hesitated a fraction of a second and said, 'Tell me about it.' His eyes had narrowed.

'Privileged information. You know that.'

'Look, Pinkert, this is a murder investigation. I've been up with it all night. I don't want any shit from you. Is that clear enough? Now answer my question.'

'Get a warrant.'

'If I have to go to the magistrate for a warrant, I'll be in bad temper and you'll go to nick for letting this gentleman see your notes. It'll be your licence, too. Now, I can get a warrant. Can you get on in life without a licence?'

Pinkert gave Denton a look of hatred and pushed past them, began opening wainscot-high cupboards on the other side of the room. He pulled out brown accordion files in stacks, cursed when one of the stacks slipped. At last he came back with a file. It didn't look the same size as the one Denton had seen before, and he realised he'd been sold: Pinkert hadn't even had the real Snokes file out for him.

Pinkert threw notebook pages on the desk. 'That's what this *gentleman* saw. I made bloody sure there was nothing there to see, so don't go saying I violated my licence!'

'That's good, then I won't have to run the gentleman in for subornation. Now show me something with meat to it, please. These notes are worthless.'

Pinkert pulled larger papers from the file. Denton got a flash of copperplate handwriting, probably a copy of the report the detective had given to Mrs Snokes. Pinkert put his nose into it and said, 'I followed her husband twice to a house in Cherrytree Street. He stayed for hours. I told the wife. She didn't do anything. Usually, they cry or they go red in the face or they tell you what swine men are. She did none of it. Block of wood, that woman.'

'You read the morning paper?'

'Haven't had time.'

'Woman was murdered in the Artillery Ground.'

'Heard that.'

'Her address was 39, Cherrytree Street.'

Pinkert glanced at the papers in his hand, then at Denton, then at Guillam. Guillam waited, then burst out, 'Is it the same address or isn't it?'

'It is. Followed him there twice.'

'How recently?'

Pinkert was suddenly nervous. He scrabbled through the papers. 'Ninety-nine. Nearly five years ago.'

It wasn't the answer that Denton had expected, nor apparently the one that Guillam had wanted. Guillam said, 'Five bleeding years! You're sure of that?'

Pinkert pushed the papers at him. 'It's there in my report. I'll show you my office log, if you want. It'll have her visits, payments. I tell you, that's when it was!'

Guillam rubbed his forehead. 'All right, you come to the station before six and I'll have somebody take a statement. Get your paperwork together, including those logs and any invoices, financial stuff; we may want it in court. You been a copper?'

'What if I have?'

'You know how it's done, then.' Guillam got up. Seconds later, they were in the outer office, the coffee mugs deposited on the boy's desk. The boy said, 'Here! You're going right by the stall, ain't you?'

Guillam walked out. Denton gave the boy a helpless shrug and followed.

On the street, Denton said, 'It doesn't make any sense.'

'Not yet, it doesn't.'

Even exhausted, Guillam was as fast a walker as Denton. Denton glanced up at the corner and saw the street name on a building. *Worship Street.* He had seen the name several times before, but now his conscious thought was that it would make a good book title. And then he saw it. *It's the protagonist's life, a worship street. But then I'd have to start in London; he's born on Worship Street; he has the accident here; he becomes…*They crossed City Road and Denton looked down to his left and saw the coffee stall. Well, they hadn't actually passed *right* by it.

When Denton stopped the car at the station, Guillam got out but held on to the door as if he meant to prevent the little machine's driving off. 'You know more about Snokes than you've told me, I suppose.'

'And the wife. They've got a son who's strange. They're a strange lot, in fact.'

'Snokes spread himself around among the women. I'll want to hear about that. The wife, too. You free tonight?'

Denton had planned to wait for Janet and try to take her to the Italian eatery behind the grocery store. She'd be late, however. 'I can be.'

'Come to the station at seven.' He let go of the door.

'When do you ever go home?'

But that was too familiar for Guillam. He scowled and turned away. Denton rolled the car forward.

CHAPTER

13

Hyam Cohan had fought under the name 'the Stepney Jew-Boy' fifteen years before, and now he ran a boxing school called The Massada Academy of Self-Defence in the East End. He had been almost killed the year before when three anti-Semitic toughs had worked him over with brass knuckles and burned his school out. He had lost an eye and he still had a limp, but he was back to teaching kids from the Jewish streets how to fight. He lived in the bottom floor of Janet's house; his wife was her housekeeper, dress-maker and, Denton thought, confidante.

Cohan and Denton were in Denton's attic, where he kept his practice pistols and his dumb-bells. Denton had cleared a space in the middle of the attic where he could put down a worn carpet. He and Cohan boxed there one or two days a week. Mostly, Cohan held up his palms for Denton to throw blows at, and then Cohan would throw blows that Denton tried to block. Even one-eyed and wearing carpet slippers, Cohan was better than Denton.

'Faster!' Cohan rasped at him. 'Bing-bang, bing-*bang*. You are going bing, bing, bing like I am going to wait for you to hit me. What you think fighting is, politeness?'

'I don't want to hurt you.'

'Ha-ha, you making me laugh.' Cohan shot out a fist and caught Denton on the cheek, more a slap than a punch.

'Hey! I'm supposed to be doing the hitting.'

'Oh, is that how boxing is! One fella hits, the other stands still. Some idea of it you got, Mr Denton. Come on, bing-*bang*, bing-*bang*—better. Better. Good!'

Denton was stripped to the waist and sweaty even though the attic was cold. When he heard the downstairs doorbell ring, he thought he would ignore it: Atkins was out; people should know better. When it rang again, longer this time and seemingly louder, he made a disgusted sound but kept on punching at Cohan's palms.

When it rang the third time, Cohan dropped his palms and said, 'Maybe it's the police. They ring like that—long. Next, they bang the door. Then they knock it down.'

'This isn't Poland.'

'I feel better if you answer. You and me about done, anyway. You all sweating; me, my leg hurts.'

'Agh.' Denton pulled off the light gloves he had been wearing, pulled on a shirt and trotted down the stairs. In his bedroom, he grabbed a high-collared robe and got his arms into the sleeves as he went down the next flight, jumped over the comatose Rupert, who in the absence of Atkins came up to be with the second-best human, and was buttoning up the front as he reached the door. As he did so, the bell rang again.

'I'm coming, dammit—'

He wrenched the door open. Rosamund Gearing was standing on his step. She was there only an instant, and then she was in his lower hall, saying, 'I knew you were here!' and going past him. 'Am I interrupting something?'

'I was exercising.'

'Ah, yes, it's how you keep that very fit look.' She was going up the stairs. 'Are you going to stand down there?'

'Miss Gearing, I'm not really able to, mmm, receive anybody now.'

'Oh, but I'm not "anybody".' She laughed and disappeared through the door into his sitting-room. When he got there, she was dropping her coat on his armchair. 'I thought your man would be out this afternoon. Was I right?' She began to pull pins from her hat.

'It's his afternoon out and my afternoon to be, ah, unsociable, Miss Gearing. Another time—'

'I'll just step into the convenience, if I may. I stood so long at your door ...'

Denton wondered what he was going to do with her. He didn't like to ask her to leave in just those words. Or tell her to leave, which would be worse. Maybe put on some clothes and take her somewhere. Put her into a cab.

Tell her to go to hell.

He got a tea towel from his alcove and wiped his sweaty face. Above, he could faintly hear Cohan straightening the attic, something he knew he didn't have to do, something Denton could do for himself. Denton was getting fed up with the servant business—first Atkins, now Cohan. Could he live with no servant at all?

He looked at himself in a small mirror above the mantel. He tried to brush his hair with his fingers.

If I said, I'm sorry, Miss Gearing, I'll really have to ask you to go because...Because what? What the hell, being greeted by a man in a robe should have been enough to tell her she shouldn't be here.

He moved away from the mirror. At the same time, he saw two things—above on his right, Cohan's slippered feet started down the stairs towards the sitting-room; only slightly to his right and at the end of a short corridor, the door to the downstairs WC opened. Then things happened quickly: Cohan came down, and Rosamund Gearing, wearing only pink knickers with a wide band of ecru lace at the knees, walked towards him along the corridor.

Denton opened his mouth.

She stopped so that she was framed in the arch between the sitting-room and the corridor and, spreading her arms a little and extending a hand, she said, 'Come.'

Cohan said, '*Oi, gevalt!*'

Denton said, 'Unnnhhh—'

Rosamund Gearing screamed and ran back to the WC.

'Mister Denton!' Cohan said. 'Mister Denton!'

'It isn't what you think, Cohan.'

'You like mice playing while your missus is the cat working all day! What kinda shenanigans is these?' Cohan, although a self-described 'bad Jew', was nonetheless a moralist.

'Mr Cohan, I didn't know that was going to happen!'

Cohan looked at him with his good eye, as bright as a crow's studying a diamond. 'All right, I am believing you. But some *bristen* she got on her, yeah? If you want to tell me you was tempted, I believe you.'

'I didn't know she was going to pull her clothes off, and I'm not tempted.' Denton stared angrily at the closed door of the WC. *And yes, she has nice bristen. And hips and legs and…*He snorted at his own stupidity. 'I never should have let her in.'

'I better go home.' Cohan started for the stairs down to Atkins's quarters and the rear garden.

Denton grabbed his sleeve and pulled him back. 'You stay here! You're my witness.'

'Like in court? The police?'

'Just stay here.' The two men stood together, Denton still holding Cohan's sleeve. When Rosamund Gearing came out, both seemed to lean back just a little. Without looking at them, she swept down the corridor and into the sitting-room, red-faced, where she picked up her coat and her hat and, without putting either on, went to the door. Not looking at them, she seemed ready to say something, then ducked her head and went out.

'Now can I go?'

'Not until I know she's gone.'

He waited. After a time—he supposed she was putting in hat-pins—the front door slammed. He went to the front window, stepping over Rupert and pulling Cohan along, and looked out. She was striding quickly up the street towards Holborn.

'All right.' He almost said, *We're safe.*

'What did she want?'

'A baby.'

Cohan took that in. '*Oi, veh.*' He looked out the window again. 'I am allowed to tell Leah?' Leah was his dour wife.

'Please do. Tell everybody.'

Cohan went down the room, making little ticking sounds with his tongue. He again stepped over Rupert, who, woken by all the activity, wagged his stub of a tail. Cohan went down the stairs.

Denton bent and scratched Rupert's head. 'You want to get to Sophie to make a baby, and you can't. That woman wants to get to me to make a baby, and I won't. It hardly seems fair, does it?'

He met with Guillam at King's Cross Road, but Guillam was in such a rush that Denton could give him only the outline of what he knew. Guillam's purpose had shifted in the few hours since they had left Pinkert's; Denton wondered if he had slept at all. What Guillam wanted now was control of the case, which meant taking it away from Masefield despite its being Masefield's by rights because the first murder had happened on his pitch. Denton knew Guillam's hunger for promotion, guessed that Guillam saw the case as a possible springboard to loft him back to Central, from which he'd been busted for abusing his power (in a case involving Denton, in fact).

'There's no reason other than tradition that Masefield should have it,' Guillam said. 'He's done nothing except take a man to magistrates' court and have it thrown out. He botched it. Masefield doesn't know of Snokes's connection with Cherrytree Street, and I don't want him to learn of it, you follow me? Not until I settle who's in charge. It's late, but I've kept some people in their offices at the Yard to decide it.'

'You're going over your super's head?'

'I am not! Divisional chief inspector's on my side; we went together to the super, he sees the rightness of it. If we solve it, it goes on our sheet and we all share the rosy glow. Give me a ride to the Yard, will you? I've got Donnie Munro waiting for me— he thinks it's all a lark, but he'll back me.'

'You wanted me to tell you about the Snokeses.'

'Tell me as we go.'

That was why he found himself shouting the Snokes history over the noise of the engine and the pounding of hooves behind them and the grind of iron rims ahead. There was hardly time to mention Walter Snokes and his confinement. The only question Guillam asked about him was 'Is the boy big enough to kill a woman?' Denton said he was but he was locked in, might as well be in a prison.

'We'll see.' Guillam might like a mental case for a suspect, he thought, but Guillam was focusing just then on Walter's father. Two amours, private detectives, the wronged wife: Guillam apparently was seeing it from the press's point of view.

Guillam slammed the car door. 'I'll let you know when I want to see you. This is all privileged information now—you keep it to yourself!' He ran to the entrance of New Scotland Yard.

Denton drove home, more amused than offended. Janet had just got home when he arrived, the car put away in its garage. Minutes later, they were in a cab and then at a table in the rear of the Italian grocery. Tinned food stood on shelves around them; two hams and five cheeses hung from hooks in the ceiling; a long table filled most of the space, four paying customers at one end, the family at the other; two smaller tables, of which they had one, were pushed in under the hanging food.

Hard-crusted bread appeared as soon as they sat down, with it a bowl of murky grey-green fluid. Denton looked at the young woman who was serving, probably a daughter of the family. She said, 'Scarola ieri,' and turned back to serving somebody else.

Janet said, 'Escarole yesterday,' as if she had to translate for him. She dipped the bread in the fluid. She put it tentatively in her mouth. 'Oh, Denton!' They decided that the escarole had been cooked with anchovies and red pepper and something sweet—raisins?—and was delicious.

When they were dribbling olive oil down their chins from a plate of *antipasti* that also had appeared without their ordering it, he told her about Rosamund Gearing. Janet was eating toasted bread dipped in olive oil and garlic, following it with onions in vinegar and sugar, smiling once, sipping the Montalcino he had ordered.

'Cohan said she had nice *bristen*.'

'What's that—lavalieres?'

'I think, from context, yes.'

'But she'd kept her knickers on. There's a theory that half-nudity is more arousing than nudity. It suggests, though, that she was more interested in what she was doing than her "scientific" approach might suggest. I suppose you behaved like the second act of *Thaïs*.'

'I didn't behave like anything. Yes, I behaved like somebody in a farce. Thank God Cohan was there.'

Janet selected a slice of roasted red pepper and two black olives. 'She'll give you trouble.'

'She's already given me trouble. But I think she's shot her bolt.'

'Hell hath no fury.'

'But I didn't scorn her. Cohan intervened.'

'She'll feel scorned.'

A small plate of *piselli pasta* came, followed by osso bucco and bitter greens that Denton didn't recognise, cooked in olive oil and hot pepper and garlic. There was no menu and there were no choices; they ate what they were given. The bill was ridiculously small. They sipped coffee. The girl who served them recommended the Italian ice cream up the street.

Janet said in Italian that she couldn't eat any more. '*Non posso mangiare più.*' Once in Naples she had said '*Sono stuffata*' and never made the mistake again: it was slang for 'I'm pregnant'.

They walked towards Finsbury Square. 'That was nice.' She squeezed his arm. 'Nice to speak Italian again. Let's go back to Naples.'

'Tomorrow?'

She laughed. 'I can't, of course, if I mean to be a solicitor. But sometime.'

He told her about the second murder, Guillam. He had honoured his promise to Guillam and never told her about his secret life. She listened but didn't comment; Janet liked questions that could be answered, not mysteries. When they had walked a little in silence, she said, 'Watch out for that woman. I meant what I said. You think she'll be reasonable because she's educated and well-bred. She won't.'

He spent the next morning at his desk, immersed now in the book. He had scratched out the original title, *The Secret Jew*, and with it the idea that the central figure was obsessed with the delusion that he was a descendant of one of the lost tribes of Israel. He wrote *Worship Street* above it. The new title rolled out a highway for him; the idea was radiant. He didn't know the end yet, except that it was death; originally, the protagonist was to have pursued his obsession through many religions, moving from place to place, heading at last into the Canadian Arctic to die there. Now, he knew that would not be the way of it.

The second post of the day brought a note from Rosamund Gearing. Janet had been right:

> *My dear Mr Denton,*
> *I regret that we were interrupted yesterday. Had I known someone else was in the house, I should of course not have come at that time. When may I see you again? I know what must happen, as do you, I hope. We may meet somewhere else if your house cannot be private. Please reply by return post.*
> *Yrs most cordially…*

It was her closing that astonished him. She really must be mad, he thought, if she could write 'most cordially' about such a situation, the more so because they hardly knew each other. He understood the sexual appeal of strangers, even the sexual appeal of the no-nonsense, soulless poke, the casual, the accidental, the drunken. But the truth was, he now saw, that he didn't like her. In another world—a world without Janet, he meant—he might in fact have been seduced by those *bristen*, those open arms. Few men would not—which said something cautionary about most men, Denton included.

'Never turn down the poke freely given,' Frank Harris had said to him once. But Denton wasn't at all sure that this one was being freely given. Or that Rosamund Gearing was capable of knowing what 'freely' meant or what it was she was trying to give.

He wrote:

> *Miss Gearing,*
> *What you ask is impossible and something I do not wish to take place. It will be best if you try to communicate with me no more. No reply is necessary or wanted.*
> *Sincerely...*

He had hardly finished writing it when Atkins called, 'Telephone for you.'

'Our telephone?' Denton still didn't think of the telephone as a real part of his household.

'It's some copper. Name of Masefield.'

'Oh, Judas.' He threw down his pen and left the note on his desk. Atkins, he thought, would read it. He trotted down the stairs and put his mouth against the horn, which always looked to him like a bird's open beak, expecting food. 'Ready!'

'What?'

'Ready.' That's what he had learned to say in Naples. *Pronto.* Atkins, passing behind him on his way down to his own quarters, said, 'We don't say that any more, General. Say hello.'

'Oh. Hello.'

'Is this Denton?'

'Detective Masefield?'

'What the hell have you told George Guillam about my case?'

'I don't understand.'

'Guillam from G Division! The Yard just yanked my case out from under me, and you're in on it somehow! What the hell did you tell him?'

'Stop swearing and mind your tone of voice. You can be polite or I'll ring off.'

'You bloody ponce, I'll reach through the phone and yank your—What?' Masefield seemed to be talking to somebody else. Denton heard muffled voices. Somebody reminding him how coppers were supposed to behave towards the public? He waited. Apparently Guillam had got his way at New Scotland Yard. Guillam, as Munro liked to remind him, had 'friends'.

'You still there?' Masefield said.

'I am.'

'All right, I apologise if I was outspoken. Did you know the Snokes case was going to be yanked away from me?'

'I did not.'

'You have anything to do with it—going over my head, maybe using your in with Detective Inspector Munro at Central?'

'I did not.'

Masefield seemed to have temporarily run out of steam. 'Somebody put his oar in.' Denton waited him out. Masefield said, 'Your name was mentioned in connection with tying my case to the murder in the Artillery Ground.'

'I'm not responsible for rumours, Masefield. Ask Guillam.'

'Him and I aren't speaking. And like bloody hell will I take orders from him!'

'I'm afraid I can't help you.'

'Did you tell him anything about the Snokes case?'

'You'll have to ask Detective Sergeant Guillam.'

He thought that Masefield had calmed down, but he shouted, 'You bloody creeping Jesus, I'll have your poncey arse!'

Masefield rang off with a violence that Denton could feel through the receiver. The threat was meaningless, he thought, although it would have been enough to get Masefield a reprimand if Denton had wanted to make a stink. After Rosamund Gearing, however, it was a flea-bite that was best forgotten.

He put the note to her in an envelope and scribbled the address of her Oxford college and smacked a stamp on it. He trotted down the two flights and put it out for the postman, then trotted back one flight and snatched up the rest of the morning mail, which he'd forgotten in dealing with 'that woman', as he now thought of her. There were the usual bills and begging letters and a note from Snokes. He had left two of the music sheets from the piano with the porter at his office. Denton could pick them up any time.

He went back up and did another hour's work, then changed into day clothes and went out. It was raining again but warmer, the pavement a forest of umbrellas. There were no cabs in Russell Square, and he walked up to Euston Road and found none there, either, so descended into the wool-and-coal smell of the underground. Ten minutes later, he came out of Liverpool Street underground station and strode around to Snokes's office. The day porter had the drawings; yes, they had the name Denton on them; yes, that was all right then, sir. He handed them over; Denton handed over a coin. The porter insisted on wrapping the rolled tube of music paper 'because of the rain, sir'. Another coin was offered and, remarkably, refused.

He gave a perfunctory glance around for a cab, saw without really noticing her a woman standing halfway along the street under a green umbrella, and went back to the underground, emerged another ten minutes later at Charing Cross. He walked to Piccadilly Circus, the rain now more gentle than otherwise, the air windless, the sky as uniform as a bolt of grey cloth. He avoided the temptation of the Café Royal and, coming into Piccadilly, saw a flash of green behind him and thought of the earlier green umbrella, frowned, went up to Burlington Arcade and the shop of a man named Geddys. It said 'Objects of Virtue' on the outside.

'What *is* an object of virtue?' Denton said.

Geddys, if he had been taken in two huge hands and straightened out, would have been about five feet eight, but some affliction caused him to carry his back bent and his head twisted to the side, so he topped out at about five feet two. From that height, he had to turn his head sideways so as to look up into Denton's face. 'If I told you, you wouldn't understand.'

'You have a low opinion of me, Geddys.'

'I thought I hid it so well.' Geddys had a pointed beard, very dark, and a look of worn-in cynicism. His shop was cluttered, in what Denton supposed was an artistic way, with small tables and a couple of glass cases, most horizontal surfaces pretty well covered with silver, china, ormolu, Fabergé, Wedgwood, and the odd bisque shepherdess. The walls were thick with paintings.

'I still have those Scottish paintings, if you're interested,' Denton said. When he had first bought his house, he had picked up two huge paintings of hairy cattle and mountainous land-scapes to fill the blankness of his downstairs hall.

'I'm not.'

'Now, Geddys, they're not that bad.'

'You have no eye for art. None.'

'Geddys, *I'm* the one who brought back a Cimabue from Italy that *you* said was a fake.'

Geddys turned his head tighter into a corkscrew and sneered up at Denton. 'You told me you'd bought it because you didn't know what was art, but you knew what you liked.'

'That was supposed to be a joke.'

'I don't have a sense of humour. What are these?'

Denton had unrolled the sheets of music paper that had come from the Snokeses' piano. 'You tell me.'

'What is this, some sort of modern nonsense?' Geddys bent over the drawings, which Denton had flattened on an eigh-teenth-century drum head, holding them in place with several objects of virtue. Bending closer, Geddys felt with a hand over a counter-top and found a magnifier. He peered into it. 'Richard Dadd,' he said.

'Are you telling me something?'

'Don't you even know who Richard Dadd was? Really, Denton, for a famous man who makes his living *writing*, you're an ignoramus.'

'Who was Richard Dadd?'

'A painter. What most people remember about him was that he murdered his father. Spent years in Broadmoor, died there, oh, going on twenty years ago.' He was still peering at the music paper. 'This is merely derivative amateur work. A child could have done it.'

'A child *did* do it. What's the connection with Dadd?'

'You want to go see *The Fairy Feller's Master-Stroke*. Fairies or little people or something of the sort—faces peering out from everywhere, none of them more than a few inches tall, hiding under flowers and creepers and so on. Like this stuff. A child. Well, in that case it's rather good. Am I to make something of the music staff?'

'I don't know.' Denton took the magnifier from him and studied the top page, the images familiar but not identical to those he'd got from Tonk. The double-gabled building, The Oaks, was of course absent, not yet part of Walter's life when he'd drawn these. He said, 'Is it just because it's got lots of little figures that it's like your painter—Dadd?'

Geddys was standing with one hand in his back, pushing his abdomen forward as if he were trying to take the twist out of his body. 'I think you'll find that the costumes are right out of Dadd. It's Dadd's world, in fact.'

'Does that mean something?'

'How should I know?' Geddys went to the window and looked out into the arcade. 'If it weren't that I don't have any customers, you'd bore me, Denton.' He put his face almost against the glass and looked to the right.

'Maybe you should sell things people want.'

'Like Scottish genre?' He put his hands behind him, looked out at the empty arcade. 'I wish I had a Dadd to sell. Always popular.'

'Was Dadd that good?'

'People like the idea of an artist who murdered his own father. It seems so artistic. And the paintings are rather nice. Disturbingly nice, if that's possible.' He turned on Denton. 'Is the child mad?'

'The one who did these? I'm trying to find out.'

A customer, or at least a visitor, came in, a fussy young man who made a point of leaving his umbrella outside. Denton rolled up the sheets and put them in the porter's wrapping and thanked Geddys. When he was at the door, Geddys caught his sleeve and said very low, 'I've been watching the same woman go past my shop three times. That have anything to do with you?'

Denton started to say of course not, changed direction and said, 'Did she have a green umbrella?'

'Furled, yes. And eyes like a frog. I don't operate a *maison de passe*, Denton. I hope you're not making assignations here.'

Denton denied it. He went out into the arcade, turned towards Piccadilly, and saw Rosamund Gearing. She pretended to glance back, pretended to be surprised. 'Mr Denton! What are you doing here?'

Anger wrapped its fist around his chest, then his throat. He forced himself not to show it. He raised his hat an inch, put it back. 'Good day, Miss Gearing.'

He stepped around her; she tried to step in front of him but was trying to open her green umbrella at the same time and was a half-second too slow. 'You're going my way,' she cried. 'I'll walk with you.'

Denton stopped. He said, 'No, you won't. I don't want you to walk with me. I don't want you to write to me. I don't want to see you. I don't *want* you.' He raised his hat again, aware of passers-by who must see them only as two quite proper people, doubtless acquaintances, the man perhaps a friend of her father's. 'Goodbye, Miss Gearing—permanently, I hope.'

He went as fast as he could towards Old Bond Street. He heard the hard click of her heels behind him, first keeping up, then fading. She called, 'You'll regret not waiting for me!' He hurried on and turned at the corner; she had given up and was staring after him. He strode up to Wigmore Street and then to Trinity College, looking behind to make sure she hadn't followed. He was told that Walter Snokes's former teacher, Mr Reishak, was with a student. Denton wandered about, letting his anger subside, hearing again the muted cacophony of several pianos being played; he wondered if these were sounds that Walter Snokes still heard inside his head. He looked into shadowed corridors and doorways for Rosamund Gearing.

When Reishak was free, he led Denton to some sort of common room where a couple of other men, presumably teachers, were lounging as if dying of exhaustion. One was chewing a sandwich that he kept putting back into a leather satchel on the floor.

'These are very sad,' Reishak said when Denton had spread the drawings in front of him. He pulled a tiny folding magnifier from a pocket. 'But talented, yes? Walter was a talented boy.'

'These were done after his accident.'

'Yes, yes, I understand.'

'Was he trying to write music, do you think?'

'This is a fantastic idea. Because he used music paper? Well…It is not music. It is little people and plants.'

'But on music paper.'

'Yes.'

'His mother said that he was composing something for the piano when he had the accident. Could he have thought that he was finishing it somehow with these drawings?'

'I cannot say what that poor boy was doing. I can tell you, this is not music. If he meant for the figures to be the notes, they do not make music. They make…' He shook his head. 'Do you know Mahler? No? Well, even Mahler…' He shook his head again.

'But they all seem to be going someplace. Along the staff. Isn't that what music does?'

'Yes, in a way, but…Now, this is interesting. This *is* like music.' He was tapping a drawing of a house.

Denton looked. It was one of the places he had seen before where a building appeared, reduced, inside the staff. 'What is it?'

'When we change one staff from bass to treble or treble to bass, we put the symbol like that, smaller than when it is up here at the beginning of the measures, and we put it on the bottom line like that. If, you know, we have been playing in the bass with the left hand, which is usual, and now the composer wants us to play with the left hand up in the treble, than he puts the treble sign like this down in the bass staff, and we know to play up where he wants. So it is here as if Walter has said, "Now play in the treble." But he has no treble, no bass. Only houses!' Reishak shook his head. He put away his magnifier. 'Poor little Walter. Poor little boy.'

'Does the name Richard Dadd mean anything to you?'

Reishak said it didn't, added that he had to go. Denton kept him to ask if there was anything Walter might have seen that would have given him the idea for the drawings—the tiny people, the costumes, the leaves and flowers. Were there pictures in the rooms? In the corridors? Reishak raised his hands and shook his head, then looked at the drawings again with his magnifier and suddenly strode out of the room, beckoning Denton to follow. They went up a flight of stairs, pianos and some sort of horn and a deep-voiced string playing all around them. Reishak threw open a door, startling a young woman at a piano. She stood; he waved her down, and he pointed at an engraving on the little room's far wall. It was black and white, only a tangle of lines at first, then dimly seen figures emerged, human and non-human, flowers, mushrooms and grasses and stems. At the bottom, it said, 'The Fairy Feller's Master-Stroke by Richard Dadd'.

The rain was coming down harder. That miracle, an empty cab, appeared; he almost leaped into it. Half-dozing in the damp cold, he let the horse's rhythm lull him, so that he was drifting off when the cab pulled up and the driver said, 'Here! You've got a constable!'

Woken more by the stopping than the voice, Denton looked out. He recognised his own front door, then saw that indeed there was a constable, and then Rosamund Gearing. Also Atkins, very red in the face, hovering in the half-opened door like an animal in a burrow.

'This your house all right, guv?'

'It is.' He gave the man money, but his eyes were on the tableau at his doorstep. 'Drive on.' He pushed his wrought-iron gate open and took a step. Rosamund Gearing looked at him; her expression became hard. He had seen the look before, thought again that it would be terrible to live with. 'Now then, Constable! I'm Denton. The householder here.'

'Yes, sir, relieved to see you, sir. Now, miss, if you'll just stay right here, I'll have a word with the owner.' It was the same constable he had seen with Maltby, the young cop he knew from Naples. He looked calm, perhaps imperturbable. She sneered at him, but he had already turned away and come down off the step to 'have a word apart' with Denton, as he put it, his voice very low. 'It's a bit of a situation, sir. Your man blew his police whistle. When I responded, I found your man physically barring the young woman from entering your house. Was that at your direction, sir?'

'It was.'

'He said as much. Well, now. This could be a breach, although my thinking is I'll go to the magistrate for a summons for the young woman if you wish to make a complaint.'

Denton looked at Rosamund Gearing. Her eyes had narrowed; she still had the hard look, but now she seemed suspicious, as well. Atkins, barring the doorway, was looking back and forth between her and Denton. Denton said, 'I think summoning her would be maybe a little much.'

'Well, now, I'll be the judge of that, sir. Your man has, I believe, a bruise on his cheek. I don't want to charge a well-spoken young woman with assault, but I could if I had to.' The constable came still closer and dropped his voice still lower. Denton got a breath of something he'd had for lunch. 'The young woman insists you had invited her to visit, sir. Your man says the opposite. Which is true?'

'I told Atkins not to let her into the house.'

'Is this a romantic situation, sir?'

'Not on my part. Look, Constable, the young lady's got it into her head that she wants to, ummm, know me better. I don't want to know *her* better. She's at one of the women's colleges at Oxford. She reads a lot of literature.'

The policeman nodded, his tall helmet accentuating the movement. 'Her head in the clouds, is it?'

'After a fashion.'

'You're a writer, I believe, sir? Has idolised you, is that it?' The constable turned to eye Rosamund Gearing. Denton was afraid he was going to say something about wasting education on women. Instead, he said, 'I could give her a warning. That goes in my book and in the station log. Be on the official record, but there's no charge.'

'That would be better.'

'Though I should by rights summon her.' He turned back to Denton. 'I have your word, have I, that you have done nothing to encourage her?'

Denton thought about what he might have said to her. 'No.' But had he? Something meant to say one thing, interpreted as another? He looked at her, caught the look, thought, *No, I never encouraged that.*

'I might just ask my sergeant to step round and have a word with you. The situation, although not unknown, might have repercussions. Your name and hers will go in the book. The press sometimes have a look at the book.'

'I'd rather that didn't happen.'

'Yes, sir. That's why I'll have a word with my sergeant.'

He went over to Rosamund Gearing—Denton thought of it as a cross on a stage, *Policeman crosses Right to Rosamund*, his doorway the scenery—and Denton went to Atkins, who stood aside to let him in. Denton heard the constable giving the almost ritualistic words, '...officially warn you against appearing again on these premises, lest I have to request a summons in the magistrates' court for your appearance to…'

'Rough time?' he murmured to Atkins.

'She's a bleeding Amazon! Cripes, if I hadn't had my police whistle she'd have been inside and up the stairs faster than Jack Robinson. What's your secret, General?'

'Now, now.'

The constable was writing in his notebook. She said something to him and he held up the pencil as if to silence her, wrote some more, asked her a question; she replied in a voice Denton didn't hear. The constable wrote some more, then nodded at her, and she went to the gate with her head back and the look firmly, perhaps permanently, on her face, opened it and marched up past the Lamb and out of sight.

'Thank you, Constable.'

'Part of the day's work, sir. Though I will say, in my early years on the force, I didn't meet up with young women like that.'

'It's the twentieth century.'

'Aye.' It seemed to sadden him. 'G'day to you, sir.' He started off, looked back and said, 'How's that probationer I talked to before? The young constable from Y Division, sir.'

It took Denton a moment. 'Maltby?'

'That sounds right. Very green, sir, very green, but he has the makings. A friend of yours, he said. He was concerned about the young woman.'

'Well, he was right.'

The policeman touched a finger to his helmet and went off. Denton watched him go, then turned to Atkins. 'Why are we standing in the doorway?'

'Oh, cripes. I've left my brains somewhere.' Atkins slammed the door. 'That woman! Drove everything right out of my head. I was in my sitting-room with Rupert, and— Oh, cripes! I let Rupert out and forgot him!' Atkins was shouting as he ran towards the back of the house.

Denton, his mac half off, struggled after him, pulling himself back into it as he saw Atkins go out the rear door into the garden and start shouting Rupert's name. As Denton reached the open door, he heard Atkins say, 'Rupert! He ain't here. Rup— Oh, crikey!'

Denton stepped over a puddle into the back garden. Cohan and Atkins had turned it into a vegetable patch, the rows now mostly empty except for the tops of swedes and the remains of a row of lettuces. High brick walls surrounded it; the one opposite the house had a door, now closed and locked, that led to Janet's. Atkins was staring down at the base of the wall. He looked up at Denton. 'He's tunnelled through! He's in there!' He rushed to the door and tried to pull it open; finding it locked, he began a search for the key, jamming his hands in his pockets, patting himself, muttering, 'Oh, crikey, oh, crikey—'

From the other side of the wall, a voice burst into excited, then enraged noises. The language was not English; Denton took it for Polish or Yiddish. It rose to a scream. Denton grasped the top of the wall and hoisted himself up so he could look into Janet's back garden.

Sophie stared at him with a look of puzzlement. Rupert, seeming to have been thrown over her like a huge black rug, was pumping his hind quarters with more energy than Denton had ever seen from him, his white face concentrated on this difficult problem. Leah Cohan, who had armed herself with a broom, rushed at him and whacked him on the rump, screaming insults. She might as well have hit the brick wall. She hit him again and he didn't even lose his rhythm. Mrs Cohan ran back into the house.

'Now I'm for it,' Atkins said. He had pulled himself up beside Denton. 'We've got to stop him.'

'We couldn't if we used dynamite.'

Denton dropped back to the ground. He took a leather wallet of keys from a pocket, found the right key, and put it into the door. As he moved into Janet's garden, Leah Cohan rushed back with a white ironstone pitcher and dumped its water over Rupert. He pumped twice more, shook all over, made two more somewhat shuddering thrusts, and got down. Leah Cohan screamed at him. He looked at her and lay down.

Sophie lay down.

Atkins had run to Mrs Cohan. 'Leah—it was an accident—we had a crisis. Oh, crikey, why can't she speak English? Don't kick my dog, Leah! No! No!'

'Bad! This your dog is bad!'

'It's Nature. Leah, Nature's bad! Leah—'

She stomped back to her quarters and slammed the door. Atkins looked down at Rupert. 'Now see what you've done.'

Rupert wagged his tail.

'What'll I do?' Atkins said. 'What ever am I going to do, General?'

'Let's start by taking Rupert home. Sophie, are you all right?' He was tempted to make cheap jokes. He scratched Sophie's head and behind her ears, and she looked away, still seeming puzzled. 'We'd better get Rupert inside before he gathers his forces again.'

'Oh, crikey, he wouldn't!'

'I would—wouldn't you?'

They steered Rupert back through the doorway, not without trouble, because he wanted to stay. Denton locked the door as Atkins began shovelling dirt into Rupert's tunnel. 'Impressive,' Denton said. 'That's quite a hole.'

'He's possessed.'

'You told Mrs Cohan it's Nature.'

They put Rupert indoors. Atkins shook his head. 'The missus will kill me. The missus will draw and quarter me!'

Denton patted his shoulder. 'The worst that can happen is that there'll be half a dozen more puppies in the world.'

'She'll absolutely annihilate me.'

Waiting for Janet to come home, Denton laid out all the music paper, the sheets he had got from Tonk and the ones he had got from Snokes, and studied them with his magnifying glass. He made notes, struck things out when he found they were wrong, tried to make connections, sense, sanity, and after two hours he thought he had learned very little, but he had learned something: that, if the drawings were not music, they were something that progressed; that they always began on the left at one of three structures—The Oaks, the new house Denton didn't recognise, or the terraced house; and that only two structures ever appeared as the reduced-size 'changes of clef' within the staff and partway across the page—the odd triangular building and the house with the weather-vane on the portico. Were they then destinations or were they changes of key—some sort of regeneration?

The difference he thought he had detected between the old drawings and the new was partly a difference of Walter's increased skill and dexterity: Walter had got older and he had become practised. But Denton thought he saw a difference in some of the figures, as well. They had developed individual faces, recognisable and repeated in the later drawings, and they had developed a look—passionate, driven. And they were not crawling through the foliage; they were scrambling for their lives.

About five, Atkins said that Miss Gearing was on the telephone, and would he talk to her? Denton swore and said he was out. She called again at five-twenty, at five-twenty-three, at ten to six, and at six-fifteen. Denton told Atkins he was gone for the night and went over to Janet's house.

CHAPTER 14

Janet was enraged by the rape of Sophie, as expected. He knew she would be, but being prepared didn't help. He had learned—from rather bitter experience—not to interfere and not to offer advice and not to tell her that she was tired. Her rages were infrequent and brief, awful while they lasted. Her face got red, her scar livid, her tongue vicious.

Finally, spent, she threw herself into a soft chair. 'Atkins and that dog of his should both be castrated!'

It hadn't seemed to occur to her that Sophie might escape getting pregnant. She had already shouted that 'they were at it all afternoon', which of course wasn't true. Denton wanted to suggest that she could have any incipient puppies aborted, but he didn't. She would get to that in her own good time. And did. 'I suppose you'll say I should have them aborted! Well, I won't. I won't have my dog done to that way. I just won't, so don't suggest it.'

Eventually, she accepted a glass of her awful dry vermouth.

'Play something for me.' He nodded at the parlour grand.

'I'm too upset.' She glared at the piano, at the walls, at him. 'I've had a horrible day. A hellish day. Teddy all but fired me because I made a balls of the notes for a case. My tutor scolded me for abandoning economics for the law. Now I come home to this.' She drank, then burst out, 'Say something!'

'I don't dare.'

'You do, too. Comfort me. Give me unwanted advice. Tell me I'm being hysterical.'

'You'd have my bollocks.'

She threw her head back. A moment later, he realised she was laughing. She said, 'Do you suppose she enjoyed it?'

'She looked confused.'

'Well, who wouldn't be? And that wretch Rupert, how did he look?'

'Earnest.'

'I'll give him earnest! Oh!' She made a sound with her breath, then held out a hand. 'Come sit with me. Tell me something entertaining.'

He squeezed himself into the chair with her. She wound up mostly in his lap, her legs across his and hanging over the upholstered arm. He said, 'I don't have anything entertaining. I worked; I got pi-jawed by Detective Inspector Masefield; I had Rosamund Gearing try to push her way into my house and get the police down on me.'

'Oh, tell me!'

He told her.

'I said she'd be difficult. And all the constable did was warn her?'

'That was my doing.'

'You should have let him charge her.'

'He wasn't going to charge her; he was going to the magistrate for a summons. Maybe she'll be grateful to me.'

'Of course she won't. Was it a great brouhaha?'

'A very quiet one. The best tradition of the Metropolitan Police. Of course, it was raining, too.'

'And then what?'

'She went off, and Atkins remembered he'd let Rupert out.'

'So that's how it happened! Had Atkins left that gate open again?'

'Rupert dug under the wall.'

'It's still Atkins's fault. I could kill him.' Her glass was empty. She twirled the stem in her fingers. 'What shits males are.' She tittered. 'And what fools females are. Some of them.'

'Not you.'

'No. What about this Gearing woman?'

'She doesn't seem to me like a fool.'

'I didn't mean that. What are you going to do about her?'

He knew that his face had a stupid expression pasted on it. 'Should I be doing something?'

'What if she cries rape? What if she says it was all arranged and Cohan simply walked in on the beginning of a tryst? What if she says you seduced her? You've kept her letters at least, I hope.'

'Unnhhh…'

'Denton, really! You're exasperating! Have you kept her letters?'

'There was only one. It might still be next to my chair. Unless I threw it in the grate.'

'Look for it. I mean it, Denton—I know a little now about the vengefulness that drives people to go to the law. And she'll be vengeful.'

'A young woman scorned by an old man?'

'*Look* at it, Denton! Young woman, older, famous man—he lures her to his house—'

'I didn't lure her! She came on her own ticket!'

'Prove it.'

'I told Atkins to keep her out of the house. She's called half a dozen times since five and I wouldn't talk to her.'

'Only because you'd jilted her.'

'I didn't jilt her! Oh, you're playing devil's advocate. Anyway, Maltby saw her "loitering" and apparently told the beat cop about it.'

'She was love-sick, hanging about to catch a glimpse of you.'

'Janet.' He put a hand over one of hers. 'Have you ever thought of becoming a lawyer?'

'Well, you see how somebody would put it in court. In the end, of course, it's your word against hers, and you could bring in Atkins and me as witnesses, and Cohan, and Maltby, and I suppose young Hench-Rose.'

'It would ruin him.'

'Better him than you.' She lay back. 'I'd ask you for some more of this lovely drink, but you'd have to move, meaning I'd have to move. Anyway, you've a nice lap.' Both of them were silent until she said, 'Damn Atkins, anyway.'

'And damn Rosamund Gearing.'

'And damn everybody. How nice it is to be perfect, just the two of us.'

He went back to his house because Janet wanted a bath without him, and he wanted to see if he had any of Rosamund Gearing's letters. Coming in, he told Atkins that he wasn't there, in case she telephoned again. Atkins told him that Munro had telephoned and might 'stop by'; Denton guessed that Atkins hadn't dared to come to Janet's house to tell him.

What Janet had said was now a niggling worry. He was happy to find Miss Gearing's recent letter in the pile next to his chair; he re-read it, standing there, thought that 'I regret that we were interrupted yesterday' didn't sound as if he were a vile seducer, and her 'When may I see you again?' while perhaps ambiguous, didn't fit an accusation of 'taking advantage'. Or did it? He took the letter upstairs and shut it into a drawer of his desk. Perhaps he should have a copy made. That seemed extreme. He thought he was behaving like a nervous old pensioner, frightened of shadows. Disgusted with himself, he went out and had a deliberately awful supper at a chop-house as punishment.

When he got back, a horse-drawn cab was coming down towards him from the Holborn direction. He put his key in his own door, and, prepared to go in, heard the driver's voice and then the change in the horse's rhythm. The cab was stopping. He turned, thinking *Oh God don't let it be the Gearing woman* and saw Munro heaving his considerable bulk out of the cab.

Denton walked back to his gate. 'You here to see me?'

'I am.' Munro was paying the driver.

'Social call? I'm flattered.'

'It isn't, so don't be.' Munro pushed the gate open, backing Denton towards his front door. They went together up the steps.

'Atkins is out.' Denton threw his overcoat towards a monstrously ugly thing that had brass hooks sticking out all over it like antlers. His hat followed.

Munro hung his own coat up more fastidiously. Pulling at his cuffs, then touching his necktie, he said, 'I want to talk to you.'

'I didn't think you'd come to gaze at me. Have you eaten?'

They went up the stairs, Munro growling that he'd had something in New Scotland Yard canteen. Denton asked if the food was good there; Munro shrugged. Munro was married, had several children; he boasted of his wife's cooking. Denton wondered how many evenings he actually ate his supper at home.

Denton produced whisky and glasses, then fetched biscuits and cheese from the downstairs kitchen in case Munro was still hungry. Finally, Munro burst out, 'Stop fussing and sit down!'

'I'm being the host.'

'If I have to spend the night on a cot because you're being polite, I'll have you up for interfering with the police.'

Denton laughed at him, poured the whisky, sat in his green armchair. 'What're you angry about?'

'The detective super's put me in charge of the Snokes mess.'

'Ah. I thought Guillam was after that.'

'He was, and that's why they foisted it on me. George always tries too hard. He was right to try to take it away from that blockhead Masefield, but he pulled so many levers and bothered so many folk at the Yard, they got sick of him. So the public prosecutor's taken it over, and I'm it. Now, you tell me what you know and don't leave anything out!' Munro settled back in his own armchair with his whisky.

'Didn't Guillam tell you?'

'Georgie's nose is out of joint, as per usual. He's sulking in his tent in King's Cross Road. I've a meeting with him and Masefield and a couple of other tecs in the morning, and I want to know as much as they do when I start—preferably more. Guillam tells me you know more than any civilian should.'

'Guillam asked me to help out.'

'He told me that, too. Damned peculiar, for Georgie. You got something on him?'

Denton dodged that. 'Did he tell you I saw a connection between Cherrytree Street and the first murder? All right.' He tried to lay it out in order. The order in which he'd learned things turned out not to be the right one. There was no right one, in fact: things had happened simultaneously, or in the past. Still he thought he'd got it all in.

'You're interested in the boy?'

'I'm interested in him as a boy, yes. As a human being. I'm not sure what I think about him in connection with the cases.'

'You said he's locked up. How'd he be connected with the cases, then?'

Denton shook his head. 'Both murders have—sorry, seem to have—some sort of connection with the Snokeses. The first one, Snokes admits he and the woman were having it on, and he found the body. The second one, Mrs Snokes hired an investigator who trailed Snokes to the woman's house on Cherrytree Street. Five years ago!'

'Masefield's not letting go of it being Snokes. When Guillam was finally forced to tell him about Cherrytree Street, Masefield opined that Snokes is killing off his women.'

'You mean to say he's done nothing else about the first one? It's more than two weeks.'

'He's done a canvass of Denmark Road and turned up a mysterious Jew who was "seen walking". So Masefield's spent two days looking at the fingerprints of every Jewish name in the files and comparing them with some fingerprints found on the Wilcox woman's floor. Of course he got no matches. So he's put out a "man wanted" description in *Hue and Cry* and the *Gazette*, which is about like asking to look out for somebody with a black moustache and old clothes. But he really believes that Snokes is guilty, and he's "waiting for him to make his mistake". Masefield should be back on a beat.'

'Well, Snokes was likely in the beginning.'

'My choice for the murderer would have been Mrs Snokes, if the women hadn't been sexually assaulted.'

'Jealous wife?'

'Though for the life of me I can't see why she'd wait five years to kill the Adger woman. But we were talking about the boy. Any chance it could be him?'

Denton was silent for a long time. 'He's very attached to his mother.'

'What, you think she could be using him to commit murder? And the boy raped the women while he was at it?'

'Seems far-fetched when you say it flat out like that. No, I don't see any evidence for that. But apparently she takes the boy out of the place where they have him, at least two days a week. But during the day, I think.' But he thought, *I didn't ask Tonk if she ever took the boy out at night.* 'Any chance the surgeon has the times of death wrong?'

'What, wrong by several hours? Hell's bells, Denton, if you're going that road, you might as well go back to the husband—if the wife was off with the boy in the afternoons, and the time of death was afternoon, the old man has no alibi. But it won't hang together—the first woman ran a shop; she would have been missed in the afternoon. The second one was behind a cricket club, near a road. She'd have been found if it was during the day. And the crime would have been seen.'

'What does the laboratory say?'

'Guillam and Masefield're both holding on to their reports and being horse's arses about it. I'll get them tomorrow.'

'Both women were raped, is that a proven fact? Or just assumed because they saw some white stuff and didn't check it?'

'Don't believe everything you read in the papers. But yes, apparently there really was semen in them. Or the first one, at least. Cripes, I didn't ask for chapter and verse on it. I don't know what the labs found. It's early days yet on the Adger woman, anyway; lab's slow. What should they find?'

'You might be able to get an idea of when the women had had intercourse, for one thing.'

'But...A-hum, I see what you're getting at. The semen might be from somebody else and have nothing to do with the murders. Both women might have had it on with somebody else, you mean.' Munro was making notes. 'Why is it I never mind you telling me my business? I do think of these things, you know. Eventually.' He scribbled. 'But don't think you can identify suspects from their semen. And don't tell me to collect a sample from them!'

Denton was reminded of Rosamund Gearing's 'holding up the handkerchief'. He poured them both more whisky. 'Bruising on the thighs? Of the women?'

Munro sighed. 'I'll ask.'

'Somebody suggests—is it Gross?—that bruising of the thighs is a far more reliable sign of rape than bruising in the vagina. And then their fingernails.'

'Taking scrapings is standard now.' Munro made another note. 'You're a relentless bugger. You and Georgie Guillam would either kill each other or get on like a house afire if you had to work together. You're not half alike.' Munro put his pencil in his notebook and closed it but didn't put it away. 'There isn't really anything in this boy, is there?'

Denton chewed on a finger. 'No, because I don't see how he could have done either one. But...' He looked at Munro. 'Sex.'

Munro raised his eyebrows.

'According to his father and his sister, he tried something with her when he was twelve. He doesn't...deal with other people the way the rest of us do, Munro. If he wants something, he wants it right then and he wants it a lot. If he somehow was with these women and he wanted sex…'

Munro muttered, 'A sister? Why didn't somebody tell me about a sister?' He scribbled a note. 'He might kill to get sex?'

'Apparently he can be violent—at least his sister thinks so. But I'm not sure that he understands what killing is. He might rape. But would he kill?'

'Some men kill to keep the woman from telling.'

'I'm not at all sure he would think that through. Or that he would even understand about "telling". I just don't know.'

'So maybe he could rape and somebody else would clean up—and kill? Mama? Papa?' Munro began to make notes. 'Cripes—families!' He thought about that and said, 'They're as bad as coppers fighting over a case.'

CHAPTER

15

Denton spent the next morning writing. Rosamund Gearing telephoned eight times, according to Atkins; he had begun to keep a log 'for the police, which I'll call in myself if this keeps up'. Denton stopped at noon and ambled down to the sitting-room, pushed the day's mail aside in favour of the notes that Nellie Strang had been dropping off for him. She had found several more brief articles from small weeklies about the 'prodigy', as they had all called Walter Snokes before his accident, but they told Denton nothing new. Or so he thought until he re-read them and found in one 'little Walter Snokes of Banner Street, Finsbury'. Had he known the name of the street before? It would be the place where the family had lived during the prodigious years. And then, presumably, they had moved to De Beauvoir Town.

He wondered why. The accident? Had Walter's sister said anything about it? He didn't think so.

'I'm going out,' he called down the stairs.

'Please look proper.' Atkins's head appeared at the bottom

of the stairs. 'Is that the blue lounge with the stripe? Well, that's all right. Black overcoat, I think.'

'How's Rupert?'

'We're not speaking. If that woman calls five more times, I'm calling Central and telling them to come take the telephone out. That'll get their attention.'

Denton walked to the Guildhall and went to the library, knew exactly what shelf he wanted, and plucked out a Kelly's for six years before. Arthur Snokes was not difficult to find on Banner Street—number 24. Armed with this, Denton set out again, up Moor Lane and Bunhill Row and then west into Banner Street. Number 24 was neither more nor less than he had expected, a narrow house in a row of narrow houses. It could well have been the terraced house that Walter Snokes now drew on his sheets of music paper. Two letter boxes suggested that it had two occupants; it probably had been so when the Snokeses had lived there. Maybe a promotion had lifted the family to De Beauvoir Town? He would have to ask.

He continued to the end of the road and turned down Whitecross Street, heading for Cherrytree Street to have a look at the dead woman's address. He had deliberately passed it by as he had gone up to Banner Street; now, he wasn't entirely sure why—saving it for last? That seemed an odd, perhaps macabre, idea.

Cherrytree Street was, for a house or two, rather elegant, certainly as middle-class as Whitecross Street; then it deteriorated, less in age or style than in maintenance. Many of the houses looked slovenly, some downright neglected. Several, however, were spruce and trim; there seemed to be a competition as to which way the street would go.

Denton thought he would have to look for number 39. He needn't have bothered himself about it, however. As he came closer, he could have recognised it from the constable posted outside. By then, however, he knew the house by the little portico over the front door and, on top of it, the weather-vane. And the hand-made sign in a downstairs window: *Piano Lessons Given*.

Number 39, Cherrytree Street, was a house whose picture Walter Snokes drew over and over—one of the destinations of his tiny people in his Dadd-like drawings.

Suddenly in a rush, Denton all but ran down to Moorgate Street underground and sped to King's Cross, then trotted again to his own house. Flinging his hat and overcoat aside, waving a hand at Atkins, panting, he ran up his stairs and so to the telephone.

He might as well have stayed in Finsbury. Munro wasn't at New Scotland Yard.

'Where is he?'

'I'm sure I don't know, sir. You can leave a message if you call the Yard exchange.'

'No, no, I want the man himself! Is he at King's Cross Road?' Denton had just been within a couple of hundred feet of the police station.

'I really don't know, sir. You can leave a message, as I said.'

'You did, yes.'

He rang off. Guillam's home station was King's Cross Road, Masefield's behind the Angel. Munro, he thought, would have set up shop at one or the other if he hadn't done so at the Yard. Or maybe he wasn't going to have an office for the joined cases. Or maybe it had all fallen apart.

'I'm going out again!'

He walked and trotted to his motorcar and then drove to King's Cross Road, then had to leave the car two streets away because the kerbs were lined with carriages and hacks and drays. The station sergeant told him first that there was no Detective Inspector Munro there; he had somebody in his book of that name at New Scotland Yard, sir. Denton asked about Guillam.

The station sergeant looked at a board that had coloured discs and hooks and names. 'Out,' he said.

'Where?'

'Can't say, I'm sure, sir. On a case, of that I'm certain.'

'He might be with Detective Inspector Munro. Munro's in charge of a case he's on.'

'That could very well be, sir.'

Denton drove up to the Angel. Neither Masefield, Munro nor Guillam was there. He supposed he should be glad that they were all out working. But he wasn't. Remembering that he'd given up lunch to go on this wild goose chase, he went into the Angel and ate a Scotch egg and a slice of ham and thought balefully about the difference between English and Italian food. He was still glaring at his by then empty plate when a booming voice said, 'Well, *here* you are!' as if he'd been hiding.

It was Munro, very sweaty around the forehead where his hat had rested, huge in a tweed ulster, fanning himself with the hat. 'Been looking all over London for you.'

'Munro, I've been driving around looking for you for an hour!'

'You looked in the wrong places, then. Station sergeant said somebody with a Yank accent had been by, pointed out your little car, leading me to believe that the only place you could be was here, scarfing down food while the rest of us slave. Come on, I need you to drive me to the Yard.'

Denton didn't move. 'I've got something to tell you.'

'Tell me on the way. I'm late.'

Still Denton didn't move. 'One of the houses that Walter Snokes draws pictures of is the one where the late Mrs Adger lived.' His expression was grim. 'She was his piano teacher—his first, I suspect.' In fact, he didn't *know* that she had been his piano teacher, but it was a fair assumption. He went on looking at Munro, who had stopped fanning and was looking back with a kind of suspicious seriousness. 'She was also probably one of his father's tosses—*not* his first, I suspect.'

Munro made a helpless gesture with his free hand. 'That's how they met, maybe.' He put his hat on. 'Come on.'

As they walked to the motorcar, Denton said, 'Where's Guillam?'

'Checking Snokes's mates at his office to see if he was really there like he says he was when the Adger woman was killed.'

'Guillam still sulking?'

'Not so bad. Now it's Masefield. Like a bloody infant without a tit.'

'You're well loved all round, I'm sure.'

Munro grunted. He started to hoist himself into the passenger side of the tiny Barré. 'You need a bigger motor.'

'No, I don't. You're cranking.'

'Oh, cripes.'

'Contact.'

The motor caught on the second cranking; Munro got in, threatening to tip the Barré over with his weight. Steering into Pentonville Road, Denton said, 'So what have you learned?'

'I've learned what I already knew—that Masefield's a horse's arse. I've got him doing what he should have done yesterday, chatting up the rector of Mrs Snokes's church to make sure she was really there that night, because she says she was and that'd clear her on the Adger woman's death. I don't dare let Masefield loose among the other ladies of the church cooking crew for fear they'll tell Mrs Snokes about it, and I don't want her to know I'm interested in her yet. Going to have to get her fingerprints—which bloody Masefield should have done two weeks ago—but I'm holding off, same reason.'

'Snokes said he was at work when Mrs Adger died, too?'

'Of course. Guillam had him in yesterday. Said he seemed truly shocked—more shocked than he ought to be if he hasn't seen the Adger woman in five years. Guillam opines he may still have been giving her the odd pounding.'

'Giving cause to Mrs Snokes?'

Munro grunted.

Denton cursed aloud at the London traffic. It was one thing to know the city as a pedestrian, another to drive through it, even in a car as small as his. 'Drays and cabs!' he snarled. 'Horses—plod, plod, plod!'

Munro laughed at him. Munro seemed to enjoy being driven about. At New Scotland Yard, he said, 'Pick Guillam up at King's Cross Road at two, if you please. I want you to take him to see the boy.'

'Munro, I have other things to do!'

'You work in the morning. Morning's over. Gent about town,

you can spare a little time to help the police in the thankless task of keeping the citizenry safe.' He got out, closed the little door with great care. 'I want the boy's fingerprints. Guillam'll handle that.'

'So I'm just the chauffeur.'

'If the shoe fits…' Munro raised his hat.

Guillam was waiting outside King's Cross Road police station when Denton pulled up at the kerb. Guillam got in, but Denton made a point of getting the copper petrol can from the boot—really nothing more than a space under the rear-facing back seat—and pouring the fuel into the tank. Guillam seemed not to notice. When Denton got back into the driver's seat, Guillam said, 'This fellow Tonk where the son's being kept.' He looked at Denton. 'He's a former lag. Two long terms in chokey.'

'I guess I'm not surprised.'

'Thought you should know. I may need to put the knee into him some. We going to sit here all afternoon?'

Denton thought of lashing out, instead said mildly, 'Did you see what I was doing?'

'When?'

'When I was putting fuel in the motor. Fuel costs money.'

Guillam stared at him. 'Put in a chit. Not my province.'

It was a long drive down to Camberwell. Without sunshine, the air was cold in the moving car. Guillam put his bowler at his feet, seemed to enjoy letting the wind blow over his hair. Denton would have got lost, but Guillam directed him; all of London, it seemed, was in his head. At one point, Guillam said, 'Munro lives down here somewhere. Peckham.' Denton didn't ask if they saw each other outside of police work.

Guillam's only conversation was about the case: what Snokes had said, how he had behaved. 'His mates at the office bear him out. And you had him from eight to nine the night the Adger woman was killed. It looks like he's in the clear on this one.'

Denton told him about the connection between the Adger house and Walter Snokes. 'She must have been his piano teacher. Before he went to the music school.'

'So she taught Papa to play her instrument,' Guillam said.

This seemed brutal to Denton, but on second thought it was so only because the woman was dead; coppers were often brutal as a kind of armour.

Denton said, 'The Adger house means something to the boy. It's a destination, a good destination, I think. He never puts it at the beginning of things; it's always along the way.'

'It was a place he went to, wasn't it? Maybe he's just re-living all that. Going to have his piano lesson.'

Denton thought about that. He shook his head. At Peckham Road, Guillam insisted that they stop at the local police station. 'They'll raise hell if I'm in their division without telling them.' He was out again in a few minutes, and they putt-putted down to Camberwell. Ahead of them, The Oaks stood up on its hill, narrow and, in the grey of the day, heartless.

'That's it,' Denton said.

'What, that tall place? Cripes, if they had a fire!'

When Denton had stopped the car under the last of the oaks, Guillam put a hand on his arm. 'I'll lead the charge on this one. You stay silent, if you please, unless I ask you to speak up. And let me handle the boy.'

'He doesn't like to be touched, remember.'

Guillam gave him the sort of sneering look that meant he thought that Denton was referring to his fitful, risky sex. 'I don't intend to "touch" him.'

'Munro said you were going to take fingerprints. You'll have to touch him for that, is what I meant.'

Guillam sat still. 'Oh.' He stared up into the tree. 'Anything else I should know, then?'

'He doesn't like loud noises. Don't expect a normal response from him. He doesn't seem to know about manners.'

Guillam nodded. 'Right.' He got out and they marched up to the door. By the time they got there, Tonk was standing in the opening. Tonk said, 'I can't have you visiting all the time.'

Guillam held up his warrant card. 'Thomas Tonk? Detective Sergeant Guillam, CID. Don't give me any trouble and I won't give you any.'

'I'm clean.'

'We want to see the Snokes boy.'

'First I've heard of it.'

'Well, if you don't take us to him, it won't be the last. Now move your arse, if you please.' Guillam pushed his way in. Tonk stepped back, gave Denton a look of hatred, then shut the door behind them. Wordless, he led them to the stairs and up. Guillam was looking around, apparently missing nothing. When Tonk stopped at Walter Snokes's door, Guillam said, 'This place licensed?'

'Of course.'

'I'll want to see the licence before I go. Mind you have it ready for me.'

Tonk gave him back a stare he might have learned in prison. As he had the first time, he pulled out a crowded ring of keys, picked the right one at a glance, opened the door. He started to go in, but Guillam held him back. 'That's all that's required of you,' he said. 'Hop it.'

'It's my job!'

'It'll be your job if you don't.' Guillam moved him away with the pressure of a hand, then said to Denton, 'You stay out here, too. Look through the hatch, if you want.'

When the door had closed behind Guillam, Tonk whispered, 'If he riles the boy ...' He looked enraged, probably at his own sudden helplessness. Seconds later, he stalked off along the dark corridor and disappeared down the stairs.

Denton opened the hatch and put his face to it. Mostly, he saw the back of Guillam's black overcoat. It moved; Guillam was advancing into the room and taking the coat off at the same time. Over his right shoulder, he could see Walter Snokes, who wasn't looking at Guillam but was saying, 'You're not supposed to be in here. No one is allowed in here.'

'I'm a policeman.'

'Policemen wear blue uniforms and blue helmets and are called coppers or bobbies. They used to be called peelers.'

'I'm a detective. I don't wear a uniform.'

The Backward Boy

Walter turned his back and disappeared into the 'grotto', but he was standing in there this time, not curling up on the floor. Guillam's back seemed to have no reaction, but it suddenly sank lower. Denton had to stand very straight so that he could look downwards to where Guillam was now sitting on the floor. Guillam reached for his overcoat and took a rubber roller and a small bottle from a pocket, from another a shiny sheet of metal. From an inside breast pocket, he took folded papers.

The curtains of the grotto stirred.

Whistling softly, Guillam uncorked the bottle and shook a few drops of black ink on the shiny metal. He began to roll the ink out on the metal surface, pushing it in different directions to coat the entire plate.

Walter's face appeared between the curtains.

Guillam opened the folded papers and laid them out in a row on the floor. Denton could see that they were blank finger-print forms. Guillam lined them up with what seemed to be great care, making sure that their sides were aligned and that their tops were all exactly even.

Walter stepped out of the grotto, no longer watching Guillam. He made a sound, a kind of cicada-like hum. As it grew louder, he raised his arms, then lowered them, raised and lowered, raised and lowered, faster and faster, as if he were trying to fly.

Guillam's back rose up to block Denton's view. The cloth of the suit moved, up and down, up and down: Guillam was imitating the boy. Walter's hum got louder and the arms got faster; so did Guillam's. Walter darted to one side of the room, then reappeared on Guillam's other side. The hum turned to laughter. The boy seemed manic. Denton thought he would run into a wall, hurt himself. Abruptly, he screamed with what sounded like delight and threw himself down, slapping the floor and howling his laughter, his arms no longer flapping but his heels kicking and his torso now twisting from side to side.

Slowly, he fell quiet.

Guillam's back fell out of sight, and again Denton had to try to look sharply downwards. Guillam put his right index finger on the inked metal plate, then looked at the inky fingertip, and, again aligning the pages perfectly, left his dark fingerprint in the precise centre of a square on the first page. He took a magnifying glass from his right suit pocket and examined his fingerprint.

Then he did his thumb. And then the third, fourth, and fifth fingers of his right hand. He started on the left.

Walter Snokes pulled himself up and crossed the room, came back a few seconds later with a sheet of music paper. He squatted facing Guillam and watched him as he inked two more fingers and left his fingerprints on the form. Then, as Guillam reached towards the plate to ink the fourth finger of his left hand, Walter pushed the hand away and put his own thumb on the inked plate. He was as careful, as almost ritualistic, as Guillam had been. He placed his thumb precisely on the lines of the music staff and made his mark.

Guillam laid the magnifying glass next to the inked plate.

Walter snatched up the glass and examined his own thumb print. Then he bent over Guillam's fingerprints. He was what seemed to Denton a very long time at it. When he put the magnifier down, he put it in exactly the place where he had found it.

Guillam put his left fourth finger on the form.

Walter inked his right index finger and put the print on the music staff, rolling the finger from left to right precisely as Guillam had done. He examined the print with the glass.

Guillam and the boy each did another fingerprint. Guillam had now done all ten fingers. Walter had done three.

Guillam cleaned his fingers with something from another bottle and wiped them on a rag he pulled from a pocket.

Walter went on inking and pressing fingers on the music paper until he had done all ten of his fingers.

Guillam was sitting quite still, so far as Denton could see. If he was watching Walter, his head was angled wrong, for he was looking off into a corner. After perhaps a minute, the boy began to fidget. He bounced a little. He looked around, twice glancing up at Denton. He looked at his inky fingers, grabbed Guillam's rag and tried to wipe the ink away. Unable to get it all off, he made an angry sound, a cry of pain; he shook his hands up and down as if they were wet. The cry got louder.

Guillam bent to ink his own fingers all over again. Walter stopped.

Guillam pushed one of the blank fingerprint forms over and aligned it exactly with the boy's music paper, then began to put his own prints on a new sheet. By the time he was doing his second finger, Walter was inking his own again. Three minutes later, a complete set of Walter Snokes's fingerprints had been placed neatly in the middle of the squares on the Metropolitan Police form. Guillam cleaned his fingers and pushed the bottle and the rag towards Walter.

Three minutes later, Guillam was in the corridor with Denton, 'They keep the doors locked, do they?' he said. When Denton nodded, Guillam closed the door, listened to the lock snap, said, 'Cripes.' He started for the stairs, Denton following. 'Where's Tonk likely to be, then?'

'Ground floor in the back, maybe. There's a kitchen.' As they went down the worn wooden stairs, Denton said, 'How did you know how to act with him?'

'My sister has one like that. Not as bad, but he does the arm-flapping and like that.' Guillam went down two steps and muttered, 'Poor bastard.'

'Did you get the form with his fingerprints away from him?'

'I switched for a set of mine. Of course I got it.'

They found Tonk in a small room near the kitchen, the room almost bare except for an ancient secretary and a chair. One of the lower drawers was pulled out. Papers bulged from it. Tonk, bent over it from the chair, looked up when they came in but didn't stand.

'Got that licence?' Guillam said. Tonk handed up some papers. Guillam looked at them; Denton, looking over his back, saw what seemed like several copies of the same form. *Licensing of Rooming Houses, Boarding Houses, Doss Houses*...Guillam said, 'The most recent one is four years out of date, and this isn't a rooming house. Where's the current one?'

'Maybe the lawyer has it.'

'Who's that?'

'The owner deals with him. I just keep things running here.'

'Who's the owner?'

'Mrs Truelove. In Deauville.'

'France?'

'Yah, France. She lives in France.'

Guillam looked at him with what seemed to be disgust. Still, his voice was surprisingly mild. 'Write it down for me— name and address, the lawyer's name and address. Now, look, Tonk—you're the man on the spot. I'll have an inspector out here in the morning. You know what the violations are here—I'd start with the locked doors and no fire ladders. Sanitation isn't up to standard, either. It looks to me like there's no dental care and probably no medical, either, am I right?'

'The relatives have to carry their weight on them things. This isn't a hospital.'

'No, and I won't tell you what I think it is. Look, Tonk, if there's no owner and no lawyer handy, you're going to be the man of the hour. Now, maybe I could help you, maybe I couldn't. Anything else you want to tell me about young Walter Snokes? Or his family?'

'This about some woman was murdered?'

'You know it is.'

'I don't know nothing! I'm as locked in here as the loonies are! You think I'm gadding about, visiting the lending liberry and reading the Acts of Parliament? I get one day off in a month; otherwise I'm on call here day and night, night and day. If some woman's murdered someplace, what's it to me?'

'I need information, Tonk. I'll take your word for it you've been clean. Still, with your past, it'll be hard if you're the one this comes down on.'

'I know what it'll be. What you want to know?'

'The Snokeses. How long has he been here?'

Tonk had to look in a ledger. 'Near four years.'

'Ever any trouble?'

'They're all trouble if you don't know to manage them. He's no worse nor better.'

'Is he ever violent?'

'You mean, does he threaten life and limb? No, because I don't let him. Could he? Yes, because he don't understand how to behave. If you teach him how to behave, then he's all right.'

'He ever go out?'

'From here? How would he? Have to be watched every minute—you think I or Malkin is going traipsing about the town, watching him? Not a hope.'

Guillam was making notes. 'Malkin. He here? Well, when will he be here?' Tonk said that Malkin got in food from the markets. 'Well, you tell him to stay here; I want to talk to him. He an old lag, too? Well, I'll find that out.' He closed his notebook. 'All right, the Snokes boy—I thought he goes out with his mother.'

'And so he does. At least two days a week, she comes and takes him away. All right, you want information, well, she rents a room; she takes him there. He comes back shaved and bathed. He often smells of chocolates.' He looked down at the bulging drawer, then up at Guillam, then at Denton. 'I'm trying to give information, here, Detective. I'm being helpful, am I right? At the same time, I don't want to be up for libel. I mean, if I say something that isn't exactly fact...'

'This is confidential. Police business. If you suspect something that seems to you to be important, you tell me.'

'And it comes out in court and then she sues me?'

'Tonk, what is it you've got?'

Tonk's upper teeth chewed on the right side of his lower lip. Denton heard the teeth scraping over his stubble. Tonk said, 'I think he gets off some way while he's out with her. I can't prove it. It's just a look he has. Satisfied, like. And things he's said to me. Like it was something he'd learned. He's started saying, "I want a Sally, I want a Sally."'

Denton remembered Walter's saying something about getting a sally. He said, 'Walter said something like that when

I was with him. But I thought he meant a sally, you know, like going out. But you think—a woman named Sally?'

Tonk was nodding. 'He's had a woman. I'm sure he's had a woman. I can't prove it, though.'

'You saying, Tonk, that his mother provides him with a woman?'

'Well, who else? Not his da, his da's out of it; it's like he don't exist. His mother's the one does everything. She pays his bill. She'd do anything for him, is my sense of it. She's like one of them wild jungle animals, protecting her kid. Cub, whatever you call it.'

'Sally—you heard the name Sally?'

'I heard him say Sally, but this gentleman thinks it's something else, what the hell do I know?' Tonk jumped up and paced around the room. 'Crikey, you got me all nerved up now. I can't say things about them and then have that woman come after me about the libel law! She'd do anything, that woman!'

'It won't go any farther. Sit down and think. Is there anything else? The father never visits him. How about his sister? No? Never? Only the mother, then. Anything else? She takes him away for how long, a couple of hours? Three? Anybody ever say they saw them out and about, getting on an omnibus, in one of the shops? No? So your notion is she takes him off to a room and shaves him and bathes him and maybe brings in a woman for him. Yes?'

'It's only what I'm guessing at.'

'All right. You did fine. Anything else? Anything at all? Now's the time to tell me, Tonk. Sweeten the porridge while you can.'

Tonk was shaking his head. He fell back into his chair and rested his forehead on a hand. 'This makes me right sick.'

'I told you, it's confidential. Mr Denton can be trusted. You go on doing your job and you'll be all right. Right? We'll see ourselves out. You might check the lock on the Snokes boy's door—I pulled it to, but you'd best check.' Guillam gave him a card. 'You think of anything else, you tell me. At once. Got a telephone here? No? Find one, or send a telegram. Calm down, Tonk. It'll be all right. And tell that Malkin to stay close.'

In the car, pulling his overcoat under his thighs, Guillam growled, 'Bloody scandal, keeping people like that. Poor bastards.' He pointed to the north. 'We want to go back to Peckham Road. The police station.' Denton looked at him. Guillam glanced back, sank down as far as the little car would allow. 'I want to ask them about a prostitute named Sally. It'll give the local coppers a laugh, anyway.'

Rosamund Gearing had stopped identifying herself on the telephone, Atkins said. Now, the line was silent and then she hung up. 'Of course it's her!' He'd had twenty-three calls during the day and had followed through on his threat to call the operator. They would 'look into the matter'.

Denton was dressing to go to dinner with Janet when Atkins said that there was a telephone call for him. 'Not her!' Atkins shouted. Denton groaned anyway and ran down the stairs from his bedroom, mostly dressed but coatless and shoeless.

'Denton here!'

'It isn't the boy.'

He recognised Guillam's voice only slowly; he was already saying, 'What? I didn't get that— Oh, Guillam!'

'I compared the boy's fingerprints to the ones from the Wilcox woman's floor. It isn't him.'

Denton felt an illogical relief. 'He's off the hook, then.'

'I don't know what he is. That bloody fool Masefield is in court the next three days on other cases and he hasn't done tuppence-worth on the mother. Jawed with the dominie and learned she was in the church kitchen the night the Adger woman was killed, no time, no idea when she left. Didn't interview another frigging person and apparently the church kitchen was as crowded as a tart's knickers. Now I've got to do his work for him.'

'What about the boy? I think he could still be significant.'

'Think what you like.' That was that.

Denton put the receiver on its hook and was staring at the wall when the telephone rang again, making him jump. Afraid it was Rosamund Gearing, he lifted the receiver but said nothing.

'Hello? Hello! Is anybody there?' It was Munro. 'You drunk, Atkins?'

'I thought it was Guillam.'

'Aha, Denton. Called you, did he? Called me, too. That's why I'm calling you. He told me his tale of this place where the lad is, the fingerprints. I just want your penny-worth: can we write the lad off now?'

'I still think he's important somehow. I don't know how.'

'Guillam said the boy's ma might've got him a tart.'

'Is she a suspect now?'

'I've told Guillam to go ahead and take her fingerprints; I can't pussyfoot about any longer.'

'Maybe we ought to talk.'

'They don't give me time to talk, much less think. Tomorrow I'm supposed to shepherd a herd of Dagos through Scotland Yard, and I'm expected to run this investigation up there. But yes, I'd like to talk—clear the cobwebs, maybe. How're you sevenish tomorrow morning?'

'I'll be working, but I'll give you an hour.'

Munro grunted, said he'd be at Denton's front door at seven, and the connection clicked and popped and that was that.

CHAPTER 16

The early morning was still dark, but he was at his desk and damning himself for letting Munro come to interrupt him. The novel was still racing on, almost too fast for him: he was afraid the writing would prove to be bad or it would all fall apart. But he pressed on.

He got up as the first silvery light silhouetted Janet's house against the sky, took a turn to stretch his back, then trotted downstairs and made coffee on his spirit stove. Atkins was making noises below—bumps and the odd word to the dog—but Denton knew better than to bother him this early. He carried his coffee up and sat to work again, then, when the cup was half empty, leaned back and ran his hand over his face and told himself he must remember to shave before he went out. The sky was light now, still clouded but bright as a polished platter. He stood at the window, craned his neck to look up: would it rain? He looked to Janet's house for lights: none. He looked down into his back garden. There was Rupert, squatting; as Denton watched, he stood up, made a desultory backward scrape with a paw and began to sniff along the base of the brick wall. Raising his nose, he sampled the air, rotated his head, suddenly trotted away to the right. Denton had to press the left side of his face to the glass to follow. Rupert was eating something. He gulped it, gobbled, gulped some more. *What was it?*

The dog turned and started back towards the wall, then, halfway across the garden, lurched. His head went down; one side was on the ground. Denton thought he was going to do one of those doggy slides along the grass, scratching his head and neck. Then the entire dog was down. As Denton watched, the head came up, the front shoulders, then sank again to the grass; the back arched slowly; the legs seemed straight out, rigid. The front legs began to pump.

'Atkins!' Denton was leaping down his stairs. 'Atkins—it's Rupert—the garden—'

'Oh, cripes, he ain't under the wall again!'

'He's having a fit!'

Denton burst through Atkins's sitting-room, Atkins still sitting there with a cup, a napless velvet dressing gown wrapped around him. He was frozen.

'The *dog*! He's having a fit!'

When Denton got into the garden, Rupert was still lying on his side, his back bent into a crescent. His legs were straight out again. Body and legs quivered. Urine ran from him.

'Oh, Judas!' Atkins said behind him. 'Oh, Rupert!'

'Don't touch him.'

'What'll I do? What'll I do?'

Rupert's head came off the ground, swung up and down, and he tried to push himself up on his front legs. A terrible sound came from his throat, the loud groan of pain and near-death. He raised himself higher, tried to get his back legs under him, and vomited a pile of bright-red meat and a puddle of yellow liquid on the grass. He fell back; the noise came again; he vomited more, lying on his side. He choked and went into another rigid spasm.

'He's been poisoned,' Denton said.

'Oh, crikey!'

'Run to the horse barns where I keep the car. Get somebody.'

'That's horses!'

'They'll know what to do. Atkins, go! And ask them to send for a veterinary surgeon! And bring them back in the car!'

Atkins stopped at the door. He was pulling off the robe. 'You don't think—it ain't the missus? Because of Sophie—'

'Go, man! For God's sake! And get a policeman!'

Denton knelt by the dog. Rupert's breath was coming now in hoarse groans, the same terrible sound but muted. Denton put a hand on him; there was no response. Rupert's side heaved up and down. His back bent again into a bow and his legs got rigid. Denton found he was saying, 'It's all right, boy, it's all right, you'll be all right...' A police whistle sounded, seeming distant— Atkins at the front gate.

Time stretched. Atkins seemed to have been gone for hours. Denton stroked the dog's head, walked to where he had seen him eat, found nothing because Rupert had wolfed it all down. He walked back, saw the dog now barely breathing, legs limp. He got control of his thoughts, began to study what was happening, went into the kitchen and got a metal pan, then saw an empty glass jar and took that instead. Back in the garden, he scooped the vomited-up meat and fluid into the jar, then washed his hands and covered the jar with a rag.

A constable appeared, not the one who had been there a few days before; this one was younger, a bit officious. He walked about, taking notes and measuring things with long paces; Denton had no idea what he thought he was about. Saying he would send the sergeant, the man left.

Still Atkins had not come.

Denton knelt by the inert black body. He stroked it, felt no life, thought Rupert was dead until another spasm started and the back arched and the legs pumped and another attempt to vomit produced only slime.

'Here, here...' He heard Atkins's voice as he came through the house. 'Back here...'

'I'm here!' Denton shouted uselessly.

"How is he? Is he—'

'He's alive; he's breathing.'

'Where is he, now?' A large man in a bowler and what looked like a duster, no necktie, strode past Denton and made for the dog. He was carrying a valise of peeling leather and some brass contraption that looked like a syringe the size of a cricket bat. 'There he is. Well, now. Poison, well, nasty stuff. We don't know *which* poison, do we?' The man knelt by the dog's head. He looked up at Denton, his eyes sharp, very dark, his black moustache like an ink stroke on a chalky face. 'Went into convulsions, did he? Stiff as a board? Had the heaves, your friend said. Tossed it all, I hope. Pissed himself. Bowels moved, too, I see. Well, we'll make sure he got rid of it all.' He put the oversized syringe down and opened the valise. 'Water.' He looked at Atkins. 'Water!'

'A glass? More?'

'A bleeding bucket! What good'd a glass do? I ain't going to drink it to cool my thirst!' He looked up at Denton again. 'He the animal's owner?' When Denton nodded, he said, 'Nervous type.'

Atkins came from the back door, tilted by the weight of a slop-pail full of water.

'That's the ticket. Now we're moving. Now, doggy, just you lie there.' He upended a pint bottle over the pail, the glass bright blue and winking in the morning light. Denton looked into the bucket: the water was now a transparent green.

'You're a veterinary surgeon?'

The man laughed. 'I'm a groom. Never you mind. I know what I'm about.' He nodded at Atkins. 'Surgeon's been sent for.' He picked up the syringe, started to flourish it over the bucket, said, 'My name's Alf Nevercot.' He plunged the end of the huge syringe into the bucket and pulled on a handle at the other end. The level of the liquid in the pail went down until half of it was inside the brass cylinder. Alf Nevercot raised the end out of the coloured water and held it up rather as the Statue of Liberty in New York held up its torch. He burrowed in the satchel with his free hand and brought out a flexible rubber hose, brass fittings on each end.

'Now, then, if you'll just open the doggy's mouth.'

Atkins looked panicked. 'What're you going to do?'

'Going to give him a drench, ain't I? Open his mouth. And take care, for if he goes into another fit, that mouth'll close like it's on steel springs. Get it open, now—open, man, for Judas Priest sake!'

Atkins was trying not to hurt his dog. Denton, not so involved and with a lifetime with horses behind him, bent, nudged Atkins out of the way with a hip and a thigh, and put the fingers of his two hands along the edges of Rupert's front teeth and prised the jaws apart.

'Now, then,' Alf said, 'don't let go.' He put the brass-clad end of the rubber hose into the opened jaws. 'Steady, now—hold him still...'

He was pushing the hose down Rupert's throat. Atkins made a sound. Alf clenched his jaw and bore down. 'The trick is to get it into the food tube and not the lungs...' He peered along the hose as if he were sighting a gun. 'Smallest tube I could find—made for calves and colts—not so much bigger than this creature...'

Rupert made the horrible sound. Atkins yelped. Denton said, 'Do it.' Half of the tube had disappeared. Alf pushed, and several inches more went the same way.

'I think we're there,' he murmured. He pushed on the handle of the syringe. Green water dribbled, than bubbled from Rupert's mouth. Atkins said, 'No, no,' and Alf told him to shut it. Alf pushed the handle farther; more green water bubbled out. Rupert tried to get on his feet.

'There we are!' Alf cried. 'Out comes the tube—hold on, now, they never like this part...'

He drew the hose to him, along with more green water and what looked like blood. Atkins groaned. Alf nodded at Denton, who let go of the jaws, and Rupert clawed halfway up, his back legs now splayed on the ground and pointing behind him, and began to vomit green water. Huge quantities of it. More, Denton thought, than could possibly have gone down his throat.

'What is that stuff?'

'Foster's Emetika. Sovereign remedy. Remarkable what horses and cattle get into. And sheep! Lord help us, too stupid to live, mostly; they'd eat rat poison and ask for more. There, see—he's sicked it all up for now. Good chap! Let's get the rest down him.'

Atkins said that was enough, but Alf insisted, pointing out that he was the only one there who knew what he was doing. Denton got the mouth open again; the hose went down; more vomiting followed, then convulsions and another period of rigidity. When it was over, and Alf had packed up his satchel, he said, 'It may be I was called too late. I done what I knew to do.'

Atkins was cradling Rupert's head. Alf looked at him and then at Denton. Denton was slow to get it, finally did, said, 'What do we owe you?'

'Whatever you think is right, guv. Bearing in mind that I done my best, and if I was too late, it wasn't my fault.'

Denton ran up the stairs and fetched money, handed over too much. That it was far too much was clear when Alf grinned and said it was a lovely way to start the day. And no, he wouldn't take a ride in that motorcar again; he'd walk. Denton saw him to the door and noted that the Barré was up on the kerb in front, sticking out into the street at the back.

'We need to move the car,' he said when he reached the garden.

'He's dying.'

'We don't know that.'

'He doesn't know me. He'd know me if he wasn't…' Atkins teared up and couldn't speak. When he had pressed his lips tightly together and shaken his head and looked away, he said, 'It wasn't the missus did it, was it? She doesn't hate him that much, does she?'

'No, it wasn't the missus. You know it wasn't.'

Atkins nodded. 'I just…It was my first thought. She's better than that, isn't she?'

Twenty minutes later, Denton heard the front bell and went to the door to find a tough-looking little man in a dark blue frock coat who said he was the veterinary surgeon. He looked Rupert over, studied his gums, studied his eyes, used a stethoscope, and said, 'It's nip and tuck. The groom did pretty much the right thing. I'd have used something gentler, but the effect is the same. You say he ate and voided at once; that tells me the meat was poisoned, and poisoned very strongly. It's nip and tuck.' He stood. 'I'll give you something for him, but he's going to go on having those convulsions; if he survives, he may always have them, less and less often as time passes.' He looked off over Denton's left shoulder, his eyebrows rising. Denton turned his head. Munro was coming from the house.

'I walked in,' Munro said. 'Front door's wide open.' He nodded at the veterinary surgeon, looked at Atkins and the dog. 'What's that about poison?'

'The dog.'

'As I was saying,' the veterinary surgeon said, self-importance surging through the words. 'You kept a sample of what the animal ingested? I'll have it tested, then I'll prescribe. If it's arsenic, as I think...' He shook his head. 'Give him two of these every hour for four hours, then one every two hours. I'll come back tomorrow, shall I? That'll be six shillings for the house call and eightpence for the medicine.'

'He thinks Rupert's going to die,' Atkins said as Denton came back into the garden from steering the vet to the front door.

'He said "nip and tuck".'

Munro was writing in his black notebook. 'Poisoning is serious business.'

'Not Yard business, is it? A dog?'

'In meat?' Munro was looking around the garden. 'Thrown over the wall? That'd be her house, not likely. You having trouble with the neighbours? No? Then...' He pointed at the narrow gate that led along the side of the house to the front. 'Leads to the street, that does?'

'It's latched on this side.'

Munro grunted and went to the gate. He looked up, looked at the gate, unlatched it and went out.

Atkins said, 'Maybe we should take him inside?'

'I don't think we could get him inside, could we? Maybe if we put him on something, drag him…'

'I just hate to leave him out here—it might rain…'

'Atkins, we'll get the person who did this.'

'I'd rather have my dog.'

With that, Munro came back, a different uniformed policeman behind him. He latched the gate and walked towards them carrying a piece of brown butcher paper by a corner. 'I need something to put this in. Fingerprints. Get fingerprints from anything now. Five years ago we hadn't heard of them. This is Sergeant Gunn.' He looked down at Atkins and Rupert. 'Let's get the poor beast inside.' Munro put his hat on the ground, crown down, and put the butcher paper in it, then gestured the sergeant over, and both bent and put their hands under the dog and with a grunt lifted him in their arms. 'He's a big 'un, I must say. Open the bloody door, will you?'

Settled in Denton's sitting-room fifteen minutes later, Munro said, 'That horse-doctor sure it's poison?'

'He said it was. I'll have it analysed at a chemist's, too.'

Munro shook his head. 'We'll do that. It's in my notebook, so it's police business now. "Never erase, never cross out." Once it's in the book, it's police business.' He frowned at Denton. 'I told the sergeant I'd take your statement, and so I will. Any idea who did it?' He poised his pencil above his notebook.

'We were going to talk about Mrs Snokes.'

'Anybody who'll poison an animal will poison a man. Answer my question.'

'Yes.'

'Atkins says he doesn't know; you say you do. It's Atkins's dog, isn't it?'

'I think the person thinks it's mine.'

'Somebody taken against you? Another admirer gone off his nut?'

'A woman, I think "scorned".'

Munro didn't seem as surprised as Denton thought he should. 'Poison's a woman's weapon, more often than not. Which is not to say they won't use knives, guns, clubs or anything they can lay their hands on. I'll want her name and particulars.'

'I thought I'd see my lawyer and get some advice about how to handle it.'

'I told you, it's a police matter now. You say "scorned". This going to make you trouble with the lady?' He bobbed his head towards Janet's house.

'No, no, not that. But...she's attached to one of the Oxford women's colleges. An Old Student.'

'You know she did it for a fact?'

'Not yet I don't. I'm going to hire a private investigator. You know Doty?'

'Doty's the best—almost as good as we are. Well, it'll take leg work. Here and in Oxford. She's done other things to bedevil you?'

Denton was acutely embarrassed. 'I suppose you'd say she's been bothering me, more or less.'

'Ever report her?'

'The beat constable came when she tried to push past Atkins at the door. He put it in his notebook and warned her.' He remembered Maltby. 'There's also a probationer—Maltby, the one who got shot helping me—he's been in our street off and on, I think looking for her. He might have seen something. Y Division.'

'All right, what's her name?'

'Munro, let it lie for a bit...'

Munro was tapping his notebook and shaking his head. 'The name.'

'If I'm wrong, I'll have got a young woman in trouble and maybe hurt her future. And other women's, as well. Maybe you don't care about that. Because of Mrs Striker, I do.'

Munro looked slightly contemptuous. 'I'll get it from the constable if I don't get it from you.'

'Munro! Dammit!' He told him about Ivor Hench-Rose's visit but didn't use the young man's name. 'It isn't just the woman, Munro. Let me handle it myself!'

Munro looked him in the eyes, pushed out his lips in thought, then shook his head quickly. 'If it wasn't poison, I might go slower. Hire Doty if you want. You might want to bring a civil action; what he finds would be useful. But don't be so bloody squeamish because she's an Oxford girl and the boy thinks he'll look better in grey pants than brown. What's her name?'

'By God, you'll make me angry, Munro!'

'And you'll get over it. Name?'

Denton told him. Munro nodded as if it was exactly as he had expected. 'Stop by Bow Street before this evening to sign the statement. It's their division. You remember Markson, don't'you? I'll try to get him to take it.' He put the notebook away in an inner coat pocket. 'Now—what about the Snokes woman?'

'You're relentless.'

'And busy. Give me some help in how to handle Mrs Snokes. What's she like?'

'Like what you'd expect. Proper, conventional, stolid. Mrs England.'

'Not so proper if she brought in a tart for her son. And not so conventional if she's murdered two other women.'

Denton let his anger subside. 'You believe she did it?'

'I don't believe anything until I have the proof. But if Masefield hadn't bollocksed this so completely, we'd know by now. Masefield isn't a bad tec when he's in his speciality, which is getting information and chatting up his narks. He's a demon on local crime—burglaries, assaults, gang tussles. Got a load of commendations. But he was miles out of what he's good at when it came to the first murder, and his chief should have known that and taken it away from him. As it is, he's wasted the very time—the first twenty-four hours after a crime—when a good tec figures to collect the evidence and make an arrest. Now I'm stuck with it.'

'Why the interest in Mrs Snokes now?'

'Because we've got nothing else. Masefield had some notion about a Jew—or was it a gypsy?—seen skulking around; that's come to nothing but a lot of false sightings to take up his time. On the Adger killing, it's just as bad. The blood on the building was hers, of course, but we expected that. The footprints they made casts of would be useful if we had some feet to compare them with, but we don't. Police surgeon says she was killed with something heavy but a little soft, if that makes any sense. Sounds like a kid's riddle, eh? Well, the answer is some sort of tube filled with sand or shot or something. There were some grains of sand in the woman's hair. Didn't match the soil in the Artillery Ground. So it was some sort of cosh, maybe leather, but probably cloth if some of the grains leaked out. Not Snokes's weapon of choice, I'd guess, nor his missus, either.'

'Professional.'

'That's the thinking. Bloody Masefield's giving testimony at the Old Bailey today and the next two days, maybe; when he's out, I'm going to have him quizzing his stags to see if somebody's gone on the run or boasted of killing a woman.'

'And no handbag.'

'The purse. Could have had so little in it, somebody killed her and then left it. Or whacked her, took the purse, got so mad when he saw how little was in it, he killed her.'

'You canvassed Adger's street?' Munro's expression of disgust told him that of course they had. 'Anything?'

Munro stared into the dying grate. 'Keep this to yourself. One woman who's lived there a while says she knows Snokes. She says she's seen him there *recently*.' He looked up at Denton. 'She thinks maybe—*maybe*—she saw him the night that the first woman was killed.'

It took Denton a few seconds. 'When Mrs Snokes says she was with her husband?'

Munro nodded. 'Makes you wonder.'

'You mean—if she alibied him, she also alibied herself. And if she lied...'

Munro nodded gloomily, as if the capacity of human beings for mischief was beyond him.

'But why would he let her? Ah, if he was with Mrs Adger...
But Mrs Snokes would have to know he'd let her tell the lie.
Wouldn't she have to know where he was, in that case? And that
he'd want to hide it?'

Munro stretched far out to get the poker, then gave the
almost dead coals a rattle. 'If she was going off to kill the Wilcox
woman, she'd for damned sure want to know her husband was
set for a while. If she knew he was tucked in with the Adger
woman, that would do it, wouldn't it?'

'It'd mean that Snokes was poking both women, and that
he went straight from Mrs Adger to Mrs Wilcox, because that's
when he found the body.'

Munro put the poker back and then stood in front of the
fire, trying to warm his backside. 'It doesn't hang together real
well. The Wilcox woman had had sex. It wasn't likely with
Snokes, not that night—whatever he is, he doesn't poke corpses.
So it would have to mean she was having it on with somebody
else. I find it hard to believe that that many in the middle class
are carrying on two affairs at a time. So we're back to rape and
murder, and we're barking up the wrong bloody tree. We're in
the wrong bloody *forest*!' He rubbed his buttocks, shivered. 'I'll
have Mrs Snokes brought in today for fingerprints and a talk. It
can't just be coincidence...'

'It could.'

Munro stared at him as if he'd broken wind. 'I have to go.
Sorry about that dog.'

When he was gone, Denton went downstairs; Atkins was
sitting on the floor next to Rupert. He shook his head when he
saw Denton. 'No change. He had another fit.'

Denton went up to his bedroom. Writing did not begin
again easily. Emotion could become a wall between him and the
writing. Still, he thought he should be able to sit down and go at it.

He couldn't.

He went through the gardens to Janet's and told her what had
happened. Within minutes, she and both Cohans were in Atkins's
sitting-room; minutes later, Mrs Cohan was making tea and then

running back and forth between her kitchen and Denton's with food. Janet sat with Atkins, smoothing the rough hair of Rupert's head, telling them both that he would be all right. Privately, she said to Denton, 'I told you that girl would be dangerous.'

'If she did it.'

'Don't be a fool. You are going after her, aren't you?'

'Munro's doing it.'

'Don't leave it to the police! Go after her!'

Denton made himself more coffee and drank it while he dressed. The work day was ruined. He would go off and see his lawyer, hire Doty, get an investigation started. Then, maybe this afternoon he could write a few pages. And forget the Snokes business, just get out of it, tell Munro and Guillam—

The telephone rang. He trotted down the stairs, braces dangling, no boots. If it was that bloody damned Gearing woman…

'Denton here!'

'It's Guillam. Tonk's turned all his loonies out. He's flown the coop.'

'Out of The Oaks?'

'One of the coppers I talked to at Peckham Road yesterday gave me a shout. Somebody saw the loonies wandering about and went after the beat constable to do something. One of them was out in Bushey Hill Road. Nearly got killed, they said, but who knows? The constable went up there and apparently found three or four of them standing about. Front door open, no Tonk, more of the inmates in the corridors. Every door open, so far as he could tell. Peckham Road've sent a crew.'

'The Snokes boy?'

'No idea. He could still be in his room, or—he could be anywhere.' Guillam gave Denton time to say something, then went on. 'You want to drive down there again?'

Two minutes before, Denton would have thought it was the last thing he wanted to do. 'Meet me at the garage? I have to get dressed.'

'Fifteen minutes.'

Denton tried calling Munro, but he was 'out'. Probably hosting his 'herd of Dagos' to tea and cakes.

The Oaks rose on its slope above Bushey Hill Road like an animal looking for prey. Seeing it, Guillam muttered, 'Thank God he didn't put a match to it.' He already had his warrant card out when they reached the decrepit gate; the uniform there waved them through. Figures seemed to be scattered all over the scruffy grounds within the old wall—a few uniforms, two women whom Denton took to be relatives of inmates, probably from somewhere close by, and a few civilian males who might have been inmates or relatives. Guillam looked at them and said, 'They all look ordinary enough. There's one over there got an Oriental look, I suppose he's one of them. Otherwise, you can't tell if they're a loony or a journalist, can you?' In fact, three journalists were being held back at the gate by the constables.

Denton stopped the car and looked around more carefully. One figure was curled in the grass below them. Another was standing still, hands at sides, looking towards the north as if he had turned to stone. Down the slope, an elderly woman was looking at him and weeping.

'Come on.' Guillam gave Denton a push towards the front door, where another constable stood.

'Can't go in, I'm sorry, sir.' Guillam held up his card. 'Right, very sorry, sir…'

The lower hall was empty. Guillam turned back to say to the constable, 'Anybody inside?'

'Not so far as we know, sir. Couple of our chaps going room by room. My sergeant's at the back if you want to talk to him.'

Guillam grunted and went up the stairs. Denton, coming behind him, thought how familiar it was becoming: the smell was the same, the shabbiness of everything. It was quieter, however, the muffled voices now silent.

The Backward Boy

Guillam was heading for Walter Snokes's room, he thought. Nonetheless, on the second floor they detoured down the central corridor towards two dark figures silhouetted against a window, recognisably constables by their helmets despite the blasting effect of the light behind them. Guillam showed his card and said, 'What's the situation?'

'Just writing some notes, sir. Been up and down, opened every door. There's three of them still in rooms they won't come out of. You'd think they would, being locked up in this place, but they won't. It's home to the poor devils, I suppose.'

'Any trouble?'

'Nice as lambs. Won't speak. Must be hungry. I believe the woman that cooks is out there somewhere or was; she made a ram-sammy when we wouldn't let her in. Said she had to cook.'

'There's a man ran the place—Tonk.'

'They're looking into that, sir. We're waiting for the inspector to sort things out.'

Denton said, 'There was another man supposed to work here, too. I can't remember his name.'

'Malkin,' Guillam said.

'I'll make a note of that. It's a right tangle.'

Guillam led him away and up more stairs, then along to Walter Snokes's room. The door was open wide. Guillam looked in the 'grotto', found nobody, then stood in the middle of the room and turned in a slow circle. Denton went to the desk. Blank music paper lay there but no completed or even half-finished drawings, and no pencils or watercolours. 'I think he took his drawing stuff.'

'I thought he was afraid of the outside. Other people.'

Denton thought that a book was missing from the shelf but couldn't remember which book it would be. The clothes in the minuscule chest of drawers seemed to fill it without gaps. The chamber pot was partly full of urine and two large masses. He said, 'I don't remember seeing an overcoat. But it's going to be a warm day.'

Going back down, Guillam looked into every room. They found the three residents who wouldn't come out. Two never looked at them; one did, however, his mongoloid face in a perpetual smile, but he made no move to come with them. Guillam held out his hand, and the boy—boy or man, Denton couldn't tell—toddled forward and took Guillam's hand and allowed himself to be led downstairs. At the door, Guillam turned him over to a constable. 'Don't let go of him. You understand me? He's your responsibility now. Tell your sergeant. This one's not competent to be left by himself.'

He pushed Denton back inside and searched the rooms at the back, from the little room where they had talked with Tonk to the kitchen and the pantry and the space where Tonk had got the drawings from the dustbin. A door that might have led to the cellar was locked. Going back towards the front, Guillam stepped into the room with the desk and pulled out the drawers. They were still stuffed with papers.

They went around to the back, where a kind of command centre had been set up under a shed roof. A sergeant and a constable were taking names and making notes, and in what had once been a wire-fenced garden, two policemen were trying to control five former residents of The Oaks, the reminder of the recent South African concentration camps perhaps inescapable. Denton was surprised by the ages of the former inmates: one looked to be in his fifties, another far older and, he thought, perhaps senile rather than like Walter or the others. Another, his back to Denton, was flapping his arms as Walter had done. Guillam watched but made no move, this time, to imitate him.

'Well?' Denton said.

'I feel responsible for them. You'll say that's bollocks. I pushed Tonk too hard, and look what's happened.' Guillam's pocked, hard face was bleak. 'I didn't think he'd be such a fool.' He sighed. 'I never learn.'

They walked around to the front and moved from person to person, asking about Walter Snokes. Another uniform was trying to interview the few outsiders who seemed to be relatives.

A stout man in civilian clothes came up the slope with a good deal of authority. A constable saluted him. Guillam placed himself in the man's path and presented his warrant card. 'Detective Sergeant Guillam, sir, G Division. We've an investigation that may involve one of the residents.'

'Hm. I'm Superintendent Wilfley, Camberwell. Don't I know you from the Yard?'

'I used to be at Central, yes, sir.'

'Bad thing, this. Reflects badly all round. What're you doing in my division?'

'One of the patients, sir—a case jointly in G and N.'

Wilfley looked displeased. 'Remember you're not on your home ground. And be careful—I don't want this blown all out of proportion in the press.'

'I don't speak with the press, sir.'

'Good man.' He looked at Denton. 'And you are...'

'Denton.' He put out his hand. 'I ran Detective Sergeant Guillam down here in my car. I'm familiar with the family of the, mm, patient he was investigating.'

Wilfley appeared to have a totally bald head; certainly, his black bowler revealed no hair below its brim but sat high on his bare skull as if too small for him. He had somewhat made up for the lack of hair with moustache and eyebrows, which he now aimed at Denton as if they were siege batteries. 'You understand about the press?'

'Of course. Absolutely.'

Guillam said, almost *sotto voce*, 'Mr Denton's a friend of Detective Inspector Munro's. The Saterlee case? And the hermorphadite that killed the painter—Hinkle, was it?'

'Himple,' Denton said.

Wilfley aimed the batteries at Denton again, then tilted his face so they would fire over Denton's head. 'You're not a policeman.' He braced his shoulders. 'So long as you understand about the press.' He turned on Guillam. 'The first thing to be done here is to restore order. The second is to sort out the inmates and find temporary berths for them. I don't want any interference with those tasks, is that understood? You may talk to the chap you're interested in, or whatever you *need* to do, but I won't have you using my people or taking up their time. Make your inquiries within those limits. Is your chap here?'

Guillam explained that they'd been inside and searched the rooms but hadn't found him.

'I'll have a proper sweep done when I have enough men. Until then, the building's closed. Could be he's hiding in the cellar or places we don't know about. There are some outbuildings, I understand. If you find him, turn him over to my people at once. I don't issue threats, Sergeant, but I am not happy if my orders are disobeyed.'

'Understood, sir.'

'See that it is.'

'A bit officious,' Denton said when Wilfley was out of earshot.

'He's got his life's dream—divisional super. He doesn't want to lose it.' Guillam was looking down at the large crowd that had gathered at the gate. 'I'm worried about that boy.' He pointed his chin towards the rest of London. 'If he's out there, they'll eat him alive. Come on, let's have a look in those outbuildings.'

Denton followed. It started to rain, first fine drops almost like mist, then a drizzle. They looked into a disused brick privy, then a collapsing garden shed, then a wooden building apparently once intended for a carriage and two horses, now derelict. The remains of yet another, smaller building were behind it, but it had collapsed so far that there was no way into what was left. When they came back by the wire enclosure, the boy who had been flapping his arms was standing with his face turned up into the wet and a joyful grin on his face. 'It's *raining*!' he cried.

Guillam stopped at the open shed where the constables were trying to make sense of it. He said, 'Got the name Snokes?' He held up his card.

One constable looked at a list. 'Inmate? Haven't got it. Want me to add it to the list?'

'Walter Snokes. He's missing.'

'A lot of them are missing. We've got six here now; they tell us there's two more upstairs. It'd help if we knew how many there's supposed to be.'

Denton said, 'Thirteen. Or that's what I was told when I came here last week.'

The constable was dubious about that until Guillam vouched for Denton, and then he said, 'Thirteen, crikey. We're missing five, then.'

'If the number's right,' the other said. 'Have to be confirmed.'

'How many relatives so far?' Guillam said.

'Three.'

'You'd best notify the others.'

'Names, sir. We need the names. Addresses. It's like trying to get a grip on a jelly.'

Denton went to the front again. Fewer people were out there, none recognisable as patients. The superintendent was halfway down the untended lawn, three uncertain-looking people near him probably the relatives. Wilfley was making a sweeping gesture with an arm; below him, along the old wall, two constables were walking slowly, looking back to him for direction.

Guillam came along more slowly, talking with another man in plain clothes, a detective, Denton guessed. Detective Constable Mendoz, as it turned out. 'We're just talking about Walter. He thinks he's located Sally.'

Mendoz, who was young, deferential to Guillam but careful, said, 'I haven't *located* her, sir—identified her is what I said.' He looked at Denton. 'A woman named Sarah Blessing. Not exactly a streetwalker, but, well...'

'Of the sisterhood,' Guillam said. 'I want to talk to her. She may have spent time with Walter in a room his mother rents here somewhere. She can tell us where it is, maybe.' He turned to Denton. 'That's the first place I'd look for him. Mmm? It's probably the only place he knows.'

Denton thought of the buildings in Walter's drawings but didn't mention them, said instead that Guillam's was a good idea. 'His parents should be notified,' he said.

'You want to take that on? You know them.'

Denton looked at his watch, saw that the morning had fled. 'I don't want to. A constable could be sent.' He saw Guillam's disgust. 'Oh, all right. Munro was going to have her in for finger-printing today. She might be at the station now.'

'She might, and she might be in Timbuc-bleeding-too. There's nothing to be done here, not at least by you. I don't have a telephone here; the world isn't full of constables who can go running off to deliver messages; you've got nothing better to do.'

Munro would have gone himself or sent another copper, Denton knew. This was Guillam at his worst, his judgement unhinged. Denton realised that Guillam was truly worried about Walter Snokes. He had a nasty moment of wondering if this was an aspect of Guillam's sexual life, then remembered his taking the hand of the man to lead him out of The Oaks. 'All right, I'll go. If they're out, I'll leave word with the station sergeant at the Angel that somebody should be given the message and the Snokeses should be told. That acceptable?'

Guillam nodded. 'I'll be looking for this Sally.'

'Telephone me if you find her.'

Guillam met his eyes, shrugged, pushed his fists into his overcoat pockets and turned away to mutter with Mendoz.

Denton got in the car, feeling excluded.

CHAPTER
17

Mrs Snokes heard the news of her son's disappearance with what looked like blank incomprehension; then she exploded into outraged questions. What did he mean? Where was Tonk? They couldn't have looked; he'd never have gone out into the streets alone; where were the police?

'The police are there, Mrs Snokes; they're looking.'

'Then he hasn't disappeared! If they're still looking, you don't know that he's disappeared. Why do you worry me with things that aren't true?'

'Mrs Snokes, the doors were left unlocked and the man in charge—Tonk—is gone. Some of the patients were found outdoors. When I left, Walter hadn't been found.'

'Why didn't you come at once? You say it's been hours! How can you have been so inconsiderate?'

'It's a very confused place. They don't have all the names, all the relatives—they're still trying to—'

'I don't care what they're doing! What I care about is Walter! Get out of my house!'

Denton understood the psychology of this; still, he was angry. She would have said the same thing to anybody who brought her such news. He said, 'I thought maybe he'd head for the room that you rented down there.'

'What room? *What room?*'

'Tonk said you had a room where you took Walter. When you visited.'

'Tonk is a liar.'

Denton started to say that Tonk had seemed truthful, but he knew how asinine that would sound. Tonk probably *was* a liar. She seemed absolutely certain. Maybe there was no room.

'What's going on?'

Arthur Snokes was standing in the doorway, tying the sash of a flannel robe. Framed by dark wood on each side, dark sawn work and a green swag overhead, he looked small and sheepish, as if he expected a hiding. He cleared his throat and said, 'What's all this, then?'

'Go back to bed.' His wife headed for him. 'I'm going out.'

'You just got in.' She went past him into the hall. Snokes said to Denton, 'She's been out all morning having her fingerprints taken. What's all that about?'

Denton shook his head.

'You don't know or you won't say? I'm getting fed up with all this. I'm supposed to be sleeping—have to work tonight, like every other night. What're you doing here?'

Denton, still standing in his wet overcoat but with his equally wet hat in his hand, told him about The Oaks.

'Walter's hiding?'

'I don't know where he is. We couldn't find him.'

'He's hiding. In his room somewhere. He wouldn't leave his room.'

'He wasn't there.'

'You don't know him.'

Mrs Snokes appeared behind her husband, a black cape over her dress and a black hat on her head, the total effect deeply unattractive. Snokes said, 'Where are you off to?'

'I'm going to find my boy.'

'I'll come with you.'

'You!' She might as well have spat on him. She looked past him at Denton. 'And you! I don't want to see you in this house ever again. You know where they had me this morning? At a police station, giving my finger-ends! Great dirty smears of black all over my hands; I'm sure it's on my clothes! Well, they'll pay for new ones, I can tell you. I suppose you had something to do with it!'

Snokes was trying to say, 'Now, now—now, Annie...' and she gave him a hard shove and stamped away, and the front door slammed. Snokes looked at Denton and gave a feeble grin.

'I'll be going,' Denton said.

'She doesn't mean half she says. He's the apple of her eye.'

'I understand.' He squeezed through the doorway, chest to chest with Snokes. As he put on his hat in the shadowed, cold hall, he said, 'Might Walter come here?'

Snokes hunched his shoulders as if cold. 'He might. But... this house wasn't...'

'Did his accident happen here?'

'Oh, no. No. It happened where we used to live. Banner Street.'

Denton thought it was a time to stay silent, to see what might get said. Snokes seemed to have come to an end, but after several seconds he said, 'When he was little, Walter never went out. It was always the piano, piano, piano. He should have been running about, playing outside. You know. I took him out sometimes. Just to some places where he could see people playing and flying kites and doing things, you know. She didn't like it.' He sighed. 'That day, I took him out to walk down to the Artillery Ground. We'd only got over the road when she called him. Called him back. It was like he was on a string—he turned about and flew into the street.' Snokes leaned back against the dark woodwork. 'There was a delivery wagon, empty, so he was going too fast. It was like he got tangled in the horse's legs. Then it dragged him.' He shook his head. 'Never the same after that. Never the same.'

'Is that why you moved?'

Snokes shuffled into the parlour. 'You might as well sit down if we're going to talk.' He shrugged. 'I'm awake now.'

Denton went a little back into the parlour but didn't sit. Snokes stood on the green-tiled hearth. 'Did you move here because of the accident?'

'I had an increase in salary.'

'And you moved here at once?'

'Oh—we took the let of this house in 1899. April. Moved up in the world. Anna's a great believer in moving up in the world.'

'Your promotion was in 1899, then?'

'Yes, well...'. He looked around, then tried to place an elbow on the mantel in order, maybe, to seem relaxed, but he wasn't tall enough. 'There were other factors.' Snokes fidgeted. Finally, he said, 'A little boy about our lad's age disappeared from our street. Never found. Anna was frightened out of her wits. Moved away.'

'So you put your son in The Oaks as soon as you moved here?'

Snokes's elbow slipped off the mantel. He tried to prop it up there again, gave it up and said, 'He was a month or two with us here before, ah...'

'You put him in The Oaks because he had behaved improperly to his sister?'

'Did I tell you that? I might have done. But I wouldn't say that, not just like that—it wasn't *actionably* improper. He didn't, didn't...'

'You told me before that he had his Johnson out.'

'Well...yes...' He looked anguished. 'He wasn't like other boys.'

'Mr Snokes—I know this is prying, but—how much does Walter understand about sex?'

Snokes simply shook his head.

'Did you ever have one of those talks with him? Explain about...'

Snokes shook his head again. 'He wouldn't have understood. It was like him being a baby in a man's body. I couldn't...reach him, you know?'

'Could his mother?'

Snokes looked towards the doorway as if there were evidence piled there that he had to study before he could answer. 'She was better with him. She *said* she could...deal with him. We had a terrible row when I found that place to put him. But I wouldn't take no for an answer that time. Because of Eunice. I had to choose between them, see?' He seemed to want Denton's pity for making that choice: a little pathos, drama. He puffed out his cheeks and blew out his breath. 'I'm sure you've guessed, this isn't the happiest house in London, Mr Denton. Walter's always here between us. Drove his sister away. Drove me...You know I've been no saint. But—'

'I asked you once before and you didn't answer, Mr Snokes. Is Walter dangerous?'

Snokes turned his face to Denton's. Denton believed from what he saw that the man really was suffering. Snokes said, 'I put him in that hell-hole, didn't I?'

Denton drove to Chancery Lane. He was depressed by his time with Arthur Snokes, then by poor Rupert and Atkins. A hundred yards from Snokes's house, he was distracted by the car, which gave a jerk and an abrupt stop and start that was like a bucking horse. He thought he'd done something wrong. He drove on, holding the wheel tight, wondering if one of his feet had been in the wrong place, and, when he was sure that he was doing every-thing right, the car did it again. Denton felt his body try to sail over the bonnet, then bang back into the too-low back of the seat. His head snapped back; his neck hurt. Then the car went on for several streets and all seemed well. And then it did it again.

He was within a few streets of the shed where he stored the car. He could take it there and have somebody come to look at it. Or he could drive it down to the place where he'd bought it and have them look at it. He remembered, however, that that had been on the old Wych Street, and Wych Street had been gobbled up by the construction that was supposed to become the Aldwych. They were probably not even there any more.

He decided to go on. It wasn't far.

The motor died when he was two streets from Sir Francis Brudenell's office. Denton felt the buck, the push forwards, the push back, the snap to his neck. When he recovered, the motor was no longer running and the car had stopped in the traffic lane of Gray's Inn Road.

'Oh, *hell*!'

Two workmen who were enlarging a hole in the pavement watched him with a good deal of pleasure: *Gent Gets What He Deserves*. Denton got out and disengaged the gear and pushed the little vehicle to the side of the road. When he pulled the hand brake into position, one of the men said, 'It ain't going nowhere, governor!'

Denton thought of how he'd have reacted twenty years earlier in the American West. Fist-fighting in the street wasn't as acceptable in London. And fist-fighting across class lines was really out. So, instead of laying down a challenge, Denton laughed and said, 'I should have bought a horse.'

The man laughed, too. Both of them were suddenly his pals—their way of saying, he supposed, that he'd taken it all right. One of them said, 'We'll watch her for you, mate.'

'Well, as you said, it isn't going anywhere.'

He walked down to Sir Francis Brudenell's and threw himself on the mercy of the young man who served as Sir Francis's Cerberus. Dressed in black, hair parted in the middle and very slick, pince-nez on his aristocratic nose, he listened to Denton's tale of his immobilised motorcar and disappeared into the inner regions. As Denton had hoped, Sir Francis was enough interested in motors that he made room on his afternoon schedule for him.

'I told you that you should buy my Benz. Now look what's happened.'

'You also told me never to drop in without an appointment.'

'Ah, but that time your motor was running. How about my Benz?'

'In a word, I haven't the money. What I need is Doty.'

'Doty? What's Doty to do with motors?'

Denton told him about Rupert and the poisoned meat. Sir Francis, as Denton knew, had dogs of his own. He was severe about anybody who would use poison on one. 'Fully actionable in a civil court. I even know which justice I should try to put it before. Also a dog lover.'

'Munro's taken it to the Yard.'

'Munro's an admirable fellow, but the police have too much to do as it is. You're wise to think of Doty. Though, if you can't afford my Benz, I'm not so sure about Doty. You will, anyway? Noble of you.' Sir Francis wrote down the particulars. 'A woman—dreadful. Women are becoming very distressing. I'm happy to say I have no daughters.' He pushed his notes away and joined his hands on the desk. 'I shall ask Doty to visit you. The sooner the better, I think—tracing the poison is of the essence. If it's arsenic, she'll have to have signed the poison book some-where. It would be easier if we had a photograph. Have you a photograph?'

Denton was glad to say he hadn't. He told the solicitor about the telephone calls; Sir Francis's eyebrows went up. 'Harassment by telephone! Promising—there may be records. She's at Oxford? I doubt she telephoned from there. I'm not sure they even have telephones at the colleges. Far more likely she was in London, thus perhaps at an hotel. I shall make a note of that for Doty, too. Are we done?'

Denton supposed that they were. Sir Francis offered a ride to his house in the Benz, but Denton said he could walk it as fast. 'I suppose I'll have to have the car towed. By a horse.'

'You could simply leave it and hope someone steals it. Oh, that was unkind of me. Goodbye, Denton—goodbye...'

As it happened, Atkins had 'a pal in the automobile trade' who would have a look at the Barré *in situ*. Rupert was still breathing, no longer vomiting, less inclined to go into convulsions. 'He's going to make it,' Denton said.

'Don't say it,' Atkins muttered. He pointed upward with a thumb. 'Shiva's not the elephant one, but he's got big ears.' He had been seventeen years in India. 'Let's see what the vet says tonight.'

Denton had hardly got upstairs when the front bell rang. He started down for it, thinking Atkins busy with Rupert, but Atkins was there ahead of him. 'I ain't been ruled medically unfit, General.' Denton backed up the stairs; Atkins opened the door, and Denton heard Maltby's voice. His reaction was to wish the young man somewhere else; his conscience urged that Maltby was young, alone in London, overworked. Denton still wished he hadn't come.

Maltby came in looking as if he'd been out in a bright day in the Alps instead of a warmish day in London, very red-cheeked and brisk and smiling, and wearing his constable's uniform without his arm-band, meaning he was off-duty, but with his helmet tucked under his arm as if he were a dragoon. 'You're looking uncommonly well,' Denton said.

Maltby got right to it. 'My sergeant got me out of bed at the service house to tell me to report to Bow Street in *uniform*. I thought I was for it! But what they wanted was anything I knew about a woman who's been loitering on your street. I was so relieved I was weak in the knees. Didn't know what I'd done.'

'And what did you know about the woman who's been loitering here?'

'Has she? Has she really? I wasn't sure. I thought so, though.'

'I've seen you. What in the world were you doing, Maltby—following her?'

Maltby blushed. 'I want to make detective. It isn't for a couple of years, but I want to be on my toes. This seemed a ready-made chance. I told you, remember, I'd seen a woman—remember, over the way—'

'I remember, yes.'

'Well, I *did* think she was loitering, and, between you and me, frankly I don't have a lot to do when I'm not on duty, unless it's my turn to do the latrine at the service house. So I came here now and then to, umm, surveil her. As it were. Once or twice in, mm, ah, disguise.' He looked stricken. 'Do you mind?'

'Why would I mind? Did they tell you I think she poisoned the dog?'

Maltby looked aghast and said that if that wasn't criminal under 12 and 13 Victoria, it was under the Wild Animals in Captivity Act, 1900, although perhaps it wasn't because the dog wasn't wild, was he? At any rate, it surely was criminal under common law, although perhaps he wasn't allowed to arrest, but only summons. 'And there are the poison statutes,' he said.

'What did you tell them at Bow Street?'

'I showed them my notebook. I had four entries on her, one when I'd talked to PC Wither, your beat policeman. I identified myself and he said I was "a good lad", by which I suppose he meant he thought I was fresh as paint and twice as green as grass, but he wrote it in *his* book, so there's that evidence as well. And I told them about my photos, of course.'

'Of her? You got photos?'

Maltby grinned. 'From a hansom. I knew she'd see me if it was just me. It was five to one I wouldn't get her, photographing from a moving cab, all that shaking and bouncing, but there she was, and I took the risk. I'm on my way back to Bow Street with my photos, which I didn't know I'd need the first time, of course, so I went back to the service house and I just thought I'd stop by here to tell you, as it has to do with you.' He frowned. 'I hope I haven't done anything that will pain you. Bring down the *press*, and so on.'

'You have your photographs with you? *With you?*' Denton held out a hand. 'For God's sake, Maltby...'

Maltby put his helmet down on the floor and bent to the side to get to some inner pocket. He produced three photographs, all about the size of a postal card. Two were mostly of the houses along Lamb's Conduit Street, but one was unmistakably of Rosamund Gearing. 'By God, you're a wonder!'

'Oh, no...' Maltby guffawed with pleasure.

'But why? You saw her once and thought she was—what?'

'Suspicious. A policeman has to be alert for suspicious persons.'

'But she's a tutor or something at one of the Oxford colleges. She's very well-dressed.'

'She looked suspicious. Her face had an expression of... intent.'

'Intent to do what?'

'Intentness.' Maltby retreated into hurt dignity. 'It's a sixth sense.'

Denton laughed, apologised for not offering him something and suggested sherry, but Maltby said he was going on duty soon. He had yet to go back to Bow Street, return to the service house for his supper ('eggs and bacon, over and over—we have to cook our own'), and be at his divisional station house by quarter of ten. He was saying again how terrible it was about the dog when the doorbell rang.

'What now?' Denton looked out into the street. A cab was at his gate. 'If it's that damned woman—'

Atkins's head appeared. 'Visitor name of Doty.' He opened the door a bit wider and handed in a card. 'Investigator, he says.'

'Oh, my God. Oh, good. Show him up.' Denton put a hand on Maltby's shoulder. 'We're in luck. He's going to look into the poisoning. The best private investigator in London, they say.'

Maltby frowned as if private investigators were as suspicious as Rosamund Gearing.

Doty came in, minus hat and overcoat, shook hands with Denton and raised his eyebrows a fraction of an inch as he was introduced to Maltby. Doty murmured something; Maltby was stiff. Denton explained in a sentence why each of them was there and held up the photograph. 'PC Maltby has a photo of my suspect!'

'Has he really.' Doty's mild voice suggested that he had reached the peak of his abilities to show enthusiasm. 'A recognisable photograph?'

'A lallapalooza!'

Doty looked at it, then cocked an eye at Maltby. 'You took it while…?'

'Keeping said woman under surveillance.'

Doty smiled at the photograph. 'Is the entry-way in the background recognisable as…?'

'Three doors down and over the way. I'd testify to it in court.' Maltby drew himself up. Denton wondered if Maltby had yet actually been in the witness box.

'Three doors down and over the way…' Doty turned his small smile on Denton. 'Quite fortunate, Mr Denton. I thought it was too much to hope that you would have a photograph, unless there had been—'

'There hadn't! She was an acquaintance, nothing more. Nothing.'

Doty asked Maltby if he had the negative, then, as he did, if copies could be made. Maltby in fact had the negative with him, as a detective at Bow Street wanted it. 'E Div are investigating the matter,' he said.

'They are, yes.' Doty seemed to accept E Division as his equal in the right to investigate. 'They'll look into the criminal; I'll look into the civil. Of course, the two overlap. Now, PC Maltby, would you allow Mr Denton to have prints made from your negative before you take it to Bow Street?'

Maltby swallowed, turned red, and frowned. 'I should need their permission, I'm afraid.'

Doty nodded. It seemed to be exactly what he expected. 'Then let us go along to Bow Street now and ask for permission. I know a few people there. Mr Denton, if you'll ring for my hat and coat…?'

The hat and coat arrived, and the three of them went down the stairs in a swirl of counter-invitations, excuses, postponements and evasions. Doty turned back at the door and murmured, 'I'll just drop back if I may to fill in some details.' And they were gone.

Denton was glad they were gone. It was still not yet four-thirty. Maybe he could get a little work done. Instead, he fell asleep in his chair.

Denton awoke to hear the door. It was the veterinary surgeon; a few minutes later, the door banged again and he was gone. Denton tried to lure sleep back, but it was no good. He opened the door to the downstairs and said, 'Well?'

'It was arsenic.'

'How's Rupert?'

'No worse.'

'You're being intentionally pessimistic.'

Atkins put a foot on the bottom step and leaned, his arms folded, against the wall. 'He gave me boluses were made for an elephant to force down the poor fellow's throat. It's already sore from that engine the groom used. Cure is always worse than the disease, it is. How I'm going to get these things down him, I don't know.'

'That Doty's coming back.'

'You and the missus going out?'

'She's working until nine or ten. You going to Mrs Johnson's?'

Atkins set his jaw. 'I told her that was off until Rupert's… better or worse.' He took his foot off the step, started to disappear, put his head back into view and said, 'You want me to fetch supper from the Lamb?'

Denton looked at his watch. It was barely six. 'Maybe later.'

Doty returned at six-fifteen. The photographic prints, he said, would be ready first thing in the morning. 'Invaluable, Mr Denton. I think we may—I say only "may"—know a good deal by tomorrow evening, thanks to the photograph. You'll pay the fare to send a man to Oxford? The poison was probably bought there. Not the meat, I think.'

Denton said he supposed he must. 'Was Maltby terribly officious with you?'

Doty gave his tiny smile. 'PC Maltby is young.'

They went over the details of Denton's recent history with Rosamund Gearing. He showed Doty her letter. Doty had him repeat everything twice, sometimes three times. Doty made notes. Denton showed him the telephone log that Atkins had kept. Doty's eyebrows rose the fraction of an inch that meant he had been pleasantly surprised. 'And you complained to the exchange?'

'He threatened to tear the telephone out of the wall.'

'That's probably not as unusual as you may think. Still, they'll have a record. Did she telephone from Oxford, do you think? Well, that remains to be seen. We must work out when she was here and when in Oxford; your Maltby's notes will help there. If here, she may have stayed at an hotel. Or hotels. More use for the photograph.' He closed his notebook. 'I never make promises, Mr Denton, but I believe that with a bit of luck, we'll know more by this time tomorrow than we did yesterday.' His departure overlapped a visit by a detective constable from H Division about the poisoning; finding that Atkins, not Denton, was Rupert's owner, he disappeared into Atkins's part of the house.

At eight, Denton went to the Lamb to order something sent over for him and Atkins both. At a little after nine, impatient to see Janet and feeling ill-used by the world, he had a visit from Guillam.

'I feel like hell,' Guillam said, throwing himself into a chair.

'Whisky?'

'If I drink, I'll fall on my face. Nothing to eat since morning, and I'm jiggered up, absolutely jiggered. You have beer?'

Denton ran down the list—beer, ale, Guiness, sherry, claret...

'The India's fine; don't go on about it.' Guillam groaned. 'Mrs Snokes's prints don't match the Wilcox woman's floor.'

'Prints' didn't register immediately. When it did, Denton was leaning into the stairs and asking Atkins for biscuits and cheese, a slice from the ham, if they still had any—

'Yes, yes, yes. Hungry lot, coppers...'

Denton turned back to Guillam; he realised what he had said. 'So it isn't her, either.'

'And you know what?' Guillam was gesturing at Denton with a finger, his expression baleful. 'Those three bleeding fingerprints on the Wilcox woman's floor? That we've all been saying were in the victim's blood? They were in fact in preserves! Red. Redcurrant jelly, most likely. Do you admire that? In a police department? We take photographs of the fingerprints but we don't take a sample because of course it's blood, isn't it, it's bound to be blood, the place was thick with blood! Like bloody hell it is; it's something the Wilcox woman dropped from her breakfast muffin or it's something she was going to stuff into a cake, or what the hell! It could have been there for weeks.' Denton held out a bottle of ale and Guillam took it and drank as if he hadn't drunk all day. 'I stopped at King's Cross Road on the way here. It's bloody Masefield all over again. So I ordered the fingerprint people to go back and do the whole place again—everything this time, every implement, every underside of every bleeding bit of furniture, every inch of the floors, and the damned ceilings where they can be reached!'

Atkins put a platter of two kinds of cheese, bread, mustard, two thick slices of ham, two sorts of biscuits, and a dab of anchovy paste next to him. Guillam growled, 'How's the dog?'

Atkins was startled. 'Holding his own, sir. Thank you for asking.' He looked at Denton with an expression that meant *How did he know?* Denton raised his eyebrows to suggest he didn't know, but he guessed that Munro had told him. Atkins went down his stairs, not opening the dumbwaiter so he could listen; Guillam had complained of his doing that before.

Guillam sighed. He was putting mustard on a slice of bread as if he were spreading concrete on a brick. He cut a thick slice of cheddar. 'It's too late, of course. The Wilcox woman's relatives have been in the house now. Masefield gave the word it was all right.' He slapped the cheddar on the mustard and took a huge bite, then said while chewing, 'The whole thing's a bollocks. Masefield ought to be walking a beat.'

'So Mrs Snokes is clear?'

'No more nor less than anybody else.' Guillam swallowed hugely. His black hair, shiny in the artificial light, hung down over his forehead. Denton thought that he looked as if he needed a haircut, wondered when he had the time to get one. Guillam said, 'She showed up at the station house on Peckham Road while I was there this aft. Made a great lot of noise about her "poor boy".' Guillam lowered his head over his food. 'Well, he is a poor boy, she's frigging right about that. That kid's out in London somewhere right now. Cripes.' He swallowed again, finished the bottle, dipped the cheese knife into the anchovy paste. 'When she shut up for a moment, I asked her if she'd been to her rented room. She had; he wasn't there.'

Denton was getting another bottle of ale. 'She denied to me it even existed.'

'You're not a policeman.' Guillam ate half a slice of ham. Denton brought him the second bottle, which Guillam with a jerk of his head ordered put on the mantel. He swallowed the ham and said, 'I talked to that Sally.'

'Well, that's something.'

'Scared out of her noggin, she was. Married woman— husband doesn't know, she says. Insists she's not a "professional", sometimes does "medical benefactions" for gentlemen who're invalid, as a service. That means just what you think it does. Bit sickening when you think about it.' Guillam's jaw clenched. He drank a quarter of his ale from the new bottle. 'I'm nobody to talk.'

'How'd she find Walter Snokes?'

'The Snokes woman found her. "Through a friend." I don't believe it. Some sort of advert somewhere would be my guess. "Special nursing for gentleman clients in medical need", or some such. But she's local in Camberwell. Could be Tonk knew her— worth asking if I ever find him.' He cut more ham and then took a slice of bread, then the mustard. 'Or is it? Why do I care?' He cut a slice of cheese.

'Anything new on Tonk?'

Guillam drank again, making a kind of sandwich with one hand as he did; he shook his head as he drank, and the bottle waved back and forth. He took the bottle down, wiped his mouth with thumb and forefinger and said, 'Tonk's not my main interest, anyway, is he?'

'Walter?'

Guillam grunted. 'Did I say that Mama was looking for him at her rented room? I followed her there.'

'Did Sally say she'd been there?'

'Not right out, but often enough, would be my guess. She was clever—after all, if it was more than a year ago, he was underage and she'd be actionable. Although with the mother there, I don't think Sally'd get much from a judge.'

'Mrs Snokes was in the room when she—did whatever she did?'

'Not clear.' Guillam used the end of the cheese knife to spear a morsel of ham. 'She said something like "Whatever nursing services I performed, his mother approved."'

'What did she do?'

'The mother?'

'Sally.'

'She didn't tell me, did she? What'd be the significance of her using one part of her body instead of another?'

Denton shrugged. 'Only an idea.'

'Cripes, I was supposed to telephone you when I found her, wasn't I? I didn't have anything else to do, did I, nor anywhere else to go.' He threw down the cheese knife and leaned back in the chair. 'Your grub saved my life. What's your idea?'

'It doesn't matter now.' Guillam's face telegraphed a question. Denton shook his head. Guillam shrugged.

A few minutes later, Janet came in. Guillam was embarrassed, the ravaged platter probably the reason, and took himself off. When she had pulled off her hat and coat and gloves and fallen into a chair, Denton said, 'Apparently it wasn't Mrs Snokes. Hers weren't the fingerprints on Mrs Wilcox's floor.'

'Are you surprised?'

He shrugged. She told him about her day; he sketched his own. They commiserated about Rupert. He got her a glass of claret to go with the end of Guillam's platter, which she had appropriated. Denton watched her eat, smiling, and poured himself a whisky. When she was done, he said, 'How would you get sperm into a vagina? Other than the usual way?'

She leaned back, one arm curled above her head. 'Just in there, or all the way in?'

'All the way, I'd think.'

She thought for some seconds. 'The better shops sell a sort of syringe thing for the douche. A clyster.'

'Like the thing they put down Rupert's throat.'

'Well, a bit shorter, I hope. Are you having as disgusting an idea as I think you are?'

But he was sipping his whisky and looking into the darkness beyond the window.

CHAPTER

18

He forced himself out of bed a little after four next morning and worked until seven, then dressed and went down. The Barré was parked at the kerb by his front gate. He trotted down another flight to tell Atkins that his pal had done a splendid thing, but Atkins wasn't there.

The rear door was open an inch, cold air sneaking in. Denton went out. Atkins was looking into the garden but turned at Denton's step and said, 'Rupert's having a pee!' He might have been announcing the Second Coming: his face was bright, his smile huge. 'He's up and walking!'

In fact, Rupert was staggering more than he was walking, but he was making a kind of tour of the garden, sniffing here and there, even standing, legs wide apart, to stare at the filled-in tunnel under the wall. When Atkins called his name, the stump of tail moved, moved again; Rupert turned, lurched, almost fell on a front shoulder, recovered enough to cross to Atkins and collapse at his feet. 'He walked all the way round the garden!' Atkins said.

'Maybe he's hungry.'

'Oh—I don't know—maybe a bit of milk?'

'Water, anyway.'

'Well, he's full of water, isn't he? That drench! Though it seems to have done some good, I guess. Pissed it all away now, I suppose.' Atkins bent and stroked the great head, and the little tail vibrated. Atkins looked up at Denton. 'You really think that young woman done this?'

'I certainly do.'

'Just because you wouldn't do the mm-hmm-mm with her? Seems mad.'

'More than a bit. Do we need to carry Rupert inside? If we can?'

Atkins called Rupert. The head came up; the tail gave a single wag. Atkins went to the door, called again. Rupert tried to get on his feet, and Denton straddled him and put his hands under his gut and lifted, and that way they crossed to the door, Denton with his legs wide and his back complaining. 'He's heavy as a dead minister,' he said.

'But worth it, General. Worth every ounce.'

Denton left Atkins to care for Rupert and got himself a kind of breakfast on his spirit stove—Italian coffee, a couple of scrambled eggs—and toasted bread at his coal fire. He had to go down twice, once for the loaf and once for the Society Best Marmalade. He propped Walter Snokes's drawings on a chair and stared at them while he ate, then fetched his magnifying glass and studied them some more. At eight-thirty, he said he was going out. Janet, he knew, would be going to church. 'And give your pal something extra for the car. It was good of him to bring it over.'

'Brisk out there, Colonel; that duster ain't enough.'

'I'm wearing it over the kashmir. Stop worrying about me and take care of your dog.'

'I am, I am, good cripes...'

Before he went out, Denton called King's Cross Road for Guillam, was told that Guillam had gone to N Division behind the Angel. Denton telephoned there and was told that Guillam wasn't there, and then that he was just coming in the door. Guillam seemed to have forgotten any cameraderie they might have developed the night before.

'What now?'

'I want the address of Mrs Snokes's room in Camberwell.'

'Why?'

'I might find Walter.'

'P Div put a uniform at the door.'

'I want to talk to her.'

'Munro doesn't want her agitated, Denton.'

'That was before the fingerprints didn't match.'

'It's 42 Guthill Road. Just off the High Street. Don't stir her up, you hear me? We don't want her screaming harassment.'

The motorcar seemed to run better than before. Denton remembered with some guilt that he'd given it no attention since he'd got back from Italy; had Atkins, while he was away? He drove up to De Beauvoir Town and found nobody there, not even the maid—it was Sunday.

Number 42 Guthill Road had three letter boxes and a sign that said 'Rooms'. None of the boxes had the name Snokes on it, and if there was a uniformed constable watching the place Denton didn't see him, so he rang and had the door opened by a fat weasel of a man who was apparently already drunk at ten on a Sunday morning. He wore a waistcoat and a smeared necktie but no jacket, and he looked at Denton and held on to the door, clearly for support.

'Snokes?' Denton said.

The man shook his head. His head jerked again, the beginning of a lurch that would have become a fall without the door.

'I don't mean you. *Mrs* Snokes. She rents a room here.'

The man took it badly. 'Don't you come all over me! Bloody Lord's Day, it is.'

'Does a woman named Snokes rent a room here?'

The man leaned forward—his way of closing the door—until his forehead met wood and he more or less collapsed against it, pushing the door shut. Through a pane of glass and a lace curtain, Denton saw him leaning against the inside, then watched him feel his way along a distempered wall towards the back of the house. He seemed to leave a track, like a snail; it was in fact an old smear of many dirty hands. Denton thought that was that, but after a few seconds a woman began to feel her way towards him along the same dirty line. She was bent with age; like the man, she kept a hand on the wall but she seemed otherwise to be sober. The drunk's mother? Not his wife, to judge by her age.

'Well?'

'I'm looking for Mrs Snokes.'

She looked him up and down. 'You from the papers?'

'No.'

'We're that sick of you.'

'I'm not the press.'

'Police?'

'I'm a friend of Mrs Snokes.'

'She isn't here. She was here but she ain't. I don't want folk hanging about my house. Go on, now.'

'Do you know where Mrs Snokes went?'

'How would I know? Out looking for that half-wit kid of hers, I suppose. Go on, before I call a policeman. You think I won't? You got another think coming.'

Denton said an insincere thanks and backed down the steps, one hand on a wrought-iron railing and his head tipped back to look up at the house. What did he expect to see, Mrs Snokes watering a potted geranium up there? When he reached the bottom and turned, a constable was standing there.

'Help you, sir?' He, too, sounded as if Denton was a suspicious person.

'I'm looking for a Mrs Snokes. I got the address from Detective Sergeant Guillam of G Division. She rents a room in this house. She had a son in that place, The Oaks.'

The constable thawed and told Denton that the Snokeses had gone out to look for their boy, he didn't know where. Going up and down streets, he supposed.

'Have they found any of the others?'

'One wanted to be served in a public house and had no money, so they held him for the constable. Another was playing with a dog in Camberwell Square.'

'But not the Snokes boy?'

'I don't believe so, no, sir.'

Denton got back in his ridiculous car and putted up and down streets but, seeing neither Walter nor his parents, headed for Bushey Hill Road and The Oaks. Another policeman was at the gate there; he said that the place was closed and nobody allowed in.

'I was looking for a Mr and Mrs Snokes. Their boy is one of the missing ones.'

The policeman looked doubtful. 'There's a lady up there now. The sergeant made an exception for her—he's with her.' He was middle-aged, destined by his own inertia to be a constable for life, yet emanating a solidity that Denton suspected was simply lack of ambition. The constable looked up the hill, pursed his lips, perhaps doing nothing more taxing than calculating the time until his watch ended, and said, 'You could wait down here until they come back, sir.'

Denton tried to offer a description of Mrs Snokes as a bona fide but got nowhere. He suggested that the name Walter might have been mentioned. The constable allowed that it might have, but not in his hearing. Denton went back to his car.

He sat for ten minutes, contemplating what had turned out to be a wasted Sunday morning. He was thinking of looking for something to eat when he saw a flicker of movement near the gaunt hideousness of The Oaks; it became a very dark shape with a skirt and a fairly dark shape with legs. They started down the hill, became a policeman and a woman, and the woman turned into Mrs Snokes.

Denton met her at the gate. She looked swollen and sleepless; her eyes were red, her expression grief-stricken and angry. He realised that she didn't recognise him, but when he said his name she reacted away from him.

'I have a car, Mrs Snokes. Can I take you anywhere?'

'Where would that be, I'd like to know?'

'We could look for Walter, if you like.'

'And what's Walter to you? Prying, are you?'

He winced inwardly; *yes, he was prying.* 'You came to my house to ask for help, Mrs Snokes—remember?'

She looked blank. Could she have forgotten? 'So I did.' She looked around as if she didn't know where she was. 'That's a very small motorcar.'

He told her that he'd stopped at her house. 'Is Mr Snokes looking for Walter, too?'

'What good would he be?' She headed for the Barré. 'I suppose you can take me to Guthill Road.' She frowned at the car with suspicion.

He opened the sliver of a door. 'I was there earlier.'

She stepped back. 'How did you know to go there?'

'Detective Sergeant Guillam told me.'

'I don't know him.'

'I believe you met him yesterday. But there was so much going on—'

'Going on!' She teared up. 'What would any of you know about it?' She advanced on the Barré and fell backward into the seat; the car leaned like a boat in rough water. Denton closed the door, making sure he didn't touch her, got in the other side. When the car was moving, she sat upright, one hand on the door and one on the dash as if she might have to leap out.

'Where would Walter go, do you think?' he shouted over the motor noises.

'If I knew, I'd be there, wouldn't I?'

'I thought he might go to your room. On Guthill Road.'

She looked straight ahead and held on. He was aware that she was a heavy woman from the way the car drove. She said, 'I spent the night there. In case. I didn't get a wink of sleep.' In profile, her face looked as if it was filled with hatred of everything around her. 'Who knows where he'd go?'

'He might go home.'

'How? And how would he know where to go?' She said nothing, then seemed to say to herself, '*Home*! As if it's a home...'

Denton turned into Guthill Road and stopped at the kerb in front of number 42. She began to wrestle with the door latch; he ran around the rear of the car and went back and forth with her, trying to get her to let go so he could open it. It would have been comical under different circumstances. When he got the door open, she stood, still in the car, as if she meant to survey the ground for possible use of artillery, then stepped down, bending forward to grasp the seat-back and the dash with her hands before putting a heavy foot on the ground and groaning.

'I'd like to ask you a question,' Denton said.

'I'm fed up with questions.'

Two men who had been lounging on the railings of number 42, restrained until then by the constable, detached themselves and started for the car. Denton took her arm. 'Let me get you inside before those leeches bother you.'

To his surprise, she let him steer her. He went forward, warning the two men to give it a rest, let her go by, pack it in, boys! He called to the policeman, who said, 'Now, now...!' Denton went straight forward, forcing the newspapermen to separate so he could go between them; the one on Mrs Snokes's side put a notebook in front of her as if he expected her to write something down and asked her how it felt to have her son missing. She gave a sob of disgust. The other one crowded Denton, who stepped on his foot and shouldered him; the man staggered and Denton got her to the steps.

'Constable, keep them away from her!'

'Now, now...'

He went up the steps without pausing. 'You have a key?'

'Of course I have a key.' In fact, she had it in her glove already. While the constable kept the newsmen at bay, she unlocked the house door; Denton pushed it open, stepped in behind her and closed it. He smelled coal and meat. At the far end of the central hall the little old woman stepped into silhouette in a doorway. Paying her no attention, Mrs Snokes walked three steps to a dark wood staircase and started up. Denton followed.

'No male guests!' the little old woman shrieked. 'No male guests!'

Mrs Snokes was breathing heavily by the time they got to the second floor. She planted her feet heavily, bent forward, and pulled herself up along the thick banister. After stopping at the top to breathe, she walked forward, looking in a small handbag, then pulling out another key and unlocking a door. Denton stayed close behind her, afraid she'd lock him out, but she said nothing and went to a cheap platform rocker near the only window and fell into it.

'You must be exhausted,' Denton said.

She stared ahead of her and breathed. She might have been running.

'Could I get you something? A glass of water?' He saw, next to a boarded-up fireplace, a rickety table with two glasses and two cups and, on the bottom shelf, a spirit stove and a can that said it held alcohol.

'Water's in the convenience.' She gestured towards the door. 'Yes, a glass of water.'

He took one of the glasses and found a WC partway along the corridor. Somebody kept it more or less clean. There was a toilet and a copper sink. He drew a glass of water and carried it back, ready to find the door locked against him, but it was open and he went in.

'Why do you want to ask me questions?' she said.

'Because I don't understand. About Walter.'

'Nobody understands. The doctors don't. His father neither understands nor cares.' She drank off the water and held the glass out to him. 'You want to know why Walter wouldn't go home? Because of his father, that's why. Because it was his father who did this to him.' Her voice was bitter, her face hate-filled.

'I thought it was an accident.'

'It was his fault. He wouldn't have it but that Walter would go out with him on his day off. He hated Walter—because of his music. He never understood about it. He couldn't understand how a son of his could care so about music. So he took him out of the house when Walter didn't want to go. The poor little boy was crying. Trying to get free of his father's hand! But he took him over the road. Dragged him. I saw it. I was standing at the window. Walter pulled his hand loose and tried to run to our door, and he was run over. Run over like he wasn't there.' She had tucked her hands under her arms as if they were cold; perhaps they were, for it was cold in the room. She said in a monotone, 'He was a prodigy.'

Her story wasn't quite like the one that Snokes had told. He let that go and said, 'That was when you lived in Banner Street.' She didn't say anything. 'He liked Banner Street?'

'He was happy there. He had his music.'

'But you lived there for—four more years? And then you moved away.'

'My husband moved us away.'

'Because of a little boy who disappeared?' He thought he knew the answer, but he wanted her answer, not her husband's.

She sat, then leaned back so that the platform rocker's springs creaked. She came forward again. She said, 'He always liked Eunice better. He did it for Eunice.'

'Because Walter did something to her.'

'He did not do anything! Only the once. Eunice didn't know what she was talking about! Neither of them understood about... physical things.'

'Eunice was older, wasn't she?'

She closed her eyes, opened them. 'You'd expect a little boy's father to teach him about those things, but that didn't happen. That responsibility—like a lot of others—fell on his mother—too late, as I found after Eunice...said what she said.'

The door opened behind them. Denton had left it unlocked. Snokes came in, surprising Denton, paused with the doorknob in his hand, saw them both and closed the door. He, too, looked exhausted: this was the time of day when he normally slept. He said, 'What's that about Eunice?'

'Eunice told a lot of lies about Walter!' It was as if they were picking up some argument at its peak.

'Walter behaved indecently to her.'

'He didn't! He didn't know any better. If you'd been half a father, you'd have taught him how to behave. You'd have taught him about decent women and how to behave, although you never had much experience of *decent* women, did you!' She stayed in the chair but turned her body to show her hatred to him, even leaned out of the chair towards him to shout, 'You know all about that dirtiness—why didn't you teach him?'

'He wouldn't have understood a word I said.'

'So you left it for me!'

Snokes sneered. 'You! What would *you* know about it?'

She was out of the chair and pushing Denton aside. 'How do you think I felt, a decent woman, having to teach that boy about his private parts and how to do the whole dirty business of it? Because I loved him! I loved him so much I made myself do what you wouldn't. Because you were too busy with your trollops!' She looked as if she were going to attack him physically. 'I saved my little boy's life!'

Snokes backed away from her, glancing at Denton, his face red and worn. She was breathing heavily again. Her hat had come partly unpinned and was crooked, pushing hair over her forehead. She looked the opposite of decent; she looked half-drunk, truculent, cruel. She seemed to remember Denton then and looked at him for so long he felt he had to say something.

'Walter talked to me about what privacy meant and what things you have to do in private. Is that what you taught him, Mrs Snokes?'

'He had to be taught them over and over. How do you think I felt?'

Snokes snorted back in his nose. 'What, the birds and the bees? What the hell would you know?'

'I know what the male urge is! I had the example of his father before me, didn't I, who couldn't keep his flies buttoned for two nights in a row! Do you think I wanted him showing his thing to other girls the way he did Eunice? Holding it out, asking—' She stopped herself. 'He had to learn control *and he had to have relief*!'

'Relief? What the hell does that mean?'

She went close to him and put her face almost against his. 'That's a word I heard from you, Arthur Snokes—you had to have relief! So do boys! Do you think a mother doesn't find what's in her boy's bed in the morning? Do you think I couldn't *smell* it? Do you think I was going to leave him like a scared little boy when he had that thing sticking up and didn't know what was happening to him?'

Snokes gaped. 'You mean self-abuse?' He sounded at first horrified, and then he covered his reaction with a titter and looked at Denton and said, 'No boy needs to be taught about that.'

'He didn't know what was happening to him!'

It was as if only then that Snokes understood. And perhaps it was, Denton thought—perhaps, for all his philandering, Snokes was as profound a prude as his wife had at least seemed to be. And he was suddenly angry. 'You mean you *touched* him?'

She turned away. If she was still angry, it was in a way that didn't contort her face; now, she looked weary, and, when she glanced at Denton, embarrassed. Snokes, however, was in a rage. He grabbed her arm and turned her. 'Did you touch him? *There?*'

'Do you know what the law would have done to him for what he tried with Eunice? And you know what would have happened to him in gaol? *I saved his life!*'

A fist banged on the door. The old woman's voice shrieked, 'Stop that noise in there! No male guests! There's a policeman here. You stop that racket!'

The two of them seemed frozen. Denton strode to the door and opened it. He said, 'It wasn't locked.' The old woman and the constable looked startled.

The old woman said, 'Get out of my house!' She pulled at the policeman's coat. 'Get him out of my house!'

'Now, sir...'

Denton pulled the door almost behind him. 'Constable, it's a family row. They're husband and wife; they're all worked up because of their boy.'

'Arrest them,' the old woman cried.

'It isn't an arresting offence, missus; it's a summons offence. I have to go back to the station to ask for a summons.' He looked at Denton, perhaps remembering that he had at least one friend in CID. 'Perhaps, sir, if you'd leave, and I could just issue a warning to the lady and gentleman…'

The old woman glared at Denton. 'I won't tolerate male guests.'

Denton wanted to stay, then saw that there was nothing to stay for. The Snokeses would fight to exhaustion; Denton would get nothing more. He nodded to the policeman. 'I'll go. Tell them I've gone to look for Walter, would you?' He stepped away from the door. The constable pushed it open with a tentative finger, then oozed inside. Denton went to the stair; the old woman came behind him and followed him all the way until he was outside on the steps. 'And don't you lot come back here!' she said.

Denton touched his hat brim and went out to the car. It was almost one. He was hungry, but things that had been said were racketing around his brain, tantalising and confusing him.

Eunice, he thought. Maybe Walter had gone to Eunice. But would he know where she lived? Or maybe Eunice would have an idea where he had gone. Or where he would try to go. Denton had an image of Walter's trying to find his way across London, a boy who had been run down in a street, a boy who had probably never been in the underground, may have had no idea of the Thames, a boy whose geography might have been no more accurate than the geography of his drawings.

The drawings. He would want them, too, to show to Eunice. He headed back towards his house to get the drawings.

'She's out at the shops. For Sunday dinner.' The maid sounded as if it were a personal loss.

'I wanted to see her. About her brother—he's missing.' She stared at him without seeming to understand. 'I was here the other day.'

'Yessir, I remember. But she's at the shops. Mister is home, if you want him.'

Denton shook his head. 'How long will she be?'

She put her left-hand fingers to her chin and stared into the street as if there might have been a clock there. 'She's been gone since I come back from church. That was...' She looked at Denton. 'She'll be another half of an hour, I should think. She won't leave baby for long, will she? But she does have to get the dinner meat.'

Denton scribbled on a card, *Walter is missing—can you help?* He handed it to her.

'Yessir.'

'Tell her I'll be back within an hour.'

'Oh, right, yes. Goodbye, then.'

Denton walked about until he found a pastry shop that had a couple of tables and a sign that said 'Teas'; he got a cup of rather weak tea and a piece of fruity bannock that was a long way from Scotland but nonetheless edible. Fortified, he went back to try to talk with Eunice Snokes, who proved to be putting baby to bed. A cautious older man looked at him and said he was Eunice's husband and disappeared. Denton figured he was twenty years older than she.

'I've had the police here twice,' Eunice said. She looked very young, still somewhat highly coloured from being out or perhaps from boosting the baby about, but she didn't look like a happy woman. 'They were very insulting.'

Denton doubted that but tried to be sympathetic. 'They have a hard job.'

'They're paid, aren't they?' She sniffed. 'They've been pestering Ma and Pa even worse. They're supposed to be public servants; what a laugh. What do *you* want, Mr Denton?'

'You know Walter's gone missing?'

'I know it because my father sent me a telegram. A telegram! Everything that's happening in the world and he sends me a telegram about a...You know what I mean. But it's always the way of it—they both fly into hysteric fits if anything happens to Walter. Has he been found?'

'I'm afraid not. I thought he might have come here, in fact.'

'Here! Thank God, he doesn't know where I live! Wouldn't come near me, anyway, not after what he tried and got caught. He isn't so backward he didn't twig I'd shut the door in his face.'

Her violence surprised him, mostly because it was so far from the idea of the proper little wife; but maybe she wasn't a proper little wife—more a New Woman, perhaps? He winced at the expression—memory of Rosamund Gearing—and said, 'Maybe you could give me some idea of where he might be—or where he'd be trying to get to.'

'How would I know?'

'Well, you...' He started to say *You're his sister* and changed it to 'You grew up with him. You must know the places he played along Banner Street, for example.'

'Do you understand the difference that four years make? You think I wanted to play with some little kid, especially when he was practically an idiot? I *don't* think so.' She wiggled herself upright like a chicken shaking off water. 'I had my own friends. I didn't depend on Walter for company, I can tell you.'

'You must have been told to look after him sometimes, though?' He tried to make a joke of it. 'Big sister given the task of watching little brother?'

'There was some of that.' She moved her shoulders. '"Help carry the burden of our poor little boy." I heard sufficient of that.'

'Was there anywhere special you went?'

'I didn't want to be seen with him, did I? I'm sure if I was stuck with him I stayed at home. I can't help you, Mr Denton.'

'Your mother said that there was another boy who disappeared. Did you have to watch him more after that?'

She looked even more displeased. 'Bobby Vickers. You'd have thought every other kid in the street had been snatched by the gypsies. My mother was in a perfect panic. Frankly, I thought it would be best all around if somebody took Walter, but then I'm selfish and hard-hearted and egotistical.'

She looked as if she was daring him to challenge her. The words had probably been her mother's—and not, Denton thought, her father's; if Walter was the mother's child, Eunice was the father's. Trying to keep her peaceful until he had asked all he wanted, he said, 'And you moved to De Beauvoir Town because of the boy's disappearance.'

'Is that what they told you?' She let out a sarcastic rattle of laughter, four notes. 'They didn't say, I suppose, that we left because the neighbours all blamed Walter. Oh, yes. It wasn't very pleasant living in Banner Street, I can tell you. I got comments in the school yard. We had to move away, was the truth of it.'

'But Walter wasn't...How old was the boy who disappeared?'

'Bobby was—oh, my age, I suppose, though you'd never have known it. Small for his age. But a little savage. Got in a lot of trouble, off and on. Smart enough, though, in his way. The truth is, he probably ran off. His father was a drunkard, took his belt to him. Anybody who knew him knew he'd run off one day, but people didn't get it.'

'Then why did they blame Walter?'

'Because he was peculiar, wasn't he?' She looked upward at some sound Denton missed, then turned in her chair and cocked her head, but if it was the baby it was now silent. She turned back to him. 'I don't have a notion where Walter might try to go. I've a thousand things to do this afternoon.'

'Of course. One thing, and I'll be quick.' He stood, causing her to stand, too, probably with the hope that he was leaving. However, he unrolled Walter Snokes's music papers and held them against the wall, there being no flat surface in the room that wasn't crowded with knick-knacks. 'Could you look at these for just a moment?'

'Oh, those.' She was impatient. 'Where did you get those from? Ma's made an altar for them at home.'

'These are ones he's done since then.' In fact, two of them were and two of them weren't. 'I'm curious whether you recognise any of the little buildings he's drawn. See—at the beginning of the bars, and then partway along—'

'I don't recognise them.' She hadn't had time to look.

But Denton wouldn't let her go. He tapped a drawing where the musical signature would have gone. 'I think that this one is your house in De Beauvoir Town. Don't you think so?'

Interested despite herself, she folded her arms and bent a little towards the drawing. 'Could be, I suppose.'

'That's where many of his drawings start. And this is The Oaks—where he's been living the last few years—the place that—'

'I never saw it. Wild horses couldn't drag me.'

'And this one is, I'm pretty sure, his first music teacher's house. Now this one'—he tapped a drawing of the triangular building with the fairy-tale turrets—'I can't figure this one out. Do you recognise it? It's kind of three-cornered, with towers. Anything about it?'

Her arms dropped; she turned away. 'Doesn't mean a thing to me. One of his fancies, I'm sure. Him and his fairies.'

'It's very distinctive. All the others are real places, so—' Denton had followed her and was trying to hold the half-furled sheet where she could see it, but she didn't look.

'I said I don't know it! Enough's enough!' Her tone got fractionally less strident. 'Baby will want me any minute.' She went to the doorway.

'I'm sorry.' He let the sheets curl back against his fingers. 'Of course.' He picked up his hat from the floor, his coat from a chair back. 'Thank you for giving me your time.'

She shrugged. 'If it'll help Ma…'

'Yes. She's very upset.' He didn't suggest how upset—or how exercised her father had been when he had left the two of them in the rented room.

She said, 'We're all upset. You see how it goes on? And all over Walter. The whole family in a turmoil, and all because of a…' She watched the maid scuttle to get ahead of him and open the front door. When he thanked her again and said goodbye, she was standing there, arms folded, looking plainly as if she couldn't see the back of him fast enough.

Denton sat in the Barré and let the little engine bang along by itself for a bit to warm up. He unrolled the drawings again and looked at them as they vibrated with the rhythm of the two-lunger engine. *She didn't even look*, he thought. But he corrected himself. *She glanced at the triangular one. I'm sure she did. When I said 'three-cornered'.*

But she was right, it did have a fairy-tale look to it. Still, he thought there had been something. Maybe only that she had reacted to it at all. He wished he could have seen her eyes. Was it only that she had seemed to protest too much?

He steered the car away from the kerb and headed south and west.

CHAPTER 19

He had worked for the hour or two that was left of the afternoon even though it was Sunday, Janet closeted with something for University College, but Atkins tiptoed up and told him that young Maltby was back and would Denton see him. Denton groaned and went down, to find Maltby sitting on a hard chair with his helmet in his lap and an almost visible dark cloud over his head. Maltby had a rare ability to project his moods, many of which were dour: in Naples, they had all been dour. This one was black. Without going through the courtesies, Denton said, 'What's the matter?'

Maltby didn't look at him. 'I'm leaving the police.' His voice was like the lowest note on an untuned piano.

'You love the police!'

Maltby glanced at him as if he hated him. 'My sergeant reprimanded me!'

'Maltby, what the hell! Yesterday they loved you because you had those photos.'

Maltby shrivelled into himself. 'My section sergeant says I'm a discredit to the Met.'

'What happened?'

'It's the same bloody thing, the photos! And me hanging about and surveilling the woman! My section sergeant says I was…' He had to draw in a breath to speak the words. '"Over-zealous and meddlesome".' He turned very red. 'That's a quote from Lord Brampton. My sergeant made me find it in the *Code* and read it aloud at parade. In front of all my mates. He says I have to recite the whole paragraph from Brampton's "Address" at the beginning of parade every day for the next month! "Beware of being over-zealous and meddlesome. These are dangerous faults. Let your anxiety be to do your duty, but no more. A meddlesome constable who interferes unnecessarily upon every trifling occasion stirs up ill-feeling against the force and does more harm than good." See? I already know it by heart!'

Denton saw it all. 'He read you out for coming up here and shadowing that woman.'

Maltby clutched his helmet to his chest like a child with a favourite toy. 'He said I "played detective". Right in front of everybody. He said I did it out of uniform. But we're not required to wear the uniform when off-duty! But he says we're always on duty, and I forgot myself and over-reached and could have brought down a complaint against the police. And he says I did it to curry favour with a famous author and further my own career and that I deserved a reprimand.' Maltby swallowed. 'Which he has put in my file.' His voice fell almost to a whisper. 'He says I ought to be kicked out of the force. Well, I'm going to kick myself out!'

'You most certainly are not.' Denton pulled a hideous green hassock close to Maltby's knees and sat on it. He talked about discipline and learning the ropes, but he was thinking about Ivor Hench-Rose and Rosamund Gearing and how sick he was of youth and its egoisms.

When he was done, Maltby said stubbornly, 'He made a fool of me in front of the others.'

Denton jumped up. 'Goddammit, Maltby! Grow up!' He knew he was spewing his own anger all over Maltby.

Maltby looked stricken, then headed for the door. Denton rushed after him, caught him by the shoulder; when Maltby turned, Denton thought the boy might try to hit him, his face was so ugly with anger. Denton said, 'You're going to be a good cop. You made a mistake. The world isn't going to tilt on its axis because of it. Come on, Maltby.' He shook the shoulder. 'You took a bullet for me. This is a hell of a lot easier than that.'

Maltby still had his angry-baby expression. He said, 'So what am I supposed to do?'

'You recite your piece every day at parade, in a good loud voice with your back straight and your chin out. And you take whatever crap your mates hand out, which I suspect won't be much from the ones that like you. And when things have calmed down a bit, you go to your sergeant and you apologise and you say you see now that you were wrong and he was right.'

'But I don't see that I was wrong!'

'Your sergeant does. He's the one who calls the tune.'

'It's a bitter pill.'

'It is.'

Denton walked him downstairs with the hand on his shoulder. 'You're going to be a good copper, Maltby. But you're not going to be one without making some mistakes.' Maltby nodded as if this confirmed his worst fears. He shook Denton's hand, hesitated at the front door, and put on his helmet with the brim so low that he looked as if he were snuffing a candle.

Janet came over at seven. They went together down to the old kitchen, Atkins distracted by a slowly improving Rupert, and cooked more of the Italian foods from the grocery-cum-restaurant. He cut Gaeta olives while Janet smacked garlic cloves with the handle of a knife, then began to chop them. Partway through, she came to him and ordered, 'Kiss me.'

'Am I that alluring?'

'No, I've been eating the garlic.' After he'd kissed her, she popped a clove into his mouth. 'There.'

They managed to boil water and put in *penne rigate*, identified for them by their Neapolitan mentor as 'the nervous kind', by which he had meant it had lines on it. Quantity was a puzzle; they made too much. Janet put fresh broccoli in with the boiling pasta while Denton added pepper flakes to bubbling olive oil and the garlic.

'We shall be pariahs,' Janet said.

'It's in a good cause.' He was putting out squares of roasted pepper (from a jar) and pouring on olive oil. '*Carciofi?*'

'Of course.'

'I wish we had decent bread.'

'Upstairs in the sleeve of my coat. I thought you needed a surprise.'

'Where from?'

'Teddy sent Nellie Strang down to Shaftesbury Av for something; I got her to come back through Soho and buy a real loaf. She was made nervous by all the foreigners, she said.'

They carried the food upstairs. Denton hauled the plates and cutlery and glassware and the wine up in the dumbwaiter. 'Atkins works damned hard for his money,' he said, thinking of Atkins's doing it every day.

'It's an essential but largely ignored tenet of capitalism: the less physical labour you do, the more you get paid; the more work, the less money.' She gestured towards him with her fork. 'Look at you, for example.'

He started to protest, then laughed. 'If you can say that to me, I guess we're getting along pretty well.'

'We are.' She glanced at him across the crowded, tiny table. 'After the bad time I wished on us.'

'No, no.' He broke off a piece of bread, the crust cracking into big flakes, the inside soft, with big holes.

'We rub along.'

'Better than that. It's—'

'Don't.' She put more of the penne with broccoli on her plate, then two slices of the roasted pepper, as red as the red of a military coat and shining with oil. She said, 'We must ask at the grocery place what they put in the little bowl of oil they set out to dip bread in.'

'You never want to talk about us.'

She stopped with her fork a few inches off her plate. She looked at him, then put the food in her mouth. When she had chewed and swallowed, she said, 'Acts, not words. All right?'

Later, they took a cab down to Greek Street and ate *biscuit Tortoni*. He bought her a tin of almond macaroons, and they went back and lay in his bed, sprinkling the sheet with the fine, crisp crumbs. She put out her arms. 'Actions, not words.'

Munro telephoned at six the next morning. 'I knew you'd be up.'

In fact, he'd been enjoying sleeping next to Janet in the narrow bed. He tried to make his voice sound like that of a man who'd been awake for several hours. 'You're calling me for a reason.'

'The Snokes woman is dead.' Munro's voice suddenly sounded older, frailer. 'She's been strangled.'

Denton leaned against the wall. It was cold, no fires lit yet; he was wearing only a thin flannel robe and nothing under it. 'Any idea who?'

'Want to give me breakfast while I tell you? I'm at the Yard now; I don't have time to go home. I could use a wash and a shave. Go to your house, I can kill three birds with one stone.'

'How soon?'

'Half-hour. At most.'

Denton thought of Janet. 'I'll be here.' So would Janet, he thought.

He pulled on old corduroy bags and a grey flannel shirt and the decrepit smoking jacket and cleaned up the dishes they'd left the night before. He filled the dumbwaiter, then went down and hauled on the rope. Atkins appeared and was waved back to bed. Upstairs again, Denton put his sitting-room more or less to rights and then went downstairs and built a fire in the ancient iron range. Atkins wandered in.

'I told you to go back to bed.'

'I don't always do what you tell me. Rupert wanted a pee.'

'You up for good?'

'Looks like.' Atkins pulled his tatty robe around him. 'Bloody cold.'

'Inspector Munro's coming.'

'Crikey! Another day's writing lost.'

'Like hell. It's going like sixty.'

'Not if you don't sit at that desk, it don't.' Atkins started out. 'I'll have a look at Rupert in case that b-i-t-c-h has tossed something over the garden gate again.'

Denton made Italian coffee in his alcove, poured a cup for himself and put the pot on again for Janet, then raced downstairs to find the kettle boiling, made tea, and raced upstairs again in time to turn the now boiling Italian pot upside-down. He then tried his coffee, which was only partly cooled, and took his cup back down and tried to put together a breakfast—to Atkins's disgust.

'Give over!'

'Now, now, Sergeant—'

'Give over; it makes me queasy to watch you, General! Eye-talian food is one thing; breakfast is another! That Guillam didn't half eat us out of house and home, I don't mind saying. There's a slice or two still of that ham. Bangers? I got a couple of bangers. What about the lady?'

Denton was warming milk. 'I'll call her at quarter to seven. Where're the eggs?'

'No eggs.'

'What the hell! There's always eggs!'

'Eggs with milk and a drop of sherry, sovereign remedy for a tricky insides. I thought Rupert might benefit.'

'*All* the eggs?'

'He liked them.'

Denton began to rifle the ice cave, then the bin that held potatoes and, sometimes, root vegetables. He found four potatoes and three wrinkled apples. 'Is there bread?'

'Of course there's bread! What sort of household you think this is?'

Denton found two onions. 'Cut those up, throw them in a skillet, fry them. Then the potatoes. Then the apples, the ham, and the bangers. Got it?'

'All together? With *apples*?'

'It's the best we can do. Cut everything pretty fine. Chop-chop.'

'If it was India, I'd curry it. Oh, well. My thanks for starting the fire and boiling the kettle, now please vamoose.' He smiled, because Denton had taught him 'vamoose' and he thought it was a funny word.

Denton grabbed the milk and his coffee and ran back up to his sitting-room. He poured the second pot of Italian coffee into a cup, added hot milk, threw in two spoons of sugar, and ran the cup upstairs while he stirred it. He bent and kissed the still sleeping Janet and said, 'Coffee.'

'You beast, why are you waking me?'

'Munro's coming. Any minute.'

'Oh, dear God.' She sat up, pulling the sheet and blankets tight up under her ears. 'Coffee.' He held out the cup. A bare arm appeared. She drank, moaned, drank again. 'What's Munro coming for?'

'Breakfast.'

'Don't be deliberately dense.'

'He also wants to wash and shave, so the bath—'

She threw back the bed covers. 'I'll leave.'

'No, stay.'

Naked, she stood on the bed and walked to the foot and got down. He caught her waist and kissed her; she turned her face away, complaining about her teeth and meaning her breath, pushed him off and snatched up his robe and ran out. 'How soon?' she cried from the bathroom doorway.

'Any time now.'

'You should have waked me sooner!'

He thought of changing, rejected the idea, thought it over again and swore. He began to pull off the old, comfortable clothes. When Janet came back, he was wearing grey tweed trousers and a white shirt, and he was buttoning on a new collar.

'I like your outfit,' he said. She was naked.

'Just an old thing I had lying about. I want to be out of here before he comes.' She was pulling on stockings. He was aroused but let it go. She got a pair of knickers from a drawer in his wardrobe and sat to pull them on. 'I know that Munro knows all about us; I know he's your friend; but I'm still uncomfortable being seen *here en déshabillée.*'

'Does that mean in the buff?'

'It means in anything that suggests that I spent the night here.'

'But he knows we spend the nights together.'

'Yes, of course, but—it's a matter of the appearance of it.'

He kissed her cheek. 'Breakfast?'

She was tying the front of a camisole. She shook her head. 'The coffee's lovely. I'll get something at home.' She kissed him. 'You have a good day. Shall I see you tonight?'

'God, I hope so.' He was buttoning a knitted wool waistcoat, not quite acceptable to Atkins or, presumably, the sumptuary gods, but comfortable and warm. 'Shall we eat in again?'

'That was rather fun, wasn't it? However, no. My house— Mrs Cohan was talking about "baby mutton", which sounds promising.' She was pulling on the dress she had worn the day before. 'Go on, now. I'll bundle up dirty clothes and slip out of here. Before he comes, Denton—go, please!'

He trotted downstairs, had another look at the sitting-room, sniffed the air and thought that blended smells of onions and ham seemed right. 'Paprika and pepper on that hash, Sergeant!'

'Yes, yes…'

A minute later, Janet slipped past him and went down Atkins's stairs. At almost the same moment, the front bell rang and Atkins, in the midst of greeting Janet, went for it; a minute after that, Munro was in the sitting-room. He looked grey with lack of sleep and, perhaps, discouragement. He said little but allowed himself to be pointed up the stairs towards the bath.

'There's hot water in the geyser,' Denton said.

'Thank God.' Munro sniffed. 'Lovely smell. We're going to eat it, I hope.'

'Scrapple. An American dish.'

He went off. Minutes later, the folding table was up again and laid by Atkins; the teapot appeared, the jam and the marmalade, a rack of buttered toast, the castor of sugar and cinnamon. As Munro clumped down the stairs, Atkins brought two plates heaped with the brown-and-gold speckle of the hash. Munro rubbed his hands together and said, 'Ah.'

'No eggs. I apologise.'

'I get eggs at home. Not feasts like this.' Munro was chewing. 'Damned good. *Damned* good.'

Hunger the best seasoning, Denton thought. They ate in silence, not Denton's choice but Munro's. The policeman looked better, his colour up from shaving and scrubbing, his eyes brighter perhaps because of the food and the tea. When they had finished the hash and had each eaten a slice or two of toast, Munro was ready to talk. He was interrupted by Atkins, who offered porridge (refused) and took the pot away for fresh tea. Denton said, 'Well?'

'No question it was murder. Sexual violation, too, from the look of it. We'll get that confirmed by the police surgeon.'

'Strangled, not stabbed or bludgeoned?'

Munro nodded. 'Medico on the scene said so. Pretty obvious—eyes and tongue, bruising. You know.'

'Where was she?'

'That place where her kid lived. Local cops had pulled off the uniform they had up there. The place has been boarded up, no reason to watch it.'

'The husband?'

Munro spaced the words out, as if he were a slow reader getting them from a notice board. 'That's—a—difficulty. He seems to have cleared off. Nobody at home; I sent an officer up there. Didn't work Sunday nights, so no use asking at his office. Not at his daughter's. Not clear when he was last seen—trying to sort that out.'

'You been up all night?'

'Since two. She was found about midnight. Somebody came in to Peckham Road station—his tale was he'd been walking and heard something that sounded like a woman groaning. He admitted later he'd been having a knee-trembler when the noise started and scared the judy, who ran off and left him halfway there and mad as mustard. That's what got him to Peckham Road station—he wanted his own back on whoever was making the racket. Bit muzzed—he'd been making a night of it. He's still at the station, being hauled over the coals. I don't believe he did it, but you have to be sure.'

'Why you and not Guillam?'

'Oh, Peckham Road tried to call Guillam because they knew his name, but Guillam isn't on the telephone, so they called King's Cross Road. Station sergeant there's a bright lad—he knew I'd been given the two cases and knew I lived close by. Lucky me.'

'Lucky you. Judas.' A little reluctantly, he told Munro about the scene with the two Snokeses the day before. 'Right then, they hated each other. Maybe they have for a long time.'

'Hated enough for him to kill her?'

Denton raised his shoulders. 'The whole family is...broken.' He told him about the visit to Eunice.

Munro was spreading the Society Best on a piece of cold toast. 'What about the boy? You and Guillam're a bit hipped on him, aren't you?'

'Guillam said something?'

'I was a bit short with him and told him to focus on the other two dead women, and he started to go on about the kid, alone out there in the City of the Dreadful Night. There were only the two then—this was yesterday—and I was trying to make up for the time lost by Masefield. However, now Mrs Snokes is dead and the boy's missing, I see that maybe I should have listened to him.' He chewed toast and looked up, his head bent forward so the crumbs would fall on his plate. 'Kids murder their mothers sometimes.'

'I don't think so with this one.'

'But you saw it with the Wilcox woman and the Adger woman, Guillam said.'

'No, I was...trying that on. I don't see how he could have. You know who Tonk is?'

Munro said he remembered he'd had a report. 'And *he's* still bloody missing, isn't he! Everybody's gone missing!'

'Tonk said the boy never went out, except with his mother.'

'Isn't there something about the boy being able to open locks?'

'Only that he had an old kids' book about locks. Nothing says he could actually have got out of that room he was in. Cripes, Munro, if there'd been a fire, they'd all have burned alive.'

Atkins appeared with fresh tea and hot toast. Munro said to him, 'How's that dog?'

'Better, sir. Loose on his pins, but better, thank you.'

'Feed him that cold toast in a bowl of milk. Milk toast—my mum always gave me that when I was ill.'

'Thank you, sir, we'll try that. Anything else, gentlemen? I could go out and get some eggs...' Refused, he faded away, doing his perfect-servant imitation for Munro's benefit. The dumb-waiter door was of course left open so he could listen from below.

Munro lavished butter on a slice of toast and then shook cinnamon sugar on it. 'So maybe the kid couldn't get out, meaning that he'd be out of it for Wilcox and Adger. Mmm. We'll have to locate Tonks. Tonk, no *s*? Tonk. Guillam's put him in *Information* and the *Gazette*, but we'll have to send some telegrams and get people's attention. Man like that doesn't speak languages, but he might try to slip over the Channel anyway; I think Guillam's seen to that. Probably holed up with some woman no farther away than Brixton.'

'The boy could have been to the room the mother rented since I was there.'

Munro grunted. 'I'm having it checked. Or maybe it's been checked already—there were two tecs from Clerkenwell showed up before I did last night; if they knew about it, they'd check.' He threw down his napkin, sighed. 'Clerkenwell super's in a dither because I took charge; he claims the Snokes woman's death is his division's. I'd better call. Don't eat all that toast.' He heaved his big body out of his chair and moved awkwardly to the telephone, as if he had stiff joints. Denton heard him talk to Peckham Road station, then the CID office there; he told somebody what he wanted done at—here he turned to Denton and shouted, because he had been shouting into the telephone, 'Where's the rented room?'

'Guthill Road. Number...' He had to think. 'Forty-two. Second floor.'

Munro talked some more and came back to the table. 'They may have sent a uniform, but I told them they've got to send a tec. Argy-bargy. Their super's gone to the Yard to make noises.' He helped himself to toast. 'We thought the boy was out of it because his fingerprints don't match the Wilcox floor. Then we thought the boy was out of it because he was locked in. But he's not out of it for his mother.' Munro pulled a pipe from a side pocket and began to stuff it with tobacco from an oiled-silk pouch.

Denton sighed. 'I'm interested in the boy, yes. That doesn't make me blind to him. He's physically capable of raping and killing a woman. Is he psychologically capable of raping and killing? I don't know. He's in many ways a kid, but...' He watched Munro puff the pipe into life. 'His own mother? She's his world, Munro. She's everything.'

'Often a bad side to that.' Munro leaned back and blew out smoke. 'Sex?'

'Physically, he seems to be normal. That's what the Snokeses were fighting about when I left them—how far she'd gone in teaching Walter about sex.'

'So he finds her up there in the dark and he wants her to give it to him and she won't, and he rapes her and kills her. Eh?'

Munro swung sideways and crossed his legs and puffed. He stayed that way for a couple of minutes, then got up and knocked his pipe against the iron of the grate. 'I'll have to get a warrant to search the Snokes house. One of them killed at least one of the other women—we'll find something.' He straightened his tie, brushed imaginary crumbs from his trousers. 'Anything you'd like me to find there, Sherlock?'

'If you find a vaginal syringe—a thing women douche with—have it analysed. I can show you one in the Army and Navy Stores catalogue, if needs be.'

Munro lowered himself into his chair and put his pipe on the table as if it were some precious object. 'You believe she killed them, don't you?'

Denton hesitated, then said reluctantly, 'Ye-e-e-s.'

'And the boy killed her?'

Denton shook his head.

'The husband killed her?'

'Yes.'

'For killing the others?'

Denton rubbed his long fingers over his chin and moustache. 'More because of the idea of sex between her and Walter.'

'He was *jealous*?' ·

'That might be his word. But I'd think he was revolted. Sickened in some almost spiritual sense. You know about the incest taboo? It's very old. It's meant to revolt us—to be a crime that separates us from God. I think they finished their fight and he went away, but of course those things are never finished, and he went back to the rented room. Not to kill her but to sick it all up on her. The old woman who owns the place doesn't like noise; she, or maybe Mrs Snokes, got them out. They walk back to The Oaks—it's a magnet for her; she thinks maybe Walter's up there. All that hatred pours out up there in the darkness, and he can't stand it and he rapes her. To teach her a lesson. And strangles her.'

'Or the rape is to make us think it's the son.'

Denton made a face. 'Snokes thinks that he loves his son. I suppose he could try to put it on him, nonetheless. Or maybe just put it on somebody else male. But rape is possession and it's anger and it's revenge. Teaching her a lesson.'

They sat together without speaking. In that silence, the sounds of the street became audible, the city now awake. A barrow passing made the only recognisable sound, but under it were the grumbling and the sighs of the city itself, the millions of feet on the pavements, the wind at a million corners, the hooves and the wheels.

Munro pocketed his now cold pipe and said he had to go. Standing, he growled, 'I always ask myself when I get to this point in a case, why did they do it? Why didn't they just *let it go?*'

'Because we're not made to let go. If we could let go, we'd never care about anything.'

Atkins produced Munro's coat. He struggled into it, a big, already weary man facing a long day. Denton walked down the stairs with him. At the bottom, Munro said to him, 'You're a fine story-teller. You weave it all together and when I hear it from you, it makes perfect sense. And you're often right about these things. But I have to have proof. Facts. I need fingerprints or bloody clothes or somebody who saw somebody for sure at a certain time in a certain place. You may be right, but I can't take it to the public prosecutor. What I need is, I need to find Snokes and I suppose I need to find this boy. I've got a list a yard long of people who have to be interviewed again—the Snokeses' maid, the daughter, people up and down their street, folk from Snokes's office. I need to get a warrant to search the Snokes house. I need chapter and verse of how the Snokes woman died and when. I need a PM, and I probably need to sit in on it. I need a *fact*—one solid, certain fact!' He put his hat on and looked at Denton with a little smile. 'I can't sit at home by the fire, like some, and weave convincing tales.'

CHAPTER

20

Doty came late that afternoon and told Denton that things had come along very nicely. He had found a chemist's in Oxford that had sold arsenic to a young woman who matched the photograph of Rosamund Gearing but who had signed the poison book as Mrs John Fitzwilliam. He had found a butcher in Marchmont Street who remembered serving the young woman in the photograph but didn't remember what she had bought. He had found three small hotels within half a mile of Lamb's Conduit Street where staff said they remembered the young lady, and he expected to find at least two more. He had, with the help of 'contacts' at the Post Office, identified four of the London telephones from which the bothersome calls to Denton's telephone had been made, and he had located two more in Oxford. 'Young lady didn't make much effort to hide her trail,' Doty said. 'Egotistical, would be my guess, for what it's worth. We come across that type more often than you'd think.'

'Believing it can't happen to them?'

'That, and a belief that if they've thought of it, it must be something too clever for the rest of us to follow. And of course young ladies of this sort have no knowledge of crime and police methods, and so they lack the criminal's caution. Still, she was remarkably foolish. Using a false name in the poison book is a felony crime.' Doty was having a glass of Denton's sherry. 'How would you like to proceed, Mr Denton? Shall I give this to Sir Francis and let him do with it what he thinks best, or would you like it to go to the police?'

'Both.'

'Very good.' Doty put down his empty glass. 'I'd like one more day to finish the hotels. Shall I bill you through Sir Francis?'

Denton said that that would be fine, shuddering inwardly at what the bill would be. He saw Doty out, then went slowly back upstairs, wondering how best to deal with Miss Gearing. He was still meditating on it when Janet came in, pink with walking from Teddy's office, full of exasperation and wry amusement at Teddy's clients. 'I'm going right off to my own house to have a bath, but I thought I'd tell you I was alive. You can come over in an hour, if you like.'

He told her about Doty. 'Now that I have her, I'm not sure what to do.'

'Don't be squeamish.'

'It's her career if the police move on it.'

'It's what she did, Denton.'

He took a turn up the room, hands in pockets. 'She's awfully young.'

'She poisoned a dog—out of spite.' She touched his arm as she went to the back stairs. 'Don't lose your fine head of outrage.'

He thought about it for another half-hour and wrote a note to Sir Francis Brudenell to tell him to start civil proceedings against Rosamund Gearing. 'Doty is to give the police his infor-mation, too. I believe they will move to a charge.'

He tried to telephone Guillam, then Munro, but neither was reachable. He felt left out of whatever was happening. He acknowledged the inevitability but felt a fierce curiosity, none-theless. Most of all, he wanted to know what had happened to Walter Snokes, but he had to admit that his interest was merely personal and perhaps unhealthy. The newspapers were full of the new murder, and they included Walter as 'the missing mental case', but missing he seemed still to be. The more lurid did a lot of chop-licking over the obvious connections between the murders of Mrs Snokes and Mrs Wilcox, Snokes the tie that bound them. Most of them mentioned the Adger murder but didn't tie Snokes to it, probably because of the libel laws.

One paper, however, had discovered that Mrs Adger had been Walter's first piano teacher and hinted gauzily at 'a possibly irrational connection in the mind of the missing mental patient, Walter Snokes, now said to be a powerful young man whose violent tendencies are well remembered on Banner Street, Finsbury. It was five years ago that little Robert "Bobby" Vickers disappeared from his home, only five doors along from the Snokeses, never to be seen again. It was within weeks of that tragic event that the Snokes family decamped from Banner Street, leaving behind a foment of speculation and recrimination. If violence has followed in the wake of the Snokes family, suggests one resident of Banner Street, it began there, its first victim a mere lad and a playmate of the Snokes children.'

Denton went to sleep knowing he'd put himself too close to Walter Snokes and that he was useless to Munro because of it. Munro wanted facts; Denton could give him only feelings, those only of a kind of identification with the boy. If Walter represented for Denton a lost childhood, a gleam of memory no more real than moonshine, to Munro he could be only a possible suspect. And he was somewhere in the London streets, as frightened and starved as a lost dog...With that, Denton was asleep.

He woke in the first gloom of pre-day. His body felt strengthless. He threw off the bedclothes and lay there, letting the cold of the room bring him back. He felt shadowed, pessimistic—one of those moments, usually felt in the black of the first hours after midnight, when all plans seem bad. He had been dreaming but could recapture nothing. The dream must have been an ugly one, failure or loss; he felt deeply unhappy.

Then it came back in bits. A seven-year-old Walter was crossing Oxford Street. Denton remembered fearing that the boy would be run down, but he seemed light-footed, carefree, dodging the horses and the wheels. He walked away towards a group of other boys, all walking east towards Holborn. Denton must have called after them—he had some recollection of expecting some sign, even if only a turned head—but Walter went on, merged with the crowd of boys, was gone.

It was a dream of death. Denton understood that without knowing how or why. But Walter Snokes hadn't died. Not literally. But the child he had been had died.

As, Denton now saw, his own childhood had died. *He lost his soul.* He sighed, forced himself out of bed.

Once up, however, his face towelled, his upper body washed in cold water, he felt the mood lift. This power of the night to depress him was a force he respected, perhaps feared, although less a force than his own waking mind, which wrestled with those things that couldn't be thought in the light and usually won the fall.

'Walter,' he said aloud. Of course—the fragment, the boys walking away along the street. That it had affected him so much meant that it had been about himself: himself as Walter, Walter as him. He wondered if Guillam had the same dream.

Denton shaved and put on old clothes and went downstairs. Twenty minutes later, he was at work. The grey hangover of the dream lasted half the morning. He forced himself to push through it, concentrate, lose himself in the work. He was writing the opening chapter, in which the protagonist suffers the childhood accident that makes him what he is as an adult. Of course he had dreamed about Walter—what was it but Walter? He knew that Walter now, could write about him. What he didn't have yet was the ending of the book: Walter at the end. And it was in hopes of seeing that, perhaps, that he pursued the boy.

When he had been at it for four hours, the telephone rang and Atkins called him.

'Get the name; I'll call back after one.'

'It's that Guillam. He says he wants you now.'

'Oh, *hell…*' Maybe they had found Walter. He let his heels bang on the treads as he went down, like an unhappy child. 'Denton here.'

'Walter Snokes attacked a woman in Banner Street. Less than an hour ago.'

'His old house?'

'How'd you know?'

He started to tell him about the houses in Walter's drawings, changed to 'It was one of the places he knew to go. What does "attacked" mean?'

'She screamed and he hit her, drew blood. She was on the ground unconscious when the constable got there. It's bad, Denton.'

'But he can't have just attacked her. What did she do?'

'We're trying to work that out. A local medico's with her, so far won't let us talk to her. He also tried to stab the constable.'

'Judas Priest. With what?'

'The neighbours say they saw a knife. There's a rip in the constable's tunic, but it's not a knife cut, to my eyes; I think he tore it when he fell. Maybe. Look, Denton, it's a right mess there— some of the neighbours, bloody women, started screaming about some kid they say he murdered when he lived there. Then the vultures descended; cripes, there's flash powder blasting like it's the charge of the Light Brigade. If the men hadn't been at work, we'd have had a riot.'

'Have you got Walter?'

'Walter's done a bunk again. The women—some of the women, at least three—had him and were hitting at him. The constable came and made them let him go. He says he put a hand on the kid to restrain him, and the kid pushed him down and ran off. Constables are trained to deal with that sort of crap; this one's overdue for retirement, a couple of stone heavy, and slower than treacle in Russia.'

'Judas, how did he ever get all the way to Banner Street?'

'One of the women said he looked like a down-and-outer, looked like he'd been living rough. Looked like he'd been fighting, too, she said—scratches on his face and blood. I heard one of them shouting, "The Jew, it was the Jew!" That's our reward for Masefield's putting all that out about some Jew on Denmark Road. They're a pack of bloodthirsty idiots, the great British public.'

'What can I do?'

'What can anybody do? We've sent half a dozen uniforms up there to keep order. Detectives are taking statements. As soon as I can, I'll talk to the injured woman.'

'He was looking for his mother.'

'Yah, lot of good that'll do him now, her lying in the mortuary. Yes, there is something you can do, Denton—find that boy. Once the newspapers come out, half the folk'll be locking their doors and hiding under their beds, and the other half'll be out looking to beat the tar out of him. All we need is for the injured woman to say anything that suggests it was sex. Cripes, it would go up like a cracker then!'

'Does Munro know?'

'I called him first. I've got to go back to it—I'm at King's Cross Road and a hansom's waiting. Don't try to come to Banner Street; it's a madhouse. If you have an idea where he might be, go look for him.'

'The other houses in his drawings. You might put a constable on Mrs Adger's house—that's one of them; he might go there. Their house in De Beauvoir Town, too, although—'

'We'll try that. Just don't talk to anybody or stir things up. Couple of hours, it's going to be bad. "Lunatic Murderer Maims Woman in Banner Street".' You know the drill. "Is Any of Us Safe?" Bloody leeches.' He rang off.

Denton went down the stairs to Atkins's rooms and sat on the bottom step. Atkins was sitting on the floor watching Rupert, who was staring around with what seemed to be blind eyes. 'He had another fit,' Atkins said. 'I thought he was done with them.'

'He looks as if he doesn't know where he is.'

'He doesn't. I don't think he can see or hear right afterwards. Poor old chap. I hoped he was done with them.' Atkins was near tears again.

'The vet surgeon said he might always have them. He comes out of them.'

'It scares the life out of me every time. It frightens *him*. He was so healthy before!'

'Well, we're going to get that young woman, anyway.' Denton stood. 'I'm going out. You eaten?'

Atkins nodded. 'I didn't want to disturb you. Grip of the muse.' He was watching Rupert move around the room, seeming to try to reacquaint himself with the space. 'Shall I bring something up?'

'I'll get my own. You stay with Rupert.'

He got bread and cheese and ate while he dressed. Looking for Walter Snokes was foolish now, he thought; the boy would be hiding somewhere. He thought of Walter's crawling into his 'grotto' and curling up like a sick animal. What hell had he been through in crossing London, Denton wondered? Scratches and blood on his face sounded bad: the police, even Munro, couldn't be blamed if they saw this as implicating him in his mother's death. Denton believed it impossible that the boy could be violent to his mother; she was, he thought, the only stability and the only warmth in his life. But that wasn't an argument that would be fool-proof in court. Or a police station.

He got the motorcar and drove to Finsbury, avoiding Banner Street; he went on to the Artillery Ground, drove down next to Bunhill cemetery and along behind the cricket pavilion. On an impulse, he stopped the car and checked the door to the pavilion, found it locked and no other way into the building. To have thought that Walter might have been there was to admit that he might have killed Mrs Adger; well, he told himself, he must still allow for that possibility.

He drove around the Artillery Ground, back up to Worship Street, feeling a pang as he saw the street sign that had been his road to Damascus—it seemed months ago. He circled farther north, Tabernacle Street, Old Street, then headed south, Whitecross Street to Chiswell and so east again, then up City Road and back on Featherstone Street, down Bunhill Row and west on Coleman Street, again avoiding Banner Street. And so he went, up and down, back and forth in the narrow lanes between Coleman and Cherrytree. These were miserable alleys, some of them, the houses run down or derelict, here and there one with bright paint and a look of braving it out. Men lounged and leaned, eyed his car with disgust; they had no work. He saw three clearly drunken women, one lying by a kerb and unable to get up but still hitting feebly at another woman who semed to be trying to help her. Or rob her. Walter might lose himself here if he were a smart, street-wise tough, but these were streets where, as Guillam had said, they would skin him alive. Skin him for his coat or his necktie or his shoes, skin him for the possibility of a penny somewhere in his clothes. Skin him because he was different.

Cherrytree Street was more genteel, at least on its western end. Mrs Adger's house looked like all the others now, except for the weather-vane, lace curtains closed at the front windows. The newsmen were gone. Both the constable and the news hacks might well be in Banner Street now, he thought.

He drove again around the Artillery Ground, again erratically through the maze between Coleman and Cherrytree Streets. Nothing registered. He wondered what the loafers and loungers and drunkards would say if he showed them Walter's drawings. *Do you recognise this building?* He didn't think much of the answers he'd get.

He turned into Errol Street, not too decrepit where it was opposite a brewery but quickly decaying as it headed east. Where it joined an unnamed alley at an acute angle, half a dozen men were standing as if they were waiting for him. Behind them, some ancient attempt at improvement stood like a theatrical backdrop—windows boarded, half of a building caught in a cage of scaffolding from which hung the tatters of old canvas coverings, now raddled by the wind and deeply stained. It cast its sinister atmosphere around the waiting men, two of whom, Denton saw as he came close, had pieces of lumber in their hands. One beat his on his open palm.

Denton had to stop the car or run them over. In seconds, they were on each side of him.

'Lost something, governor?'

He thought of what Guillam had said about mobs looking for Walter to beat him. 'What of it?' He knew at once it had been the wrong thing to say.

'If you think you can drive up and down here looking for a bit of stuff, you got another think coming. We're respectable folk, whatever you think, sitting in your bloody motorcar. Now you move your arse off our street, or you'll find that big nose laid in a new direction on your face.'

Denton eyed him. The man was bluffing, he knew, probably self-appointed as spokesman. Blowhard. But they were six and he was one. It wasn't worth trying to make some gesture out of vanity. He said, 'You're absolutely right. I must look a right ass, driving about. I'm looking for a boy who's run off from home.'

A voice said, 'A boy, is it! Somehow I'm not surprised.' The laughter was harsh, dangerous, and another voice said, 'Not one of our boys, you're not!'

'I'm looking for a lad about sixteen, small for his age—dark hair, probably looks like he's been living rough. He's a little... backward.'

'That's the one raped the woman in Banner Street!' a small man on the other side of the car shouted. 'That's the one we're after!'

The self-appointed leader, seeming to feel himself losing his position, shouted louder than any of them, 'Is that the truth, then? Are you looking for this bloody rapist?'

'The police have asked me to look for him. If you'll take your hand off the car, I'll do so.' He pulled the low-gear lever.

'Oho, the police! Oh, yes, the police. Looking to tear off a bit among our girls, you say the police!' The man looked triumphant. With his eyes on his fellows, he reached for Denton's coat front. Denton had a flash of thought, *touching is battery*, and yanked the reaching hand towards him, planted his left fist in the man's eye and at the same time accelerated. He brushed two of the men; a third looked terrified and froze directly in his way. Denton swerved, swerved again. Within seconds, he had to take the acute angle to go along the far side of the brewery. A piece of lumber struck the back of the car and cannoned off. The pursuit, once they had left their own narrow street, however, became half-hearted. By the time he was accelerating into Lamb's Place, they were giving up.

That was stupid, he thought. They'd have that all over western Finsbury in an hour. And Guillam would lecture him on stirring people up. *Oh, hell.* He drove up to De Beauvoir Town and looked in a desultory way for Walter. Automobiles were less rare there, the urge to take mob action absent—Banner Street and Walter's 'attack' was a distant rumour—and so he had no more adventures. He passed the Snokes house once, saw a uniform and a few people, avoided the street thereafter. But if he avoided it, what chance was there he might see Walter? Although, he admitted to himself, if he read Walter's drawings correctly, the house in De Beauvoir Town was not a house he would go to; it was a house from which his creatures fled. They always moved towards Mrs Adger's house, the Banner Street house, and the unidentified triangular building; those were the ones that were represented as 'changes of clef'—surely changes for the better? Or was that Denton's hopefulness?

He kept it up until seven. His heart wasn't in it, nor his mind, either, after the debacle on Errol Street. The hunt in De Beauvoir Town had been purely perfunctory. He had gone south of the canal, north into Kingsland, but what was the point? Walter would never come to that house.

He threw himself into his armchair and stared at the day's mail. He might as well have stayed home and read it, for all the good he'd done. He slit envelopes and threw things into the grate. The only item of interest was a big, flat packet from Geddys, the art dealer: it contained a chromo of the Richard Dadd painting.

The Backward Boy

'"The Fairy Feller's Master-Stroke",' Denton read aloud. He pronounced it the way it was written, 'feller', not remembering that the -er was the British establishment's way of representing what they saw as the lower-class pronunciation 'fella'.

He had seen it only as a black-and-white engraving. The chromo was colourful but hardly less confusing than the tangled-looking black-and-white on the music school's wall. Denton wanted it to give him a clue to Walter Snokes, but he might as well have asked for literal truth from his own dreams. *The Fairy Feller* was a dream, too, he thought, but Richard Dadd's, not his, and Walter had transmuted it into a waking dream of his own. Denton saw now the source of Walter's leaves and tendrils, of the odd daisy that now and then appeared, the chromo's figures and shapes becoming clearer as he studied it. The major figure, which Walter also drew, was, he thought the Fairy Feller himself, although Walter put him in bright green and not in the painting's earthy brown. He thought he recognised a few of the other figures, too: a little old man or gnome who cowered under a mushroom; a woman with wings and fantastically pointed breasts and huge calves that tapered to tiny ankles and looked like nothing so much as the legs on the Snokeses' piano; a tall, threatening man with a high metal helmet and another pair of enormous calves; a trumpeter; perhaps others, but so distorted by Walter's limited artistry and his tangled meanings that Denton couldn't identify them. And Walter had done what Dadd had not—added buildings, so that Dadd's dream (or nightmare?) in the understory of grasses and flowers and twigs had become a flight, a quest, from building to building along the lines of the musical staff.

'It's one of those things that you bring your own meaning to,' he said to Janet when she came in.

'That's true of everything, isn't it?' She had thrown herself down in his armchair, the chromo in her hand. 'It's wonderful. And frightening. As if they're all waiting for something horrible to happen.'

'For the Feller to split the acorn or whatever it is with his axe, I think.'

'Or fail to split it. Perhaps there's a penalty if he doesn't split it or doesn't split it exactly in half or something. The axe is rather threatening, isn't it? There's something in Shakespeare about splitting a nut—doesn't Titania or somebody ride in a carriage made of a split nut?'

'Maybe Walter Snokes saw himself in the Feller—that's usually the way, isn't it? You see yourself in the central figure? Egoism. What was it that Walter was supposed to split, do you think?'

'Perhaps his music. He saw this at the music school, you said. Maybe he had this sort of threat surrounding the music—do it perfectly, or suffer some consequence. Split the nut perfectly, or...' She shrugged.

'Anyway, it doesn't tell me how to find him.' He had already told her about Walter's supposed attack in Banner Street, and about his own wasted hours looking for him. 'Worse than a needle in a haystack—I don't even know where the haystack is. Some of the local layabouts thought I was on the lookout for women. Or boys.' He shook his head. 'There'll be hell to pay if they find Walter.'

'We'll go out first thing in the morning. First light. Scour the streets before anyone's up.'

'We?'

'Teddy's closing the office for tomorrow; the university wants nothing from me until Tuesday. I shall sit beside you and be your lookout.'

'He'll be holed up somewhere. The way to find him is to send a hundred constables poking into every hole and dustbin, which I'm sure Munro will do when he can collect the men. And even then...'

She held up a hand, wanting him to pull her up. 'Sleep on it. Let's have supper somewhere and get a night's sleep. It will look different in the morning.'

He pulled her to her feet. It would not look different in the morning, he knew.

CHAPTER

21

Not at first light, but before the feeble sun reached halfway down the houses, they were in the motorcar. He had been up at four, trying to work and failing. Janet had got up an hour later, run to her own house for clothes and, as he saw when she came back, a picnic basket. She rarely irritated him, but this morning she did: what was for him a desperate and futile labour was for her a holiday.

He rolled up Walter's drawings and put them in an overcoat pocket, then had the sense to add his magnifying glass. He took his derringer, as well, remembering the louts on Errol Street.

'Do you have a plan?' she said as she settled herself in the Barré. Denton snorted in disgust. 'Don't be bad-tempered, Denton. Come, we shall find him.' She was wearing brown wool with a fur collar, a hat like a pill-box, also fur; she had a muffler wrapped around her throat because the morning was chilly. 'We'll find him.'

'How? *How?*'

'Not by being rude, I suspect.'

He apologised and patted her knee and put the motor into gear. 'I have no plan.'

'You know he won't go to De Beauvoir Town, and he probably doesn't know where his sister lives. That leaves what, the piano teacher's house?'

'Guillam's put a constable there. But they should look to see he hasn't got inside somehow—he may be able to pick the lock or some such. I should have reminded Guillam of that.'

'Guillam's a detective; he isn't stupid. But that's all of it, is it—his old house on Banner Street and the Adger place?'

'There's the triangular building. Unless it was pure invention. It's what I drove all over half of London looking for. A sort of castle, with pointy roofs—turrets? New Scotland Yard would qualify, but I can't believe he meant that. I was sure it would be near Banner Street, something he saw when he was a little kid, something that meant—not home but, mmm, pleasure or safety or—play? Judas Priest, it could just be something he saw on the way to the music school. Something he saw from a 'bus.'

'You should show the drawings to his old neighbours.'

'After yesterday? If they recognised it, they'd go there and kill him if they could find him. I suppose I could have photos made of the drawings, give them to the police to show around. I should have thought of that yesterday. Or as soon as he was out of The Oaks. Christ, what was I thinking of?' He pounded the steering wheel with the heel of his hand.

She put her hand over his to stop him. 'You showed it to his sister?'

'I asked her and I showed her a drawing; she said she didn't know anything about it.'

'Well, who knows his old neighbourhood? Is there a pub? We could ask there. Or a post office, a corner shop. Oh, Denton, of course!' She was holding her hat on with her left hand; she grinned at him. 'The beat constable!'

'The one he knocked down?'

'You said all he did was tear his coat. Didn't you say he was due for superannuation? He's old, then—don't policemen like him stay on the one beat forever? He'll know, Denton, if anybody does!'

Denton started to say it was a waste of time, then muttered, 'If anybody does, yes.' He was on Holborn, headed towards Finsbury, but he jerked the wheel abruptly and swung left into Farringdon Road. She yelped, then laughed. It was still early morning, the traffic so far light; he had endangered nothing but the car's springs. He laughed, too. 'I had the beginning of a plan. An improvement, anyway. Guillam.'

He drove to the King's Cross Road station and asked for Detective Sergeant Guillam. Denton was ready to hear that Guillam was somewhere between there and his home, but the station sergeant said he'd already woken him, so he was probably trying to find something to eat. He sent a constable off; almost at once, Guillam shambled through a rear door, puffy and exhausted-looking and holding a mug of tea.

'Like the bad penny,' Guillam said.

'Want to ride with me to Banner Street?' Seeing that Guillam was going to say no, Denton said, 'I want to talk to the regular beat copper there. The old one. The one who got pushed down by the boy.'

'I sent him home yesterday. But he wants his pension; I daresay he's back. I suppose you mean you want *me* to talk to him.'

'Show him Walter's drawings. Ask him what one of the buildings is. He won't do it if I ask him.'

Guillam said that probably he would; he was a polite old duffer, even if he was as stupid as an ox; but he supposed he could ask him. 'I haven't anything else to do, of course.' He swallowed a huge gulp of tea. 'You've got the car?'

'Nice open-air ride to sweep the brain clean.'

'I don't have a brain any more. You saw the newspapers?'

Denton said he hadn't bothered.

'The raving ones are all but saying he murdered all three women. Sub-head on one, "Did He Kill His Own Mother?" Also, "Where Will He Strike Next?" Masefield had to put his oar in, too. He got his super's permission to talk to a newspaperman, no name—"a senior figure in the investigation"—to the effect that Walter Snokes is a proven lunatic who was probably being let out on purpose by "his ex-convict keeper" and, disguised as a "southern European or a Jew", has been a person of interest to his—*his*—investigation. There was more. Munro was beside himself. The only good thing is that Masefield's cooked his goose: coppers aren't supposed to talk to the press unless approval comes from on high. And his "on high" in this case isn't the old crock who supers N Division; it's Munro. About all Masefield accomplished was to stir everybody up—he advised citizens to check all their locks, look out for dark strangers, and make sure that there's a male in every house. Genius, Masefield. You wonder how he does it.' He put down his cup. 'That's why I slept here last night. We're waiting for somebody to shoot a neighbour or club the rate-collector with a coal shovel. Let's go.'

'You'll need a coat and hat.'

'Hell.' Guillam felt his cheeks, which he'd managed to shave. He ran towards the back of the station, disappeared, came back still running with a coat over one arm and a hat tipsily on his head. When they got outside, he saw the car and saw Janet and said, 'You don't mean I'm sitting in the rear.'

'Unless you want to drive.'

Guillam's mood was not sociable as they putt-putted down to Finsbury. Of necessity, they were sitting back-to-back; Guillam, as Denton saw when he looked over his shoulder, was hunched in the small, rear-facing seat with his knees up and his fists under his chin. When they stopped in Banner Street, however, Guillam was polite to Janet, even solicitous. His look at Denton was not so friendly.

Guillam spoke to the constable stationed outside the Snokeses' old house, came back and said that Rush, the beat constable whose coat had been torn, was probably down along Bunhill Row. 'There's a bakery that opens early down there. If he's taking free cakes from them, I'll have his hide.'

Rush, however, was not taking free cakes; he was checking the padlock on a garden shed behind a house whose owners were away—Bunhill Row was fairly well-to-do. He accepted the introduction to Denton and Janet with a rather doglike resignation. He had a drooping white moustache and a fringe of white hair below his helmet; not over-tall, he looked rather fragile for a policeman. Denton had a suspicion that about half of what he was seeing was uniform, that the thick wool might in fact be what was holding him up.

'Feeling better, Rush?'

'Yes, sir, a bit better.'

'We haven't caught the lad yet, but we will.'

'Lunatic, yes, sir. Dangerous. Going to have thirty constables make a sweep today, they say.'

'I'd like you to look at a picture, Rush, and tell me if you recognise a certain building.'

'In connection with the incident, sir?'

'You don't need to know about that.' Guillam nodded at Denton, who produced the drawings, pulled out one with a good rendering of the triangular building, and passed it over, along with the magnifier. To Denton's surprise, Rush put on a pair of steel-rimmed spectacles that made him look like a genial grandfather. Rush, Denton thought, should be spending his final years in a safe, warm station house and not walking a beat. He looked at Janet and tried a wink. She grinned.

'This one, sir?'

'The triangular one, yes.'

'With the pointed roofs, sir?'

'Yes, that one.'

Rush studied it. Perhaps he was savouring being consulted, small compensation for yesterday and its humiliations. 'Yes, sir, I'd say I recognise that building. Or I recognise something *like* that building. Like a building that used to be, I mean.'

'Used to be?' Denton said.

'Yes, sir, two of them pointed roofs, built triangular because of the streets around it, it was. Jolly place in its day. Gone now.' Rush handed back the sheet and the magnifier.

Guillam scowled and said in a voice that couldn't help being bullying, 'What does that mean, "gone"?'

'It was the Cask and Pump, sir. A pub. Closed this ten years and more. Twelve years. It closed the year of the burglary in Morehampton Street. Three men made their way into the side window of the porcelain works by way of the area, using a—'

'That isn't relevant, Rush.'

'It could have been eleven years ago. I may be wrong about the year of the burglary. Carleton Bingham was my sergeant; I do remember that.' He looked at Guillam, then Denton, then belatedly at Janet, as if to see if anybody was going to correct him. Denton said, 'You remember little Walter Snokes, Constable?'

'He's the one attacked me!'

'I mean, do you remember him as a little boy?'

'Yes, oh, yes. Played the piano. Always at it. Always knew with my eyes closed where I was by that piano. Solemn little chap. You never know how they'll turn out, do you?'

'Was this building, the triangular one with the pointed roofs, still standing when Walter Snokes was a little boy?'

'Well, of course it was. He lived here—let's see, I remember the pink ribbon on their door when I was—it must have been the year that—'

'Constable!' Guillam's voice was like a gunshot. It certainly had that effect on Rush. 'Would the boy have seen this building or wouldn't he?'

'Of course he would, if he went down to Errol Street. Though that's hardly a neighbourhood for a well-raised boy who plays the piano. Though he stopped playing the piano, you know. Just stopped. Something happened to him.'

Janet said, touching the policeman's arm, 'Did you ever see him down there, Constable?'

'Didn't I caution him and tell his mother? It's in my notebook, I'm sure, on the shelf at home. By then, of course, he wasn't right. Not right upstairs, if you know what I mean. I couldn't go too hard on a boy who wasn't right.' He looked from one to another for approval or at least sympathy.

Denton said, 'So the, mm, the pub—what did you call it—is gone?'

'The Cask and Pump, yes, sir, Gone. A considerable loss to the loafers and layabouts of Errol Street. Though in its heyday, when I first came on this beat—in seventy-one that was—it was a place of some reputation. The street not so far gone then.'

Denton was thinking of Errol Street—the gang of men and the sinister background of dangling, filthy canvas. He said, 'I was down there yesterday.'

'Was that you, sir? I had a complaint of a gent in a little car whose description would be the spit of yours. First thing I noticed when you drove up. I was going to have a word with you before we were done.'

Guillam seemed to be grinding his teeth. 'He was looking for the boy, Rush. For *me*.'

'There was an altercation, sir. A man was struck.'

Disgusted, Denton said, 'There were six of them, some of them with clubs! They were menacing. One of them reached for me.'

'Did you explain, sir, that you were looking for the boy and had been enlisted by the police?'

'I did.'

'Ah.' Rush got out his notebook. Guillam took off his black bowler and rubbed his forehead and, after a look at Janet, as if to ask for understanding, he said, 'Rush, is there anything else you know about this pub?'

'Yes, sir, it was right there that the gentleman had his altercation and was, he says, menaced.'

'You said it was gone.'

'It is, sir. Closed this dozen years. Or eleven.' Again, he looked from one to another. Something that he saw made him seem to be pleading. 'But *part* of the building is there where the gentlemen was menaced, I mean.'

'The scaffolding and the canvas!' Denton burst out.

'Yes, of course, sir. There was a scheme, six—no, seven—years ago to raze the place and put up something modern. They got as far as taking down the pointed roofs and boarding up the alley, but then, one thing and another, they stopped. Ran out of money, was what was said. Left it like you saw it yesterday. Bit of an eyesore.'

Denton moved closer to him. 'Let me just be sure of this: inside the scaffolding, behind the canvas, is what used to be the triangular building with the pointed roofs?'

'Used to be, indeed. Yes, that was the old Cask and Pump. Striking, when you saw it from the upper end of Errol Street. Couldn't miss it!'

'But it was triangular.'

'It was, sir, and still is, I daresay, if you got inside them tarpaulins. There was an alley ran along the backside of it, hardly room for two dogs to walk side-by-side, but it made the old Pump triangular, yes, sir. You'd see it if you made your way in there—there's a hoarding at each end now that closes off the alley. It was going to be built over, was the scheme, join it all to the building across the alley. Many's the time I used to go there in the night to check the locks. Problem with dossers getting in until the council boarded it up.'

Denton looked at Guillam, who gave a nod and rapped, 'Walk your beat, Constable!'

'Thank you, sir. I'll be late completing my round. I hope I was some help, gentlemen. And lady.' He touched his helmet with a hand.

Back in the car, Janet said, 'Poor old thing! I wanted to offer him my arm.'

Guillam growled, 'I wanted to offer him my fist. He ought to be put out to the same pasture as bleeding Masefield!' He swivelled around to say to Janet, 'You didn't hear that, I'm sure, madam.'

To Denton, she said, 'You *know* this place?'

'I passed it twice yesterday! I stopped in front of it and had the wrangle with the locals. Hell's bells!' He was driving too fast along Coleman Street. He shouted back to Guillam, 'You want me to take you back to the station?'

'Is he going to be in this old pub?'

'He damn well better be!'

'I'll stick with you for a bit.' They drove another street and Guillam said, 'He could be dangerous.'

Denton said, 'I brought a gun,' and felt immediately ashamed. He thought that Guillam groaned. Denton slowed, turned, turned again into Errol Street and stopped where they could look down it and see the tattered ruins of the pub. Guillam rose partway in his seat and turned around to look. 'Like a ghost ship.'

'What?'

'The sails.' Guillam let himself down but stayed turned forward, now kneeling in his seat. 'Proper procedure is for me to get a squad of men. Maybe notify the Yard and have them send their sharpshooters.'

'Christ, he isn't an anarchist bomber, Guillam.'

'You *think* he isn't, and maybe I think he isn't, but he did attack that woman yesterday and he did assault a policeman. I know, I know; don't argue with me! I'm telling you how it'll be seen. You think you're going to go in there and talk him out, don't you?'

'If he's in there.'

'And how are you going to do that? You told me yourself, he doesn't like you.'

Janet turned to face him. 'Oh, but he'll like me.'

'You're not going in there.' The voice was Guillam's, but Denton said the first two words with him and then stopped.

Janet looked at Denton. She looked at Guillam. 'You don't know this, Detective Sergeant, but *he* does: I don't do what men tell me.' She jerked her head at Denton. 'Drive on.'

'What if I said I don't do what women tell me?'

'I'd think you a fool. Drive.'

They came to the place where Denton had had his run-in with the loafers, and there some of them were, several faces familiar to him. He went on past them, seeing two or three step out into the street, one shaking his fist. Denton pulled up beyond the canvas-shrouded building and stopped the car at the kerb. As they got out, the knot of men came closer. Guillam made a single motion of jumping out and heading towards them. He stopped when they were a dozen feet away and held up his warrant card.

'I am Detective Sergeant Guillam of the CID. If you lot so much as open your mouths, I'll run you in for interfering with the police.' He seemed a very large presence in the otherwise empty street, his black overcoat as huge as a bearskin, his height above any of theirs. He held the card well up, as if it were a torch. 'Are we all clear about what I just said?'

One of the men—not the one who had led them yesterday; Denton had already noticed he wasn't there—said, 'His nibs there and his little car was down here yesterday, endangering our women! What's he doing now with a rozzer, I want to know!'

'He's assisting in a police investigation, as he was yesterday. You lot go on about your business, now. This doesn't concern you.'

From the group came a voice crying, 'You after this madman that murdered the women?'

Guillam turned away from them and nodded towards the derelict pub, then altered his route to head for it. Denton and Janet followed, Janet darting back to the car to pluck the picnic basket from it; when she caught up with Denton she said, 'He'll be hungry.'

From the other kerb, Guillam was watching the men disperse. When two of them looked back, he said, 'And I don't want that motorcar touched. I've got a memory for faces.'

Guillam turned and ran a hand along a filthy canvas until he found an edge, lifted it and held it until Denton and Janet had passed into the gloom within. When he followed, he murmured to Janet, 'I don't want you coming any farther.' He passed her and looked at what lay ahead.

The tarpaulins were streaked with soot and rain and bird lime, sagging in long arcs from their anchors high up on the scaffolding but still enclosing a space that felt huge and somehow empty despite its being criss-crossed with beams and littered with debris. Dim light came through the canvas; more oozed down through the gap between the canvases and the building they masked, the light partly blocked by a narrow platform of rough lumber twenty feet above. The space at ground level smelled of damp and urine. Denton saw an old pile of excrement. People had used the space as a rubbish tip, sometimes fairly neatly— a pile of ash and cinder rose a few feet along—and sometimes haphazardly, things flung in wherever a gap had been found. Making their way forward, they had to step around and over broken crockery. A pair of woman's shoes, the two five feet apart, lay nearby, along with the remains of a wooden dry sink and a can that had once held golden syrup.

Guillam led them to the narrow point of the old building, Errol Street on their right. Denton looked up. Over them, a round shape bulged from the building above the second storey, big corbels supporting it. *One of the turrets*, he thought. He touched Guillam's arm, pointed back the way they had come, then at himself; he turned back and hurried to the end of the building, passing two doorways as he went. At the far corner, he looked up to see another of the round extrusions, this one all but dismantled, open sky showing through its underside. Beyond, to his right, was a wide, now boarded-over doorway, then a narrower one still marked 'Private Bar', and, at the far corner, the remains of a third turret. Between the two, looming over the doors, was an overhang of half a dozen feet that ran almost from turret to turret.

He hurried back to the others. Guillam was leaning against the corner of the building; almost languidly, he pointed to his left: the hoarding that blocked the alley that made the building triangular. The planks were rotten, their limewash all but gone, only traces of white caught in the grain. A board near the building had been pushed in at the bottom. Guillam pointed at it, put his finger to his lips, bent and squeezed his hefty body through. Janet followed, her skirts a difficulty; she handed the basket back and Denton came last with it.

The alley had no longer any reason for being but must have had a history. Bricked long ago, it was buckled and hollowed, kerbless. On their right, the long-boarded windows and doorway of another building stared sightlessly into the semi-darkness; on their left, the old pub rose, straight and unadorned, to the grey sky. This had been the back; the entrances had been on Errol and the cross street. The scaffolding extended only as far as the hoarding, leaving the length of the passage clear and surprisingly clean-looking; except for one wicker baby carriage, missing its wheels and stove in, Denton saw little else—a few bottles at the far end, he thought. Partway along, a doorway suggested the pub's rear exit; high up, a beam showed where a block and tackle might once have hung. A row of tall windows in the first storey seemed all of a piece, behind them perhaps a large room, perhaps a ballroom or even a music hall.

Guillam went to the doorway and knelt. He studied the doorknob, then the lock; he gave Denton a look and nodded. Denton hurried forward, handing the picnic basket back to Janet. Guillam's thick, hairy finger pressed against the lock where three fresh scratches showed in the darkly patinaed metal.

This, Denton thought, was Guillam's point of no return. He should, indeed, go back to King's Cross Road and get a squad of constables. If he went in, he was doing exactly what Maltby had been reprimanded for. But Guillam was ambitious. Guillam wanted to be a detective-inspector, and he wanted to get back to Central. And he was touched by the boy.

Guillam moved Denton back with a hand and took something from his trouser pocket. Masking with his other hand, he put a tool into the lock and slowly twisted back and forth. Denton, glancing at his face, saw the rapt look of a man taking a piss or having a serious think about eternity. With a slight grinding, Guillam twisted his fingers hard; his expression changed, and the door started to open. Guillam held it.

'Tell your lady friend to go back to the car,' he whispered.

Denton shook his head.

Guillam put his mouth closer. 'If something happens to her, it's my career.'

'If something happens to her, it's my life. Don't be an ass.' Denton put his mouth almost to Guillam's ear; when he spoke, he could feel his own warm breath reflected. 'She works for his mother's solicitor. The boy likes women, Guillam. Be it on my head: you go in. You've warned us. You can say you left us out here.'

Guillam looked over Denton's shoulder at Janet. He shoved Denton aside and went to her and whispered something and then without another word pushed the door slowly open, preventing it from squeaking, and went in. As he tried to push it closed, Denton put one boot in the opening and the door met it, stopped, tried again to close, and stopped.

'What did he say to you?' Denton whispered.

Her smile was wry. 'He said he was sure that I would obey him and stay outside.'

Denton nodded. 'Very wise.' He opened the door.

The rear of the pub had been a warren of little rooms strung along the alley side of the building like little caves, leaving most of the space on the ground floor for the bars. Straight ahead from the doorway in which they stood was a dark corridor that faded into blackness. Denton drew her in and shut the door, then switched on his flashlight. Moving forward, he could see a varnished dark door, under his feet fallen plaster and lengths of lead pipe with torn and twisted ends. Their feet crunched the plaster. He squeezed through the doorway and found himself in the remains of the public bar, the place made comprehensible by a swing of the flashlight. The counter was intact; the rest was destroyed or gone—beer pulls, glassware, bottles. Beyond was blackness, a thin line of light where a boarded-up window stood.

He had thought they would find Guillam there, but Guillam had gone his own way, probably wanting to find the boy first. Denton saw no sign of him now, heard nothing, although they paused several times and listened. They did the saloon bar and the private bar, finding only ruin, then went back and searched the kitchens and pantries and storerooms that were strung along the rear wall. The place was gutted, even to the gas fixtures and the piping of the group urinal. All that was left was fallen plaster and exposed lath, and rat smell, broken piping and crockery.

At the far end of the narrow hall that ran along the rear rooms was a staircase that went up six steps, turned and went up again, its match-boarded sides vanishing into nothingness. He looked at Janet, raised his eyebrows: up?

She nodded.

The stairs were cleaner than the passage below, the match-boarding having been left intact and so no plaster underfoot. On the first floor, the stairs turned again and went up, but ahead was an open door—Guillam? Denton went through and down a short corridor and found a sudden surprise of space and light. He remembered the row of windows he had seen from outside: here they were, running the entire length of a vast and high-ceilinged room, matched on the other side by an identical row. More light came from those on their left, the passage side; the other side—Errol Street—was shrouded in canvas. The room was asymmetrical, the long walls following the triangle of the exterior but not meeting because the far end was a short wall, beyond it, presumably, the point of the triangle. Two rows of slender columns marched down the room.

To their right they found a stage, the front curved, holes cut in the stage floor for oil lamps, at the rear a tattered drop still hanging—a wood, some sort of temple-like thing in the distance, flowers in the foreground. *Of course—the backstage is the bulge over the far end*. A door stood at an angle on each side of the forestage.

'Ballroom and music hall,' Janet whispered. 'I've seen them just like this in the East End.' She pointed into the far corner, a pair of double doors. 'Public entrance from the street.'

Denton hoisted himself up on the stage. He opened the stage-left door with care, put his head in, flashed the light. Rough boards, a passage wide enough for one person, an even narrower stair going up. He clambered down and said to her, 'Little stairs.'

'Dressing rooms. Must be the size of closets.'

Denton thought of going up those stairs: would the boy be up there? But he'd seen no tracks in the dust. Save them for later. He motioned to Janet to stay where she was and went the length of the big room on tiptoe. Three doors stood in the far wall. He went through the first. It held three toilet stalls, the toilets long since ripped out. A women's room, he thought; the toilets had a sort of anteroom. He went to the next door, found a short corridor and what had probably been an office with windows on each side of the building's point. A few old papers were ground into the floor; one was a handbill for the Celebrated Comedy Pierrots, Newest Coon Songs and Ditties, at the Cask and Pump Public Rooms, *Three Nights Only*! He thought of the bunch who had stopped his car, didn't think they would have cared much for comedy Pierrots—or perhaps they would. Or tastes in Finsbury had changed.

He bent and looked out and up. The turret bulged above him, its corbels in fact framing the windows. This might have been a pleasant office. Like the prow of a ship—

A piano began to play. The sound made Denton jump, nerves already a little ragged from tip-toeing through the dark building. The piano, too, was particularly eerie, almost unrecognisably out of tune—the ghost of the comedy Pierrots, perhaps; he half-expected the shuffle of ghostly feet, the thin coughs of an audience long dead. Then common sense asserted itself: the music was not a coon song but something 'classical', of which he had only the dimmest consciousness. *Walter?* He hurried back to the main room, worried about Janet.

He stood in the doorway, looking down the room. The stage was shadowed, the window light not penetrating much beyond the footlights. A figure stood back there, just visible against the painted woods and flowers. The music came from Denton's left: halfway down the room, Janet was sitting at what was left of an upright piano. Its top was gone; one end had been bashed in; its castors were broken and it was down on the end nearest him. Yet, using a wooden box for a stool, she was sitting there, the picnic basket beside her, playing something that Denton thought was supposed to be light and quick but that sounded lugubrious because some keys didn't play and nothing was in tune.

'Mummy! Mummy!'

The figure shot forward from the back of the stage and hurled itself down and ran towards Janet. '*Mummy!*'

She stood. Walter stopped, even backed half a step. Denton grasped that the boy was dishevelled and bloody, that he limped, that he had lost his coat, but that was all in an instant, and he was watching Janet, afraid for her.

'You're not Mummy!'

'Mummy sent me, Walter. She thought you must be hungry.' She bent and picked up the basket and took a step towards the boy. He took another hunted-animal step back.

'You're not Sally, either.'

'I have chicken and ham and some very nice biscuits. I think it's time to eat, Walter.' She sank down to the floor, doing some sort of curtsey inside her skirts that made it look as if she had no legs but was being lowered by machinery. Folding her legs under her and sweeping her skirt around them, she opened the basket. 'My name is Janet.'

'I want Mummy.'

'I know you do, darling. But I think you're hungry. You've been on the streets for a long time, haven't you?'

'Since—since Tonk left all the doors open, which was very careless of him. I went looking for him but there was nobody except the others and I'm not supposed to talk to them, so I went to the room, but Mummy wasn't there, and then I went home but a woman I didn't like touched me. People are *not* supposed to touch me!'

Janet had put a chicken leg and bread and a slice of ham on a plate. She set it on the floor, stretching ahead to do it and putting it where she wouldn't threaten him.

Walter looked at it and moved a step towards it. 'Don't you touch me.'

'Oh, no—I know better.'

'She touched me and she tried to push me. I told her I lived there but she didn't care. Then a policeman came. *He* touched me. He took my arm. I *told* him he wasn't to do that.' He was gobbling the chicken. 'I had to run away. They were terrible people there. Policemen are terrible people. They take you away and lock you up.' His mouth was full; his cheeks puffed out. He ate like a starved animal. Denton thought that at that moment there was nothing touching or pathetic about him; he was only a mouth and teeth, revolting to watch. The boy said through the food, 'I had to push them. I have to make people understand. More chicken!'

'Of course.' She held up another chicken leg.

'On the plate! You have to put it on the plate, stupid! You might touch me if I took it from you. There.' He snatched the food off the plate and again began to gorge it down, but this time he half-fell, half-sat beside the plate. His words, muffled and mangled, came out through chews and swallows. 'The towns between Camberwell and Finsbury are Kennington, Walworth, Newington, Lambeth, and the City of London.' If he hadn't known the names of the towns, Denton wouldn't have understood them. 'I met some very bad people who hit me very hard and took my coat. They laughed, too. My nose bled for a long time. It's all down my front.' He threw the chicken bone on the dusty floor and picked up the ham slice and forced it into his mouth, folding and collapsing it on itself to make it fit. With so much in his mouth he could hardly be understood; he shouted, 'Sweet! I want a sweet!' *Shwid! I wa' shwid!*

Denton was aware of movement. He looked away from the boy. Guillam was standing in the stage-right doorway. How long he had been there, Denton couldn't say.

Janet set a green bottle of water on the floor and then a small basket, from which she produced biscuits. She put several on the plate. Walter crammed them into his mouth. Spitting crumbs, he said, 'I crossed the River Thames on the Southwark Bridge.' *Fa Shoufwak Burge.* 'There are seven bridges between the Tower of London and Big Ben. These are Tower Bridge, London Bridge, Southwark Bridge, Blackfriars Bridge, Waterloo Bridge, Charing Cross Bridge and Westminster Bridge.' *Westminster* was completely lost in a spasmodic swallow.

Janet said, 'You walked all that way?'

The boy swallowed again, hand on chest, and got it all down and became understandable. 'Ran some, but I got tired. The goblins wouldn't let me sleep. A man offered me part of a pie if I'd pull his dinkus. I was hungry.'

'Where did you learn all that about London?'

'From a map. Where do you think I'd learn it?' Then, to Denton's surprise, he lay down between the plate and Janet, his back to her. Janet looked towards Denton. She crooked a finger. Surprised, he took a step, then another; he hadn't thought she'd known he was there. She put a finger to her lips, then held her hand up, palm towards him. He stopped.

The slight scuffing of his boot was enough. Walter looked up, looked away just as quickly. 'I don't *like* him!' he shouted, as if Janet had suggested that Denton was his best friend. Walter lay down again, lying now on his back with his knees up. He rolled his head towards Janet. 'I don't like him.' It sounded quite conversational. He moved his head again: Guillam was climbing down from the stage, then crossing the room towards them.

'I don't like him, either.'

Guillam tried to smile. He waved his arms up and down as he had at The Oaks, but this time, it was as if Walter didn't see him. His head again rolled towards Janet, and he said, 'I used to do what you were doing. Making those sounds.'

'At the piano?'

'When we used to come here, I'd want to do that and Eunice would say, "Oh, you can't, you're so stupid, you half-wit, they'll hear from the street and they'll come in and that will be the end of it," and she wouldn't let me. But when she'd go off with Bobby, I'd try it with the *sostenuto* pedal down and nobody could hear. But it didn't matter anyway because I couldn't do it any more. They'd come and taken the music out of me. It was magic.' He laughed, an adolescent boy's coarse, brutal laugh. 'Eunice was too stupid to know there was a *sostenuto* pedal!' He clutched himself and rolled back and forth.

'You and Eunice used to come here,' Janet said.

'Of course we did. But I'm not supposed to talk about that.'

'Who said?'

'Mummy said, and Eunice said. I can't talk about that any more. Where's Mummy?'

Janet produced a roll of paper from the basket and unfurled the biggest sheet. It was the chromo of *The Fairy Feller's Master-Stroke*. She held it up in both hands where he could see it. The effect was startling: he became still, caught almost in mid-gesture, half up on his elbows, mouth open. He sat up violently and snatched the chromo and shouted, 'The Fairy Feller!' He pronounced it the way Denton did, the -er like that in brother. He opened the chromo on his now crossed legs, holding the ends so they wouldn't curl again. 'His coat is brown!' he cried. 'It's brown! And I've made it green! Why didn't they tell me? I've done everything wrong!' He clutched his head. The ends of the chromo spiralled to the middle. Walter rolled on his side and pulled his knees up and held his head tight between his hands. A sound came from him that was like a closed-mouthed scream. It got louder, became a noise of rage, the mouth still closed. He rolled on his back and drummed his heels on the floor.

Janet had picked up the chromo. She seemed quite calm. She opened the chromo again and spread it on the floor next to him, putting herself that much closer to him. 'Tell me what the picture is about.'

'I just said, it's Richard Dadd's Fairy Feller, stupid.' He had taken his hands away and rolled up on his right side so that he was almost touching her. '*The Fairy Feller's Master-Stroke*. The Fairy Feller has an axe and he has to split the nut or everything will end.'

'Who are all the other people?'

'They aren't *people*! They're elves and gnomes and some fairies, and one or two *are* people, like General Haig.' He stabbed the sheet with a finger. 'Up at the top, the soldier. That's General Haig.' He stabbed something else. 'That's the queen of the fairies; she's very small.'

Janet touched the picture. 'And who is this?' Denton thought it was the woman with the pointed breasts and the piano legs.

Walter said, his voice muffled, 'That's the sister. That's the *bad* sister. The other one is the good sister.' He squirmed himself into a position with his belly on the floor and his cheek on his left hand. 'The bad sister tells on you and won't let you do things you know she does with Bobby, but the good sister is nice and tells stories and shares her sweets.' His finger stabbed the paper again. 'That's a mushroom. That's a daisy.'

'Which one is you?'

Walter put his hands flat on the floor, one on top of the other, and put his chin on his hands. 'Two of them are me.'

'Which ones?'

'Well, the Fairy Feller, of course, because he's being tested. He has to do it just right or the world comes to an end. And the other one...You mustn't tell.'

'All right.'

'Nor either of them.' He waved a hand at the room without looking at Denton or Guillam. 'Tell them they can't tell, either.'

Janet looked at Denton and then at Guillam. 'You mustn't tell.' Guillam started to make some gesture, but she cut him off, saying to the boy, 'They won't tell.'

The boy wriggled closer to her but didn't touch her. He put a finger on the paper and all but whispered to her, his face almost in her lap, 'That one.' Denton thought it was the little white-bearded gnome who stared at the Fairy Feller with such fear—or was it hatred?

'Why are there two of you?'

His voice was very low now. Denton lost some of his words. 'I have to be...disguise. Because when I...Feller, they made me... disguise.' He rolled on his right side and then, sighing, sank back, resting his head an inch from her thighs. He looked up at her face and chuckled, the sound mature and comfortable.

Janet said, 'Who is the very tall man with the helmet?'

Walter hesitated. 'That's the mother.'

'But it's a man.'

'That's a disguise.'

'But he has a beard.'

He sat up. 'That's what disguise means, stupid! When you're in disguise, you wear a beard!' He scuttled away from her, crab-like on hands and feet, back to the floor. 'I don't like you any more.'

'Do you want to look at the picture some more?'

'No.'

'Do you want to eat something?'

'No.'

'Should I play the piano?'

'No! You play very badly. You make mistakes and they'll punish you because you're stupid.' He looked around, saw Guillam, and said to him, 'I want Mummy.'

Guillam started to move towards him, but Denton said in a loud voice, 'Sally.'

Walter seemed never to look right at anybody but Janet, yet it was clear he was talking to Denton. 'Where is Sally? I'd like Sally to be here to do me. Sally comes and sees to my needs and gives me relief, because boys and men need relief. You do it in a private place and she sees to your needs and there's nothing wrong with it because she's a nurse. If you do it to yourself it's a sin, but not if Sally does it.'

Janet said, 'Did you need relief often?'

'Twice a week, except once, no twice, when Sally couldn't come and Mummy said that today it wasn't a sin if I want to, and she made me private and gave me a cup—I think it was a cup, it was black and had a funny bottom—and said put your relief in here and you won't have to clean up. I think that's why it wasn't a sin.' He became thoughtful, looking at one of the windows. 'Tonk said it wasn't a sin, anyway. He said it was Nature.' He frowned. 'But you have to do what the Mother says.'

Denton said, 'Do you remember what days those were, when Sally wasn't there?'

'It was...when I was in Tonk's house.'

'Before or after I visited you?'

Behind the boy, Guillam shook his head at Denton and scowled to show that he meant it.

Denton changed his attack. 'Bobby,' he said. The boy's head swivelled towards him, but his eyes were looking into a corner of the room. 'Bobby Vickers.'

'I don't like him!'

Denton wasn't sure whether this meant him or Bobby, but he went still closer and knelt down and said, 'You came here with Eunice and Bobby.'

Walter frowned and hesitated. 'I'm not supposed to tell.'

'You knew all about locks and could open the door to get in.'

'Eunice said it was all right.'

'So—'

'Denton!' Guillam's voice was like a hammer striking glass. 'No more!'

Denton looked up. Guillam was serious, he saw, very serious. This was not the compassionate Guillam, the Guillam who had taken Walter's fingerprints and waved his arms and led the idiot out of The Oaks; this was Guillam the policeman. Denton stood. Guillam took his arm, the way policemen are told to take people into custody, and muttered, 'You come with me.' He led Denton down the room and to the doorway to the stairs. He stopped, keeping his hold on Denton's arm. As he talked, he kept his eyes on the boy and Janet. Walter was lying on his back again and they were whispering.

Guillam's voice was grim. 'You can't go on questioning him in my presence if there's any possibility he's going to be a suspect. We can't question somebody once we've decided to charge him.'

'You haven't decided to charge him—have you?' Denton pulled his arm free. 'Guillam, he didn't have anything to do with the deaths. His mother took his semen to make the murders look like rape; you heard him! And he was crossing London on foot when she was killed, for Christ's sake—he was nowhere near The Oaks!'

Guillam's expression might have come from grief, his pock-marked face heavy with fatigue and a little shiny, as if from sweat, although it was cold in the derelict building. 'I don't know,' he said hoarsely. 'Every word that comes out of his mouth, I think he's going to damn himself, and he isn't competent! What good is it to read him the caution? "For a Constable to press any accused person to say anything with reference to the crime of which he is accused is very wrong." They drill that into us.'

'He hasn't been accused of any crime. He isn't going to be accused!'

'How do you know that? You're off on this wild hare about Bobby somebody—how do I know where that leads?' Guillam shook his head. '"Great care and discretion are necessary to avoid any suggestion of an endeavour to extract an admission from someone, *and he should be cautioned before the question is put*, that he need not answer, and that if he does his answer may be used as evidence against him." Vincent's *Police Code*.' He pulled his shoulders forward as if he were cold. 'I can't caution that boy. He's got no notion of evidence or what "against him" means.'

'Of course you can. He understands more than you seem to think. Guillam, now's the time to question him. He's *talking*.'

'I'm here about the murders of three women. Don't you drag in every goddam unsolved case in the Met!'

Denton straightened but kept his eyes on Guillam's. 'We're still in your division. The missing kid was from your division. Don't give me some crap about dragging in cases!'

'I could have had that boy out of here fifteen minutes ago. You're going on and on.'

Guillam set his jaw and stared. Denton met the stare and said, 'Guillam, *please*. Let me ask about this one thing. Just that—all right? When you think I've gone too far, jump in with your caution—but God help you if you stop me and he gets put in a cell on remand because I couldn't ask him the one question that would prove him innocent. That kid's not a killer, and you know it.' Guillam started to move away; Denton caught his arm. 'How about it?'

Guillam looked at Janet and Walter, still whispering, and muttered, 'I'll give you two minutes.' He started towards the pair on the floor. Denton followed, going faster so that they arrived together within a few feet of the boy. Before Guillam could say anything, Denton said, 'Walter, what happened to Bobby Vickers?'

'I don't like you.'

'What happened to Bobby Vickers?'

The boy looked at Janet, in whose lap he was almost lying, not quite touching her by less than an inch; the two, she seated on the floor with her legs under her, he on his back, sprawled, made a strange, a grotesque *pietà*, like statues Denton had seen in Italy. It was a vision that struck him like a blow. *It's how the book ends.* He looked at Janet. She looked down at Walter and nodded to him.

Walter said, 'I'm not supposed to tell. Mummy said not to tell.' He still wouldn't look at Denton. It was as if the boy and Janet were alone as he looked up at her again. 'I'm not supposed to tell *ever*.' Suddenly, he was agitated. He shouted at her, 'It isn't fair! They don't understand. I can't tell and I have the dreams, and every day I have to go looking and trying to make it right, every day, and at night it's horrible and I pee in my bed and Tonk takes away privileges, no eating or emptying your pot for a day and a night! It isn't fair! I don't know what I'm supposed to do. I shouldn't have to think about it, but I can't help it. It isn't fair!' He sat up, put his hands over his ears, eyes shut, and began to rock, an angry moan coming from his closed mouth. 'I can't keep them out of my head!' The moan got louder. The rocking turned to a side-to-side twisting, his head going lower until it was almost striking the floor. 'Make them stop!'

Janet said almost in a whisper, 'Maybe if you tell, the dreams will stop.'

'I can't. Mummy said so.'

'Why?'

'Because of Eunice!' He jumped to his feet, his agitation now making him walk back and forth in quick, small steps. 'Mummy said that if I tell, the police will come and take her away. I don't want them to! The police will hurt her—Mummy said so!'

'I'm a policeman, son.' Guillam sounded like a man in deepest despair. 'I won't hurt her.'

The Backward Boy

Walter stopped. He looked right at Guillam, a rarity. 'You're not a policeman. You're the one who played with me.'

'But I'm a policeman.'

'Have you come to take me away? I didn't tell—I didn't, I didn't!'

Denton stepped around Guillam, who had, probably without knowing it, moved closer to the boy. Denton said, 'What happened that you can't tell, Walter?'

The boy looked much younger, suddenly vulnerable. He appealed to Janet. He said softly, 'It's telling.'

'Yes. But it isn't fair to make you bear the burden of it. Eunice is married now; she has a baby. She hasn't been shut up in that place with Tonk. She doesn't have the dreams.'

Guillam drew his breath in. 'That's enticing him,' he muttered.

The boy lay down again, now curled almost into a ball on his right side, his back to Janet. 'We were here. We came here to play. I was the one who'd found it. I was the one who could open the lock. Eunice and Bobby went off to be private, which means nobody can see you or hear you. They did that because she played with his dinkus. I know because I spied on them. She gave him relief. Sometimes I stayed down here. I played in the woods.' He raised his head and looked at the old scenic drop at the far end of the room. He put his hands over his face.

'And then what?' Denton said.

When the boy started to speak, Denton realised that he was weeping behind his filthy hands. 'This is the telling part.' Tears ran down and he snuffled them back. 'Eunice came where I was in the woods and she said please help her. Please please, she said. She was being the good sister. Please help me, Walter.' He looked at Janet. Tears had made pale tracks through the dirt on his face. 'I went up with her. Up above. Bobby was lying down. She said please please. Bobby didn't move at all, even when I poked him. He didn't have trousers on or underpants. After a while, Eunice said please please. Do something. Help me do something. So we did.'

Guillam looked at Denton and said hoarsely, softly to the boy, 'Walter Snokes, I have to warn you, son, that you don't have to say anything more, but if you do, anything you say now can be used as evidence in a court of law. Do you understand?' He was anguished. 'Do you understand?'

It was as if he hadn't spoken. Walter lay on his back and folded his hands over his chest. 'Now I've told.' It was as if he were preparing himself to die. His eyes popped open. 'Don't tell Mummy.'

'Where's Bobby now?' Denton said.

Guillam whirled on him, his face contorted; Janet flinched. Guillam shouted at Walter, 'You don't have to answer that!'

An arm rose from the floor, pointed straight up.

'Bobby's on the roof?' Denton said.

'Not on the roof, stupid!' Walter pushed himself to his feet. 'You'll see.' He started towards the door through which Janet and Denton had first come. Guillam went after him, close behind; Denton put a hand out for Janet, pulled her up. Walter was already on the stairs leading up, Guillam right behind him. They all went up into darkness, turned again, then again, came out on a small landing with a door. Walter turned a big key; the door opened on the bright, silvery light of the outdoors. They stepped out on the roof of the Cask and Pump.

Most of the roof was a low hip, probably never visible from the street, Denton thought. It tapered to a point as the building did, but the roof was smaller than the perimeter and left a para-peted walkway all around, a waist-high wall on the outside, and a deeper space at the building's wide end over the bulge of the backstage. There, an area thirty feet by ten feet made a kind of terrace, tarred and covered with small pebbles. At each end, a turret had once risen. Now, the turrets were mostly gone, but Denton could see that they had been only shells left open on the back. Walter stopped in the middle of the terrace and looked towards the remains of the farther turret. He pointed.

'Eunice brought you here?'

He pointed again. Denton walked down to the partly dismantled circle. He looked back at Walter, who was staring off over the roofs of Finsbury. Guillam and Janet were watching him.

The shallow-pitched roof had narrow eaves; below them, gutters, now broken and hanging, had carried water to four-inch pipes at their ends. The pipes ran across the gravelled tar of the roof and disappeared into what had been the shadow of the turret. Denton walked closer. The pipes in fact ended in an elbow that plunged into the gravelled tar and disappeared.

The turret's shape had hidden a water tank.

Denton went inside the circle of the turret and scuffed a shoe-sole in the gravel. In the middle, the stones fell away to show a ring like a manhole, in the centre a bar with a cut-away area underneath for a handhold. He tried to lift it, couldn't move it. Sweeping away more stones with his hands, he found a padlock.

'Guillam!'

Guillam came reluctantly. Denton knew he was afraid of losing Walter Snokes; he was also furious with Denton. Denton watched the boy and Janet, then went to them as Guillam got down on his knees. Denton was ready to grab the boy if he tried to run or—as he expected—to throw himself over the parapet. But Walter seemed to have sunk into something like a waking sleep.

Denton watched Janet's face. She was watching Guillam. He saw her begin to frown, then wince, then close her eyes. Guillam's feet ground towards them over the gravel. Guillam said, 'Walter Snokes, I have to warn you again that anything you say may be used as evidence. I'm advising you, boy, not to say anything now. Do you understand me?' Walter wasn't going to say anything anyway, it seemed. Guillam nodded at Denton.

Denton strode back to the turret. The cover was open. He got on his knees, feeling the pebbles, like nails being driven into his kneecaps. He got his flashlight and bent very low, shielding his eyes against the outdoor light and shining the flash down into the tank.

Bobby Vickers was down there in a few inches of water. A pair of trousers lay a dozen feet from him. The body was badly decomposed from years of wet, many of the bones visible. Denton supposed there had been rats.

When he straightened, he was alone on the roof. He hobbled to the door, his knees complaining. Starting down the stairs, he thought he could hear the others below. He hurried, taking the stairs too quickly in the dark, almost fell; he caught himself on the loose banister and went on, down past the ballroom-theatre, down to the level of the kitchen and the bars. Ahead, the other three were a single dark shape in the murk. Denton called out but no answer came.

He ran through the plaster-covered debris, tripping again, catching himself, reaching the back door just as it closed behind them. He hurled himself through and saw them in the brick-paved passage.

'Janet!'

She turned, held her finger to her lips. Guillam said something and Walter, walking between them but touching neither, stopped. Guillam turned to look at Denton. When he came close, Guillam said, 'I want the boy to have a solicitor. I'm not saying another word to him, nor will I let you or anybody else, until he has legal advice. This is for my good as well as his. You're finished here, Denton.' He glanced at Janet. 'Mrs Striker says she works with his mother's solicitor, but she's away. His father had a lawyer who did pretty well by him.'

'Drigny. In Clerkenwell.'

'You get in that little car of yours and go get him. It's the least you can do after what you've done today.'

Janet murmured, 'It's all right, Denton. Do as he asks.'

Guillam grunted. He said, 'The sooner he gets legal advice, the sooner he can get help. That's what you can do for him.'

Guillam turned his back and spoke to Walter, and the two of them and then Janet moved towards the hoarding at the end of the passage. Guillam held back the board; Denton took it as Guillam went through, then the others. Coming last, Denton saw them making their slow way through the thicket of wooden scaffolding and rubbish. Ropes hung down from above, twisted now by the wind around uprights and cross-pieces, a fantastic parody of nature. It struck Denton as it had not when he had first come in: this was Walter's fairy wood—these were the vines twisted around the straight lines of the musical staff.

When he parted the damp, heavy canvas and stepped out, he was astonished to see Munro on the pavement opposite. Three constables and a plain-clothes detective stood around him; two others were off to the sides. Over Janet's shoulder, he saw at the next corner of Errol Street two more constables and, beyond them, a knot of people.

Munro was crossing the street. He spoke to Guillam, not to Janet or Denton. 'Is this Walter Snokes?'

'It is.'

Munro looked at Walter. 'You've had a bad time, lad. We'll see you right.'

Guillam said in a policeman's voice, 'I don't want him spoken to, Munro. He's been given the warning and he's to be asked no questions. Mrs Striker and I are taking him along to King's Cross Road.' His voice was thick with meaning. 'Denton is going for his solicitor.'

Munro looked at Denton, who nodded, then looked again at Guillam and got some signal. Munro said, 'Would a cab be better transport than the police van?'

'Yes,' Janet said. 'Dear God, yes. Please.'

Denton started to say that he could take him in the motorcar, but she shook her head at him and Guillam looked at him as if he no longer remembered who he was. They all began to move away.

Denton was left to feel like a pariah and to find that he was angered by Guillam's judgement of him—then, and worse, to know that the judgement was just, because Denton had pursued the boy to use him for his own ends. He had asked his questions; he had got his novel; he had endangered the rest of the boy's life. No wonder he was a pariah.

CHAPTER

22

ome again after delivering lawyer Drigny to the King's
Cross Road station, where he expected Drigny to prevent the boy
from saying a word, Denton put his key in his front door and was
pulled inward by Atkins, who said, 'Heard the gate, came as fast
as I could. You've got a baronet in the parlour.'

Denton, wanting solitude and silence, said, 'Young
Hench-Rose?'

'The same. Quite agitated.' Atkins took his overcoat. 'You
want to be announced?'

'I'll announce myself.'

He went up the stairs, smoothing his hair on both sides
with his hands. He was still lost in the mess he'd made of
Walter Snokes—King's Cross Road had been in a dither,
Munro sending detectives off to talk to Eunice, shouting after
them, 'Get a statement!'; Guillam disappeared somewhere
with Walter, Janet not to be seen. Denton, ignored by everybody, had felt neglected all over again, then self-reproachful,
then flat. Drigny had thanked him with a nod, rubbed his

hands together and bellowed at the station officer, 'Where's my client, then?'

So Denton had come home.

'Well, well!' His geniality sounded false even to him. 'Sir Ivor. This is a surprise.'

The young baronet had been sitting on a hard chair. Now he rose, stood rather tragically by the mantel, head lowered; Denton thought he had seen an engraving of the actor Mounet-Sully in the same pose. The young man said, 'My life is ruined.'

Denton thought, *Christ, what now?* and said cheerily, or at least aggressively, 'I certainly hope not! Tea? Coffee? Too early for spirits, I think.'

'Nothing.' He made it sound like an emanation of his inner self.

'Ivor, Ivor—what is it? What's happened? And do sit down—not there, somewhere comfortable. Here...'

But the unhappy young man wanted the hard chair. He sat with considerable solemn grace. 'I've had a letter from Miss Gearing, threatening to tell all.'

'I thought we settled that.'

'It's this vendetta you have against her.'

'I don't have anything of the kind.'

'She says you've put private agents on her and are harassing her and have made false statements to the police.'

'If she really thinks that, she should take it up with the police. Yes, I've got a private investigator beating the bushes. She poisoned our dog!'

'That's simply not true!' He took in Denton's frown and backed off. 'That's what she says.'

'She's lying, at which she seems to be pretty expert. Look, Ivor, the private investigator's the best in London. He's traced the poison; he's traced the meat she put it in; he's tracked a lot of telephone calls. She's guilty of poisoning an animal and of small stuff having to do with harassment and home invasion and God knows what-all. And the police have everything.'

The young man, seeming younger still as he listened to this, said in a strangled voice, 'You have to stop them.'

'I wouldn't if I could, and I can't; it's their case.'

'She says she's been summoned!'

Denton put up his palms. 'Then it's out of my hands. See?'

Ivor jumped up, the tragic persona forgotten, and said, 'You can stop them if you want! They'll do what you say. You have influence!'

Annoyed, ashamed of the day with Walter, feeling pushed to an edge, Denton forced himself to say nothing. He despised the idea of having 'influence', despised more the idea that he would use it. Despised himself. Despised Ivor.

Hench-Rose made a charge at the empty grate, then charged back. 'She says if you don't cease and desist she'll tell my commanding officer everything! I've been accepted into a good regiment, Denton—I'd be ruined!'

Annoyed even more by being called Denton, no 'Mister', by a pup hardly out of the nursing basket, Denton again tried to say nothing but burst out nonetheless, 'Like hell I will!'

'It's my life! I'm terribly sorry about your dog; I love dogs myself; we have several in the country—but…a dog…' He opened his hands as if to say *A dog is expendable.* With the implied *and I am not.*

Denton decided that he really did despise young Hench-Rose. Not even for his father's sake would he do what he asked. He said, 'Sit down.' Hench-Rose frowned and recovered, straightened to show that he didn't take orders of that sort, and then sat down, carefully smoothing the new-style crease down the front of one trouser leg. Denton said, 'I've just come from a boy a few years younger than you who's lost his mother and father and whose brain doesn't let him see the world as you and I see it. He's probably going to Broadmoor or to a private asylum. He has no future. How greatly do you think I care which goddam regiment you wind up in?' He held up a hand to stop Ivor's whine. 'If the police don't convict Miss Gearing of animal poisoning, I'll get her in the civil court. You and she need to learn the same hard lesson: acts have consequences.'

'But—you can't!'

'Can and will.'

'But you're being...puritanical!'

This seemed to be the farthest reach of Ivor Hench-Rose's behavioural judgement. Denton said, 'I think you mean priggish, or maybe authoritarian. Call it what you will. I'm not going to be liberal or open-minded or soft-hearted, that's for sure. Tell Miss Gearing that.'

'There must be some middle ground.'

'In a poisoning?'

'But the animal didn't die. I asked your man, and he said it was doing very well.'

'That was service talking to aristocracy. The animal, as you call it, is still having fits and has probably had its life shortened. Atkins is frightened for it and heart-sick, and although Miss Gearing doesn't believe that he has a heart—nor you, perhaps— I do. And my heart is sick, partly over the dog, and partly that Hector Hench-Rose's son is standing in front of me and speaking this selfish nonsense.'

Ivor stared at him. 'My mother was right about you.'

'I'm sure she was.'

'She said you were a jumped-up working man with no fine sense of things!'

Denton, disgusted now, gave a snorting chuckle and shook his head.

'*Please!*'

Denton was afraid the baronet would get down on his knees. To forestall him, he said, 'I've said what I have to say, Ivor. You've said what you have to say. I think you'd better go.'

The young man rushed to the door, pulled it open as if he had expected it to fight back. 'You have ruined my life!' He sped down the stairs, shouting for his hat and coat, of course not remembering Atkins's name. 'You there! You! My coat and hat, you!'

When he had gone, Atkins came up the stairs. Denton said, 'You heard?'

Atkins nodded. 'Rupert *is* an animal, General.'

'But not as in *"only* an animal".'

'You find that Snokes kid this morning?'

'For better or worse, yes.'

'He do it?'

Denton shook his head.

'None of them?'

Denton shook his head again.

'He's sane, then?'

Denton shook his head.

Munro and Janet arrived together about five o'clock. Hearing the cab, Denton looked down from his window in time to see Janet vanish into the passage beside his house; she would be going through the back gardens to her own house, he knew. Munro, having seen her down from the cab, being very courtly in his heavy, faintly (probably unconsciously) ironic way, waited until she was gone and then came slowly up Denton's steps. His weight and his age showed.

'Inspector Munro,' Atkins said as he stood aside for the detective. He looked at Denton. 'Tea, sir?'

Denton was so unaccustomed to being called sir by Atkins that he let the question go by, realised a moment later that he was meant. 'Yes. Anything. Oh, yes—Inspector Munro needs sustenance.'

Munro fell into a chair. 'Sustenance, my hat; Mrs Munro will have a heavy supper waiting for me. In, what is it? Three hours.' He looked at Denton. 'I'm bushed.'

'Tiring day.'

'It's the accumulation of it. That lawyer, Drigny! He'd have kept us there until Doomsday and smiled the whole time. I've got to warn the public prosecutor about him—he's a corker!'

'What about the boy?'

Munro heaved his big body in a single chuckle. He rubbed his eyes. 'Bailed. By the station officer. We wanted to take the boy to the magistrates' court. Your man Drigny said—not in so many words—"not so fast, there's things to be decided first".' Munro chuckled again, this time more sincerely. 'Those "things" took up three hours. Well, there was a lot of sorting-out to do. Guillam was in a state; I've never seen him like it before. Because of the boy. I believe he thought we were going to ask for immediate remand to the adult gaol.'

Atkins appeared from the stairs and put a tray on the bottom shelf of a rolling cart and disappeared. Munro watched him, licked his lips. 'Just discovered I didn't eat lunch.' He shook his head as if to clear it. 'King's Cross Road was a madhouse. I wanted to move the case to Islington, which I'd a perfect right to do, take it to the Newton Abbott station, but Guillam was opposed. We had a bit of a ram-sammy. I saw his point— moving to Islington appeared to give Masefield more weight, and Masefield's about to have a brick wall fall on him.'

Atkins appeared with another tray, this one filled with teapot, cups, hot water and the rest. He wheeled the cart down the room and pushed it between them. 'Who's pouring?' He laid white napkins across their laps. Denton gave him a look to show he thought Atkins was spreading it a bit thick.

Denton said he'd pour. Munro peered under the top shelf of the cart, all but disappeared, and came up with a plate. 'Beef and some sort of green stuff. I suppose they call it lettuce. I grew better lettuces in my cold frames when it was freezing cold out.' Cocking an eye at Denton. 'Not to be ungrateful for the hospitality.'

Denton urged him to eat and to for God's sake get on with his tale. He poured tea.

'Your lady was back and forth to the telegraph office in Euston station like it was next door. Her and her lawyer boss or whatever she is were batting telegrams back and forth like shut-tlecocks. She got permission for Drigny to represent the boy; she insisted that the age of both the boy and his sister be determined on the day when the other boy—Vickers?—disappeared; she instructed Drigny not to let us go to court until we'd re-examined both the beat constable and the woman that young Snokes was accused of assaulting. Which somewhat waxed Drigny, who'd already done all those things. All of which didn't please us coppers much, as it was like saying we hadn't done our job, and anyway we were only taking a charge to the magistrate, not pleading in the House of Lords.' He started on his second sandwich.

'Did he plead?'

Munro's mouth was full. He shook his head. He held up a finger, swallowed, sighed. 'Drigny argued he isn't competent to plead. I agreed. Of course Guillam did. On what did or didn't happen five years ago—it was five years ago, by the by, putting the boy out of it because he was well under fourteen, so, any road, whatever happened he wouldn't have known it was wrong even if he'd been normal: crucial element in law. As for the "assaults" on the woman and Constable Rush...' Munro shrugged and looked under the tea table again.

'Are you going to place a charge?'

Munro reappeared, red-faced. 'Remains to be seen.' He put a plate of sliced cake on a corner of the loaded table, then moved the sandwiches to the mantel and repositioned the cake. 'A detective had already taken a statement from the "assaulted" woman and three of the neighbours, and it wasn't crystal clear that the boy was the first to do anything. It looks like what happened is, she put her hand on him to push him out of the doorway. Drigny said if we went to the magistrate today he'd go into the boy's condition and show he can't bear to be touched—everything becomes self-defence. Plus if she put a hand on him it's battery. Same with the constable. Old Rush is a decent sort; he admits now that maybe the tear to his coat happened when he fell, and he admits for certain that he put a hand on the boy to detain him before the boy touched him. So from assault and battery and assault on a policeman, we went to battery by the woman and failure to comply with the lawful order of a policeman by the boy, and I think that by tomorrow we're going to withdraw the charge because of the boy's competence.' He chewed on a slice of cake. 'If I decide to murder Masefield, I'm going to hire Drigny to get me off.'

'Where's the boy now?'

'Your lady's put him in a private nursing home where they know about such things, she says. The kid was released on her recognisance by the station officer—she's a householder, after all, known to me, Guillam, et cetera.' Munro lifted an eyebrow. 'And no, there was no mention of her past. Nobody there to mention it, in fact.'

Munro had cautioned Denton more than once about doing anything that would drag Janet into court, where he warned that her husband's death and her own incarceration would be trumpeted, not to mention her two years in a whorehouse.

Denton said, 'Did she thank you?'

'Of course not. She's a lady.' Munro rubbed the tips of his fingers against each other, hand against hand, and wiped them on the white damask that Atkins had dropped in his lap. 'That saved my life.' He eyed his tea. 'I suppose you wouldn't offer me a bottle of beer.'

'I suppose I would. Beer or ale?'

'The India pale has been good here before.'

Denton heaved himself up and went to the alcove. 'What about the sister—Eunice?' he called down the room.

'Oh. Mmm. Some question there.' He accepted the bottle, squinted at the glass, then poured into it. 'I sent two detectives over to take a statement, but they never got anything she'd sign. She's in a state—her mother's death, missing pa. Changed her story a couple of times but the essence was she was never in the old pub. Knew Bobby Vickers, yes, saw him on the street, never friends. Her brother's mind is gone. He may have played in the old pub; she didn't know about that. Appears that when they mentioned the body, she reacted pretty strongly—pale, then red, agitated, said she didn't know what old pub they meant, et cetera. Then she wanted a lawyer, although they swear they didn't hint at a charge and certainly hadn't made one. So they left it that she'd come to King's Cross station with a solicitor tomorrow and we'll start the game all over again.'

'But the boy's free on the body we found?'

'Free as a bird, although if he was competent we could charge him with hiding evidence of a murder, disposing of human remains, et cetera, et cetera. The sister the same, but it won't stick. No evidence but his testimony, and how could the prosecutor move on that alone? However, I stayed at the pub while they collected the body—no easy job, I don't mind saying—and I had a look around. There might be something there to show that the sister was there. Anyway, I left two uniforms and a couple of tecs to search the place, fine-toothed comb, all that. Plus fingerprint people to go over every inch if they have to.'

'Five years old?'

'If nobody's smeared them in the mean time, her prints might have stayed put. We'll see.'

'You accept Walter's version of what happened?'

Munro drank half of his beer, puffed out his cheeks. 'Guillam does. Georgie's a good copper. He's got himself too involved in this one, but he's a cop. I think we have to proceed "as if". Medico said the dead kid had a broken skull, but that could have happened when he was dropped into that bloody tank.' He gave a shudder. 'Creepy place.'

'You said "as if"—as if the girl killed Bobby Vickers?'

'Something like that. It would have been manslaughter, if she did. Maybe self-defence. What did she do—push him because he tried to go too far? She could plead pretty well whatever she wants: there's nobody to contradict her. Her lawyer'll see to that. But there's no charge unless we find somebody who can place her in that pub. Or we find something of hers there. Or a fingerprint. The boy's tale is out of it.'

Denton sipped tea; Munro sipped beer. After a full minute of silence, Denton said, 'Any sign of the father—Snokes?'

'Not yet.' Munro drank, put the empty bottle on the mantel. 'When we searched the Snokes house, we turned up one of the female things you talked about. Syringe thing for, you know. New-looking. Hard rubber.'

'Black?'

Munro nodded. 'It's at the lab. Also six lady's glove buttons in the wood range. And part of something made of canvas that we think was a home-made cosh, nice job of sewing. Got another statement from the maid yesterday; she'd smelled something burning in the house one day, couldn't remember what day. Bad smell. I've asked them to go over the remains of the canvas for grains of sand—if they find any, we'll look for a match with the sand from the Adger woman's hair. Also to test for blood, but not much hope of that after the burning.'

'That could be either the husband or the wife.'

'Also found a pair of men's shoes behind the kitchen wain-scoting. His size. Either Snokes or his wife could have hidden those, too. Mud on them—being checked.' He took out his pipe and put it back. 'She could have worn his shoes on purpose, of course. Hide the fact it was a woman, also cast blame on him.'

Denton got up to get him another bottle of ale, but Munro said he was going back on duty and shouldn't. Denton sat again and said, 'She killed both women.'

Munro raised his shoulders as if to shrug, held them there. 'Jealousy? For *Snokes?*' He dropped his shoulders, looked at Denton.

'She knew about his women. It could have been the fact of his carrying on with both of them at the same time that drove her too far, but what was wrong with that family had been going on for years! They all blamed Walter for a breakdown that was really just *them*—the father blamed Walter's change for his philandering; the mother blamed the boy's change for her losing status and maybe some fantasy of fame and money; the sister blamed Walter for driving her away from home. The splits ran deep and they were *old*. His philandering was the icing on a very sad cake.'

'Why not kill *him?*'

'Then she wouldn't have had a husband at all. I'm not joking. She made herself the alibi for her husband on the first murder; that gave her power over him. I think she thought it would bring him to heel—"Give up the other women or I'll tell the police you weren't with me that night." But it didn't work; he kept on with Mrs Adger. So she killed *her*. In a rage, I think. A fury. She didn't even give herself a proper alibi. She'd lost control of herself.' He poured himself half a cup of cold tea. 'Guillam said something when he first got on the case about Snokes not leaving her because they were bound together, husband and wife, the common history. She may have been like that, too—killing off his women so she could have him to herself, *even though they hated each other.*'

'We'll never prove it. Though we don't have to, any more.'

'And then he killed her after she told him she'd helped the boy "get relief"—the ultimate insult to a father. Incest.'

'Families, dear God.' Munro leaned back, lowered his head and busied himself with a fingernail. 'Theoretically, we're still looking at the boy for the mother's death, but it'll never wash. We've asked the divisions to inquire about him on the pertinent days and nights he was crossing London. Somebody will have seen him, talked to him. Sure, you can argue he could have gone back and forth across London twenty times by underground and tramcar, but could we prove he had money? Or that he knew how to use the underground and the trams? Lawyer Drigny would have a fine old time with that.' He pulled a pocket-knife from his waistcoat and went to work on his fingernail. 'From what you say, the sister won't take Walter to live with her. Nor will the father, I daresay, if he turns up alive and doesn't hang. The boy'll have to go into some sort of institution.' He looked hard at his little knife. 'And that's the end of that family.'

Denton said, 'The sister told her father that Walter had exposed himself to her, or something of that sort. But that was right after the death of the kid in the pub. Maybe what she wanted was to see Walter put away someplace where he couldn't talk. Although I think that the sister had told her mother what had happened, because Walter told us that both the sister and his mother had warned him he must never tell. So there was a kind of ghastly family conspiracy to get rid of him, and although they all said it began with Walter's "change", in fact a lot of it began with the death of Bobby Vickers—with which I firmly believe Walter had nothing to do.'

Munro was nodding. He said, 'So Sis tells Ma, but if she was as scared as I think she was at fifteen, what she told Ma was that Walter had killed Bobby Vickers. Ma's terrified that her boy will be put away for murder. Then Sis tells Pa that Walter came on to her, when what she may really have been describing was what Bobby Vickers tried to do to her. She's the apple of Pa's eye, so he right quick throws Walter into The Oaks. And they move away and find that they're still the same people and they still hate each other and there's still all the old grievances.' He shook his head in disgust. 'No, I don't think Sis will take Walter in out of pity or sisterly love.' Munro brushed his lap with a hand and got up, closing the little silver knife. 'I've got to take myself off.' He stretched. 'Back to the Yard to help protect the British family.' There was a sound below them; Munro's eyebrows went up. Denton heard Janet's voice. 'The lady,' Munro said.

'Stay a bit.'

'Can't. She saw enough of me today.' He asked for his hat and coat. Janet came in; they smiled and each said something about the day, as people will who have been through an ordeal together. Atkins brought Munro's hat and coat, and he was off.

Denton kissed her. 'Did somebody tell Walter that his mother was dead?'

'I did.' She pushed away from him. 'I thought he'd have a tantrum—attack me. But he did nothing. *Nothing.* I thought he hadn't heard me and I said it again and he simply walked away. He's gone into a kind of trance.' She shook her head. 'I thought it would kill Guillam. Guillam's very emotional, did you know? Yes, I suspect you did. I thought he was a brute until today.' She went to the table beside his armchair and took a cigarette from a box. 'I may have found a place for Walter, actually.'

'Munro said something about a nursing home.'

'No, not the nursing home. That's temporary.'

She lit the cigarette with a wooden match and strode around the room smoking, still restless from the day. As if finally realising where she was and who he was, she said, 'How are *you*?'

He shrugged.

She came closer. 'What is it?'

He didn't want to tell her. It had been hard enough, telling himself. Nonetheless, he said, 'I've been belly-aching about people's egoism—the Gearing woman, Hench-Rose, Maltby. Egoism! Narcissism! And how was what I did to that boy any different?' He put his hands in his pockets and stared into the cold grate. 'I hunted him down like one of those blowhards who hunt wild animals so they can get their names in Rowland Ward's. For a book! Christ, what's the matter with me?'

She touched the back of one shoulder. 'You found him and you saved him. If the locals had found him first, there'd have been violence. Even if the constables had found him first. I think you're allowed a little egoism.'

He shook his head. 'What's ever going to happen to him?'

'There's a school in Leominster. Teddy knew about it. For "special cases".'

Denton said, 'For the rest of his life?'

'If what they do works, it won't be for the rest of his life. There's hope for him, Denton.'

'And you'll pay for it?' He took her silence to mean yes. 'Could I pay part of it?' He tried to smile. 'Penance? Blood money?'

She tossed the cigarette into the grate and held out a hand. 'Take me to supper. Somewhere that doesn't smell like a police station.'

He came back from her house through the gardens. She didn't want him to sleep at her house that night: she said she was tired, but he knew there was more. She had the look she got when she thought of Ruth Castle. Grief had tiptoed back, disguised now perhaps as Walter Snokes, as his future. Janet was, as she had said of Guillam, 'very emotional'. Like Guillam, he thought, she hid it. Like him, too.

He went in his front door because he'd got leery of intruding on Atkins's space. Almost as soon as he was upstairs, however, Atkins appeared; behind him, Rupert came more slowly, his breathing announcing he'd made heavy weather of the stairs. As soon as Atkins stopped near Denton's chair, Rupert threw himself down.

'I'm honoured,' Denton said. 'First time he's been up here since it happened.'

'It wasn't for lack of wanting to. He admires you, General.' Atkins stood looking at Denton. 'Anything I can get you?'

'Go to bed.' Denton was pouring himself a whisky. He looked at Atkins to ask if he wanted some; Atkins shook his head. Denton sat again, sipped, picked up a newspaper, realised that Atkins was still standing there. 'What?'

Atkins put his lower jaw on one side. He examined a fingernail. 'I said something a while back about a wedding. Well, it's off.'

Denton had pretty much forgotten in the whirl of the Snokeses. Still, he wanted to say the right thing. 'I'm sorry, Atkins.'

'Thanks. Wasn't meant to be. I realised it after...you know. After Rupert almost took the long trip.' He sighed, looked again at his fingernail. 'I told Lily—that's Mrs Johnson—that I couldn't give him up. She said that was that. Not in so many words. A certain amount of tears. But...it seemed to me—it seemed to both of us, I suppose—that it wouldn't be much of a marriage if one of us would stick at a dog. So, Rupert and I'll be staying on, if that suits you.'

'It suits me very well.'

Atkins nodded and bent to scratch Rupert's neck and then, hands joined behind his back, walked to the window and looked into the dark street. 'Funny, that a man would prize a dog more than a woman. If that's what it was. Maybe it's something about me.' He sighed. 'Life's a puzzle. Life's a puzzle.'